Praise for Lois Richer and her novels

"Richer portrays the struggles of her flawed but
redeemable characters realistically in this sweet
story."
—*RT Book Reviews* on *A Doctor's Vow*

"[An] emotionally heartwarming story."
—*RT Book Reviews* on *Twice Upon a Time*

"*His Winter Rose* is a wonderful, warm love story."
—*RT Book Reviews*

"Richer delivers a touching, evocative, wonderful
story of selfless love."
—*RT Book Reviews* on *A Cowboy's Honor*

LOIS RICHER

A Doctor's Vow
&
Perfectly Matched

HARLEQUIN® LOVE INSPIRED®CLASSICS

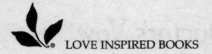

LOVE INSPIRED BOOKS

Recycling programs for this product may not exist in your area.

ISBN-13: 978-1-335-21890-2

A Doctor's Vow & Perfectly Matched

Copyright © 2018 by Harlequin Books S.A.

The publisher acknowledges the copyright holder of the individual works as follows:

A Doctor's Vow
Copyright © 2012 by Lois M. Richer

Perfectly Matched
Copyright © 2013 by Lois M. Richer

CONTENTS

Lois Richer loves traveling, swimming and quilting, but mostly she loves writing stories that show God's boundless love for His precious children. As she says, "His love never changes or gives up. It's always waiting for me. My stories feature imperfect characters learning that love doesn't mean attaining perfection. Love is about keeping on keeping on." You can contact Lois via email, loisricher@gmail.com, or on Facebook (loisricherauthor).

Visit the Author Profile page at Harlequin.com for more titles.

A DOCTOR'S VOW

Search me, O God, and know my heart;
test my thoughts. Point out anything you find in me
that makes you sad, and lead me along the path
of everlasting life.
                                    —*Psalms* 139:23–24

This book is dedicated to the One who makes dreams come true and does so far beyond what we can ask or think. Thank You, Father.

Chapter One

Fire!

Pediatrician Jaclyn LaForge quickly ushered her patients out of her brand-new clinic to safety. Her relief was short-lived when the clinic's nurse grabbed her arm.

"Randy McNabb and his mom haven't come out," RaeAnn whispered. "I think they're still inside."

The volunteer fire department of Hope, New Mexico, wasn't here yet and Jaclyn wasn't going to wait for them. She kicked off her high heels.

"Wait," RaeAnn begged.

"No child left unattended, RaeAnn. That's our motto." Jaclyn raced inside the building, praying Randy and his mom were safe. Surely God would answer this prayer.

Inside the clinic, she moved from room to room. When choking black smoke enveloped her, she dropped to a crouch, calling Randy's name as she squeezed her burning eyes closed. Reopening them, she saw nothing. Her hand clutched air. Her lungs gagged on thick heavy smoke. She ripped off her jacket and held it over her face, trying to stem her terror.

Jaclyn reached for a shadow and knocked something over. She knew she couldn't stay in the clinic, but when she rose to move ahead, shards of broken glass pierced her foot. She collapsed in pain.

Don't let me die, God. Not before I've kept my promise to Jessica.

A gloved hand curled around her arm. Another nudged her jacket away from her mouth to plant a mask over her face.

She lifted it. "Randy—"

"Keep it there," a gruff voice ordered. "And hang on to me."

Jaclyn obediently inhaled the pure, clear air in gasps. Her rescuer heaved her over a very broad shoulder and carried her through the building. For the first time in years Jaclyn relinquished all control and allowed someone else to be in charge of her life.

As they emerged into the sunny spring warmth, Jaclyn pushed away the mask and inhaled, forcing her burning lungs to clear as she shot a prayer of thanks heavenward. Her rescuer gently set her on the ground. She lay still, overwhelmed by what had almost happened.

"Are you nuts? You don't go into a burning building. Not ever." The fireman in front of her ripped off his headgear and glared at her, his lips tight in an angry frown. But his fingers took her pulse with gentleness. He carefully eased her sooty jacket from her hands and tossed it away before checking her for burns. "Can you breathe okay? Do you need more oxygen?"

He tried to replace the mask but she pushed it away.

"I'm fine." Well, that would be true if her stomach hadn't just flipped in reaction to his touch. Jaclyn peered into cobalt-blue eyes and wondered who he was.

"Why would you go into a fire?" he demanded.

"A little boy—Randy—" She blinked at the familiar bellow that came from her left. "That's him. Where was he?"

"He and his mom used the old fire escape on the side of the building. They're fine."

"Good." She kept her gaze on the fireman, fighting not to look at her clinic. "I'm fine, too." She accepted his outstretched hand to help her stand, winced and quickly sat down again. "Except for my foot. I stepped on some glass."

The fireman called for a first aid pack, shredded what was left of her stockings and examined the soles of her feet with a tender touch.

"I took off my shoes, you see," she said, as if that would explain everything.

"If those are your shoes, I'm not surprised you got rid of them." He shot a scathing glance at her spiked heels lying not ten feet away. "I don't know how you can even walk in those things." He glanced up, his blue eyes darkening to navy. "This is going to hurt."

"It already does. Go ahead." Jaclyn leaned back on her elbows and watched him delicately remove bits of glass from her foot. She tried to ignore her pulse-thudding reaction to him by trying to remember where she'd seen eyes so richly blue before.

Her rescuer's forehead pleated in deeply tanned furrows. So he was an outdoors guy, good-looking with the kind of massive shoulders that not even the bulk of a fireman's jacket disguised. He'd shed his headgear to reveal a face that appeared chiseled from stone.

His jaw clenched and unclenched as he worked, a tiny tic in his throat betraying his concentration. His hair—dark, almost black—lay in a ruffle of tight curls against his scalp—

"Kent?" Jaclyn whispered in disbelief. "Kent McCloy?"

"Yeah?" He lifted his head, blinked at her.

"I didn't recognize you. It's me. Jaclyn. Jaclyn LaForge." She waited. But Kent only nodded once and went back to work on her foot. "Thanks for getting me out of there."

"No problem. It's what firemen do." His drawl, like his face, gave nothing away.

Oh, no, her soul groaned. Kent was just like the rest of Hope's biased locals who couldn't believe the former bad girl of Hope could be a real doctor. Jaclyn was sick of that attitude. As if a mistake from her past made her completely unqualified to actually treat patients.

Kent squeezed the arch of her foot in preparation to draw out yet more shards. The last one was large enough to make her yelp in pain.

"Sorry." His fingers belied his gruff tone as he gently held her foot and poured antiseptic over the wounds. He began to wrap her foot in gauze—his bandaging skills were as good as or better than hers. "Okay?"

"It's fine." Actually his touch was more than fine, which was utterly confusing because Jaclyn had never reacted like this to anyone ever.

"I think I got it all but you should have somebody at the hospital check." He set her foot down and tied off the gauze. "No stitches needed, though I suspect it will be painful for a while. And wearing those shoes? No way."

Who cared about shoes? Jaclyn caught a glimpse of her dream—Jessica's Clinic—and groaned.

"It's ruined," she whispered, swallowing tears that would make her look weak. "It's totally ruined."

"Yeah, fires tend to do that." Kent offered a hand to help her rise. When she was upright, he slid his arm around her waist, as if he understood that only force of will and his help kept her standing. If he hadn't been there she'd have burst out bawling.

"But how could a fire start?" She looked from him back to the blackened, smoking building. "I had the place checked out. I had everything very carefully checked out."

"Then somebody missed something. Or it's an accident." He shrugged. "Sorry, but the place is toast. In my opinion it isn't salvageable." Despite his harsh assessment, his blue eyes glowed with sympathy.

Jaclyn didn't want sympathy. Forget Kent McCloy with his midnight eyes, big broad shoulders and the gentlest touch she'd ever felt. Her dream was going up in smoke.

"I just opened." Despite her best efforts, a tear slipped out and trickled down her cheek. "I worked so hard to make this dream come true."

"Then you'll start over." Kent turned her to face him, his voice softer. "It's just a building. Compared to your life, losing a building doesn't matter. Besides—" he waved a hand "—Hope is full of empty buildings. I should know. I own that one over there."

She nodded, recognizing it. "Your dad's old law office."

"Uh-huh." He shook his head. A faint smile tugged at his mouth for a millisecond before it disappeared. "You can start over, Jaclyn. Take your choice of where." He waved a hand, as if it were simple to start again.

She blinked, surveyed the street then twisted to look at Kent again. If he wanted her to reopen he couldn't be holding her past against her. Maybe he'd even help her.

"Many of these places look worse than the one I was in."

"Probably are. Unoccupied buildings deteriorate fast." He turned away as one of the other firemen came over to speak to him. "She's okay. She should be checked out at the hospital for smoke inhalation. I removed the glass in her foot."

"Fire department volunteers aren't supposed to render that much first aid," the other fireman reminded, eyes dancing. "At least that's what you said at our last meeting, Chief. I can see why you did it, though." He gave Jaclyn a smile that should have made her heart throb.

Jaclyn wanted to tell him to save it for someone who would appreciate it, that she was devoted to her work—except for when Kent McCloy made her pulse race by taking glass out of her foot.

"Generally we don't. Do first aid, I mean." Kent's tanned face turned a shade of burgundy.

"Just couldn't help yourself this time, huh?" the fireman teased.

"The fire, Pete?" Kent reminded, dark brows lowered.

"Under control. But I'll take the hint and get back to work." The other man left smirking.

"What did he mean you couldn't help yourself? Are

you a doctor, Kent?" Jaclyn frowned. "But I met the local doctors. At least, I thought I had."

"Vet," Kent corrected with a mocking smile. "I can't stand to see things hurting, though I usually treat a different species."

"Oh." She glanced at her foot. "Well, maybe you should broaden your practice. I'll be a reference if you like."

"You want me as competition in town?" His chuckle made her stomach quiver again.

"I'm not sure it would matter much," Jaclyn mumbled. "I could hardly have fewer patients." She gulped, regrouped. "It's good to see you again, Kent. It's been a long time since we were in high school together. We'll have to catch up sometime." She'd been so focused on the clinic she'd met hardly anyone—it would be nice to have a social life.

His beautiful smile disappeared, his face tightening into an unreadable mask.

"Sure." He looked around as if he wanted to avoid further conversation. "The ambulance is here. You'd better go with them, get your foot checked." His arm left her waist.

"I'm fine." Jaclyn studied him as she balanced on her uninjured foot, feeling suddenly bereft. "Have you lived in Hope since high school?"

"No." Kent's response didn't invite further questions. He turned his head, nodding when one of the other firefighters motioned for him to join them. "I have to go."

"Well, thanks for saving my life." She waited until he'd taken a few steps away. "Kent?"

"Yes?" He turned back, his impatience to get back to work clearly visible.

"Was anyone else hurt?" She held her breath as she waited for his answer.

"Just you." He studied her for a moment longer, then grabbed the gear he'd thrown down and strode away looking larger than life.

Not that he needs any help there, she thought noting the badge at the top of his sleeve. "Fire Chief Kent McCloy is already the stuff of heroes. But that doesn't matter to me," she said aloud, as if convincing herself. "I have no time for relationships. I'm not back in Hope for a high school reunion."

So what was with her reaction to him?

"Jaclyn, you're talking to yourself." RaeAnn frowned. "How much smoke did you breathe in?"

"I'm fine."

"No, you aren't. Your foot is injured. For once, stop trying to be in control." RaeAnn slid an arm around her waist for support. "I'm taking you to the hospital."

Maybe they could get her head examined while she was there, Jaclyn mused. She checked over her shoulder one last time and saw Kent motion for another fireman to direct his hose on the back of the now-smoking building that had housed Jaclyn's clinic. That clinic had been the focus of her dreams for more than ten years. It was the place where she was finally going to earn the life she'd been given. The life Jessica had lost.

Why? That was the question that always haunted her. Why had her twin sister gotten leukemia and not her? In all the years since Jessica's death, she'd never figured that out.

"Ready?"

Jaclyn shook off her stupor and concentrated on getting into RaeAnn's car while her assistant retrieved her shoes. It must have been smoke addling her brain that made her notice Kent's broad shoulders again because Dr. Jaclyn LaForge was not interested in men—especially not Kent McCloy, no matter how good he looked in his gear.

Guys like Kent, even though they're gorgeous, have no affect on me, she thought as she sat alone in a treatment room, waiting to be examined by a colleague. But all the denials in the world couldn't disguise the way her heartbeat had raced when Kent had touched her.

How was it that the only guy she'd ever had a crush on in high school—the guy who'd stuck by her when everyone else had turned against her after Jessica's death—still had the power to make her shiver?

Didn't matter. Overpowering reactions notwithstanding, Jaclyn had no time for personal relationships. She had a duty to her twin sister to get the clinic up and running again. Despite losing the building, she would find a way to do it—no matter what.

Kent left the fire hall late in the afternoon after learning the fire was the result of an overtaxed electrical outlet. Thankfully no one had been seriously hurt. But the incident reinforced his long-held belief that it was time to get an emergency procedure plan in place in town.

He took his time driving home, surveying the land in its burgeoning spring glory. The last rays of sun sank below the craggy tips of New Mexico's mountains, bathing the world in a rosy glow as he drove into his driveway. It should have made him feel peaceful.

But the usual post-fire adrenaline surge had left Kent antsy. He walked around the yard and thought about the town's new pediatrician.

Kent had forgotten a lot of things about Jaclyn La-Forge since their days in high school—that silver blond hair of hers, for one thing. Then she'd worn it long; now her short, precise blunt-cut caressed a chin that said she was all business. The silky strands cupped her face, drawing attention to her delicate cheekbones and big brown eyes framed by long lush lashes. How could he have forgotten those lashes?

The pediatrician oozed class, from her red silk suit to her spicy perfume. Jaclyn, the rebel teen whom he'd known so well had been totally erased.

In an instant he time-traveled back five years.

"Kent, slow down. I can't keep up with you wearing these heels."

His wife would have envied Jaclyn her fancy shoes—they were the kind Lisa loved but said she could never wear in Hope.

"This is Hokey Ville, Kent." Three years later and Lisa's accusing voice would not be silenced. *"You said we wouldn't stay. You promised we'd go back to Dallas."*

A promise he'd made but never kept.

Uncomfortable with the memory of his betrayal, Kent clenched his jaw. Rescuing Jaclyn from that burning building had knocked his world off-kilter. He doubted he'd ever forget seeing her through the smoke, but he needed to restore his carefully managed equilibrium because blocking out the past and focusing on the present was how he got through each day.

Oreo, his old Springer spaniel, strolled up to him and

rubbed against his knee. Her white-and-gold patches gleamed from the brushing he'd given her this morning. As usual, the dog seemed to sense his mood. She nuzzled under his hand until it rested on her head, then laid her head on his knee.

"Did you get the pups straightened out, girl?" he asked. Oreo's daughter had given birth to ten pups the week before. Grandmother Oreo seemed to think it was her duty to ensure each one of the offspring received equal attention from their mother.

The dog's responsive yowl made Kent laugh. Her throated growls sounded as if she was asking him about his day. Since Lisa's death he'd gotten into the habit of talking to the dog. Oreo had become his companion so he told her what was on his mind.

"Hope needs a kids' doctor. Jaclyn's clinic is unusable, but Dad's old building might make a good replacement." The dog shifted and he nodded. "I know. It's probably a wreck."

Kent didn't want to admit how much seeing Jaclyn had affected him. He was grateful when a car's lights flashed as it climbed the hill to his ranch house. Company would be good.

He gulped when Jaclyn climbed out of a sky-blue convertible and walked toward him—limped, actually. She had on a pair of jeans, a perfectly pressed candy-pink shirt and a pair of white sneakers that looked brand-new. Typical city girl.

"Hello." Her smile displayed perfect white teeth. Everything about her was perfect.

"Hi." He motioned to a chair. "How's the foot?" he asked when she'd sat.

"Sore." She tucked some of the glossy silver blond

strands behind one ear before she bent to pet his dog. "But fine."

"Good." Suddenly he could think of nothing to say.

"I wanted to thank you again for saving me this afternoon, Kent. I would have died without your help." Her big brown eyes stared earnestly into his.

"Don't thank me." He heard the gruffness in his voice and wished he could sound less affected by her presence. He didn't want her to guess how much seeing her again *had* affected him. "One of the other guys would have found you."

"But you were the one who did and you treated my foot. So thank you." She paused a moment.

"Sure. Anything else?" It was rude and ungracious but suddenly Kent didn't want to talk to Jaclyn. She upset his carefully regulated world.

"Yes, there is. You mentioned your dad's office building."

"Yeah." He kept it noncommittal.

"I noticed it's unoccupied. Is renting it an option?" Her voice became businesslike.

"I don't know. I haven't been through the place in ages." Why had he ever opened his big mouth? He wanted to avoid her, not build a relationship. When hope flickered in her eyes he blurted out the first excuse he could think of. "There could be some issues with the place."

"Can you check?" Jaclyn rubbed the sweet spot behind Oreo's ears and smiled at the dog's growled appreciation. She refocused on Kent. "It's really important to me to get the clinic going again." Her eyes held his. "Please?"

"I've got the ranch and my practice," he reminded. "I'm pretty busy."

"I'm sure you are." She kept staring, waiting.

"Fine," he relented when it became obvious she wouldn't back off. "I'll look as soon as I can." In the meantime maybe she'd find something else and he could forget her and go on with his normal life.

In his dreams. He remembered Jaclyn's tenacity too well.

"If you'd let me know when you go, I'd like to come along." Her smile blazed. "The clinic has to be fully operational, treating a certain number of patients, in three months or I jeopardize my financing. This is March. That means I'd have to move in by the end of May."

"I said I'll get to it when I can and I will." He swallowed his harsh tone and focused on his manners. She was his guest and he hadn't offered her anything. His mother would be appalled. "Do you want something to drink?"

"Iced tea? If it's not too much trouble."

Kent went inside and reached for the fridge door. To his shock, Jaclyn followed him and was now looking around the kitchen. He wished he hadn't offered her a drink. Or anything else. He didn't want her here, seeing the starkness of his kitchen and realizing that it mirrored his life. He didn't want her leaving behind the scent of her fancy perfume. Mostly he didn't want her seeing how pathetic he was.

He held out a brimming glass.

"Thanks. Do you have any lemon?" She accompanied the request with the sweetest smile.

Kent hacked off a wedge of lemon and held it out.

"Oh." She took it daintily between her fingertips—

perfectly manicured fingertips with pale pink polish. "Um, thank you." She moved to stand in front of the sink, pinched the lemon into her glass and stirred it with a finger. "Lovely." She held the piece of lemon between two fingers, searching for a place to discard it.

Kent handed her a sheet of paper towel.

"Thanks." She wrapped the towel around the lemon wedge and set it on the counter before she took another sip. "It feels cool out tonight."

Meaning he could hardly lead her outside to the patio again. He motioned to one of the kitchen chairs. Jaclyn sank onto it with graceful elegance. Kent couldn't help noticing her expensive jeans, her tailored blouse and her three pieces of jewelry—two small gold hoops in her ears and a thin gold chair around her neck—that made her look like a princess slumming it.

"Are you still holding that night at the church against me, Kent?"

"What?" He jerked to awareness, embarrassed that he'd been caught staring at her. "Of course not. Why would you say that?"

"You act as if you're mad at me." Her smile grew wistful. "I never came back to Hope for any of the reunions and I haven't seen you since the night of high school graduation, so I'm guessing your attitude has to be about the night I wrecked the church. I'll apologize again if it means you'll forgive me for letting you take the blame for that night, even for a little while."

Forgive her? He was the one who needed forgiveness. But what he'd done was unforgiveable.

"Am I forgiven?" Her smile faltered.

"Nothing to forgive," Kent told her, his voice hoarse. "You were hurting. Your sister had just died. You were angry that God hadn't healed her the way you expected and you lashed out. I understood."

"You always did." Jaclyn's voice softened to a whisper. "Of all the people in Hope, you were the only one who did. But I shouldn't have let you take the fall, even for the few days it took to get my act together. I'm sorry."

"I'm glad I could help." High-school Jaclyn had drawn his sympathy, but this woman disarmed him. His throat was dry. He took a sip of his tea but it didn't seem to help. Nor did it stop the rush of awareness that she was the first woman to come into Lisa's kitchen since—

"You helped me more than you ever knew. I won't forget that." After an introspective silence her expression changed, her voice lightened. "I don't suppose we could go into town and look at your dad's building tonight? Don't answer. I can see 'no' written all over your face. How about tomorrow morning? Say, seven-thirty?"

"Do you ever give up?" he asked in exasperation.

Jaclyn stilled. "Not when it comes to my dreams."

"This clinic is your dream?" Kent knew it was from the expression on her face. He also knew he wanted to help her achieve it. "I'll ask a friend of mine to check out my dad's old office as soon as he can. But be warned it will probably need a painting, at the very least. The company that opened the new silver mine on the other side of Hope was in there last and they weren't gentle."

"Your dad's retired now, I suppose? He and your mom were such a loving couple. I remember she once told my mom the ranch was your dad's weekend toy but he intended to make it a full-time job after retirement." She tilted her head to one side, studying the fancy kitchen. "Your mom must love this. Everything here looks brand-new."

"It is. My wife had it redone several years ago. My parents died in a car accident, Jaclyn. That's why I came back to Hope." Kent clamped his lips together.

"Oh, no!" She shook her head sadly. "Losing your parents must have been hard."

"Yes, it was."

After a long silence, she asked, "Is your wife here? I'd like to meet her. There aren't a lot of the kids from our class in Hope anymore. Since my parents sold our ranch right after I finished high school, I've kind of lost touch."

Kent stiffened. But he had to tell her. She'd hear it from someone in town anyway. Better that he laid out the bare truth. Maybe when she knew, she'd stay away and let him get back to his solitary life.

"My wife was Lisa Steffens."

"I remember Lisa—"

"She's dead," he blurted out.

"Oh, Kent. I'm so truly sorry."

"She died in a fire. A fire I set." Kent wished he could have avoided rehashing the past.

Jaclyn blinked. She studied him for several moments before she said, "You didn't do it deliberately. I know you and you couldn't have done that."

"You don't know me anymore, Jaclyn."

"I don't think you've become a murderer, Kent." She held his gaze. "Do you mind telling me what happened?"

Jaclyn's presence in his house made the place come

alive as it hadn't in a very long time. She brought color to the cold stainless steel, life to the gray tones that only reminded him of death and guilt. From somewhere deep inside a rush of yearning gripped Kent, a yearning to share his life with someone who would talk, listen and laugh with him. If only he could enjoy Jaclyn's company and the hope that was so much a part of her aura—just for a little while.

"Not tonight." He drew back, regrouped.

Once Kent had dreamed of happiness, a family, a future on this ranch. He'd failed Lisa and he'd never have that now. But he had to go on; he couldn't get sidetracked by his crazy attraction to Jaclyn LaForge, no matter how strong. He admired her courage in returning to Hope, in sticking to her promise to her sister, but he desperately needed to resume his carefully structured world because that was the only way he could survive the guilt.

It wasn't his job to get Jaclyn a new clinic. He didn't want to get involved. He didn't want concerns about whether her foot would heal properly or get infected. And he sure didn't want his heart thudding every time he saw her.

Every instinct Kent possessed screamed *Run!*

"I'll meet you at the building tomorrow morning at eight," he heard himself say.

Chapter Two

"This is a beautiful building. The windows give amazing light."

"Say it, Jaclyn. There's a lot of work needed here." Kent leaned against a doorframe, probably running a repair tab in his mind. Then his gaze rested on her.

Jaclyn frowned. Maybe he was waiting for her to say she didn't want to rent his father's building.

"Correction—more than a lot of work." Kent kept staring at her.

"Perhaps once all the borders are removed?" Jaclyn trailed her finger across a wall.

"My mom went a little over the top with the borders," Kent admitted. "She loved the themes and colors of southwest decorating."

His wife definitely hadn't. Jaclyn wondered why Lisa had chosen the gray color scheme for her kitchen. High-tech certainly, but it seemed clinical, with nothing to soften the harsh materials or unwelcoming, austere colors. Her curiosity about Lisa's death had been tweaked by Kent's admission that he set the fire. Jaclyn knew there was no way he'd have deliberately hurt her. Kent had been in love with Lisa since seventh grade.

While Kent became all business, talking about support beams and studs, her attention got sidetracked as her eyes took in an unforgettable picture. The handsome vet probably couldn't care less what he looked like, but he was without a doubt what Jaclyn's friend Shay would say was hunk material.

A moment later Kent's dark blue gaze met hers and one eyebrow arched.

She'd missed something. Heat burned her cheeks. "Sorry?"

"I said it's going to be a while before you can move in here."

"A while meaning what, exactly?" She hadn't been staring. Well, not intentionally.

Liar.

"Are you okay?" Kent tilted his head to study her. "You look kind of funny."

"I'm fine." Jaclyn cleared her throat. Business. Concentrate on business. "You're telling me there's work that has to be done here, which I know. How long will that take?"

"I can't tell you that." Kent frowned. "Since the mine opened last spring, a lot of locals have gone to work there. The place offers good wages, decent benefits and steady work which means there aren't a lot of qualified trades available in Hope anymore."

"But? I can hear a 'but' in there." She smiled and waited.

"I'll start on the demolition. I can do most of that myself and some of the actual renovation. There are a couple of guys I can probably persuade to do other work but it is going to take time." He looked like he was waiting for her to say "never mind."

But Jaclyn wouldn't say that—getting this clinic operational again was her duty. The clinic had been her dream since the day after she'd buried her twin sister. They both should have graduated from high school, but Jessica's diagnosis had come too late because of the shortage of doctors in Hope. The traveling doctors that visited each week didn't catch the leukemia early enough. That wouldn't happen to another child—not if Jaclyn could help it.

She had already checked the other buildings in town. This place was the best of the lot, but Kent was right. It needed a major overhaul.

"I have just over three months until I have to open. Can you do it?"

He frowned, his deep blue eyes impassive. Only the twitch at the corner of his mouth told her he'd rather be somewhere else. "I *believe* I can."

Relief swamped her, stealing her restraint. She threw her arms around him and hugged.

"Thank you, Kent. Thank you so much."

He froze, his whole body going stiff. After a moment he lifted one hand and awkwardly patted her shoulder before easing away. "I haven't done anything yet."

"I can see it finished." She twirled around, her imagination taking flight. "Reception will be here, of course. I don't remember what your dad had in this corner before, but I'll get a child's table-and-chair set for coloring. And we can put—"

"That was Arvid's corner."

"Arvid?" She stared at Kent as old memories surfaced. "Your dad's parrot!" She grinned. "That's an idea."

"You'd put a parrot in a doctor's office?" His nose wrinkled. "Isn't that against health regulations or something?"

"Not as long as the cage is kept clean and the animal isn't dangerous. It's actually a great idea. I wonder where I'd find a parrot around here."

"At the ranch. I've got Arvid out there, hanging in the sunroom for now. He stays there during winter, but soon I'll have to bring him into the main house so he doesn't get overheated." Kent made a face. "He's never really adapted to the ranch. He doesn't like my dog. Or me," he admitted.

"You're sure it wouldn't be too much for him? Would the kids overwhelm him?"

Kent laughed. She hadn't heard that jubilant sound in years but the pure pleasure filling his face captivated her. In the moment, he looked carefree, happy.

"*Overwhelm* him?" His eyes twinkled. "You must not remember Arvid very well. The only thing that ever overwhelmed that bird was my mother's broom."

She giggled, sharing his mirth. But a moment later Kent's eyes met hers and his smile melted away. In a flash his glowering expression was back.

"You're certain you can get this place ready for me to use in time?" Jaclyn wished she could make his smile appear again. But she reminded herself that she didn't have the time for personal relationships with grumpy vets, not even the ones who made her heart skip a beat.

"I'm not certain but I think so. I spoke to a couple of tradesmen this morning."

"This morning?" *And I thought I got up early.* "And?" she asked.

"They'll stop by later today to take a look. Then I'll have a better idea." He rubbed a hand against his freshly shaven chin. "You understand I can't guarantee anything. At the moment there are just too many unknowns. All I can say is that I'll do my best."

"I understand. Your best is good enough for me."

"I'm not sure you do understand." He tipped her chin so she had to look at him. "Listen to me, Jaclyn. I have my practice and the ranch. I'm the fire chief, the mayor and I sit on several local boards. Right now Hope is a town divided over allowing the mine to open. Some folks saw potential, of course. But a lot thought the mine would bring problems. Which it has. And it's cost us some of the small town security we've always enjoyed. That's just a few of the reasons which caused a big split and left a lot of people hurting. I'm trying to help heal that rift."

"You're saying you will have to juggle a lot and that the clinic isn't necessarily first on the list." She nodded. "I get that and I accept it. I have to. I don't have another option. I have a lot invested in getting this clinic going and I'm willing to do whatever it takes." She caught his skeptical glance at her hands and smiled. "Just because I haven't lived on a ranch for a while doesn't mean I don't know how to work hard."

"Okay then. I'll do the best I can." Kent nodded once.

"And I'll help however I can. Just ask." Her beeper interrupted. Jaclyn glanced at it. "I have to go."

"What will you do for offices in the meantime?" Kent asked.

"The hospital gave me a room to use for consulting, for now. Not that I need much. People here don't seem willing to trust me." She tried to swallow the bitterness.

"Folks in Hope take a while to embrace outsiders." He blinked, obviously only then remembering that she wasn't exactly an outsider. "I had my own struggle after Doc McGregor died. It took forever for people to let me treat their cattle."

"And you weren't even guilty of almost burning down the local church." She grimaced. "Nobody's going to stop seeing me as that stupid kid. Maybe it was dumb of me to think I could come back here."

"No, it wasn't. People here will get to know you. Some will remember you were just a kid who lost your sister. Besides, you and your parents repaired the damage. Not that it matters anyway. The church is in bad condition now."

"Maybe I could find a way to restore it," she murmured. "Maybe that would make them forget."

"It's a nice thought." His tanned brow furrowed. "But it's not just your past. Your family only lived here for a few years, Jaclyn—your parents left when you did and neither they nor you ever came back. I'm not trying to hurt you, but to folks in Hope, you *are* an outsider."

"But I'm trying to help them!"

"I know." Kent nodded. "But while you've been away things have changed. Because of the mine, people here are more suspicious than ever before."

"Is that even possible?" she quipped.

"Oh, yeah." He didn't smile. "I told you the town had split over the mine, but I didn't tell you that the split was caused by outsiders who set friends and neighbors against each other, using scare tactics, among other things. Everyone's suspicious of everyone right now. But folks will come around. We need your clinic, Jaclyn."

We need your clinic? She liked the sound of that.

"Don't give up on your dream, okay?"

"No chance of that—I owe it to Jessica." The beeper sounded again. "Thanks, Kent." Jaclyn waggled her fingers as she strode toward her car.

After she had treated the baby who'd ingested his brother's marble, she sat and enjoyed her first cup of coffee of the day, recalling the note of earnestness in Kent's voice when he'd told her not to give up.

Remembering the forlorn look on his face last night when she'd visited his ranch, she wanted to repeat it back to him.

But now she wondered, what *were* Kent's dreams?

Dr. Jaclyn LaForge possessed remarkable powers of persuasion.

As he watched her drive away, Kent couldn't quite quash his smile. He walked through his dad's building a second time, remembering her insistence that she would help with renovations. As if those manicured hands would know how to grip a hammer.

His smile faded as he noted issues he'd missed. He should have been in here before this.

He should have done a lot of things.

Like not notice how Jaclyn's smile made her eyes as glossy as black walnut fudge. Like escape that hug she'd laid on him. Like ignore the way she'd lured him into helping her reach that goal of hers. The hurt in her eyes when she revealed that she'd been rebuffed by the locals had nearly done him in.

Kent drew on his memories of the LaForge twins. Jessica had always been the serious twin, Jaclyn the prankster. But after her sister's death, Jaclyn had bottled up her pain and anger until she'd finally exploded on graduation night. He'd understood why. Jaclyn had put so much faith in believing God would heal her sister. She couldn't reconcile Jessica's death with that faith. That's why she'd torn up the newly planted flower beds at the church. It was the reason she'd spray painted the walls and made a mess that had scandalized the entire town. Jaclyn had needed answers that night and she hadn't been able to find any that satisfied.

He knew how that felt. He'd asked why so many times. He still didn't have the answer he craved. He wondered if Jaclyn had ever found hers.

Uncomfortable with the direction of his thoughts, Kent reconsidered Jaclyn. She was still stunningly beautiful, but she'd lost the easy, confident joy in life that had once been so much a part of her. Jaclyn now seemed hunted, as if she had to prove something. He recalled her words.

I owe it to Jessica.

Kent knew all about obligations, and about failing them. Boy, did he know. He veered away from the familiar rush of guilt and recalled instead the closeness between the sisters. He, like others in their youth group, had attended many prayer services for Jessica in the small adobe church. But Jessica had died in spite of Jaclyn's insistence that if they just asked heaven enough times, God would respond.

Clearly the obligation to her sister still drove Jaclyn.

Brimming with questions that had no answers, Kent continued his inspection of the building. He pressed the wall in several places where water leaks had soaked through the plaster and left huge spots of dark brown. Each time he pushed, hunks of soggy plaster crumbled and tumbled to the floor. It would all have to be removed.

His former tenants had complained about something in the bathroom. Too busy with Lisa's depression, the failing ranch and his own pathetic practice to tend to the matter himself, Kent had hired a plumber. He now saw that the work was substandard. The bathroom would need to be gutted.

There were other issues, too. The roof, for one. Some of the clay tiles had cracked and broken away. Summer rains in Hope were aptly named monsoons. This past summer, the water had managed to find a way in, ruining large portions of the ceiling.

Kent made four phone calls. Then he took off his jacket, rolled up his shirtsleeves and got to work hauling refuse out to the newly arrived Dumpster he'd ordered. He'd been working about two hours before a phone call sent him back to his clinic at the ranch to treat a family pet. One thing after another popped up until it was evening. He wanted nothing more than to sprawl out in his recliner and relax, but he'd promised Jaclyn that building and her deadline would roll around too soon.

After a quick meal, Kent filled a thermos with coffee, grabbed an orange and headed back into town. At sunset his high school chum Zac Enders stopped in.

"Out for the usual run, huh, Professor?" Kent used the old nickname deliberately because it bugged Zac. He tossed yet another shovel full of plaster into a bin.

"Yeah. What's going on here?" Zac grabbed a

push broom and slid a new pile of rubbish onto Kent's shovel. "You sell the place?"

"I wish." Kent dumped the load, stood the shovel and leaned on its handle. "You didn't hear about Jaclyn's clinic burning?"

"Actually I did. I was out of town for a two-day conference but someone at the office filled me in." Zac had become the superintendent of Hope's school district the previous fall. "Shame."

"Yeah, it is." Kent waved a hand. "She wants to use this place. She's got to be up and running within three months." He gave his buddy the short version.

"This time you've really bitten off a big piece, cowboy." Zac smirked when Kent's head shot up at the old moniker. "Aren't high school nicknames fun?"

"Yeah," Kent said with a droll look. "Real fun."

"This place is a disaster." Zac glanced around, his eyes giving away his concern. "I hope you believe in miracles."

Kent didn't believe in miracles. Miracles would have saved his wife from the depression that took hold of her spirit and never let go. Miracles would have made him a better husband, would have helped him know how to help her. Miracles would have saved Lisa from getting caught between a wildfire and the backfire he'd set to stop it.

"I didn't make Jaclyn any promises," he told Zac. "I'll do my best here and hopefully it will be enough. But I don't know what I can do about Jaclyn's other problems." He shook his head at Zac's puzzled look. "Apparently the good people of Hope are reluctant to go to Jaclyn for medical help."

"Ah. The vandalism is coming back to bite her. But you can change that, Kent."

"Me?"

"Yes, you," Zac shot back. "Everybody in Hope thinks you're God's gift."

Kent snorted. "Hardly." God's failure, maybe.

"It's true. They look to you for leadership and they do whatever you say. All you have to do is put out a good word about her clinic and Jaclyn will have more patients than she can handle. I should know. That's how I got my job."

"Not true. You got your job because you were the best candidate."

"And because you put in a word with the board chairman." Zac smiled. "I heard."

"I only said it would be nice to have someone with a PhD running things." Kent avoided his knowing look.

"So? You can do the same for Jaclyn." Zac paused, frowned. "Can't you?"

"I've already tried. But she's big city now, Zac." Kent stared at the shovel he held. "Designer everything. You know how that goes down in Hope."

"I do know. Everyone still feels conned by the city jerks that came here, promised the moon and have yet to deliver. But so what?" His friend studied him for several moments then barked a laugh. "Surely you can't imagine Jaclyn will leave? Don't you remember high school at all, cowboy?"

"Which part of high school?" Kent remembered some parts too well. Like how he was going to marry Lisa and live happily ever after.

"Dude! The Brat Pack, remember?" Zac nudged

him with an elbow. "Jaclyn, Jessica, Brianna and Shay? Their dream?"

"I had forgotten that." Kent recalled the closeness of the four, the way Shay and Brianna had rallied around Jaclyn while her sister suffered. He vaguely remembered the friends discussing some future project they'd all be part of.

"They were going to build a clinic. Then Jessica died. The others decided to make the clinic as a kind of monument to her. They were each going to have a specialty. Jaclyn, the pediatrician who made sure no child ever had the lack of care her sister did, Brianna wanted to practice child psychology and Shay was going to be a physiotherapist." Zac slapped his shoulder. "You've got to put in a good word for Jaclyn, man. She's spent a long time nursing that dream."

"Ah, yes, Brianna." Kent frowned. "You wouldn't still be waiting for your former fiancée to come back to Hope to work in this clinic, would you, Professor?"

"No." Zac shook his head, his eyes sad. "I gave up that dream long ago when I heard Brianna had married."

"Then what's your interest?" Kent raised his shoulders.

"I live here. I knew and liked Jessica. I think it would be cool if Jaclyn finally got to make her dream come true and cooler still if you helped her do it. But that's up to you." He looked around, flexed his arm. "Want a hand? I haven't got anything going on tonight."

"Great. You're better at cleaning than me," Kent teased.

"If you consider this place clean, then I certainly am." Zac and Kent worked as a team for several hours.

As usual, Zac brought the conversation around to discussing his first love—Hope's schools. "Are you listening to me?" he asked.

"Sure." Kent blinked, grinned. "Not really."

"Thinking about Jaclyn, huh?" Zac snickered. "I hear she's changed."

"I told you, she's turned big city." Kent shrugged.

"That doesn't mean she's different inside." Zac drank from his water bottle while Kent sipped his coffee. "She's still focused on that clinic."

"I'd substitute 'driven' for 'focused.'" Kent sat on an upturned pail. "It's like the clinic will happen or she'll die trying."

"What's wrong with that?" Zac asked.

"Lots." Kent waved a hand around them. "What's going to happen if I don't get finished in time? She'll lose her funding. But Jaclyn doesn't hear my warnings and, far as I can tell, she doesn't have an alternate plan. It's the clinic or nothing."

"So you finish this place." Zac blinked. "What's the problem?"

"The problem?" Kent made a face. "Oh, just a few insignificant issues, like finding someone to do the work, paying for it, spending time here that I should be spending on my own practice or the ranch—take your pick." Suddenly the magnitude of what he'd agreed to swamped him. "I don't want to be responsible for ruining her dream."

"Her dream? Or Lisa's?" Zac tilted his head to one side, his expression sober. "It wasn't your fault Lisa didn't get her dream."

"Yes, it was. I'm the one who dragged her away from the city. I'm the one who wouldn't leave the ranch when she asked me to." The guilt multiplied every time Kent thought about his actions. He'd loved Lisa yet he'd hurt her deeply.

"How could you have walked away from the ranch?" Zac asked quietly. "You would have lost everything. That's not what a responsible man does."

"Not even at the cost of his wife's happiness?" Kent growled.

"There's no evidence that moving would have guaranteed happiness. Lisa was sick. You told me the doctors said moving would change nothing."

"They said it, but I don't *know* that. Maybe if I'd forced her into treatment—"

"You can't force someone to be well, Kent," Zac said, his voice somber. "You did what you could."

But Kent knew he hadn't done enough. He'd tried to force Lisa to see the good things about living on the ranch, but all she saw was a trap that kept her from the fairy-tale dream in her mind of a happy, party-style life in the city.

Zac helped awhile longer then offered some advice before he left.

"Lisa's gone. Leave her with God. He knows you did your best. He loves you and understands. Move on."

God loved him?

After Zac left, Kent tidied up the place, gathered his thermos and shut off the lights while thinking about Zac's words. Kent felt he couldn't accept God's love because he wasn't worthy of it. Lisa would still be alive if not for him. So what if they'd lost the ranch? He'd persisted because he wanted to make his dad's dream for the place come alive when he should have let it go and started again.

Shoulda, woulda, coulda.

The awful truth was that he'd chosen his father's dream over his wife.

Kent wouldn't make that mistake again. Somehow he'd get this building ready for Jaclyn, no matter what it cost him. It couldn't bring Lisa back or erase his guilt over her death, but maybe it would ease Jaclyn's grief.

He had to remember only one thing.

No matter how beautiful or how interesting Jaclyn was, no matter how many times he felt that zing of attraction when she smiled at him, there could be nothing between them.

Kent's love had failed the one woman he'd pledged to cherish. That would not happen again because as far as he was concerned, he had nothing to offer a woman but failure.

Jaclyn was a friend, but that's all she could ever be.

Chapter Three

"I'm begging, Pete. I know you're full-time at the mine, but I just need a couple of hours of your time. That's all."

Jaclyn paused in the doorway, struck by Kent's tone. Were plumbers so hard to get? She hadn't considered that. She'd figured Kent would pick up the phone, hire someone to do the renovation and she'd move in. But he sounded almost desperate.

"I didn't realize you had an exclusivity clause. Maybe if you asked them to waive it, they'd let you help with the clinic. It's for a good purpose, for our town's benefit. That's what their people promised when they begged us to let the mine in." He paused for effect. "This would be a good opportunity to keep that promise." There was silence as he listened. "I really appreciate it, Pete. Thanks."

Not wanting to be caught eavesdropping, Jaclyn waited a few moments before she let the front door bang behind her. "Hello?"

"Hi." Kent blinked at her. He was covered in a chalky dust that turned his dark hair gray. He'd been putting on goggles but now pulled them away, his blue eyes meeting hers. "Are you slumming?"

"Pretty fancy slum you've got here," she teased.

"Not yet, but it will be if I can get it done." He frowned. "Did you need something?"

"No. But I thought you might. I came to see if there was something I could help you with this evening." Jaclyn made a face. "Emergency was busy today— an issue with the mine. I need to work off the stress. I figured if you were into demolition, I'd channel my energy into that. Have you eaten dinner?" She glanced around amazed by the mess he'd created.

"I haven't had time for dinner." Kent gave her pristine clothes a dark look. "You can't work here dressed like that. Leave this to me, Jaclyn."

"Nonsense. I make a perfectly good gofer assistant and I can clean with the best of them. Besides, I've got the clothes issue covered. But first we eat. Deal?" She waited for his nod before setting down the two bags she'd carried in. She removed containers of Chinese food from one. "Come on. Let's sample this while it's hot."

At first it seemed as if Kent would refuse. Maybe he was used to working alone, or maybe he thought she'd get in his way. Either way Jaclyn wasn't going to let it dissuade her from pitching in.

"Thank you," he said when she handed him a loaded plate of stir fried vegetables.

"Welcome." She separated her chopsticks then speared a piece of pineapple. "Yum."

"It is good. Thanks," he said again, looking directly at her, his blue eyes bright.

"I don't know if Chinese is rancher's food but nobody in town has takeout steaks." She giggled at his droll look. "I'm guessing by that kitchen of yours that Lisa was a gourmet cook."

Kent's hand froze halfway to his mouth, his face pale at the mention of his wife.

"I'm so sorry," she said, feeling a fool. "I didn't mean to bring back painful memories."

"No, it's okay." He inhaled slowly then let out his pent-up breath before he spoke. "Lisa liked to cook if it was for entertaining—invite people over and she would go all out."

"I remember some parties Lisa invited me to in high school. She was a fantastic hostess back then, and an amazing cook." She watched the sadness of his face ease. "I suppose entertaining does provide an incentive to create. Not that I'd know. I can do basic cooking, which means I can open soup cans." Jaclyn took a bite, waiting to see if Kent would continue talking about Lisa or if he would change the subject.

"What happened at the mine?" he asked. "Anything serious?"

Note to self, she thought. *Stop bringing up Lisa.*

"A chemical explosion left burns on a number of miners. Emergency was swamped. This isn't the day for the traveling doctors so the hospital asked me to help. There were no critical injuries, so that's a blessing." She shuddered. "I loathe treating burns."

"Why?" Kent studied her with a puzzled look.

"Because of the pain. Kids or adults, it doesn't matter. Burns are the worst for continued pain. After initial treatment there's always the task of debrading the scar tissue to allow new tissue to grow—very time-consuming and more pain for the patient." She blinked. "As a firefighter, you probably know that."

"Since I've been on the job we've never had anyone badly burned, thank heaven," Kent said.

"That's lucky. Now—" Jaclyn lifted out a surprise "—I scored this from the bakery. Are you interested?"

"Who wouldn't be interested in key lime pie?" Kent raised an eyebrow when she cut a slice.

"What?" She studied the piece then chuckled. "Too small? Well, okay then." Jaclyn whacked out a much larger hunk of pie with her plastic knife. "Better?"

"Much better. Thank you." He dug in with relish.

"I'll have to jog for hours after this." She tasted her pie and sighed.

"You can join Zac. He's always jogging." Kent told her about their other school friend, Nick, and she shared the latest on her best friends Shay and Brianna.

"I remember Shay was offered some kind of contract just after her dad lost his job," Kent said.

"Modeling, yes. She felt she couldn't decline it because they needed the money so badly. Her father was broke. But he's gone now and she's finishing her physiotherapy degree. And Brianna is a practicing psychologist now in Chicago."

Kent finished his pie and added the plate and plastic fork to his garbage load.

"Both Shay and Brianna have gone through tough times." Jaclyn gnawed on her lower lip. "It's difficult to understand why things happen. Sometimes it seems to me that God expects too much of us humans."

"I'll second that." The words spilled out of Kent in a rush of bitterness.

"I'm sure you miss Lisa," she said before she could stop herself. So much for not bringing her up.

He nodded, accepted the cup of coffee she offered and they drank in silence for a while.

"I'm on call tonight so I might have to take off at any moment. We'd better get to work." She cleaned up the remains from their meal then met his gaze. "What can I do to help?"

"It's not necessary, really, Jaclyn." Kent glanced at her clothes again then quickly busied himself donning his mask and gloves. "The meal was more than enough."

Jaclyn let him go back to work then put on the white paper coveralls she'd brought, along with gloves and a mask. She began tapping the wall, trying to imitate Kent's motions on the plaster surface. She must have tapped too hard because huge chunks dropped down at her feet.

"I'm not sure I need this much help," he said, blue eyes twinkling.

"So tell me what I can do to help because I'm not going away." She met his stare head-on, relieved when he finally gave a half nod.

"How about stripping the wallpaper?"

"I can do that." She followed his directions and for the next hour worked feverishly, spraying, scrubbing and peeling away the old borders as she forced the stress from her mind and her muscles.

"How's work going? Are you swamped yet?" Kent steadily removed the damaged material from the walls, never missing a stroke as he spoke.

"Ha! I wish. My practice is on the way to failure. People won't even look me in the eye when I meet them on the street. Especially since I asked about the church and how it could be restored." She yanked extra hard on a strip of paper and smiled as the entire piece came loose. "At last."

He shrugged. "It might take a while but you'll break through their reserve."

"When will that be?" she demanded. "The day after the clinic closes because I don't have any patients?"

"It's not that bad," he muttered.

"You think not? A woman came into the hospital with a sick baby today. I tried to help, but the mom took the kid away, saying they'd drive to Las Cruces. You know how far that is, especially for a sick child?" Frustration leached through though she tried to suppress it. "If this continues, it won't matter if I open this clinic or not." She gulped down her panic. "I need patients, Kent."

He put down his hammer and turned to her.

"I'm really sorry this is happening, Jaclyn. It must feel terrible to be treated like that when you're just trying to help."

"I don't care about me," she sputtered. "It's the kids that matter. Their parents won't let me help."

"None of them?" His voice softened, flowing over her with compassion.

"Not many. Officially I have eleven juvenile patients on my books. Eleven, Kent, in a population of— what's the population of Hope? Three thousand?" She clenched her left hand as tears welled in spite of her efforts to suppress them. "I came here because I'm trying to make sure no other kid gets missed like Jessica did. Why is that wrong?"

"It's not wrong." He rested a comforting hand on

her shoulder. "It's a wonderful, unselfish, kind and generous thing to do."

"It can't be that wonderful." She dashed the tears away. "I know that God has a purpose for each of our lives, something only we can accomplish for Him. I believe the clinic is my purpose. I've been praying about it for years. I'm here. I'm ready. So why doesn't God help?"

If only Kent McCloy were privy to God's thoughts.

"I don't think I can explain God's actions." Kent lifted his hand off her delicate shoulder and turned so she couldn't see his face. "I think I'm on a need-to-know basis with heaven."

"Because of Lisa's death, you mean?" Jaclyn sat down on an old sawhorse he'd brought from home, watching him carefully, her big brown eyes inviting him to share. "I can't even imagine how hard it must have been for you. Do you want to talk about it?"

Hard didn't begin to describe it, but no matter the release he might find sharing with Jaclyn, Kent wasn't going to do it. He knew he was to blame. He didn't want to watch the pity fill her eyes.

"No, I don't." That came off sounding harsh so he changed the subject back to her. "Eventually people will get to know you and realize your heart is right." The last thing Hope needed was to lose yet another doctor. "Don't give up."

"Oh, I'm frustrated, Kent. But I'm a long way from giving up." She rose, took another swipe at the wallpaper. "So how do I go about getting to know the people of Hope?"

"I'm not sure." He carried a bucket of refuse out

to the Dumpster. When he returned, Jaclyn was grinning. "What?"

"I have a great idea. I'm going to join some of their local groups. I can't cook and I haven't got a clue how to quilt, but if those groups exist here, I'll join them." Her chin lifted in determination. "You'll have to tell me what kind of activities Hope offers because this place isn't at all as I remember."

"It's the same place, but we've gone through some issues. When the town split over the mine almost two years ago, there were a lot of hard feelings. Cliques developed." She frowned at him and he sought an example to illustrate his point. "Like there used to be a ladies' aid society, but it's for the pro ladies now," he told her. "Pro meaning pro-mine. The ladies against the mine and the problems they thought it would bring to their families left that group and started their own. That one is called Hope Circle and it has no relationship with the other group."

"Should I join one, or both?" She frowned, rubbing her chin.

"Don't ask me. I don't even know what they do in their meetings." Kent shrugged. "I only know they do not do it together. We used to have a family bowling night. Everyone came out, brought their kids and had a great time together. Now we have the Christian night and the Followers' night."

"You're kidding me," Jaclyn said with a wry smile. Despite her messy work, she still looked as if she'd stepped out of a magazine. Her white paper suit did nothing to disguise her beauty.

"I wish I were kidding." Kent forced his gaze off her. "The rift goes a lot deeper. Neighbors don't talk to neighbors. Old friends don't have coffee together. Fellow citizens bicker over fence lines and every other petty issue. It's bad. They even insist on different services at the church. The place needs repair badly but nobody is willing to work with anybody else on it." Talking about this made him feel worn-out. "I was a town councilor when it happened. Now I'm the mayor. It's my fault things got so bad."

"You feel responsible?" Jaclyn blinked at him. "Why?"

"I couldn't find a way to mediate, to bring them together." Painful reminders of arguments he'd interrupted, friends he'd tried to reunite and the bitterness underlying everything weighed on his soul. "In the end the town voted on it, the majority won and the mine went ahead, but the issues remain."

"Democracy worked. How is that your fault?" When he stored his hammer in his toolkit, Jaclyn asked, "We're finished for tonight?"

"I am. I'm beat. I had a very early morning." Kent turned away as she shed her paper suit.

There was so much about this woman that spoke to him. Her beauty, her determination to give, her spunky grit in coming here to help him and her strength of purpose in keeping the vow she'd made her sister all demonstrated a woman filled with resolve and fortitude. Her determination astounded him—joining town groups after being virtually ostracized by the community was a gutsy move.

This was one amazing woman.

"There's a long way to go with this place, isn't there?" Her voice was quiet, almost solemn. She stood, holding the leftover pie, waiting for his answer as he locked the building.

"It'll be tough, but it can be done." Kent hoped he wasn't going to regret saying that.

"But it's costing you a lot. I should have considered that." Under the streetlight, Jaclyn's pale hair glowed like a halo around her heart-shaped face. "If you want to back out, tell me. I can find another way."

"Can you?" Kent doubted it.

She looked so small, so delicate. A sudden urge to protect her from the gossip and the hurt she might endure overwhelmed him. Silly. He barely knew Jaclyn anymore.

And yet Kent did know her. He knew her heart was for her patients. He knew her commitment was total. After tonight he also knew her resolve was firm.

"I shouldn't have asked you to do it. You have enough on your plate." A tight little smile curved her very kissable mouth. "I don't want to add to your burdens, Kent."

"Too late." He grinned. "I want to make this clinic happen, Jaclyn." In that moment he realized it was true. "If they could forget their differences, the pristine countryside they've lost, the promises made and broken, the hurt feelings because they didn't see things the same way—if they could only see that their differences are making us all weaker—" He sighed. "Maybe if they could unite in your clinic's cause—well, I guess I see it as a sort of rallying point for people in Hope."

"You do?" A fan of tiny smile lines appeared at the edge of her shining eyes. "How?"

"Your clinic isn't part of the old system. It's new, different. Maybe it can help undo past damage and end some of the bitterness. Maybe that's God's plan in all of this." Kent had no business saying that since he wasn't in touch with God anymore. But his idea about the clinic felt right.

"Thank you for saying that, Kent. I admit I was a little discouraged when I came here tonight, but I feel reenergized now. You can't know how much that means to me." She stood on tiptoe and brushed her lips against his cheek before shoving the pie at him. "You're a wonderful man, Kent. Lisa would be proud of you. Good night." Jaclyn got into her car and drove away.

Lisa would be proud of you.

The surge of hope Kent had experienced drained away. Lisa wouldn't be proud. She would know he was trying to make up for past mistakes. She would recognize that he was trying to redeem himself by getting this clinic up and running.

As if you could redeem yourself for causing your wife's death.

God has a purpose for each of our lives, something only we can accomplish for Him. The clinic is my purpose. Jaclyn's words echoed inside his head as he drove the familiar route home.

What's my purpose, God?

But as he pulled up to his house, memories of the past crowded out whatever answers God might have whispered.

If only Kent could have a chance to start fresh, like Jaclyn. He'd do so many things differently.

Maybe if he worked hard enough on her clinic, he could finally rise above his regrets.

Chapter Four

"But Dr. LaForge is a member of our group."

"She can't be! She's a member of ours."

Two days later the presidents of Hope's two women's committees glared at each other on Main Street—because of her. Jaclyn gulped. What had she gotten into?

"Can't I be a member of both groups?" She heard the timidity in her own voice. Two heads swiveled to stare at her.

"Pro ladies have no relationship with Hope Circle. We stand for different things." Heddy Grange's rigid shoulders tightened even more.

Jaclyn swallowed hard and searched for some middle ground.

"But at the last meeting you discussed doing something to start restoration on the church. Hope Circle is also going to initiate fundraising for that." The moment the words left her lips, Jaclyn knew it was the wrong thing to say.

"You copied our project?" Heddy's voice rose with every word. "How dare you?"

"How dare you?" Missy Sprat snapped back. "We chose it first."

"No, you didn't."

"Ladies, please. Does it matter that you have both chosen to help the place where we all go to meet God?" Jaclyn thought the role of peacemaker ill-suited to her, but in this instance she had little choice. This was her fault. "Aren't both of your groups really trying to extend God's love? Can't that be done better by working together? Won't He bless all efforts to restore His house?"

The two frowned at her. Their silence lasted only a few seconds before the wrangling began again. Jaclyn laid a hand on each arm.

"I'm sorry, ladies. Perhaps it's better if I resign from your groups," she told them in a no-nonsense tone. "The church is an important part of my faith which is why I wanted to help restore it. I never meant to cause problems between you. I apologize." Then she turned and walked down the street, aware the women were staring at her retreating back.

"Trouble?" Kent stood in front of his father's building clad in jeans and a faded chambray shirt. His blue gaze hid behind sunglasses. "The three of you don't look very happy—you least of all, Doc."

"Happy? No, that would not apply to me at this precise moment in time." Jaclyn grabbed his arm and pulled him forward. "Please, can we go inside?"

"Need to escape, huh?" His rumbling chuckle shook his shoulders as he unlocked the door. "As mayor, I've come to know that feeling very well."

"Why didn't you warn me about what I was walking into?" Jaclyn flopped down on the sawhorse and exhaled. "I've probably ruined any church restoration plans."

"I doubt it." He chuckled and shook his head. "Those two were vying for supremacy long before you showed up in Hope. I don't think your presence here has changed much."

But Jaclyn couldn't laugh. She'd added to the friction in town and she felt awful. "I should have minded my own business."

"What happened?" he asked. Before she could finish her explanation he burst out laughing.

"This is not a laughing matter!" She glared at him.

"Sometimes you have to laugh. Or cry at the stupidity of it all." His smile disappeared. "It really isn't your fault. They would have found something to argue about. That's how stupid this quarrel is."

"But I want to be part of the town. That's why I joined those groups, to work toward a common goal. I had this dumb idea that maybe I could make up for the past." She bit her lip. "Instead, I've probably alienated them so much they'll never speak to each other."

"Oh, they'll speak to each other. Otherwise holding the grudge would be pointless." He smiled at her. "Forget about it. You tried to help. Let it go."

"I can't. Somehow I've got to do something to restore that church. If I can do that, maybe the town will find healing there." She blinked, suddenly noticing the floor. "What happened?"

"Mildew. I had to tear out the carpet. Then I found some of the floor boards damaged. The roof leaked during the summer." He scuffed his cowboy boot against a newly installed sheet of plywood. "Renovating this place is like removing an old woman's makeup. You just keep pulling away layers."

"I'm not sure I like the allusion." She frowned. "Why do men always use women as their scapegoats? Cars are 'she.' Fires are 'she.'" Jaclyn saw his shoulders shake with laughter and sighed. "Now I'm bickering! It's contagious."

"Yep. That's why I say forget it. It can get you down if you let it." Kent pulled off his sunglasses and studied her. "We can't afford to lose you, or let you get caught up in somebody else's feud. You've got things to do in Hope, remember?"

And suddenly she did remember. "Oh, brother, now I've done it."

"What?" After a moment he stopped and leaned nearer. "You look funny."

"I feel sick." She slid off the sawhorse onto an upended pail. "How could I be so stupid?"

"What?"

"Kent, I promised I'd speak at those ladies' groups." She watched his smile die.

"What, both of them?"

She nodded. "Separately, of course."

"Well, in light of today's argument, maybe they'll cancel and find somebody else," he offered.

"By tonight?" She shook her head. "Heddy told me how hard it's been to get speakers. Hope isn't exactly sitting in the mainstream of a speaking route. She seemed to like my fundraising ideas and wanted me to tell the Pros about them. Truthfully I was kind of looking forward to it, too. I thought it would make things easier if I provided a little history about my night of terror." She groaned. "Why didn't I shut my mouth? Why did I even try?"

"Because you are generous and trying to help. Relax." Kent pulled out his cell phone and dialed. "Hey, Margie. This is the mayor." He listened for a minute, laughed and then said, "Is there a ladies' group meeting tonight?" His blue eyes twinkled as he listened to the response. "Okay. Sounds like a good time. Thanks." He flipped the phone closed. "It's on and so are you. Apparently the word has gone out about your fundraising ideas for the church and a fair crowd is expected. Margie said she just talked to Heddy and nothing's been canceled, not tonight and not tomorrow night."

"I guess I'll show up then." Jaclyn got hung up on the dimple that sometimes appeared when his eyes crinkled with laughter. "Thanks, Kent. I hope you'll pray for me while I'm there. It's funny but walking into the church's basement makes me feel like Daniel going into the lions' den."

He chuckled but he didn't say he'd pray.

She checked her watch. "Yikes! I've got an appointment. I have to go."

"So I guess that means you won't be by tonight to work," he teased before she dragged open the door.

"I'll stop in and give you the gory details after," she promised. "I'll help you, too, if you want. I have a hunch I'm going to need a good workout before the evening is over."

"Positive thoughts," he ordered.

"I'm positive I was an idiot to even consider this. Nobody can say Hope is boring." She stepped outside to the musical sound of his laughter echoing through the building.

Jaclyn consulted on two cases that afternoon. It felt good to be needed. Later she hurried back to her town home to prepare shrimp salad for the potluck dinner before the meeting. The recipe was Shay's. If it got any accolades tonight, that would be enough. Tiny steps, she reminded herself.

She took her time getting dressed, striving for professional yet not stuffy. The chocolate-brown pencil skirt coordinated perfectly with the pinstriped white-and-brown shirt, and her dark brown heels encased her healing foot like a velvet glove.

"Okay, Lord. That's the best I can do with what You gave me. From here on in it's up to You." The phone rang. "Hi, Mom. How are you?"

Jaclyn winced as her mother launched into a tirade about her father. She suggested her mother discuss it with him.

"He's never here. Golf and more golf. That's his true love."

"Mom, I'm sure Dad loves you as much as he ever did."

Her mother scoffed at that. Clearly her parents' rocky relationship was not improving. In fact it had gone steadily down since the day of Jessica's funeral.

"I found a new site for my clinic," she said, hoping for a diversion.

"When will you give up that silly idea, Jaclyn? You're our only daughter. You should be here, near us, in a profitable practice."

"Mom, I promised Jess. I have to do this." It was always the same argument and tonight Jaclyn didn't want to get into it. "I'm the speaker at a ladies' meeting in a few minutes. I have to go. I'll call you later," she promised and hung up quickly.

The church parking lot held at least fifty cars. The white stucco church, cornerstone of her childhood and teenage faith, now showed its age. The exterior needed a new coat of paint and repairs on the corners, as did the crumbling stairs. The few undamaged stained windows were cloudy with dust and grime. It looked like birds had taken over the bell tower, and the rosebushes Jaclyn had helped her mom plant as repayment for her vandalism badly needed tending. The carved wooden door she'd ruined ten years ago had been repaired, but it still looked sad and uninspiring. A frisson of despair rippled through her as she saw the gouges she'd made that night. No wonder people hadn't forgotten her vandalism.

But inside Jaclyn was amazed at the transformation of the tired old basement, thanks to candles and some beautiful spring flowers in the center of each table.

Someone took Jaclyn's salad. A moment later Heddy appeared. The woman's beaming face showed no sign of their previous altercation.

"I'm glad you're finally here. I'll introduce you to some members who weren't at our last meeting."

Jaclyn knew she'd never remember all the names so she concentrated on learning about interests and ended up agreeing to take a couple of classes. It was a relief to finally sit down to dinner.

Jaclyn had never tasted anything as delicious as that potluck dinner. She spared a thought for Kent slaving away at her clinic—maybe she'd ask for a plate for him. Before she knew it, Heddy's introduction was over. Jaclyn stood, her knees quaking at the expectant looks.

Please don't let me mess this up. Let me be a help to this hurting community.

Jaclyn started at the beginning, emphasizing God's role in her life and the pain of her twin's death despite so many prayers. She admitted she'd done a lot of damage at the church that night and how sorry she was for it. Then she focused on her reason for returning to Hope.

"I want to be more than just your children's doctor though," she said. "I want to give back to the community." She laid out her ideas for restoring the church. By the time she finished Jaclyn felt she had the sympathy of those listening, but whether or not they'd accept her wasn't clear.

"It's hard to know if I reached them," she told Kent later as he sampled the food she'd brought. "They smiled, thanked me and wished me well, but nobody said they'd bring their kids to see me."

"Give it time." He paused and watched her as she looked around the room. "Well? What do you think of the place now?"

Jaclyn wasn't exactly sure what he expected her to say. She couldn't see any real difference in the room, except that he'd hauled out more garbage. So she simply smiled and said, "Looking good."

"You don't see it, do you?" He shook his head. "No reason why you should, I guess."

Jaclyn tracked his gaze to the window, studied it for several moments.

"I put in a new one," Kent explained. "Zac helped me. He's working out back."

Jaclyn inspected it. "It looks exactly the same," she mused. "You can't tell it's been altered at all."

"That's what I wanted to hear." He grinned. "My dad was big on southwest architecture so I'm trying to preserve the integrity of the structure."

"He'd be very proud of your work here, Kent." She thought about the ranch. "He must have had plans for the ranch, too."

"Some." Kent's face closed up. He quickly finished his meal and tossed the plate and plastic utensils into the garbage. "That was delicious. It seems like you're always feeding me. It's my turn next time."

"Okay." She smiled at the prospect of sharing another meal with him, until her brain kicked in a reminder that she wasn't here to enjoy Kent McCloy. She was here to keep her promise to Jessica. "Anything I can do to help?"

He looked at her, moving his gaze from her head to her toes. "Um, I don't think so. Not dressed like that. Besides, you'd wreck your nails and muss your hair."

"You're always commenting on my appearance." Jaclyn frowned.

"I don't comment on your appearance all the time. Do I?" He lifted one eyebrow as if he found her comments surprising. "I don't mean to. It's just—"

Jaclyn waited for Kent to complete his thought but when he didn't, she finished it for him.

"Just that I look out of place, like I don't belong here?" She stuffed down the hurt.

"I never said that."

"You didn't have to." She straightened her shoulders and looked directly into his vivid blue eyes. "It's sort of reverse prejudice, isn't it? But I can't do much about it. I look the way I look. I wear the clothes I have. I am who I am. You and everyone else are just going to have to accept that. Or not. Your choice."

"Jaclyn—"

"Good night, Kent." She turned and walked out the door, surprised by the sting of betrayal. She didn't care what Kent McCloy thought of her.

You just keep telling yourself that, said a voice in her head.

"You're an idiot, cowboy." Zac emerged from the back room wearing a grim expression. "I can't believe you just did that."

"Did what?" Kent muttered.

"Jaclyn offered to help and you shoved it back in her face."

"Did you see what she had on?" he bellowed. "I can hardly ask her to start sanding the wall compound in high heels, can I?"

"Not the point and you know it." Zac's harsh voice left no room for excuses. "You're cranky with me and that's fine. I'm used to your orneriness, but I don't think Jaclyn deserves it. She's only trying to help."

"In those clothes?"

"Oh, get a grip! As if she couldn't have gone home and changed. All she wanted was a chance. But you can't see past her appearance to the heart of her. I never thought you'd be so self-centered, Kent—that you of all people couldn't see past your own biases." Zac dropped the tool bag he was carrying.

Kent didn't know how to answer. But his brain mulled over Zac's words.

"Pete gave me that tool bag. He said he'd be around

tomorrow morning and he'd need it then. I have to get home." Zac walked toward the door.

"Professor?" Kent waited for him to turn around. "Thanks for your help."

"No problem. But can I offer some advice?" Zac didn't wait for an invitation. "When you get home tonight, take a look in the mirror and tell me if you're any different from the rest of the naysayers in this town who've already judged our new pediatrician."

"I haven't judged her." Kent ground his teeth at the accusation.

Zac scoffed. "Forget Jaclyn's clothes, her hair and her mannerisms. Jaclyn isn't Lisa, Kent. When you accept that, maybe you'll begin to see past Jaclyn's exterior."

A moment later Zac disappeared, leaving Kent gaping. His best friend had just called him biased. Was that true?

Kent replayed his words to Jaclyn as best he could remember them. He'd said nothing wrong. Except that expression in her eyes—he couldn't get that sad look out of his mind. Like a wounded puppy that expected better of you and was utterly disappointed when you didn't meet her hopes.

Zac was right about that. But he was right about something else, too. Something that was hard for Kent to accept.

Jaclyn did remind him of Lisa.

The two women were nothing alike and yet every time he looked at Jaclyn he saw her clothes, her hairstyle, her fancy shoes—and all of it reminded him of how much Lisa had wanted all those things, and how she'd never gotten them because they'd moved to the ranch.

His phone broke through his musings.

"Hello?" He almost groaned aloud when Heddy, the town's biggest troublemaker, began speaking.

"Thank you for suggesting we ask Dr. LaForge to speak to us, Kent. Some of us remember the damage she did to the church. It's hard to forget. But tonight we realized how much she regrets her past actions. I think we are all impressed by her commitment to re-open the clinic after the fire. According to her, you are the reason she can do that." Heddy paused for breath.

"I'm happy to help." Kent rushed to get a word in before she took off on a new tangent. "I think her ideas to fix the church are amazing, though it's going to take all of us pitching in to make that and her clinic a success." Was that a broad enough hint? Just in case it wasn't, he added, "It takes a lot of patients to make a clinic like hers successful."

"I'm sure it does." Heddy was backing off—he could hear it in her voice. "Of course, I have my own doctor in Las Cruces and anyway, Dr. LaForge is a children's doctor, but I'm sure she's very good at it."

"She certainly comes with high references." Kent paused. He decided to enlighten her, knowing it would flash through the town like wildfire. "She had offers from six other communities, but she chose to set up her practice in Hope."

"Is that right?" Heddy sounded surprised.

"Yes, it is." He paused a moment then added, "I hope we won't make her regret that choice."

"Oh, Kent, dear. Don't worry. There are other

doctors to be had." Heddy's breezy, know-it-all tone glossed everything over.

"Then why aren't they here?" Kent saw red at her easy dismissal of the generous doctor who'd slaved night and day trying to give to this town. "Where have they been for the last umpteen years? We need Jaclyn in Hope, Heddy. I would think everyone here could see that after the trouble we've had keeping the hospital functioning."

"Are you getting a little too personally involved, Kent?" The snide undertone irritated.

"I am personally involved," he shot back. "So are you. So is everyone in Hope. Jaclyn lost her sister because of inadequate medical care in this town, and yet she's put away her sorrow so she could come back to help us. I hope we won't be responsible for driving her away because we can't forgive a teenager's mistake. I think we've all made blunders we need forgiveness for. All of us." He paused a moment, added a goodnight and hung up. Let Heddy think on that for a while.

But as Kent cleaned up the job site and drove home, his brain kept replaying Jaclyn's face just before she'd left. She reminded him of Lisa when he'd told her he wouldn't move off the ranch. Worse, she reminded him of Lisa's condemnation.

"You hurt people, Kent, because you close yourself off. You won't let anyone, even me, see the vulnerable part of you. What are you so afraid of?"

Once, a long time ago, Jaclyn had asked him exactly the same thing.

He'd been on his way home from dropping off Lisa after the graduation celebration when he'd seen a figure in pale yellow in front of the church.

"Jaclyn?" Kent barely recognized her in the ragged and torn dress. Her eyes were bloodshot and black-ringed from tears that streaked mascara down her cheeks. Then he saw the chaos she'd created. "What are you doing?"

"He's God, isn't He?" Jaclyn sprayed another red jagged line on the white adobe wall of their church, her brown eyes seething with fury. "He wouldn't help Jessica, but He should be able to repair His own church, don't you think? God. The great One. He's supposed to fix everything. Isn't that what they taught us here, Kent?"

"Stop it." He wrenched the paint can out of her hand. "This won't bring Jessica back."

"No, it won't. Nothing will." Jaclyn picked up a stone and hurled it, shattering the small stained-glass window of the youth room. She tore plants from the flower bed and tossed them on the pavement, ignoring the cactus barbs that tore her delicate skin.

"Jaclyn, stop." He'd grabbed her hands, held them in his. "Just stop."

"Stop what—hurting? Stop feeling like God abandoned me, left me hanging when I needed Him most? I wish I could." Her chin thrust forward, her jaw tightened. "Jess should have been there tonight, Kent. She should have been the valedictorian, not me. She should have worn the dress we chose last winter. Why wasn't she?" Fury vibrated in that question. "Because He sat there and did nothing. God let her die."

A second later she'd yanked her hands free and raced to the front door. After removing her shoes, she started hitting the wooden doors with them, antique doors that had guarded entry to the church for almost a century. The gouges from her pointed heels went deep.

"Jaclyn, stop it!" He'd grabbed her arm, tried to drag her away. But anger made her strong. She wrenched free, grabbed the spray can he'd stuck in his pocket and continued her vandalism. Kent tried to stop her but she kept evading him. At last he grabbed her hand and pulled.

"We have to get out of here," he urged when she didn't move.

"Why? What are you afraid of, Kent? That your reputation will be shot 'cause you're here with me? That people will find out you're not the Goody Two-shoes you pretend to be?" she laughed. "Or are you afraid they'll figure out you're not the good little Christian boy they think?"

Kent remembered flashing police lights strobing across her face and the way Jaclyn had pushed against him, hard. She'd dropped the spray can by his feet and run off, her shriek of laughter ending in a muffled sob. He'd stood dumbfounded while the police jumped out of their cars and arrested him.

Oreo drew Kent back to reality, shoving her head against his hand. He'd never forgotten Jaclyn's words. Never stopped wondering how Jaclyn had seen past his carefree facade to his ever-present fear that he failed his parents.

Kent wondered if Jaclyn knew that even after all these years, the fear was still there.

Chapter Five

❧

"We might as well close early, RaeAnn," Jaclyn told her office nurse. "We won't have more appointments or drop-ins this late. Besides I'm dead after being on call last night. Two heart attacks, a broken arm, a broken leg, suspected meningitis and an accident with a chain saw were enough." She grimaced. "Not that I'm complaining. At least people trust me in an emergency."

"They'll come around. Hang in there." RaeAnn patted her shoulder.

"That's what everyone says." Jaclyn pocketed her phone. "So far I feel like I'm hanging out to dry."

"Hey, where's your faith?" RaeAnn challenged. "God is working. You just have to give it time."

Time. Something Jaclyn was running short of with only two months left before she lost her funding. Unless Kent got her clinic ready in time.

"Well, if you're serious about quitting early, I'm going to enjoy a half hour of sun before I get to work on dinner." RaeAnn shut down the computers and grabbed her handbag.

"I'm going to have a nap. Then I have a supper meeting at a service club."

"Another one?" The nurse frowned. "You just got in with that speech-making group. You're sure joining a lot of things. Don't you think you're taking on too much?"

"I'm trying to fit in so people will see I'm not the same dumb kid they once knew. And I haven't exactly joined the second service club yet. I'm still a guest," Jaclyn told her. "I'm hoping I can make a few friends there."

Except that no one hung around to talk to her after the meeting. Everyone seemed to have a place to be—except her. Jaclyn deliberately drove past the clinic site, as she had twice every day for the past two weeks. She was getting frustrated. How could she get patients if she didn't have a professional place to see them? That pokey room tucked into an unused corner of the hospital wasn't going to inspire confidence in new patients.

Jaclyn climbed out of her car and tried the door of the clinic but it was locked, and no one answered her knock. She'd hoped to work off some of her stress tonight by assisting Kent. Manual labor would go a long way toward making her feel like she hadn't lost all command of her world.

But Kent was not at the building. Again. Two whole weeks and as far as she could tell, nothing was happening with the clinic. Two weeks of no lights, no noises of construction, nothing. It was as if Kent had completely forgotten about her clinic.

Desperation edged in on her already strained nerves. When was he going to finish the place? Had he given up? And if he had, why didn't he just come right out and tell her?

"I'm trying to help," she said through gritted teeth. "What does it take to get some cooperation in this town, God?"

Fuming, Jaclyn climbed back in her car and headed for the McCloy ranch. If Kent had given up or changed his mind, she had to know now. Not that it was likely she could make alternate arrangements at this late date, but she couldn't just give up, either. She had to *do* something.

The scenic beauty on the drive to the ranch eased some of her frustration. The valleys burst with lushness. She reveled in the beauty of the hills, and was reminded of the days she and Jessica had saddled up and ridden over the hills of their own ranch, searching for a perfect patch to lie on and peer into the heavens, full of dreams and plans for the future.

Only Jessica never had the opportunity to fulfill her plans.

"I want you to live all the things I won't, Jaci," she'd said, lying in her bed. "Don't be angry at God. He knows what He's doing."

"Jess—" Her sister had stopped the words with a pale, thin finger against her lips.

"Do all the things we planned. Be a doctor, start the clinic. Live, Jaci. Do it for me. I love you." That night Jessica fell into a coma. She never awoke.

The only way Jaclyn could appease her pain was to take action. So Jaclyn worked, trying to earn the gift of life that had been taken away from her sister. She'd strived so hard to make her parents proud of her, but the pain of Jessica's loss was too great and they'd all fallen away from each other. Neither parent approved of her decision to return to Hope.

In the recesses of her mind, Jaclyn had never achieved Jessica's peace about God's failure to heal. That angst was bearable only when buried under a cloak of activity. She had to get Kent to complete the clinic.

In the McCloy ranch yard, heavily scented pink blossoms on fruit trees mingled with the blush of spring flowers newly opened, their whimsical fragrance filling the air. Kent's truck was parked in the side yard so he had to be around, though no one answered her knock.

Jaclyn headed around the side, toward the paddock, and saw him saddling a big bay stallion that danced with anticipation. Kent seemed totally engrossed in his task and never even looked up as she approached.

"How are you, Kent?"

"Hey." He blinked at her, smiled then continued cinching the saddle. "What are you doing out here?"

"I came to talk to you." When he didn't respond, she added, "About the clinic."

"You should have phoned. I would have told you I can't talk right now. I'm on the way to check on some cattle." His answers were short and brisk. He didn't look at her.

"But—"

"I'm busy right now." His tone made it clear he wasn't about to relinquish his plans.

"I'll go with you to check the cattle." The words slipped out without thought, but Jaclyn knew it was the right decision. "Maybe we can talk on the way."

She looked toward the horses in the paddock. "Is there a certain one you'd prefer me to ride?"

"Jaclyn." Kent studied her for several moments. After a moment he sighed. "How long is it since you've ridden?"

"High school." She held steady under his stare, breathing deeply only when he turned away to whistle. A pretty chestnut mare trotted over.

"This is Tangay. She was Lisa's." Kent frowned. "Think you can handle her?"

"I'm sure she'll be fine." Confident words when she wasn't confident at all. Jaclyn hoped Kent couldn't tell.

"Not that I'm complaining, but are you going to ride in those clothes?" he asked in a careful tone.

She glanced down. "I have gym clothes in my car. I'll change and be back in a second."

"Use the house. I'll saddle her up." He waited until she'd walked about fifty feet before he asked, "Are you sure you want to come? It's not an easy ride."

"Kent." She tsk-tsked. "You should know nothing worthwhile ever is easy. You should certainly know that 'hard' doesn't stop me." She grinned at him then walked to her car.

In record time she'd changed into jogging pants, a cotton shirt and sneakers. Not exactly ideal riding wear, but it would do for now. When she returned to the corral, Kent was waiting, obviously eager to leave. He handed her the reins and offered her a boost up into the saddle.

"Hello, Tangay. Be gentle with me, will you? It's a long time since I went for a ride."

"You don't have a hat." Kent frowned.

"I doubt I'll get sun stroke this late in the afternoon."

"Are you sure—"

"Unless you want to get off that horse and talk to me here and now about the clinic, I'm going on this ride." She gave him the fiercest look she could manage.

"Okay, okay. Let's go." He led the way but glanced back to say, "But don't blame me if you're stiff and sore tomorrow."

"Like riding a bike," she said airily. "Nothing to it."

The dirt path soon disappeared. Kent motioned her to ride beside him.

Jaclyn reveled in the glorious green of the hillside. "Look at that valley. The sun's lit a kind of aura around it."

"Uh-huh." Apparently he was too used to it to get overly excited.

"Where are we going?"

"Sore already?" he teased, ignoring her dark look. "We're going over to Shadow Ridge. We used to go there for campfires with the youth group."

"I remember." Shadow Ridge was where she'd first asked the other kids to pray for Jessica.

"Some of my cattle trespassed onto my neighbor's property. Again. I need to see why." He made it sound as if it was a repeated chore he did not enjoy.

"How do you manage the cattle, all this land and your practice?" Jaclyn was beginning to understand Kent's reluctance to take on the clinic renovation. He had to be exhausted juggling so many demands on his time.

"I have help with the ranch," he told her. "Two men usually, but one is off sick and the other's on holiday. So today it's just me and the dumb cattle. Normally I don't have much interaction with them."

"Why is that?" Jaclyn caught an undertone in his voice. "You always loved animals."

"Most animals," he corrected. His mouth slanted down in a grim line. "I've never liked longhorns."

"Why?" The funny tone told Jaclyn there was a lot he wasn't saying.

"Since we moved to this ranch, I've been stabbed, kicked and mauled by longhorns."

"Surely that's not unusual. You must have had animals bite you. I've had kids do that. Part of the job." Jaclyn studied him. "Isn't it?"

"Maybe. It's a little different when you're staring down a two-thousand-pound animal with horns who just wants you out of the way." His voice grew tight. "I grit my teeth and treat them when I have to but that doesn't mean I like them."

"Then why keep longhorns on your ranch?" There was something Kent wasn't saying so Jaclyn pressed, even though she knew she shouldn't.

"Because they were Dad's." The words burst out of him in an annoyed rush. "He loved them, said they were a breed to honor. Dad spent hours choosing, trading one animal so he could get another." Kent adjusted his reins, avoiding her eyes. "I can't just get rid of his handpicked herd. It would be like selling the ranch."

Jaclyn didn't remember his father being so obsessed about cattle but then she hadn't known him that well. She rode in silence, struggling to recall Kent's parents. She remembered something else instead.

"Weren't you the guy whose yearbook blurb said he was going to build a petting zoo, or a sanctuary for wild animals? Something like that. What happened to that plan?"

"It's on hold." Kent stopped at a tiny stream and dismounted. He offered a hand to help her down. "Let them have a drink," he said. "Then we'll head up the hill."

Once she was off the horse, Jaclyn sank onto a big, flat sun-warmed rock. Kent would tell her the rest of the story when he was ready. She hoped.

He led the horses to the water. As they drank he ran a hand down his stallion's flanks, his touch gentle on the glossy black coat. Clearly he loved his horse, though he only patted Tangay once before moving away.

"Why didn't you sell Tangay?" she asked in the gloaming of the riverside.

"She's got medical issues. I couldn't charge anyone knowing that and there aren't many ranchers who want a problem horse."

"Is it okay for me to ride her?" Jaclyn worried.

"Oh, yeah. Tangay doesn't get enough exercise. But she's not up to anything more demanding than an occasional ride." Kent dragged off his black Stetson and raked a hand through the riot of curls that shone ebony. He sprawled on a nearby rock, a piece of grass in his mouth. Kent McCloy was a very handsome man.

"Thank you for bringing me here." Jaclyn inhaled the peace and beauty surrounding her. "I needed a break to readjust my thinking. You may have guessed I have control issues."

Kent raised one eyebrow, smiled, but said nothing.

"I need to have things arranged just so."

"I noticed." He winked at her.

"Well, I'm working on remembering God's in control." His wink had her flustered.

They sat in silence until Kent held out his hand to help her stand.

"Time to go," he said, his smile slightly crooked.

His touch against her skin sent a heat wave up her arm that had nothing to do with the waning sun. Jaclyn scrambled back on her horse, pretending nonchalance as they rode up the hill.

"There they are." He halted on the rise and pointed a finger at several cattle perfectly content to graze on someone else's land. "How— Oh, I see. The fence is damaged. I'll have to drive out with the truck tomorrow morning and fix it."

"I can help now if you want." Jaclyn saw his smile peek out before he composed his expression into a bland mask.

"Thanks, but I didn't bring my equipment." He shrugged. "This was just a trip to reconnoiter. Oh, look." He pointed to a sleek, dark form racing across the open. Then it slipped into the shadows of a clump of trees. His voice dropped to a whisper. "I think it's the same one."

"The same one what?" Jaclyn peered, but the gloomy shadows hid the animal.

"A wolf. I came out here about a month ago." Seeing the wolf, Kent's demeanor underwent a complete transformation. "A young wolf cub had injured himself and was trapped in some cactus brambles. Took me a while but I got him free, gave him some water and cleaned up his cut."

"He let you?"

"I think he realized he had nothing to fear from me. Whenever I come to this area, I usually see him. I always leave something for him so now I guess he's come to expect a treat." He dug in his saddle bag and pulled out a plastic zipper bag. "This won't take long."

Jaclyn watched him remove a large steak. Kent laid it on a boulder, tucked the bag back into his pocket and got back on his horse.

"He'll wait till we're away from here then he'll come over to check. Do you want to watch?"

"Yes." Jaclyn followed Kent for a minute, then they dismounted and sat on the ground, holding the horses' reins.

"I've come across lots of different injured animals since we moved here when I was a kid," he told her, his voice low and even. "I try to help them if I can. Some of them remember." His hand stilled hers as she reached to touch her hair. "Don't make any sudden moves."

"What kind of a wolf is it?" she breathed.

"Mexican wolf. Not too many of them left. Come on, fella. Come and taste your dinner." Kent kept up a low monotone until the animal emerged from the woods and loped toward them. "Okay?" he asked.

"Stunned, but yes. I'm fine." She tightened her grip on the reins as Tangay shifted. "It's okay, girl. I think this is a friend."

"It is," Kent assured her. "He'll inspect the area first. He doesn't know your scent so he may be a bit shy. But the scent of that meat will bug him and eventually he'll take it. Just don't move."

"Not going anywhere," Jaclyn whispered and threaded her fingers through his without even thinking about it. When she realized what she'd done, she hesitated. But she could hardly jerk her hand away now. "Here he comes. How his coat shines."

The wolf halted about fifty feet in front of them, lifted his head and sniffed the air.

"Talk calmly. Don't raise your voice or you'll frighten him. He's not a people person."

She leaned close to Kent's ear and whispered, "I'm not sure I'm a wolf person, but I'll try to behave properly."

Kent's eyes met hers in a connection that sent frissons of shock waves straight to her heart. He didn't let go of her hand until Tangay's whinny broke the spell that held them.

"Give me those." He slid the reins from her nerveless fingers and with a whisper calmed the horse.

The wolf studied them from his safe vantage point. Kent studied him just as hard. Riveted by the expression on the vet's handsome face, Jaclyn couldn't look away. This was a Kent she'd never seen.

"Look, our boy is coming a little closer." Kent's lips grazed her ear. "Stay as still as you can."

Breath suspended, Jaclyn watched the wolf pace off the area, constantly sniffing, occasionally lifting his head to check out some movement. Finally he stopped about twenty feet away from Kent's left side.

"Hello, big fella. You're looking good. You been riding herd on my cattle?" The wolf tossed his head. Kent grinned. "Well, thank you. I appreciate that. I left you a little snack. I know hunting's not as good as it once was. A guy has to work hard to get a decent meal, doesn't he?"

Jaclyn didn't move, entranced by Kent. His entire demeanor altered as he interacted with the animal. The irritation that had permeated his behavior when he'd talked about the longhorns was completely gone. Now his voice was full of tenderness. Totally relaxed and in the moment with this magnificent wild animal, Kent's face radiated bliss.

"You enjoy your dinner, fella. And take care of yourself. We'll meet again."

The wolf waited a moment, as if to signal his agreement then loped toward the steak. After several sniffs he grabbed the meat in his powerful jaws and raced across the valley, heading into the trees. He turned once to look back, as if to say thanks, then disappeared. When she could see him no more, Jaclyn finally let out her pent-up breath.

"That was amazing!"

"Yeah." Kent grinned at her. "They're incredible animals. Clever, resourceful and extremely intelligent."

"He certainly responded to you. I've never seen anything like that before." She looked at him carefully. "You should get to work on your animal shelter—you do still want to build a sanctuary, don't you?"

"Yes." He sat up. "I often get to treat injured wild animals but they usually end up going to a zoo or something. If there was an area where they could be free instead of confined to cages or stalls..." His voice drifted away.

"Forget those longhorns, Kent. Your calling lies elsewhere. I think your father, if he were here, would agree."

"My father was all about ranching." Ice cracked his voice.

"But—"

Kent cut her off. "We should head back before it gets dark." He helped her rise and handed Tangay's reins to her. "Ready?"

The vibrancy that had transformed his face and sparkled in his sapphire eyes dissipated. The impassioned wild-animal caregiver had changed into a cattleman doing his duty.

Oh, Kent.

But all Jaclyn said was, "Ready." She mounted up.

He led her back on a different route, this time more open with sweeping vistas on all sides. The silence between them stretched until they arrived at the rear entrance to his ranch.

"You know, I understand why you came back to the ranch." She felt oddly diminished and yet expanded by the beauty of his land. "I feel very close to God out here."

"Do you?"

"It's almost like I can reach out and touch Him."

Kent didn't respond.

As she followed him into the barn, she noticed blackened sticks poking from the earth. "How did the fire start?" she asked quietly.

"Lightning. It was a very dry year and everything went up like tinder." His voice hardened, his words emerging short, clipped. Gone was the gentle whisper. Cold, hard anger burned in his eyes as he removed their saddles. "Once lit, the wildfire became massive." His fingertips whitened as he gripped the curry brush and swept it down his horse's sides.

She wanted him to talk about it, to let out the festering hurt. That's what the counselor had told her parents when Jessica died, though they'd never done it, at least not in Jaclyn's presence. Maybe that's why they were so far apart now.

"And Lisa got caught in it." Jaclyn began brushing Tangay.

"Not exactly caught." He stopped brushing and inhaled. When he spoke again, his words emerged in tight, controlled snaps. "I lit a backfire to stop the wildfire. It was so dry. We didn't have enough water. I was desperate. The barns, the sheds, maybe even the house were in its path."

"So you had to cut off its fuel." Jaclyn waited while he put the horses in the paddock to nibble on the fresh grass. "Do you have any iced tea? I'm terribly thirsty." She didn't want to leave him with the sad memory of Lisa's death. He needed to talk; she needed to listen. Maybe that was the only way she could help him. "What I don't understand is why Lisa would go out in it."

"Nor do I." He waited till she was seated at the kitchen table before sitting opposite her. Condensation ran down their glasses and puddled on the table. He studied the surface, avoiding Jaclyn's eyes. "I doubt I ever will."

"Maybe she didn't understand what you were going to do?" Jaclyn suggested.

"She understood. I told her. And yet she walked right into it." He sucked in a breath. "I'd already lit the fire when I saw her. I tried to reach her, but it caught fast and I couldn't control it." His gravelly voice became hoarse. "I couldn't get to her. The flames were too much."

"You saw her?" Horror shuddered through her at his nod. She could only imagine carrying that image around every day and the blame that would magnify over time. Jaclyn took his hand, cradling his icy fingers, speaking fast, urgently. "You listen to me. It was not your fault, Kent. Do you hear me? It was not your fault."

"Whose then?" The bleakness in his voice matched the utter despair in his dark eyes. "God's? Hers?" He gazed at their clasped fingers then slowly drew his hand away. "I made her stay here. Lisa never wanted to come back to the ranch. But after Mom and Dad died, I had to come here, to straighten things out and try to make a go of it. I owed them that."

"You were their son, Kent. Of course you handled their estate." His tortured voice touched the deepest part of Jaclyn's heart. She'd suffered with Jessica's death, but at least she'd never felt she caused it.

"I didn't have to stay here." His head lifted and he stared at her.

"What do you mean?" Jaclyn didn't understand the blazing anger on his face.

"I could have sold everything and left. But I broke my promise to Lisa that we'd go back to Texas. I kept her in a place where she was desperately unhappy. And do you know why, Jaclyn?" Harsh laughter cracked the silence as he waited for her answer. "Of course you don't. Nobody does."

"Kent, this is upsetting you and I never meant to do that." She wished she hadn't pushed him to talk just to satisfy her need to know what happened.

"Can't take the truth, huh?" His smile didn't reach his eyes.

"I blamed myself for Jessica's death wondering if I would have done this or that, if it would have made a difference. But it wouldn't have—it couldn't have. So you go on."

"Is that what you're doing?" Bitterness flashed in those vivid blue eyes. "Are you going on with your life, Jaclyn? Is joining every group you can the way you're getting on with your life? Or are you postponing your life so you can make amends?"

She bit her lip at the accusation. "Stop it."

After a moment, Kent touched her hand, his face ashen. "I'm really sorry. I'm lashing out at you and you don't deserve it." He shook his head. "Let's just leave it alone, okay?"

"Okay." *For now*, she thought. But sooner or later she'd discover why he felt duty bound to keep his father's cattle, and why he'd stayed here when he could have left. This man was in deep pain and she ached to help him. If only she could figure out how. "So, the reason I came out tonight was to talk about the clinic. Is there anything I can do to help get it moving again?"

"No." He sighed. "I was waiting on some material. I heard this afternoon that it's in so I'll be back there tomorrow." His voice was devoid of all emotion.

"Thank you, Kent. I appreciate all you've done." She rose. "I need to get home. I've got a meeting. Thanks for the ride."

"Sure." He walked her to her car, silent and darkly brooding.

"Call me if you need help. With anything." He didn't respond. All Jaclyn could do was drive away. She glanced and saw him standing there, alone.

Something's wrong, God. It's like he's drowning. Please help him, she prayed as she drove down the hill and back into town. *Please help me to help him. And most of all please help the clinic. I've got to get it running.*

The prayer made her feel a bit selfish. How could she push her own agenda when Kent seemed so broken?

She recalled the touch of his hands on hers, the protective way he'd helped her on and off Tangay. Most of all she remembered the way he'd stood there, alone, watching her leave. She'd wanted to turn around, go back and assure him he wasn't alone.

But she couldn't. Jaclyn couldn't afford to get sidetracked by Kent McCloy. Besides, she knew what happened to love. It died, just the way Brianna and Zac's had, and the way her parents' had, so that now it seemed as if they barely tolerated each other. Romantic love didn't last and Jaclyn had no intention of going down that path. Still, her heart longed to find a way to help Kent.

Nothing wrong with that. As long as she didn't let it become more than friendship.

Chapter Six

Kent drove through Hope the next morning with a sinking feeling in his stomach that had begun at 7:15 a.m. with Heddy's phone call.

"Can you be at the library at ten-thirty, Kent? We need to talk."

During his first months as mayor, he'd learned that ignoring Heddy's demands was done at his own peril. So now, as he pulled into the library parking lot, he hoped she'd get it over with quickly, whatever it was. He had plans to spend some time on the clinic today. Jaclyn was right—he had been putting it off, mostly because finding the trades he needed seemed impossible. But he wasn't giving up. Not yet.

Kent had barely crossed the threshold of the library when he spotted Jaclyn. He jerked to a halt at the sight of her sitting on the floor, surrounded by preschoolers, their faces rapt as they listened to her.

"Quite a sight, isn't it?" Heddy directed him into a room where he could still see Jaclyn through the floor-to-ceiling windows. "She's a natural storyteller."

"Is that what you wanted to talk to me about?" Kent

tried to keep his gaze from straying to the pretty blonde and her big, wide smile, but Jaclyn was a magnet that constantly drew his attention. She looked perfectly at home on the floor, as if she was having as much fun as the kids were.

"Certainly speaks to her character."

"It does?" Kent blinked. Heddy was now the doctor's champion? His instincts went on alert. "Why?"

"Jaclyn heard our story-time team couldn't show and volunteered to help." Heddy's face glowed as he hadn't seen it in ages. "She's an amazing woman."

"Also a very good doctor. So why don't you use her services, or tell your daughter to?" he challenged.

"I intend to do both." Heddy smiled at his surprise. "Why not? My grandchildren need a good physician nearby."

Kent was dumbfounded.

"Oh, don't look at me like that," Heddy scolded. "Aren't you the one who's been telling everyone in this town to look at things in a new way?"

"I have." He never imagined Heddy had taken his comments seriously.

"Well, I have examined my attitude and decided to change it." She sighed. "I admit it's taken me a long time to get past what happened all those years ago. You have to understand, Jaclyn wrecked the doors which my grandfather donated to the church." Heddy's face lost some of its glow. "Those doors commemorated the death of his wife—my grandmother—and I loved her dearly."

"You don't have to explain to me, Heddy." Kent was surprised by a rush of compassion for the woman who had so often made his life a misery.

"I do." She dabbed her eyes and cleared her throat. "I watched my grandfather sacrifice to buy those doors—he endured hardship to commemorate his wife's life. Every time I went into that church, I looked at those doors and relived so many happy memories of my grandmother."

"I see."

"Those doors cost a mint to refinish and even when they were done, they were never the same," Heddy sniffed.

"I'm sorry, Heddy. And I know Jaclyn is."

"Yes, she apologized to me back then but I never believed she was genuinely sorry. But after hearing Jaclyn talk about losing her sister—I could see how her hurt still hasn't left her." Heddy's gaze pinned him. "Kent, she doesn't want the clinic because she's trying to make a name for herself. She's trying to make amends for living."

He frowned, hoping Heddy wouldn't spread that insight around town.

"When she talked about the bond she had with her twin, it made me realize I'd never accepted that she was mourning way back then." Heddy shrugged. "So when Jaclyn called yesterday to offer to have the doors refinished, I refused."

Pride surged up in Kent that Jaclyn had reached out to Heddy. He turned to look at Jaclyn.

"Are you listening?" Heddy demanded when Kent didn't respond right away.

"Why did you refuse?" he asked patiently.

"Doors are just things and Grandfather never put things above people." Heddy beamed. "I've forgiven Jaclyn."

"That's very generous of you." Kent could hardly contain his amazement. In the years since he'd been in Hope he'd never known Heddy to openly forgive anyone until she'd exacted whatever retribution she felt entitled to. Yet Jaclyn had softened her heart in a matter of a few weeks.

"It's very generous of Jaclyn to give us this clinic," Heddy said.

Laughter penetrated the glass windows. When Kent looked, he saw the kids doubled over with the giggles. Jaclyn was making faces.

"Whatever she's reading them seems to be a hit," he said.

"Oh, she's not reading anything." Heddy's pale eyes danced with excitement. "Not yet. She's giving them a talk about health."

"Health?"

"Yes. She has this fuzzy worm, Ernesto. And she's been using him—well, just look. You can see for yourself." Heddy tilted her head sideways, indicating the circle of children now avidly involved in what was happening.

Kent looked at the doctor clad in her white coat, a green wiggling puppet covering one hand. Just then Jaclyn glanced up, saw him and winked. Every single mom nearby turned to look at him. Even Heddy grinned.

Kent's face burned.

"She has an amazing knack with kids." Heddy chuckled when one little boy cuddled onto Jaclyn's lap. She wrapped her free arm around the child and continued speaking, unfazed. "I never imagined she'd know how to reach them," Heddy said. "To look at her, you'd think she was all about fashion."

Another snap judgment, just like his. Kent winced. It wasn't just Heddy who'd been unfair. But as he stood watching her, he wondered if Jaclyn had agreed to fill in this morning in a deliberate attempt to win over moms and kids for her clinic.

He immediately chastised himself for the thought. What did it matter? The doctor had found a way to fit in here. He found himself feeling proud of her again.

Though he had no business feeling anything for Jaclyn LaForge.

"So what did you want to talk to me about, Heddy?" Kent was desperate to leave so he could get his attention off the doctor.

"The Pruitt boy." Heddy pursed her lips. "His mom told me this morning that Jaclyn is insisting Joey sees a specialist."

"That's a good thing." He saw her frown. "Isn't it?"

"No. That family was decimated when the boy was injured. You've seen how many times they've hoped for some new treatment and then had their hopes dashed." Her eyes misted. "Those poor people have been on a roller coaster. Each time they see another specialist it happens again, but the result is the same. Joey's condition is untreatable."

Kent had heard that, too.

"The family has come to grips with Joey's problems and Joey's adapted. Another examination, another test—it won't help. It will only get their hopes up only to have them crushed again."

"You told Jaclyn?" Heddy nodded. "What did she say?"

"She won't listen to me."

"Jaclyn's the doctor. I'm only a vet. I'd no more ask Jaclyn to listen to my advice about her patients than I would take hers about mine."

"Be that as it may, you must try to dissuade her about this," Heddy insisted. Her fingers closed around his wrist.

He didn't get this. "You just said you trusted Jaclyn. I thought you'd be glad she's taking an interest in the boy's treatment." He drew his arm away from her tight fingers.

Heddy's eyes brimmed with sadness. "I know you don't believe it, but I want this town to heal and I'm trying to help."

"How?" He didn't understand the source of Heddy's fierce glower.

"Think and you'll realize the damage this could do, to Dr. LaForge, to Joey and to his family. The doctors have all said the same thing. Joey's spine was damaged too badly in the car accident. He'll never walk properly."

"I'm sure Dr. LaForge has that information in Joey's records," he said.

"Then why does she want Joey to see someone else?" An indulgent smile creased her mouth. "I want her clinic to succeed. But if she keeps pushing the Pruitts, she'll only get their hopes up and when they're disappointed again, the whole town will turn on Jaclyn." There were tears at the corners of Heddy's eyes. "Hope will suffer again, Kent. Jaclyn has good intentions but please, ask her to stop."

He studied her, surprised by Heddy's about-face to Jaclyn's side.

"It may be a moot point," he told her.

"What do you mean?"

"Jaclyn must open her clinic by May and right now it looks like that won't happen because I can't get an electrician to certify the building." He waited for the usual caustic comment, but Heddy surprised him.

"Well, of course her clinic will open. It can't be that hard to get an electrician. My son is one. A very good one." She preened. "He even has his own company over in Whiteville."

"I know. But your son isn't here. Hope's only two electricians are at the mine and can't be released from a non-compete contract." He held up a hand when she would have interrupted. "I've tried asking. The mine company made an exception for the plumber but they won't allow this. If I can't get that building rewired, I can't let Jaclyn move in. And if she doesn't move in, her clinic won't happen. She may even be forced to move away."

Heddy was finally silenced.

"So you probably have nothing to worry about." Kent shrugged, pretending it didn't matter to him, when in reality he absolutely did not want Jaclyn to leave. She made a difference in his life and he had begun to like that.

Heddy was silent for a long time. Her birdlike gaze moved from him to Jaclyn, to the mothers sipping their coffee, and back to him. Finally she spoke.

"If I can get whatever electrical work is needed in that clinic done, will you ask Jaclyn to stop pushing the Pruitts to see another specialist?"

When he didn't answer, she poked his chest.

"Is it a deal, Kent?"

He made up his mind in an instant.

"If you promise to get the wiring done, I'll talk to Jaclyn. But it's very unlikely she will discuss a patient with me. I'm not a medical doctor, Heddy. I don't keep up with the latest treatments. But I'm sure Jaclyn does. She may know of something that can help the boy." He gulped, stunned by his own temerity. "I'll try to find out why she's so determined to get Joey to another specialist, but if she insists on going ahead, that's her business."

She patted his shoulder. "Thank you, Kent. I know Jaclyn feels a close connection with you, probably because you're the only one of us that's been a real friend to her. That's why I thought this admonishment would sound better coming from you than me."

"Heddy!" he sputtered in outrage. "I'm not going to admonish—"

"I must go. It's snack time."

Heddy scurried away so fast Kent felt like he'd been had. At least he got an electrician out of the deal. He only hoped it wouldn't backfire.

"Hi. Do you come to story time often?" Jaclyn stood in front of him, amused.

"Only when Heddy summons me." Jaclyn was radiant. Her eyes sparkled with happiness. "Looked like you were having fun."

"I was. I love kids." She tilted her head to one side. "And you?"

"Me? Yeah, I like kids. Listen, Jaclyn, have you got time for a coffee?" Better to get this over with. But he wasn't going to challenge whatever decision she made.

"I have no patients this morning, but I may have gained one or two today." She tossed him a wink. Her teasing smile died away when he didn't respond. She grabbed her bag and followed him out of the library.

As Kent walked with her to the nearest café, it dawned on him that he knew little about Jaclyn personally beyond her desire to get the clinic operational. She always coaxed him to talk about himself. In the café, Jaclyn held her cup and stared him down.

"What's going on, Kent? What's this about?"

"Heddy. And the Pruitts." He launched in, relaying Heddy's worries bluntly, embarrassed he'd agreed to be part of this. "So I said I'd mention it to you."

"Okay. Now you have." She rose and reached for her purse.

"Jaclyn, I'm not trying to tell you how to practice medicine." Kent touched her arm.

"Good," she snapped. "Because you're not qualified."

Uh-oh, she was steaming. Well, who wouldn't be? He'd questioned her professional judgment. And yet he also wanted to save her grief, if he could.

"Please sit down, Jaclyn. Finish your coffee and talk to me about this."

She sat. But the firm jut of her chin told Kent his soft tones weren't working.

"I do not discuss my patients," she said. "You should know that."

"I do know. And I respect it. But I've known the Pruitts and Joey for years. I've seen what they go through each time their hopes are built up and what happens when they're dashed. I've watched the people of this town rally round them." Kent struggled to voice his thoughts inoffensively. "We might bicker and argue among ourselves in Hope, but underneath we still feel responsible and look out for each other."

Her eyes glittered like polished granite. "Why the sudden concern about me trying to do my job? Last night you were all gung ho about encouraging me. You told me to have faith. Now you're questioning my ability to do my job."

"No!" He backtracked. "I just wanted to be sure that you knew—"

Hurt filled Jaclyn's eyes. A nerve flickered in her neck as she steeled herself and in that moment Kent wished he'd never started this because now there was no way to make it right. He'd overstepped the bounds and he knew it.

"It's none of my business. I'm very sorry, Jaclyn," he said simply.

She studied him for so long he wanted to squirm under that look.

"Thank you—for that, at least." Then she rose and walked out.

Kent spent a long time with his coffee. It took a while to examine his heart and realize that he'd just hurt Jaclyn to spare himself. He'd grabbed at Heddy's offer to get an electrician because he wanted to get the clinic finished. He wanted to get Jaclyn moved in so he wouldn't have to go through another visit like she'd made last night, wouldn't ever again have to risk her seeing his weaknesses. He wanted her office finished so he could feel he'd done something for the town. Mostly he wanted to get back to the hermit's life he'd carved out before Dr. Jaclyn LaForge crashed his world.

But his crime, Kent admitted to himself, was worse

than that. Far worse. He'd spouted off to a whole lot of people, including Heddy and Jaclyn herself, that he trusted her judgment, that he was confident she was the doctor for Hope. Pretty words. But his actions made a total lie of what he'd said. And though she'd said not a word to condemn him, Jaclyn knew it.

Kent paid for the two untouched coffees and walked out of the café. Okay, he'd messed up badly. Guilt rose as he realized that if there was any chance for Joey, he might have just killed it. No wonder God had washed His hands of Kent McCloy.

His mouth grim, Kent headed for the clinic and got to work. It was time to put his money where his mouth was, though even if he got the clinic finished in time, it wouldn't likely restore Jaclyn's opinion of him.

Jaclyn sat behind her desk and studied the file of Joey Pruitt. The sting of Kent's questioning haunted her. She'd been furious at first and had itched to tell him to mind his own business. Fortunately Jaclyn's temper had cooled in the past few hours. Kent's lack of belief still stung, but it also had her second-guessing her decision to pursue help for Joey Pruitt.

Kent wasn't a physician. Yet his and Heddy's concern over what the Pruitt family might have to go through was obviously genuine. She'd seen the rush of hope flicker in the parents' eyes when she'd first mentioned the specialist. She'd also seen the way they ruthlessly tamped it down to ask all the hard questions and then asked her not to tell Joey anything until they'd made a decision.

Jaclyn knew the painful rehabilitation Joey would have to go through if the surgery worked. But what if it didn't? What if it left him worse off than before? What if the whole town turned against her because of that?

My job is to find healing. I can't worry what people will think of me.

There were no guarantees in medicine.

Jaclyn phoned the specialist to talk over the case before she requested they schedule Joey for an appointment. If his parents decided to cancel, that was their decision.

Was there anything else she could do? Yes, pray.

I don't know what the outcome will be, God. I only know that You love children and You want them to be well.

RaeAnn ducked her head in to say it was five and she was leaving.

"What are you doing tonight?" her nurse asked.

"I'm going to finish this paperwork then reorganize my file cabinet." Jaclyn pointed to the stack of files on the floor. "And I have to phone that list of people for the service club."

"Always busy," RaeAnn grumbled, then said goodnight.

Jaclyn quickly completed her to-do list, but she couldn't stop thinking about Kent. Last night she'd seen a different side of the man. The way he'd changed at the appearance of the wolf stunned her. So had his angst about the getting rid of the longhorns. It was laudable that Kent wanted to honor his parent, but something else underlay his anguish.

She left the office and drove past the clinic, shocked that the lights were on and Kent's truck was parked outside. Should she offer her help again? No. He'd said he'd do it, now leave him alone.

Only, he always seemed to be alone.

Jaclyn drove home, made herself a sandwich and ate it while she watched the news. She wondered if Kent was eating, if he'd eaten all day. She finally changed into jeans, wrapped a sandwich, grabbed two bottles of juice and made a quick phone call. Then she walked downtown. The fragrance of flowering shrubs filled the air and fireflies flitted past as she waved at passersby, delighted that she could identify most of them.

She stopped outside the clinic's new glass door, brimming with second thoughts. Why was she doing this? Kent had hurt her deeply. He'd questioned her judgment. He'd claimed to trust her, to want her to succeed, but then put up barriers. Bringing him a sandwich would make her seem desperate.

He cares about the people in this town.

He's a good man.

He's hurting inside. He's lost his wife, his parents—he has no one.

"All right," she mumbled, exasperated by the amount of inner conflict one man could cause.

"Talking to yourself?" Kent stood holding the door open with one booted toe, his arms filled with junk.

"You're working here again." It was an inane remark and Jaclyn blushed at the stupidity of it.

"Free evening," he said before he tossed the broken boards into a Dumpster that sat in a parking spot. "I thought I'd get a couple of hours in."

"Oh." She trailed behind him into the room, surprised by how much lighter it felt without the dark paneling.

"On your way home with dinner?" he asked. He inclined his head toward the bag she held.

"No, I've already eaten. I thought perhaps you hadn't." She held out the bag then faltered. "Or maybe you have."

"I haven't," he said and took the bag from her. "In fact, I'm starving."

"Good." She handed him one of the juice bottles and watched as he unwrapped the sandwich.

"Thank you." He held up the sandwich, staring at it. "Jaclyn, I need to apologize to you. I never should have questioned your judgment about Joey. My only excuse is that Heddy promised me an electrician if I did and I got carried away by the prospect of actually getting this place rewired and certified. I'm sorry."

"Where's Heddy going to find an electrician?" She glanced around at the broken walls, dangling fixtures and utter chaos.

Kent kept looking at her, his blue eyes dark, worried. "You haven't said you've forgiven me," he reminded.

"You expect a lot." Jaclyn glared at him, irritation bubbling up anew. "I can take criticism, Kent. I understand that the locals are worried I'll take off at the first hint of a better job. I can understand their distrust of my motives. I even understand that they don't want Joey or his parents to get their hopes dashed again." The hurt was still there, raw, throbbing. "What I can't take is a friend questioning my medical judgment. You crossed the line, Kent."

"I know I did. And I'm sorry." He sat there, looking at her.

"Why did you do it? And don't say for an electrician."

"It was, partly. Progress here has been sporadic, and that's being generous." He sighed. "Mostly it was concern for you. I've seen what this town can do to protect their own. I don't want you to be the target of their anger."

"It wouldn't matter if I was," she said quietly. "I'd still do what's right for my patient. I took an oath and I promised God. That's why I'm in Hope. To help."

A long silence yawned between them. Kent's blue eyes wouldn't release hers. He seemed to see past her bravado to the secret fears beneath. Finally he nodded.

"I know," he said. "I apologize." Then he took a bite of the sandwich.

"Just like that?" She didn't believe him. "Why?"

"Because you're right." He munched thoughtfully for a minute then shrugged. "Bottom line, if there's even the remotest chance Joey can be helped, it's worth taking." He lifted his head when the door pushed open and Zac stepped inside. "Hey, Professor."

Zac winked at her. Jaclyn grinned, glad she'd phoned him.

"What are you doing here?" Kent asked.

"I'm here to help this damsel in distress." Zac made a motion as if he were doffing a hat. "At your service, Doc."

"Thank you for coming." She loved Kent's confusion. For once the town's do-gooder was flummoxed. "Where should we start?"

"Wait a minute." Kent rose. "What's going on?"

"We're going to give you a little push getting this place operational," Zac said. "Right, Doc?"

"Right. I—" She stopped as the door opened. A man stepped inside. "Can I help you?"

"You're the new doctor, right?" He held out his

hand. "Paul Cormer. I was told you need some electrical work done here."

"Excellent!" Zac nudged Kent. "C'mon, cowboy, show him. We've got a clinic to fix."

Jaclyn nearly laughed out loud at Kent's stunned expression. When Kent and Paul disappeared to look at the panel box, she and Zac began hauling out the accumulated refuse.

"How'd we get this electrician?" Kent demanded when he returned as Zac took a bag outside. "The mine bosses were adamant none of their guys could work here. Did you change their minds?"

"Me? What do I know about electricians?" Jaclyn blinked. "It had to be Heddy."

"Changing the mine bosses' minds?" He shook his head. "Even Heddy doesn't have that much pull." His shoulder grazed hers. He took the garbage bag from her hands and held it while she filled it, his fingers brushing against hers. "You think?"

"Who else is there?" Jaclyn struggled to control her breathing. Lately she couldn't seem to control any of her responses to him. Just a touch from him and her nerves came alive. She rushed outside with the bag, inhaling the fresh air in an attempt to regain her equanimity.

"You look funny. Are you okay?" Zac asked.

"Uh-huh." She was far from okay. Her heart hammered in her chest; her head felt woozy and funny little prickles ran up and down her arm where Kent had touched her.

"If you say so." Zac frowned.

Jaclyn took her time, waiting for him to return inside. Finally alone she sat down on the curb and practiced relaxation breathing. But it didn't help. Nothing did.

Because the truth was too hard to digest, and impossible to accept.

She was starting to care for Kent McCloy.

"Hey, Jaclyn? We could use your help here." Kent's voice broke through her reverie.

"Coming." She went inside, but while she helped, she made a mental list of all the things she could do to keep away from this building. Away from Kent.

And she knew she wouldn't do a single one of them.

Chapter Seven

"Jaclyn, this cake looks delicious," the minister's wife praised. "Everyone's going to enjoy it."

"Good. That's why I made it." Well, that and the need to keep busy. She waved an airy hand as if baking a layer cake was something she did every day instead of a major job requiring many hours, in spite of using a cake mix and store-bought icing.

"Would you be in charge of the desserts for the potluck today?"

In charge of *them*? Meaning serving them?

"Sure," Jaclyn assured the busy woman.

"Thanks. I'll find someone to help you load them later." She scurried away.

Load them?

Jaclyn tried to recall how the last potluck lunch had worked but came up blank. Oh, well. Couldn't be that hard. She stopped in the foyer to drop the quilt squares she'd cut for the quilting meeting tomorrow into the appropriate box. The task had taken five evenings and she was glad to be finished with the tiring work.

"Jaclyn!" Heddy's voice boomed across the crowded

foyer. "I hope you have those notes on leprosy that you promised me. Our missions' group wants to learn all we can so we can better prepare our care package for the missionaries."

"I have your information here." She drew the sheaf of notes from her bag and handed them over, relieved at the lightness of her purse.

"You are coming to the meeting? We need everyone's help."

"I'll try to be there." Jaclyn had joined so many groups she now needed a calendar to keep the meetings straight. Unfortunately she didn't have it with her and she didn't want to embarrass herself by asking Heddy which day.

In fact, she'd prefer to avoid Heddy altogether.

Jaclyn knew she'd taken on too much but refused to cut back. Sooner or later Hope-ites would see her as an integral part of Hope.

Jaclyn looked forward to relaxing and enjoying the service, but as she walked into the sanctuary, Heddy followed.

"How's work on the clinic?" She slid into the pew beside Jaclyn.

"You'd have to ask Kent." *Because I'm deliberately avoiding him.*

"Dear Kent. He's such a boon to this town. His concern is for all of us and he goes out of his way to make Hope a better place. It's a pity he hasn't anyone special in his life. He's such a handsome man, too."

Please God, let someone invite Heddy to sit with them.

"Have you heard Kent's taken in six miniature horses?" Heddy leaned nearer as the organ swelled.

"They were abandoned, if you can imagine such a thing. That boy has such a heart." Heddy patted her hand. "Say, you're not working today, are you? You're just the person to help."

"Help with what?" Jaclyn asked warily.

"Transport food to the potluck, of course. It's at Kent's ranch. Surely you knew that?" Heddy ignored Jaclyn's sudden silence and peered across the room. "Excuse me. I must speak with Millie. We'll expect your help later, shall we?" She hurried away.

At Kent's.

If only she'd planned something pressing after church, but this was the one day Jaclyn had kept totally free. When she saw the outside of the church, she was always assailed by memories of that awful night and the vandalism she'd wreaked. Inside, she waited for memories of tranquility to quiet her soul. Instead a panoramic slideshow of Kent at his ranch played through her brain while the choir sang their first selection.

Kent petting his horse. Kent playing with the dog. Kent speaking so tenderly to the wolf.

Kent touching her hand and leaving behind an earthquake of emotion.

Okay, so she was falling for him. But why? A high school crush was one thing, but she was all grown up now. What was it about him?

On the day of their horse ride, when he'd envisioned an animal sanctuary, he'd exposed a part of his spirit she'd never seen before. As she considered his abrupt shut down of that dream, she realized Kent had substituted Hope's dreams for his own.

Having seen that transformation, Jaclyn now realized how much Kent was giving up. She'd seen the

guilt take over, guilt so strong that he willingly relinquished his dreams. This generous, giving man had
nobody in his world to help him achieve his goals, no
one to encourage him to explore the dreams he'd held
for so long. He gave but who gave to him?

For days Jaclyn had been trying to skate around
her response to Kent, to avoid him and anything that
would trigger her overwhelming reactions to him, because those feelings made her yearn to help him. She
so longed to see him whole and happy that it scared
her to think she might be persuaded to put aside her
own goals.

If she allowed herself to get involved with Kent Mc-
Cloy, those feelings would develop and all her dreams
for the clinic would dwindle. Then she'd never earn the
approval she'd craved ever since Jessica's death—not
from her parents and not from herself. And getting that
approval was the only way she'd feel she was worthy
of the life Jessica never got to live.

The service began. Jaclyn sang the choruses from
memory. She closed her eyes for prayer but her mind
would not quiet. A thousand questions raced around it
until the minister's voice broke through.

"Spring is God's way of saying, 'Let's start again.'
It's His promise that after the drought, after the hard
times, there will be beauty and sweetness once more.
Spring can also be a time to examine our personal
growth. Where are we going? What are we striving
for? It's time to ask ourselves if our plan for the future
is all about us or centered on God's will for us. Are we
willing to change our plan, to give up parts of it, to accept failure if God gives a new vision, a new plan?"

As she listened, Jaclyn scribbled notes. The thought

that she might be off course, or worse, completely mistaken in her plans unsettled her. Was that why getting the clinic operational was so difficult? Now she was questioning her dreams.

At the completion of the service, Jaclyn reluctantly loaded the desserts for transport to Kent's ranch. And during the potluck picnic she studied him surreptitiously. But her feelings were no clearer as she helped clean up his sterile kitchen. How could she possibly help him—yet stay true to herself and her path?

"I can't think of a way to throw the kind of party my daughter wants," Carissa, a young mother, lamented to the women cleaning up Kent's kitchen.

"What kind of a party does she want?" one of the other ladies asked.

"Casey was so sick for the past two years, she wasn't able to celebrate," Carissa said. She smiled at Jaclyn. "Thanks to our fantastic pediatrician who finally straightened out her medical issues, Casey can celebrate this year."

"A little tweak, that's all," Jaclyn murmured.

"Some really big tweaks nobody else thought of. I'll always be grateful you came to Hope, Jaclyn." Carissa grinned. "Now Casey wants to make up for what she missed—she wants to do something big. I want that, too, but other than hauling her friends to a Las Cruces waterpark, I'm stuck."

Jaclyn looked out the window and watched as Kent and another man walked to the paddock with the miniature horses. The man carried a child and the three paused by the fence.

The idea sprang full-blown. Miniature horses, pets

galore. And a man who needed taking out of himself. Perfect.

"Maybe Kent would host the party here." Jaclyn was barely aware she'd spoken aloud until the other women crowded around her to watch Kent carry the girl inside the corral and show her how to feed the horse a carrot.

"Jaclyn, that's a fantastic idea!" Carissa hugged her. "Kent's amazing with kids. Look at the way he's teaching Emma."

With gentle patience he allowed the child to experience the animal close up.

"You could plan lots of games to wear off some of the kids' energy," another mom offered.

"Remember when Lisa hosted her barbecues here?" another said.

"We let her do too much," Carissa said. "That probably didn't help her depression."

"I'd be depressed, too, if I had to work in this kitchen for very long," a woman named Amanda grumbled. "It's so sterile."

They all studied the cold room.

"It is very efficient," Jaclyn said. "All it needs is some color to warm it up."

The ideas continued fast and furious. If her goal was to waken Kent to the possibilities for his petting zoo, hosting a birthday party here on the ranch was the perfect way to show him the place in a new light. Maybe then he'd reconsider his animal sanctuary.

"Maybe I shouldn't ask him. Kent doesn't socialize much anymore. He's all work," Carissa said.

"Maybe having people here again would help him socialize," Jaclyn said. "It can't hurt to ask."

"Casey would love riding the horses. I'm going to

do it." Carissa wiped a tear from the corner of her eye then hugged Jaclyn. "Thank you."

Those words felt like an affirmation from heaven. Deeply moved, Jaclyn hugged back.

"What's going on in here?" Heddy demanded. "Is something wrong?"

"Everything's wonderful." Carissa patted Heddy's shoulder then walked out the kitchen door to talk to Kent.

"Is the cleaning finished in here?" Heddy asked.

"Just about." Amanda pointed to the counter. "We need to get those dishes back to folks before they leave."

Jaclyn grabbed an armful of the serving dishes and followed the others outside. She saw Heddy pick up a beautifully decorated casserole carrier.

"Is that yours?" she asked. When the older woman nodded, she said, "Would you mind telling me where you got it? It's lovely. The decoration is so intricate."

"I made it." Heddy smiled, obviously pleased by the compliment.

"She made that picture that hangs over the guest book at church, too," Amanda said. "And the runner that's on the communion table."

"I wish I knew how to create things like that." Jaclyn studied the woman with new eyes.

"I can show you." Heddy grinned. "You already know how to stitch people up. Stitching pictures isn't that much different."

"I'd like to learn," Jaclyn said.

"The question is when do you have free time? You're always on the go, rushing from one meeting to the next. Not that we aren't all grateful." Heddy stopped speaking when Kent appeared and touched Jaclyn on the arm.

"Can I speak to you privately?" he asked.

"Sure." Jaclyn followed him to an area away from the others.

"What are you doing?"

She blinked at his anger.

"Carissa said you volunteered my ranch for her daughter's party." His eyes shot angry sparks. "I'm up to my ears with your clinic. I can't take time off to host a birthday party and a bunch of kids."

"You need a break. Doctor's orders," she said as lightly as she could.

"You're a children's doctor," he snapped.

"And you're tired and overworked. Carissa will handle the food."

"And what will you do?"

"Me?"

"Yeah, you." A smirk kicked up the corners of his mouth. "Your suggestion, your party."

"But I don't know how to—"

"I'm sure you can figure it out," Kent said.

"This sounds like railroading," Jaclyn complained.

"Is it working?" His grin widened.

"Maybe." She huffed a sigh of resignation. "All right, let's do it together."

"The whole thing," Kent emphasized.

"Till the bitter end. I'll even stay late to help with cleanup." She raised one eyebrow. "Satisfied?"

"It's a start," he said, his electric blue eyes gleaming in a way that made her stomach do a little flip.

When Jaclyn's beeper went off, she excused herself,

happy for a reason to put some distance between her and Kent McCloy.

The emergency she'd been beeped for turned out to be a sprain and took only a few minutes to treat, but Jaclyn stayed at the hospital. She needed to think through this party she suddenly found herself throwing.

"Bright colors," she murmured to herself, scribbling a list. "A few balloons in the kitchen would look like we'd brought the party indoors." She thought of that forlorn room and the equipment that begged to be used and enjoyed. "Red balloons, a few red dish towels, maybe a couple of red spoons and spatulas to go in that round utensil container."

Her brain echoed with Kent's laughter when Emma had giggled at the horses' whinnies. She remembered the patience and incredible softness today on Kent's handsome face as he held a new kitten so the children could see and touch. He'd let the littlest tots take turns holding tiny chicks he was keeping in a henhouse. For those few moments this afternoon she knew he hadn't felt anything but pure joy.

You're supposed to be staying away from him.

"How can I?" she asked aloud as she drove home. "He's got a wonderful dream for that ranch and he's afraid to pursue it."

Jaclyn wanted to believe that she could help Kent make his dreams live without getting knocked off her own course, that she could help him realize his own personal dreams and not just those of the town of Hope.

"Maybe if I could understand why Kent's afraid to let go of the past then I'd know how best to help him."

Why does it matter so much? She avoided answering that by unlocking the door and rushing to answer the phone.

"Hi, Dad. What's up?"

"Your mother and I hoped maybe you'd changed your mind about the clinic and decided to forsake that horrible town and set up your practice in the city."

Where you can make a lot of money and be a success. Jaclyn heard the unsaid words.

"Your last email sounded as if there'd been nothing but problems."

"Oh, there are some issues, but we're working past them," she said, forcing cheeriness.

"And your lack of patients?"

Why had she ever confided that information? She constantly had to defend her decision to move here as it was. She didn't need to give her parents more ammunition to argue that she was making a mistake. Again.

"Jaclyn?" Her father's sharp voice cut off her introspection.

"I'm here. How are you and Mom?"

"Your mother is out right now. I'm going golfing. We were supposed to be planning our cruise to Iceland. It leaves in a little over a month."

"You won't be here for the opening of the clinic." Jaclyn struggled to mask her disappointment. "That's too bad. I wanted to show it to you."

"We told you we would never return to Hope." Her father's solemn voice echoed with pain. "Too many sad memories."

"Seeing the clinic might help erase some of them," Jaclyn said. Then it dawned on her that her parents' refusal probably had to do with her. They were ashamed and embarrassed by what she'd done, and what she was doing now hadn't changed anything.

"I have to go now. Tee time. I think your mother is having guests for dinner. She keeps quite busy with her friends." Disappointment lay buried in the words.

"I'm sorry I haven't emailed much. I'm on several committees and the time drain is enormous. But I want people here to see that I intend to be a full participant in town life."

"Does that matter?" her father asked. "You're there to treat their kids, aren't you? Not to make friends."

"Friends don't hurt," she replied, knowing there was no point in arguing it all again. "Have a good game, Dad. I love you."

"Let me know if you come to your senses and decide to join Dr. Hanson's practice. He's been asking after you."

"Bye, Dad." Jaclyn hung up, trying to shed a deep sense of discontent.

Her parents' lack of support for her clinic, despite it being named for Jessica, left Jaclyn aching and feeling empty. Then she glanced at her list for the birthday party.

"Maybe this is how Kent feels when he goes into that kitchen," she muttered to herself. "I have to do something." She poured a glass of iced tea, carried it out to her tiny patio and began to plan all the ways she could change Kent's world. Maybe she couldn't help her parents recapture the love they'd once had, but maybe she could help Kent find a new perspective on the world. Friends did that for each other.

Friend. Was that all Kent could be?

* * *

The day of the party dawned bright and sunny. Jaclyn rushed to prepare, pulling out the shopping bag she'd filled the evening before. She laid everything out on the table. Then the doorbell rang.

"Am I bothering you?" Heddy demanded.

"Not at all. Come in. I've just made a fresh pot of coffee." Jaclyn led the way to the kitchen. She reached out to scoop her purchases back into the bag.

"What's all this?" Heddy asked.

"Just some things I bought for Casey's party." Her face grew warm at Heddy's knowing look. "When we were there on Sunday I thought the kitchen could use some color. It must be hard for Kent to keep coming back into that stark room." She was babbling. "It was just an idea."

"A very kind one." Heddy accepted the coffee. "I must confess I've never given Kent's kitchen much thought. Except that it's useful for things like the potluck on Sunday and your birthday idea. I approve."

"Really?" Jaclyn sat down across from her. "I've been regretting that idea. Kent's always going out of his way for everyone. He does so much for the town and he's trying to get the clinic up and running. What am I adding to his load by suggesting he host a birthday party? It's presumptuous."

"On the contrary," Heddy reassured her. "Most of us in Hope take Kent for granted. He's the kind of mayor every town should have. He's caring, committed and he doesn't mind challenging us. But it's only since you came, Jaclyn, that I've started to wonder how many times he's put his life on hold for something we needed."

"I'm sure he took the job because he loves Hope and its people." Jaclyn glanced at the clock. Heddy was clearly bothered by something—she could hardly just hurry her on her way.

"His parents were so thrilled to adopt him. Mary once told me Kent was everything a son should be." Heddy stared into the distance. "When they moved to the ranch Kent was little. He was so polite, so quiet. Stan and Mary had to coax a smile. They found out later he was worried they'd send him away."

"I've known Kent since I moved here in junior high." Jaclyn shook her head in disbelief. "I never knew he was adopted."

"No, you wouldn't have. Stan and Mary didn't talk about it. Kent never does," Heddy told her. "He was their child. Period. He idolized them. Mary once told me Kent almost didn't take his vet's training."

"Why?" Kent had never talked of anything but veterinary training when they were in high school.

"Apparently Stan tended to go on and on about the ranch being his legacy. Kent felt that leaving would let down his father. I supposed he felt indebted. He even tried to hide his college acceptance but our postmistress knew every piece of mail that came into town and she clued Mary in. Mary read Kent the riot act and Kent went off to college. Then he married Lisa. Everything was wonderful until Stan and Mary died."

"And then Kent came back." Given this new perspective, Jaclyn now better understood Kent's reluctance to get rid of his father's cattle.

Heddy's round face filled with sadness. "After Lisa died, Kent was like a walking ghost. He just existed."

"So how did he become mayor?" Jaclyn asked.

"A child was hit running across Main Street. Kent happened on the scene moments later. When the stop signs he lobbied council for didn't happen, he ran for mayor. Got in by acclamation."

"And his mission to help Hope began." Jaclyn understood. Kent put aside his own dreams because he felt they weren't important. Somehow she had to show him that was not true.

"Heddy, don't be offended but I have to cut our coffee time short." Jaclyn smiled to soften the words. "I have some things to prepare for the party."

"I'm not offended." Heddy rose, dumped the rest of her coffee in the sink and stored her cup in the dishwasher. "Will you be offended if I purchase some materials to get you started on your needlework project?"

"No, but the truth is, Heddy, I don't know where I'll find the time to do needlework. I want to do it," she reassured. "But I'm so busy."

"You are. Sort of like Kent. Running around trying to make everyone else happy." Heddy leaned near, her voice very soft. "I often wonder when the two of you find time to lean on God and hear His direction. Nobody can fix all the world's ills, Jaclyn. Not even a wonderful doctor like you."

She patted Jaclyn's shoulder then let herself out.

Jaclyn considered her words. She wasn't being frivolous; she had a purpose in joining so many things. She already had a few new clients because people were beginning to get to know her. But to make Jessica's clinic viable, Jaclyn needed many more patients.

Jessica's clinic had to succeed, even if her parents didn't believe it would. Even if it meant she got only a few hours of sleep per night.

Yawning, Jaclyn grabbed the bag and headed for the door.

Today she'd try to help Kent. But after this party she'd draw the line between them. He was a business associate and that's all he could be, regardless of her silly heart. Her focus had to be on the clinic. Letting her emotions get control of her would only derail her goal.

Jaclyn was determined not to let that happen.

Chapter Eight

"Thank You, God, for sunshine."

Kent took a few moments to pray as he savored his coffee at sunrise. At least he called it praying. The gap between him and heaven had never seemed wider, nor had he ever felt more alone.

In a few hours the children would be here. He'd spent last evening mowing the yard and weeding the flower beds. He had groomed the animals, too, figuring that if they ran out of games, the children might like to see them.

Everything was ready.

She would be here.

Kent had pushed away thoughts of Jaclyn ever since the church potluck last weekend. He'd avoided her all week after insisting she be at the birthday party out of frustration that she'd volunteered his ranch. The potluck had been a special favor to the pastor, but this party—Kent sighed and admitted the truth.

He'd been avoiding her because he was embarrassed he'd revealed his stupid childish dream. He'd long ago accepted that animal sanctuaries and petting zoos were not going to be his lot in life. So why were those dreams still hanging around in the periphery of his mind?

Because they made the shambles of his life tolerable.

Behind him, someone coughed.

"Hey, Boss. I'm moving the herd higher up into the hills today. We're overgrazing on the lower levels. We might as well take advantage of the grass and water that's sitting up there free. It'll be gone once the heat hits." Gordon, his ranch manager, scuffed his toe against the pea gravel path.

Kent's dad had hired Gordon when he bought the ranch because of his vast knowledge. The herd had almost doubled since Stan's death. Several times the handyman had said the longhorns needed more grazing land than made up the ranch, but Kent ignored it because he didn't have the funds to expand and he couldn't bring himself to sell off his dad's prized animals.

"Okay." When Gordon didn't move, Kent frowned. "Something else on your mind?"

"I bought that land up against your southwest quarter. The price was right." Gordon coughed. "If you want to cut down on your herd, I'd sure like to buy some. Me and Stan talked a lot about when the herd got big. I have an itch to try out some of his ideas. He had some good plans."

And you—his son, his heir—don't.

Gordon knew more about the ranch than Kent. He certainly knew more about the animals. But the dream had been his dad's and Kent couldn't just sell it out.

"I'm not looking to sell any stock, Gordon."

"I know you're not ready yet. Thought if and when

the time comes, you'd know I'm interested." He clamped his Stetson back on his head. "Time to git." He turned.

"Gordon?" Kent rose. "If I'm ever ready to sell Dad's herd, you'll be the first one I talk to, I promise. And congratulations on your land."

"Thanks." They shook hands.

Kent watched the older man walk away realizing Gordon might one day leave here to run his own herd. For a few moments Kent imagined the ranch without the longhorns. Surprised by a sudden giddiness, he let the feeling linger until reality returned. He owed his father, for not being the son Stan expected.

"I aim to make the McCloy name the top one when it comes to longhorns." Kent could still hear the pride in those words. *"I love the law, but it takes second place when you look out the window and see your own cattle multiplying. Someday you'll feel the same, son."*

Only Kent never had felt that way about his father's beloved cattle.

"Good morning."

He turned and gulped at the beauty before him.

"Bad time?" Jaclyn paused, a frown marring the smoothness of her pale forehead. "Should I go and come again?"

"Of course not. I was just—" He didn't finish, mesmerized by the sight of her. She reached into her car. Out came bags and bags of things. "Must be planning a whale of a party." He moved forward to take them from her.

"I hope so." She wrestled out a bunch of colorful balloons and grinned at him. "Isn't it a lovely day?"

"Yeah." Lovely now, especially. Her smile turned

him into a blithering idiot. And he liked it. "Where do you want these?" he asked, juggling his load.

"The kitchen." She followed him, her jumble of balloons bumping him in the back.

"Is there anything I can help with?"

"As a matter of fact, yes." She instructed him to tie balloons all around the yard. "And we'll need a table out here. Actually two."

There was nothing in Jaclyn's voice to suggest she was still angry at him for trying to tell her how to treat Joey or for conscripting her into this party, but Kent felt that the doctor was maintaining a barrier between them. His fault.

"Jaclyn, can I talk to you a minute?"

"Sure." She looked at him, poker-faced.

"I want to apologize again for asking you to back off Joey. It wasn't my call and I shouldn't have done it. I'm sorry."

"No problem." She turned away and continued fastening little curly ribbons to lawn chairs, planters, everything.

"That's it?" He'd expected something more.

"I don't hold grudges, Kent." Jaclyn straightened and faced him. "Besides, I finally realized that this thing you have about protecting everyone and everything in Hope was at the root of your meddling. You want the best for everyone and I threatened that so you stood up to me." She shrugged. "When you get to know me better you'll realize that the way you feel about Hope is the way I feel about my patients. Nothing will stop me from helping a child."

He gulped down his surprise that she was willing to let it go so easily.

"Now, let's focus on the party. We're going to need some benches by those tables."

The minute he filled one request, she found another, darting in and out of the house with stuff like a bird feathering its nest. By the time Carissa arrived with a van load of kids, his yard looked like party central.

"Everything is so pretty." Casey enveloped her pediatrician in a hug. She did the same to Kent. "This is the best birthday ever."

Kent watched as Casey opened her gift from Jaclyn. Soon the kids were chasing iridescent bubbles Casey was creating from a weird arrangement of pipes and hoops. The freshening breeze picked up the shimmering circles and tossed them around the yard.

"Great gift," he told her.

"Thanks." She slid sunglasses over her eyes. "What did you get for her?"

Kent grinned. "You'll see. Later."

Kent had been planning to disappear but both Carissa and Jaclyn insisted they needed a hand. The sound of children's squeals and giggles made the whole courtyard come alive with laughter. This was how he'd thought the ranch would one day sound when he'd first moved back here. He became so caught up in their joy, he blinked in surprise when a raindrop plopped onto his nose.

A moment later jagged lightning pierced the sky.

"I'm sorry, Kent." Jaclyn watched Carissa shepherd the children into the kitchen. "We'll have to hold the rest of the party inside." She grimaced. "When I suggested the ranch, I never meant we'd all be inside your house."

"It's not a problem." Kent hurried Jaclyn. The kids'

laughter was gone. Big eyes brimmed with fear as another spear of lightening pierced the sky, its boom following a few seconds later. The festive party atmosphere had evaporated. Nobody was celebrating now. Except Jaclyn.

She handed everyone a red hat.

Kent blinked. Red pot mitts dangled from the oven door. There were red-and-white striped towels on the counter and two big white dishes with red polka dots that held what looked like party favor bags. Jaclyn struggled to fasten a Happy Birthday banner across the stainless-steel range hood. When he lent a hand, she smiled.

"You don't mind?"

"No." It was true. He didn't mind the extra touches, including the cherry-red pitcher on the counter and matching glasses. The room looked like a kitchen should—friendly, warm and welcoming. "I'll light a fire to take the chill off," he told her and soon had flames licking up the dry tinder and twigs in the adjoining eating area.

"We need some balloons for the last game." Jaclyn frowned. "Anyone interested in running outside to get them?" she asked loudly.

"Not me," the kids yelled en masse.

Jaclyn winked at him. "Anyone?" she said.

"Jaclyn, we don't need another game. Kent's done enough just letting us use his place," Carissa protested.

"I'll go," he volunteered. He raced outside to gather three bunches of balloons. Raindrops spattered his shirt, falling faster as the storm approached. He shoved the balloons into Jaclyn's arm and panted, "Gotta get the gifts," before returning to rescue the brightly colored packages and bags they'd forgotten.

When he had retrieved the last of them, he turned to leave the kitchen again.

"Kent, you don't need to get anything else," Jaclyn said quietly. "You'll get soaked."

"I'll be back in a few minutes," he promised.

"But you'll miss watching Casey open her gifts."

Kent lifted a hand to acknowledge he'd heard, but kept going. Inside his tool shed, he shook off the rain and fought to block out Jaclyn's effect on him. But he couldn't forget the image of her dashing across the grass in bare feet to avoid becoming "it" in a game of tag. He couldn't stop hearing the warming sound of her laughter when she'd been seriously splashed by a water gun. Nor could he rid his mind of the memory of her comforting a girl who'd slipped and skinned a knee.

Jaclyn pitched in whenever help was needed. Surely Hope-ites would soon not only accept her, but embrace her. Why, even Heddy had phoned this morning and apologized for asking him to intervene on Joey's behalf.

Kent hurried back to the house, surprised by his eagerness to rejoin the festivities. For so long he'd kept on the fringes of life, but Jaclyn and this silly party were reawakening feelings he'd thought long dead. It was dangerous to get involved—but suddenly Kent didn't care.

He left his box on the porch and went inside. Satisfaction filled him at the sight of kids gathered round the fireplace, laughing and talking as Casey opened the last of her gifts. The room was messy and happy and full of life.

Kent waited until Casey had finished thanking her friends for her birthday gifts. Then he carried in his and set it down in front of her.

"This is for you. Happy birthday."

Casey's eyes gaped. She froze for a minute in disbelief, then reached out one finger and touched Kent's surprise.

"A puppy! Oh, Mommy, it's a puppy." She hugged the furry little body to her chest and burbled with laughter when a tiny pink tongue peeked out to lick her face. "Can I really keep it?"

"Yes, Casey. Kent asked me and I agreed that you could have it. But you're going to have to take care of it. A puppy is a big responsibility." Carissa smiled at him.

Jaclyn's gaze held admiration. *Life is good*, Kent thought, basking in the warmth of her smile.

"I promise I will take very good care of him." Casey put the dog down and let it walk around the circle of kids, sniffing as it went. "What's his name, Mr. Kent?"

"Her, and the name is for you to decide." He glanced at Carissa. "As soon as you've chosen a name, I'll register her. She's a purebred Springer spaniel so you might as well have the papers."

"It's very kind of you, Kent. I know you usually sell your dogs. I appreciate you trusting Casey with one." Tears sparkled on the tips of Carissa's lashes as she watched her daughter roll on the floor with the puppy.

"What are you going to call her, Casey?" Jaclyn asked.

Casey thought for a moment then declared, "Marjorie Rose, that's her name. Only sometimes I'll call her Marj. Or maybe Rosie."

The dog had been well admired by the time Carissa

called the children to the table. Kent intervened before
Casey could feed Marjorie tidbits and explained the
dog could have only puppy food.

"You mean she can't have any birthday cake?"
Casey wailed.

"No." He hunkered down next to her. "Marjorie
Rose can never have treats like yours. They will make
her sick. You don't want to hurt her, do you?"

"No." Casey was adamant. She'd been sick so long
that she had no desire to inflict that on anyone or anything else. "But what can she eat?"

"Her own food. And once in a while doggie treats."
He pulled a sample from his pocket, winked at Jaclyn
then set the treat on the floor. The dog careened over
to it in a crazy bumbling scramble, wolfed down the
biscuit then sneezed.

The kids erupted into roars of laughter.

"Oh, Marjorie, you need some manners." Casey's
rapt adoration turned on Kent. "Thank you very much,
Mr. Kent."

"You're welcome, honey. Just take care of her."

"I will." Casey cuddled the puppy under one arm.

Kent sat in the corner next to a bemused Oreo, content to watch as Jaclyn helped Carissa serve the usual
birthday fare. Cooking in this kitchen always made
him feel like he was ruining Lisa's perfection. Today
he'd seen how the room should feel and sound. It was
not a memory he'd quickly forget.

The cake appeared, candles glowing. Kent joined in
the singing when Jaclyn shot him a look. Then he savored
every bite of the delicious chocolate cake.

"Seconds?" Jaclyn asked.

"I'd better not. I'm like Marjorie Rose—too many sweets aren't good for me."

"Oh, live a little," Jaclyn urged and plopped an oversize section on his plate. "I'll do CPR if you have cardiac arrest."

"Do I look like I'll have a heart attack?" He was indignant at the suggestion.

"You make it so easy," she teased.

"The sun is shining again," Carissa said. "Why don't we take Marjorie Rose outside and you kids can play with her?"

Kent could have pointed out that the dog would get dirty and have to be bathed. But instead, he followed the ladies outside, sat in one of his mom's favorite lawn chairs and enjoyed the laughter of the kids—almost as much as he enjoyed his second piece of cake.

"This has been such a lovely day. Thank you, Kent." Carissa's eyes grew moist. "Casey will never forget this birthday."

"Glad to help," he said, smiling.

Casey wasn't the only one who wouldn't forget today.

Suddenly Kent jumped out of his chair and raced across the grass as fear clamped a hand around his heart. One of the kids had used his barbecue lighter to set fire to some twigs.

"Kent?" Jaclyn said from behind him. He turned and she glanced from the lighter to his face, and took over. "That's really dangerous, honey," she told the child. "Fire can spread very easily when it's so dry. Then it's hard to put out."

"But it was just raining," the little girl protested.

"It didn't rain much. The ground isn't even muddy.

The sun has dried it all up." She ran her fingers over the ground to show the dust. "See? Fire is not for playing."

"Okay." She shrugged and rejoined the rest of the kids.

"Come on, Kent," Jaclyn soothed as she took his arm. "Have another cup of coffee. Everything is fine."

"Fine?" He turned on her, yanking his arm from her grasp. "That child could have been hurt and it would have been my fault."

"Kids get into mischief. Nothing happened." She'd turned her back so the others couldn't see, her voice soft. "God gave us a lovely day and kept us safe. Let's enjoy it."

God kept them safe? Then why hadn't God protected Lisa?

"Nothing happened, Kent."

But Kent knew exactly how quickly things could change.

Casey's party was the first and last that would ever happen on his ranch.

No matter what Jaclyn wanted.

Chapter Nine

❧

"This is the last of them." Kent set a tray of used dishes on the counter in the kitchen. "You don't have to do this, Jaclyn. My housekeeper will clean it up tomorrow morning."

"We're not leaving this for her." She kept working.

He gave a long-suffering sigh. "How can I help?"

"I can manage."

"I know that, Doc. By now I expect everyone in Hope knows exactly how well you manage to do anything you set your mind to." He grasped her shoulders and turned her to face him. "But since I'm here, we'll do it together. Deal?"

She nodded as she shrugged out of his hold. "Deal." Maybe working would take her mind off what had happened with the child and the lighter, and the strong urge she'd had to help Kent in that moment.

While she loaded the dishwasher, he wiped down counters, tables and chairs.

"Sorry I got so upset earlier," he finally said. "I just saw that flame flickering and—"

"You remembered the fire and Lisa," she finished.

She fought not to look at him lest she be bowled over by his pain. "I guessed that's what happened. It's only natural. After all, you haven't had a lot of people around since the accident, have you? Except for the potluck."

His blue eyes met hers. "You don't have to save my feelings, Jaclyn. I know I went over the top. But I couldn't stand it if a child got hurt out here."

She set the now-clean red utensils in the stainless-steel bucket on the counter then turned to face him.

"You think someone would blame you? Accidents happen, Kent. To everyone. We pick up and move on as best we can, but we can't always prevent them."

He raked his hand through his hair, sending the dark curls into further disarray. "It's so terribly dry," he mumbled, staring out the window.

"That's in God's hands. Not yours."

"Well, it's partly in my hands." He looked away from her and fell into a brooding silence.

"What's bothering you?" She sat down at the table and waited. "Talk to me, Kent. Is it about your cattle?"

"My cattle?" He frowned, his gaze confused as he studied her.

"I've been thinking about what you said about them. Can you not sell because cattle prices are low right now?"

"Not exactly." He tapped his finger on the table.

"Then what?" She searched her mind for memories of his dad. "You said your father understood about you not wanting to stay on the ranch after high school."

"He did."

"Then why would he expect you to keep his animals? I think he'd want you to be happy." Nothing about Kent's reluctance made sense to her. "Wouldn't building a sanctuary make you happy?"

"Yes." His entire demeanor changed. "If I just had an area where the wild animals I treat could be free instead of confined to cages or stalls until I reintroduce them to the wild—" His voice drifted away.

"That sounds simple," she reasoned.

"It's far from simple." His tortured voice told her the struggle went way beyond longhorn cattle.

"Because?" Jaclyn said softly.

"Because I owe my father." Desperation laced his voice. "I owe a lot to Dad and Mom, and I want to honor that."

She kept silent, waiting for him to continue, hoping she'd finally get an inkling as to why he felt so strongly about this.

"They loved me when no one else did." Kent squeezed his eyes closed. "I'm adopted, Jaclyn. No one around here knows." He got up, poured them each a glass of the lemonade his housekeeper had made and carried it to the table. He sat down, drained his own glass, set it on the table and looked directly at her.

"Heddy told me that the other day." Jaclyn shook her head before he could ask. "I haven't told anyone, but why is your adoption such a big secret?"

"My mom. She couldn't have children. She always felt bad about it. Embarrassed, I guess. Like she'd somehow let Dad down." A funny sad smile skittered across his lips. "It's understandable given how crazy the McCloys were about the heir and oldest son thing— a son to carry on the legacy. I broke the chain. I disappointed them."

"I doubt it."

"About a year after they officially adopted me, we moved here. My grandparents were gone. We had no other family. As far as I knew they never told anyone I was adopted." He shrugged. "That probably seems stupid to you."

"Not at all. I can understand wanting to keep private information to yourself, though I imagine it was hard on you."

"Me?" He blinked. "Why?"

"It's kind of denying a part of yourself, isn't it?" she asked. "You kept that secret from us, your friends. You couldn't be open and honest about it."

"I didn't want to be honest about my birth mother abandoning me." His mouth tightened. "Being adopted was the best thing to happen to me in my life and I repaid that by denying Dad his dream. All those years he'd talked about passing on the ranch to me." Kent's voice caught. When he looked at her, his blue eyes brimmed with sadness. "But he didn't say a word to dissuade me. The morning after my announcement he was talking funding for college. My father gave me my dream, Jaclyn. Now it's my turn to make his dream live."

"Kent." She reached out and laid her hand on his, waiting until he looked at her. "Cattle, longhorns— I doubt that's what your father dreamed of for you."

"It was all he ever talked about." He stared at their hands and then entwined his fingers with hers.

"Maybe all he talked of to you. To everyone else it was 'My son this and my son that.'" She smiled. "I talked to my dad the other evening. I told him you were mayor, and about all the things you're doing to improve the town. Do you know what he said?"

Kent shook his head.

"He said, 'Stan would be really proud of that boy. He used to say God brought the McCloys to Hope to make a difference. Kent is certainly doing that.'" She squeezed his fingers. "That was your father's dream, Kent. Not those cattle—they were just a game he played. You were what mattered to him, you and your integrity, the way you live your life. He taught you those things, didn't he?"

Kent nodded. "Yeah." His eyes glazed with memories. "Yes, he did."

"Maybe at first he was disappointed you didn't share his plans for the ranch. But once he saw the way you are with animals?" She shook her head. "I believe your dad wanted you to use that special gift you have and that's why he made it easy for you to get to college."

He bent his head to stare at their hands.

"Talk to anyone downtown, Kent. Go for coffee and ask them about your father. I guarantee every single person who knew him will tell you that next to you, those cattle came a distant second." She smiled at him as another memory surfaced. "We used to be in awe of you and your parents, did you know that? The rest of us kids used to wish we were that close with our parents."

"Yeah, we were pretty close. Dad used to say we were each other's cheering section and backup team." He closed his eyes.

"Exactly." Jaclyn cleared her throat. "Now are you going to live up to his dreams—his real ones—or are you going to get sidetracked?"

She could sit here and watch him forever, she thought, but handsome was only part of Kent's allure. He was strong, caring and determined to help everyone else. Here he was, ready to sacrifice his own dreams, as if they weren't worth the same effort he put into helping Hope.

"How do you do it?" Kent asked when she'd sipped the last drop from her glass.

"Do what?"

"Find exactly the right words to say." He leaned forward, brushed a strand of hair from her brow and peered into her eyes. "How did you know how to help me see what my dad was really about?"

She felt dazed by his touch. "Is that what I've done?"

He nodded, his face solemn.

"Well, maybe it's because I believe God has a purpose for each of us. You already know what I think mine is." She smiled. "Jessica's clinic."

"Like I needed to be told that."

"What you need to be told is, figure out your own purpose, Kent. I've watched you with kids, animals, the people of Hope—you really care about them. You go out of your way to make their worlds better. That is what your dad taught you. That is his real legacy to you. Not the cattle."

"See? You're so smart." He leaned forward and brushed her nose with a kiss. "Are you starving?"

Her insides melted at the kiss, innocent though it had been.

"How can you possibly be starving? You just ate a ton of cake," she said, trying to pretend she'd barely felt a thing.

"It was delicious, but it was *just* cake." He jumped up, strode to the fridge and peered inside. "Interested in a steak dinner, Doc? I'm cooking."

"Really?" She leaned back to study him. "I didn't realize you cooked."

"Actually I grill." Kent grinned. "Want to see?"

Jaclyn walked outside with him, marveling at the naturalness of his arm slung across her shoulders. He didn't seem to notice she was short of breath. She tried to ignore the warning bells going off in her head.

"Well?" He stood before a huge stainless-steel outfit built into an outdoor kitchen which Jaclyn was pretty sure would make most men drool. "What do you think?"

"That is not a grill. That is restaurant equipment." She had to step away from him in order to keep her thoughts together.

"My own personal restaurant. I'm pretty good with this." He picked up a lifter and twirled it like a juggler, tossing it up then catching it with two fingers.

"Do I applaud now?"

"Not till after you eat." Kent headed back into the house and began rummaging in the fridge.

Jaclyn stayed on the patio and searched for order in her chaotic thoughts. She was supposed to be avoiding him, but, oh, she wanted to stay and share a meal, to talk as they had been, open and honestly.

I have my work. I have the clinic. I have the committees. I don't have time for Kent or any other man in my life.

The thing was, Kent was already in her life.

For so long she'd defined herself as a doctor, indebted to God and her parents, a single twin. Was it time to rework her definition?

"You're not waiting to be served, are you?" Kent burst through the door bearing a huge platter with two steaks that flopped over the edges. "Because I was hoping you'd make a salad or something." He paused in front of her and bent to look into her eyes, one brow arched upward in an unasked question. "What's wrong?" he finally said.

"Nothing." She smiled. "I'd love to make a salad. That's one area in which I excel." She stepped inside.

A minute later she heard him humming a new song they'd learned in church last week. Jaclyn smiled as she moved around the kitchen, finding what she needed to set the table on the patio. She made tea, put two scrubbed potatoes in the microwave and threw together a salad. In the freezer there was half a loaf of garlic bread which she wrapped in foil and placed in the oven on low to heat. As she worked, Jaclyn realized the kitchen was perfectly planned out to facilitate every task. Nothing was more than a few steps away.

Just beyond the window over the sink, red roses bloomed in profusion, adding another touch of color to the room. With a few lights on and the new accessories, the kitchen looked, almost welcoming.

Some shrunken apples lay in a crisper in the fridge. She peeled them, added cinnamon and placed them in the oven beside the bread.

"Something smells good in here." Kent glanced around. "How rare do you like your steak?" His big grin made him look relaxed and happy.

"Not at all. This is to say—well done." She quickly dissolved into giggles at his offended look. "I know, it's the wrong thing to say to a rancher, but it's true. Make it well done, please."

"You mean ruin it." His face morose, Kent returned to his grill.

As she tidied up, Jaclyn found an old candle stub in a drawer. But when she lit it, it made everything feel too intimate. She was about to blow it out when Kent set two huge plates on the table.

"Enjoy," he said with a flourishing bow.

And she did. The food, the laughter, the teasing and the unfamiliar pleasure of eating with someone you liked—it made her realize how isolated she'd been. The talk soon turned to some mutual high school friends.

"I think Brianna, Zac, Nick, Shay, you and I are the only ones who aren't married." Jaclyn regretted the words the moment she said them. "I mean, you were, of course. But—"

"It's okay. I know what you mean." He patted her hand. "But I don't think it's all that odd. You, Brianna and Shay were pretty career-minded. It's hard to have it all." He pushed away his dish, leaned back in his chair. "I should know."

"What does that mean?" Night edged in around them and the rose bush filled the air with its intoxicating scent. "Is fixing the clinic getting to you?" she asked softly.

"Only because I can't seem to get it done." He sighed.

"And you want to? You're sure?"

"Of course I want you to get in there, to have a real office. I want your patients lined up and waiting because I happen to think you have a lot to give this town." He grimaced. "But that isn't exactly what I meant."

"What did you mean?" She never tired of the smooth, even cadence of his voice.

"There are so many things Hope needs and it's up

to me to get them done. People are counting on me. I can't fail them."

"I'm sure no one feels you have failed them," she protested.

"I feel it." He looked straight at her, his blue eyes unflinching. "I have a list of things I want to accomplish before my term is up and—don't take this personally—but it's about as long as it was two months ago."

She frowned, intrigued by his comment. "What kinds of things?"

"Redoing the baseball diamond so it doesn't look like our little league kids have been abandoned to a vacant lot, refinishing the stucco on the outside of the hospital, starting some kind of youth program so our kids have a place to go after school and in the evenings."

"All of them sound achievable to me," she said.

"Mostly I'd like to formulate an emergency measures plan." His face tightened. A furrow formed between his brows. "If we have another wildfire, if the mine has a major incident, or if anything else disastrous happens, Hope is totally unprepared."

"I thought I saw something about that when I signed on at the hospital," Jaclyn said.

"There was a plan developed about thirty-five years ago but things have changed since then. We need to update, to be prepared in case some kind of disaster hits." Kent fell silent, his face bearing that worried expression.

"You're expecting problems?" she asked quietly.

"I'm expecting the unexpected because that's what usually happens when you're not prepared." A taut grimness edged his tone now.

"We'll have to pray that won't happen." She saw his eyes narrow.

"Pray, yes. But I also want to be organized for whatever gets thrown at us. With such a dry year—" His voice trailed away, his eyes peering into the darkness.

"You're worried about another fire. It could happen, I suppose. I've noticed areas around the hospital are very dry." She tried to ease his worry. "But whatever comes our way, God will take care of us. That's His promise. We can always depend on Him."

Jaclyn knew he didn't believe it. He was thinking about Lisa and the fire that had taken her. Was that why he sounded so driven when he talked about the emergency preparedness plan?

"I still think we need to get all our ducks in a row, just in case," he muttered.

"It's a good idea," she agreed. "If you want some help, let me know. I'd like to be part of it."

"Thanks." Kent nodded then rose and began stacking their dishes.

Jaclyn took the cue, but his response bothered her. Didn't he want her help?

"It's getting late. I'll help you clean up then I'd better go. I'm on call tonight."

"Then you shouldn't be here working. You should be relaxing." He took the dishes from her and insisted she leave them. "You've done enough for today. Go home, Jaclyn. Relax and do something special for yourself this evening."

"But—" The word spluttered out of her before she could stop it.

"But what?" He smiled. "I am capable of doing a few dishes you know."

"I know that." She debated whether or not to say it. He gave her an odd look. "What?"

"I wanted to see your petting zoo."

"I don't have one." The familiar tic was back at the corner of his jaw, telegraphing his tension.

"You did show the kids something today—they told me. I wanted to see but I was busy attending to a bump on the head."

"The puppies. And I have a couple of birds I've worked on that are healing out in the shed. And one of the miniature ponies had a colt." He shrugged. "That's it. Oh, except for the snakes. The game wardens brought in a couple of snakes yesterday, but I only let the kids look at them."

"That's all?" Jaclyn mocked and burst into laughter. "It sounds like a regular petting zoo to me. One of the children mentioned a rabbit?"

"Yes," he agreed dryly. "There is also a rabbit, soon to be more rabbits if my diagnosis is correct. But that doesn't make a petting zoo."

"What would you call it then?" She tilted her head to one side.

"It's just a few animals that I'm treating. A petting zoo would have specific areas and pens designed for each animal." He shrugged. "I don't have any of that."

"Yet." She checked her watch. "I guess I'll have to see them another time." She grabbed her bag and slung it over one shoulder.

"It was the snakes that did it, wasn't it?" He grinned. "You were all ready to run out there and see the animals until I mentioned snakes."

Jaclyn tried and failed to hide her shudder.

"Snakes are amazing animals you know, even the

poisonous ones." He chuckled at her. "You don't believe me?"

"I guess it's all in the way you look at things." She met his gaze. "Like I look at God as someone who expects each of us to do our very best for Him so we're worthy of the life He gives us."

"Really?" Kent frowned at her. "I guess I don't see Him the same as you do. I don't feel like He's a big taskmaster who expects me to accomplish certain things or He'll disapprove."

"I never said that at all."

"You act that way. Signing up for all these committees, working yourself to death—what is that about?"

"Hardly to death." She held out her arms, fingers splayed so he could see they were not worked to the bone. "See? Perfectly healthy. And you know why I joined all those committees. I am trying to get clients for the clinic."

"I know it's been hard to get patients," he said, modulating his voice. "I know lots of folks have brought up the past and made it their excuse for not coming to see you. But I don't think you have to earn anything. God gives us His gifts because He loves us, not because we earn them. People in Hope will eventually come around. People like you, Jaclyn."

"So far 'like' hasn't been working." She studied the floor. "I don't know if you can understand this. My parents certainly don't. But the clinic—that is what I'm supposed to do with my life. It's what I *have* to do. Otherwise what was the purpose for me living and Jessica dying?"

Kent stared at her. A frown tipped down the edges of his mouth and darkened his eyes to a deep navy.

"You're trying to earn your life?" Disbelief filled his voice.

"Yes," she told him, thrusting back her shoulders and tilting up her chin so he wouldn't feel sorry for her. "That is exactly what I'm saying. God gives us opportunities. He expects us to make use of them. And if we don't—"

"If we don't—what?" he asked in disbelief.

"I'm not saying that God sends down a lightning rod to strike us dead if we don't use what He's given us." She drew her bag a little closer, trying to form the words. "But that doesn't mean God has no expectations of His children. There's an old saying. 'God helps those who help themselves.'"

Kent looked as if he wanted to argue. Jaclyn just wanted to escape. Suddenly she felt vulnerable, as if she'd opened up a private part of herself for him to examine and she'd disappointed him. She edged toward the door.

"Thank you for a lovely dinner. I don't know when I've tasted a better steak."

"I'm the one who needs to thank you," he said as he followed her outside. "You did so much work for that party."

"A party you didn't want. Anyway, Carissa did most of the work." She opened her car, set her bag inside. "I just helped."

"That's what you always do, isn't it? *Just* help. You help the girls' group, you help the ladies' committees. You help the Sunday school. You help the choir. You help the service clubs. In fact you 'help' pretty well everyone in town." Kent tipped his head to one side, his eyes quizzical in the clear moonlight. "It makes me wonder—who is helping you, Jaclyn?"

"You are," she said softly. Her nerves were doing that skittering dance again. Her pulse picked up when she caught the citrusy scent of his aftershave. Every nerve ending turned into a megawatt receptor that flashed details about Kent to her brain. "You're a wonderful man who has worked so hard to make my dream come true. I appreciate you, Kent. Good night."

He said nothing until she was seated in her car. Then he leaned inside and pressed a kiss against her cheek, right at the edge of her lips. A moment later he pulled back and closed the door. Jaclyn started the motor then rolled down the window.

"What was that for?" she asked, bemused.

"For bringing life back to this ranch," he said. "That's what you helped with today, Jaclyn. Good night."

Jaclyn had no recollection of driving home. As she stood in her own kitchen, she lifted her hand and touched her fingertips to the spot beside her mouth that still burned from Kent's kiss.

"For a doctor, you're a very stupid woman, Jaclyn LaForge. You've gone and fallen in love with him."

Kent wasn't interested in a romantic relationship. He was still reeling from the loss of the wife he loved.

"I can't love him," Jaclyn whispered. Running the clinic would drain her, physically, emotionally and mentally. There wouldn't be enough left over to give to someone else. Besides, she didn't want marriage. She'd seen how badly marriage could go with her parents, who had truly loved each other once.

Jaclyn had known she'd be alone when she made

the decision to make the clinic her life. She couldn't vacillate now.

She dug out her plans for Jessica's clinic and poured over them for hours. But always it was Kent's face she saw, his voice she heard, his kiss she felt. She wished an emergency would draw her to the hospital where she could dive into work and forget these very unsettling feelings.

Instead, Jaclyn sat far into the night, dreaming of what she couldn't have.

I'm trying to keep my vow, she prayed when sleep wouldn't come. *Please help me forget love and focus on work.*

But in her heart Jaclyn knew her work couldn't compete with what she now felt for Kent McCloy.

She was in trouble.

Chapter Ten

Two weeks later Kent sat in church wishing he'd skipped this Sunday service. It felt wrong to be here when the faith he'd once held so dear now filled him with questions. But he could hardly walk out just as the minister walked to the pulpit.

"What are you blaming God for?" he asked the congregation. "Is it a lack of money? A lousy boss? The loss of someone you loved? Do you think you're alone, that you've been abandoned? Do you feel like God is mad at you? What's your beef with God, folks?"

The pregnant pause had the entire church riveted, including Kent.

"You need help, but where is God? Where does He go when you need Him most? More importantly, why doesn't He help when you call? It's an age-old question. And the answer is—" Pastor Tom paused, waited then smiled. "I don't know."

Soft laughter filled the sanctuary.

"It's the truth, people. I don't know why it's that way. I don't know why it sometimes feels as if God abandons us. I can't explain why certain times in our lives we are unable to hear His voice or feel His presence." Again his smile flashed. "I do know we humans sometimes feel disappointed in His response. We think we have to work harder to get His attention, to be worthy of His time. And if God still doesn't respond, we feel abandoned, alone, as if we've sinned, done something so wrong He's finally given up on us."

Kent squirmed. This sermon hit a little too close to home.

"David the psalmist, God's chosen king and beloved child, had the same questions we do. Read his psalms and you'll see how often David asked God where He is, why He doesn't help. If David had doubts, why wouldn't we?" The pastor shook his head. "We have to stop beating ourselves up when doubts assail us. We need to remember who God said He is and the promises He's made. We have to stop allowing doubts and fears to overwhelm us. When problems hit us, when it seems we're at rock bottom, this is the very time we need to hold strong in our faith."

Uncomfortable with the message, Kent glanced around. He noticed Jaclyn seated two rows over in front of him. She wore a white lace sundress that showed off her narrow shoulders. On her left side, three young girls hunched forward, intent on the minister's words. Jaclyn also seemed riveted until she turned her head, as if she'd felt his stare on her. Her eyes met his and held as if some invisible electric current bound them together. After a moment she gave him a funny half smile, then turned her attention back to the preacher. Kent did the same.

"We all have dark moments when the questions

seem to overwhelm. But in David's blackest hour, he knew enough about God to know His truth. Listen to Psalm 139, verse seven." He turned a page in his Bible and began to read. "'I can never be lost to your Spirit! I can never get away from my God! If I go up to heaven, You are there; if I go down to the place of the dead, You are there. If I ride the morning winds to the farthest oceans, even there Your hand will guide me, Your strength will support me.' And then in verse sixteen he says, 'You saw me before I was born and scheduled each day of my life before I began to breathe.'"

The magnitude of that hit Kent like a sledgehammer. Somehow he'd never considered that God had known him before he was born and knew how badly he would fail Lisa. He'd never considered that God knew, before Kent had packed a single bag, that coming back to the ranch would send his wife into that tailspin of depression.

He and Lisa had prayed before they moved. They'd asked God's blessing. Kent had done everything he could to ease the transition for her. And yet even then, God knew it wouldn't be enough.

Kent struggled with the truth that God had also known how Lisa would die and that the guilt of her death would bring Kent to the very precipice of doubting his faith. Shock filled him as he realized that long before he'd admitted it to himself, God had known his questions.

If Lisa's death had been a test of his faith, Kent had failed miserably.

Lost in his musing, he suddenly became aware that

the congregation was rising, that the organ was playing. The service was over. He stood and scanned the
overhead for the words to a chorus he didn't really
know, his brain focused on clarifying the meaning of
those scriptures.

God knew of his guilty feelings, of his failure of
the one he loved the most. God knew Kent was im-
mobilized by blame and remorse and shame. Because
if he was honest with himself, that is what lay under
his guilt—shame. Shame that he had not been able to
save his wife. Shame that he hadn't loved her enough
to take her away before it was too late.

Did that make Lisa's death any less his fault?

"Hi, Kent. I'm glad you made it this morning." Jaclyn stood in front of him, breathtaking in her white
dress.

"You're glad?" Did that mean she'd noticed he'd
skipped church lately?

"I went out on a call last night at eleven. When I
came back at two, I noticed your truck was still in
front of the clinic. You keep late hours." Her wide
smile did funny things to his respiration.

"I guess you do, too. You look lovely. No one would
know you were up so late." He searched for another
topic of conversation. "Was it serious—the call, I
mean?"

Jaclyn nodded, her face solemn. When she swallowed
he saw the shadow of tears well in her brown eyes. That
vulnerability sent a shaft of pain straight to his heart.

"A little boy, only two. I lost him," she murmured.
"I did everything I could think of to save him, but
they brought him in too late because they knew I was
on duty." A tiny sob stopped her words for a moment.

"Oh, I'm so sorry, Jaclyn." He wanted to hug her.

"Thanks." She struggled to regroup. "I'm beginning to wonder if I will ever crack the barrier of trust in Hope," she whispered.

"Can you tell me who it was?" Kent was stunned when she named the child of a former school friend of theirs.

"The mom's parents never got over their bitterness about me. They advised their daughter to wait until another doctor came on duty." She dashed the tears from her cheeks and gulped. "Maybe if someone else had been—"

"No, don't think that. You can't blame yourself, Jaclyn." Kent touched her arm, her bare skin smooth against his work-roughened fingertips. "I know you. You did the best you could."

"Yes. I did everything I know to do." Jaclyn nodded. "But the pneumonia—"

"There are no buts." He smiled at her. "In a way, isn't that what today's message was about? Knowing that God is there, that we do the best we can and leave the rest up to Him. At least," he said, trying for a lighter tone, "that's my interpretation."

"I guess." Her face looked pale. "But this case has magnified my doubts. Maybe my parents were right and it's time for me to join a big-city practice." She drew her arm away from his touch then tilted her head to one side and said, "Maybe it would be better if someone else came here, someone they wouldn't be afraid to let treat their kids. Maybe Jessica's clinic was a selfish idea that I need to forget."

Kent stifled his urge to yell "no" at the top of his lungs. He wanted to beg her to stay, but then Jaclyn might suspect the depths of his feelings for her. He didn't want that, so he modified his response and tried another tack.

"That's a whole lot of maybes. I don't think you should give up just yet. I think this is something you need to seriously consider, not decide on the spur of the moment. I'm happy to act as your sounding board, if you want."

"That's really nice of you, Kent. I could use a friend."

He nodded, knowing his feelings were much stronger than friendship.

"Maybe you'd like to join me for lunch." Her hesitancy over the invitation transmitted clearly through her uncertain voice.

"Sure. Where would you like to go?"

"My place? I couldn't sleep when I got home so I tried out some recipes from my cooking class. I know it's a risk, but you could share them with me." She grimaced. "I promise I have a large bottle of antacids, in case you need them."

Though he had avoided Jaclyn this past week, sharing lunch with her sounded too good to resist. And he wanted to learn if she identified with what the minister had said.

"Kent," she said, giving a nervous laugh. "You're taking way too long to answer."

"Uh, I—"

"In my defense, I've had five classes now and turned out an acceptable dish for every one. Heddy's standing right over there. Ask her if you don't believe me."

Kent glanced around the sanctuary and saw Hope's

busiest busybody studying them. He knew in a minute she would rush over to see if he'd made a decision about her offer to work on the emergency measure plan and he didn't want that. Not now. What he wanted was some time with Jaclyn. Alone.

Jaclyn, with her generous smile and infectious laugh was getting to be a big part of his formerly solitary life.

Too big a part?

"Another time," she said, a flicker of hurt in her voice. She shrugged, turned away. "See you."

Jaclyn had made it out the foyer door before Kent caught up to her.

"I'd be very happy to share whatever you prepared," he said. "I'm sure it's all delicious."

"It's not necessary, really. I got the message, Kent."

"That's funny because I wasn't sending any message. I admit I kind of zoned out there for a minute, but that had to do with Heddy." He grimaced. "Somehow she always manages to corner me and talk me into something I don't want to do. I was trying to think up a way to decline her latest request to be in charge of the emergency measures planning committee and I wasn't paying attention to you. Sorry."

"Heddy wants to be in charge—oh, dear."

"Exactly," he agreed. "If she was in charge a lot of people wouldn't help. I can't think of a way to refuse her."

Jaclyn studied him. "Okay, lunch it is. We could go out. You don't have to eat what I made." Her perfectly arched brows lowered. "It's probably not that good anyway."

"I won't be able to tell until I have some," he said. "I'll follow you to your place, shall I?"

The drive to Jaclyn's town home was short. Curiosity built as he trailed her up the path to her front door.

She unlocked it and invited him inside. Kent glanced around. It was more or less what he'd expected—very stylish, quite modern and extremely tidy.

"Your home is lovely," he said. "I would have known it was yours."

She laid her purse on the sofa then turned to look at him. "How?"

"The red," he said. "It's your signature color, I think. I notice you usually wear some touch of red, most of the time in the form of funny earrings."

"You think my earrings are funny?" Jaclyn began pulling dishes out of the fridge. "My patients like them."

"And it's the kids that count, right?" Kent grinned when she nodded. "I figured." He watched her remove lids, clear plastic wrap and tinfoil from a number of bowls. "How can I help?"

"Set the table?" Jaclyn waited for his nod then pointed to a drawer.

"What did you think of the sermon today?" He worked quickly as he waited for her answer, wondering if he'd overreacted to what he'd heard.

"Good. But then his sermons are always good." She set the last of the serving dishes on the table and waved him to a seat. "I like the way he makes God personal. I'll say grace."

Kent bowed his head and waited until she finished speaking, searching for a way to ask the questions that rattled in his brain.

"Now help yourself. Take a little bit first," she warned. "I haven't tasted this yet myself."

"It looks good." As he sampled each dish, he decided to come right out with it. "Can I ask you something?"

Jaclyn grinned at him. "As long as you don't ask me if I followed the recipe exactly."

"Recipe or not, it all tastes wonderful to me." He chewed on a biscuit until the silence had gone on too long and he knew he had to ask. "I was wondering about something you said when you were at my house. After the birthday party, remember?"

"I remember," she said cautiously, not looking at him. The way she kept her head bent, her eyes on her food, made him think she was remembering that kiss.

He'd been an idiot to do it, but he didn't regret it.

"You were saying?" Confusion filled her pretty face.

He cleared his throat. "I don't remember your exact words, but when we were talking it sounded to me like you felt that you owe God for allowing you to live." It wasn't exactly the way he meant to say it, but close enough. "Do you really think that?"

"Yes," she said thoughtfully. "I do feel I owe God, though perhaps not the way you mean it."

"Would you mind explaining how *you* mean it?"

"Well." Jaclyn set down her fork and leaned back in her chair. "Jessica and I were identical twins, yet she got sick and I didn't. I finished high school, I took my training and now I'm able to work, to enjoy life and to think about the future. That's a gift from God and I need to be worthy of it."

"How?" he asked. "How can you make yourself

worthy of your life?" He took another spoonful of potato salad and a larger scoop of the green bean salad. "These are excellent by the way."

"Thanks." She rose and filled the electric kettle, then set it to boil. She fiddled around with a few other insignificant chores, then finally returned to the table. But she did not answer his question.

"This whole thing about you being worthy, about earning your life. Is it because you feel guilty for living? I can understand that," he admitted. "I felt like that after Lisa died, as if I should've died in her place."

"No, I don't feel guilty. It's more like…" She gave up and shrugged. "It's hard to put into words."

"I'd like to understand what drives you," he said quietly. "I'd like to figure out what's behind this burning need you have to excel at everything. Even cooking." Kent waved a hand over the table. "I mean, look at what you've created here. You can hardly call this beginner's work. One dish, maybe that salad, or even the biscuits, that would have been a good start. But you've gone way beyond that and created this meal. Not that I'm complaining. It's fantastic and I've enjoyed it very much. But it's so—"

"Extreme?" Jaclyn made a face. "I never did do things by half measures, Kent, even in high school."

"No, you didn't." Kent was beginning to wish he could abandon the whole subject. It was none of his business and he felt like he was prying, but he desperately wanted to understand why she felt so driven. "Why is that?"

The kettle started to boil so she rose and made some hot tea which she carried to the table along with two mugs. She also laid out a platter of fruit, took away his empty plate and offered him a small bowl.

"You see," she said with a smile, "I didn't go whole hog and make dessert, too."

Kent remained silent and kept watching her. When he didn't speak she sighed. She set her elbows on the table then cupped her chin in her palms.

"It's like this. God spared me, so I need to make sure I don't waste a single moment. Like I have to make up for what Jessica didn't get to experience." Her voice was quiet, defensive. "Maybe that sounds stupid to you, but it's like a drive inside of me. I need to make sure I do everything as well as I possibly can, to earn what I've been given."

"But Jaclyn," Kent asked, his gaze never leaving her face. "When will you have earned it? When will you have done enough?"

"I don't know." Gravity filled her big brown eyes. Her lashes glittered with tears. "I just know that I can't fail. I can't mess up again." Jaclyn jumped up and strode across the room. She grabbed a tangle of vivid-colored threads and held it up. Her smile flashed. "Or my life will end up like this."

Kent rose from the table and walked slowly toward her. The threads were attached to a piece of white fabric held by some kind of stretcher bar. "Needlepoint?" he asked in confusion.

"Yes, needlepoint. I joined a stitchery class. I've been taking lessons from Heddy. She makes fantastic pictures and stuff. But I'm a dud at it." She shrugged as if it didn't matter, but he saw pain lurking in the depths of her expressive eyes.

"Does it matter, Jaclyn? You're good at so many other things. Does needlepoint really matter?"

"Yes!" She swiped away a tear. "Yes, it matters. A lot."

"Why? Because it will get you patients?"

"No. Maybe partly." She didn't look at him.

"But if you don't like it why subject yourself—" A sudden thought made him wince. "You're doing it because Jessica did it."

She nodded.

"But Jaclyn, you are not Jessica. You're you. You can't force yourself to be something other than yourself." His heart ached for this beautiful woman's lack of self-confidence. "You can't be more than who you are—a wonderful doctor. Do I think you need to get some patients? Yes. But not by becoming all things to all people. I really think you're shortchanging yourself by trying so hard to compensate for Jessica's death."

"It's not her death I'm trying to compensate for," she said, her voice filled with pathos. "It's her life." Then the tears did fall. Jaclyn stood there, looking so small and bereft that Kent couldn't help but wrap his arms around her.

"Oh, Jaclyn. Jessica doesn't need you to compensate for her life," he whispered, pressing her head against his shoulder. He threaded his fingers through her hair and pushed it back, away from her face. "Jessica lived her life and lived it well on her own terms. Don't you remember?"

"Not really. Sometimes I can hardly remember her at all." Jaclyn's forehead bumped his chin, her eyes full of despair.

"I can see her burying her nose in those daisies

you used to bring her on Fridays, after you got paid. She adored them so much she wore them out just by touching them. I remember how you tried to coax her to learn how to ride bareback but she would have none of it." He closed his eyes and inhaled her soft sweet scent. "I remember she wouldn't even try certain vegetables they had in the cafeteria at school."

"Yes." Jaclyn laughed. "She was pretty stubborn about a lot of things."

"Yes, she was," he agreed. "You and I, and I'm guessing a lot of other people, remember those things about Jessica because they made her unique. As you are unique. So why do you think you have to live your life as if you are Jessica? You aren't, Jaclyn. You're you and you are the only person you owe anything to. That's what I meant about this morning's message."

She pulled away from him and frowned, which wrinkled her pert nose in the most adorable way. "What does this have to do with the sermon?"

Surprised by the loss he felt when Jaclyn stepped out of his arms, Kent scrambled to focus on what he'd been trying to get across to her. He followed her to the table, sat down and accepted the mug of tea she poured for him.

"Tell me what you mean," Jaclyn ordered.

"Well," he began, feeling his way, "David knew who he was. No matter how often he appealed to God to help him, he knew in his heart of hearts that he was God's, no matter what. He sinned, he made horrible mistakes, but he never lost sight of who he was as a child of God, or that God's love for him was unshakable."

Jaclyn studied him but said not one word. So he continued.

"That got me thinking," he continued, stuffing down his reluctance to discuss his personal life. If it would help Jaclyn, that was worth baring his soul. "I've always blamed myself for Lisa's death because I lit the fire that eventually killed her."

"But you didn't know she was there," Jaclyn protested.

"No, but I should have. I knew how depressed she was. I knew my refusing to leave the ranch would decimate her. She'd always held out hope that eventually I'd give up my plan to make Dad's dream come true, that I'd sell." He raked a hand through his hair, remembering that day too clearly. "The day she died I was tired, fed up with our bickering and the way nothing seemed to be going our way. I was also terrified that the wildfire would take everything we had. I felt like I had no control over anything and I lashed out at Lisa." He ignored the pressure of Jaclyn's fingers against his arm. He had to finish this. "Then I left to start the backfire. And she walked out into it."

"Oh, Kent." Jaclyn's eyes brimmed with tears as she met his gaze. Then something in her expression changed. Her eyes widened. "You think it was suicide. Don't you?"

"I don't know. That's what has hounded me all these years. Did I cause her to take her own life?" Kent rubbed the back of his neck to ease the tension there.

"I'm no expert on depression, but Brianna's told me about some cases she treated. Even if Lisa did choose suicide, it is not your fault." Jaclyn leaned toward him. "You cannot be held responsible for her decision."

"I feel responsible. There was a message on the phone. Maybe she came out to tell me, couldn't find me and when she was caught decided it was easier to give in than to fight. Maybe she didn't intend to get stranded. I just don't know." His voice was tortured.

"And you will never know." Jaclyn touched his cheek with her hand, her skin was soft against his. "That's the hardest part, not knowing. That's what you have to let go of."

"This morning made me realize that." He replayed the words of the sermon in his brain. "Lisa and I prayed for God's blessings on us and the ranch every single day. And still she died." It was like he was groping his way through a maze, trying to understand all he'd heard.

"So how does the sermon fit?" She leaned back, her face expectant.

"David was pursued by his enemies, injured and shamed for what seems like no reason. Yet each time he got up, faced his mistakes, rebuilt his faith in God and rebuilt his world." He glanced across the room, then smiled. "You know what, Jaclyn? I've been just like you with your needlepoint."

"You do needlepoint?" she teased, but empathy glowed in her dark gaze.

"Yeah, with cows." He chuckled at her puzzled face. "You hate needlepoint. You tangle the threads, make knots where there shouldn't be any and generally ruin the fabric. You keep pushing, even though that needlepoint is a mess and you're only making it worse."

"Well, thanks for that encouragement."

"I'm doing the same thing," Kent told her, amazed

by his discovery. "I hate ranching but I keep on doing it, just like you keep doing that needlepoint, despite the fact that we both mess things up. I keep doing things my own stupid way despite my failures. I'd have lost the ranch and ruined everything Dad built if it wasn't for Dad's friend Gordon."

"Meaning?" Dubious about his point, Jaclyn tilted her head sideways as she waiting for him to complete his illustration.

"The point is I've been trying to force myself to do something I shouldn't be doing because I thought it would somehow make losing Lisa and my parents okay." Saying it lifted a heavy load from his heart. "The message today helped me see I can't change the past. Ranching isn't my forte."

"Ah." She sipped her tea. "Good. So you're going to build your sanctuary."

"I don't know. I'm not sure that's where I should be going, either." He finished his tea, carried his cup to the sink and rinsed it. "I need to get a handle on my life, to talk to God and to think things through. Right now I need to focus on finishing your clinic and getting the emergency plan for the town operational. Then I'll think about my future."

Kent stopped, debated the wisdom of saying the rest of what was in his heart. Jaclyn was an amazing woman dealing with a lot from her past, and maybe from her present, too, given her parents' objections to the clinic. He didn't want to add to her pain or confuse her, but neither did he want her to get bogged down in guilt, as he'd been. He wanted, he realized, for her to be happy and content. He wanted the very best for her.

"Go ahead and say it, Kent." Jaclyn smiled. "I know you're itching to tell me something."

"You're doing the same thing as me. Trying to make something work that can't. You cannot earn your right to live, Jaclyn, and it doesn't matter how hard you try, you never will. Your life is a gift given to you by God because you're His child and He loves you dearly. You don't have to measure up. He already loves you."

Her face tightened with masked emotions. He forced himself to continue.

"You're wearing yourself out joining all these clubs, Jaclyn." Amazed by his own temerity but determined to make her take a second look at her life, Kent pressed on. "If the clinic is God's purpose for you, then maybe it's time for you to sit back, trust Him and let Him work out the details."

Jaclyn, her face flushed, opened her mouth to say something, but a piercing sound cut her off. Her eyes widened to huge brown orbs as she looked at him.

"Fire." Kent pulled out his keys. "I have to get to the station."

She was right behind him, closing the door and jogging to her car. "I need to get to the hospital in case there's something I can do."

He loved that she was so willing to jump into the fray and help however she could.

"Please think about what I said."

"Deal," she said. He squeezed her arm then climbed in his truck and drove away.

In the midst of a prayer for the safety of Hope's residents, Kent realized something else.

He'd broken all his own rules and fallen in love with Dr. Jaclyn LaForge.

*Oh, God, You know that can't happen. You know
I fail those I love. Please, take it away. I'd rather be
alone for the rest of my life than hurt her.*

But life without Jaclyn in it was a very bleak prospect.

Chapter Eleven

"You sound tired." Brianna Benson's voice transmitted concern across the phone line.

"I am," Jaclyn agreed. "There was a car accident outside of town today which caused a very bad fire." She rubbed her temples to ease the thudding there. "A coronary, burns, assorted bumps and bruises and a multitude of stitches were all a part of my day."

"Why you? You're not an emergency specialist," Brianna said.

"Here in Hope I am. This is a small town, remember? There aren't any specialists, per se. Lately I've been helping out on the emergency ward. This is the first time I've sat down since lunch." She smothered a yawn. "And then I stopped by the clinic."

"That sounds ominous." Brianna—a psychologist—had a gift for sensing trouble. "Want to talk about it?"

"Kent's not going to get it done in time." Jaclyn had known it subconsciously for days, but she'd kept hoping she was wrong. New water damage caused by a bad pipe had changed everything. Now there was no longer any point in pretending. "It won't be habitable by my deadline."

"Can you ask Kent to work harder?"

"No, I can't. He's already going all out." Bitter disappointment threatened to swamp her but Jaclyn pushed it back. "It's not Kent's fault. There's just too much for him to do and no one else to help," she sniffed. "I'm going to lose my funding, Brianna. The clinic isn't going to happen."

"I'm so sorry. Are you sure?"

"Pretty sure." Jaclyn told her a few of the many things that still needed to be done at the clinic.

"What about the townspeople? They used to be pretty gung ho on working together."

"That just shows you haven't been back in Hope for a while. This feud has split everyone. Nobody seems interested in helping anyone else. In fact, I still don't have many patients." Where did all this leave her, Jaclyn wondered? "Do you think I was wrong to start this?" she asked her friend.

"You've wanted to start that clinic for as long as I can remember," Brianna said. "There's nothing wrong with that."

"But maybe I've been going about it the wrong way." She reminded Brianna about all the groups she'd joined, all the ways she'd tried to become part of the small community. "I've tried to make them see I'm not the same kid that vandalized their church, but Kent was right. I'm killing myself trying to be all things to all people. Worse than that, it isn't working. Kent says—"

"Sounds like you and Kent have been talking a lot. Anything you want to tell me about him, Jaclyn?" The hint was hard to miss.

"I like him, Brianna. A lot." Understatement.

"You always did." A soft giggle. "Has he changed much from high school?"

"We all have. I suspect losing his parents and then his wife changed Kent most. He's been great, but friendship is all we can share. You know that."

"I don't know that at all." Brianna's voice softened. "I only know you've told yourself that. All these years you've been so focused on getting Jessica's clinic on track that you haven't allowed anything else in your life. Maybe it's time to rethink that."

"Nothing's changed, Brianna," she said quietly. "Marriage isn't for me. I'm dedicated to my patients."

"To the exclusion of everyone and everything else? I don't think that's healthy. We all need people in our lives."

"That's the pot calling the kettle black. Who do you have?" Jaclyn challenged.

"My son. He fills my world with joy."

"Is that all you want?"

"For now it is," Brianna said. "He's got problems right now and I need to get his world straightened out. But if I'm being totally honest, I think I had my shot at love and blew it."

She was referring to dumping Zac right before their marriage. Jaclyn had never figured out exactly why Brianna had done that and her friend had always refused to discuss it.

"Zac's still here," she said. "Every so often he shows up to help Kent with the clinic. He's still single."

"Oh." Brianna was silent for a few moments. "So I should get involved but you won't consider it yourself?"

"I can't. It wouldn't be fair to the guy." She squeezed

her eyes close and fought back the tears. "You know how my parents' marriage is, Brianna. Ever since Jessica died, they've been like strangers sharing a house. They loved each other once, but that's gone. I couldn't go through that—watching love die."

"There's no reason you have to. Not all marriages are like theirs. People can heal after a loss, if they're willing to work at it. Trust me, in my practice I've seen all kinds of rifts healed. But they have to do it in their own time and their own way. You're not responsible for them."

"But if they approved of my clinic—"

"Come on, Jaclyn, there is more broken in their marriage than your refusal to follow the path they chose for you." She paused and lowered her voice. "Anyway, it's you we're talking about. You seem to think that being a doctor is all you can be and it's not. You have so much more to give. It's a shame that you won't even consider sharing that with someone. With Kent," she added firmly.

"I can't. I'm not the kind of person who can do things part way. I want to give the best I can in my practice. That doesn't leave time for a relationship, even if I wanted one and Kent was interested. Which he isn't," she added bluntly.

"And you know this because?" Brianna never had given up easily.

"Because one night he kissed me and the next time I saw him he acted like we were just casual friends," she blurted. Brianna's silence said it all. "I'm no good at this relationship thing, Brianna. I never have been. You and Shay figured out how to make relationships work in high school. I never have."

"And so now you're running scared?" Brianna chuckled. "As a psychologist, I have to tell you that there is great healing in doing the thing you most fear."

"But what if Kent can't or won't reciprocate my feelings?" she whispered.

"Then you'll deal with it. Isn't knowing you did your best and accepting that you didn't succeed better than not taking the chance and wishing you had because maybe, maybe it *might* be something far better than you can even imagine?"

"I don't know." Jaclyn's brain was a mix of conflicting emotions.

"In your heart, you know." Brianna's voice changed into counselor mode. "You've always been an island, Jaclyn. You're strong and independent. You think if you can just be strong enough, work hard enough, do enough, you can earn what you want. It doesn't work that way. Nobody gets everything they want. Things happen. When they do, it's good to have someone in your corner to cheer you on. Don't let fear about love cheat you. After all, you wouldn't stop treatment for a patient just because they were afraid of it, would you?"

"No."

"Then don't run from your feelings. Think about Kent, pray about him and his role in your life and start imagining your life if he was in it all the time. This is *your* life, Jaclyn. Make sure you live it."

Just then Brianna's son came in and she had to end the call. Jaclyn hung up the phone with her friend's words spinning around and around her head. She made herself a cup of coffee and sat on the patio, trying to soak in the peace of the tiny space.

Essentially Kent and Brianna had said the same

thing—she had to stop trying to make up for what Jessica didn't get to experience. She had to invest in her own life. The clinic had been her dream for so long she couldn't imagine it not happening. But what if it didn't? What if God had something else in mind?

"Coming! I'm coming," Jaclyn called when her doorbell rang later. She stubbed her toe trying to cut short the bell's persistent peal and hopped across the room on one foot. "Is there an emergency?" she demanded as she yanked open the door.

"I think so." Kent surged into the room, his face glowing, blue eyes sparkling like crystal droplets from the ocean. "I have an idea."

She flopped down on the sofa, rubbing her aching toe. "Must be big for you to lean on my doorbell like that."

"Dr. LaForge, are you cranky?" he teased. Then he frowned at her. "What's wrong with your foot?"

"I hit it trying to answer the doorbell." Jaclyn gulped when Kent knelt in front of her, took her bare foot in his hands and began to massage away the pain.

"You were a trouper today." His fingertips were so soothing she could barely keep her eyes open. "I realized something this afternoon, Jaclyn. That clinic of yours could be a huge asset in an emergency. We could use it as a triage center to handle minor injuries, people who are homeless, stuff like that. You've got some equipment that would be very useful."

"Uh-huh." Heart racing, she carefully lifted her foot out of his grasp. "Thank you. It's better now." She waited until he'd taken a seat opposite her. "But the clinic would have to be operational for that and I now realize that isn't going to happen."

"You're giving up?" He bent so he could peer into her eyes. "That easily?"

"Easily? It's not easy at all." She pushed back her hair and folded her legs beneath her, fighting the urge to give in to tears. "But it is reality and I'm not the kind of person who avoids the truth. The truth is you can't get the place operational in the two weeks we have left."

"Can't I?" His blue eyes glinted with an interior fire. "Actually that's why I'm here."

When Kent smiled his grin did odd things to her brain cells, muddling them. She wanted to put her foot back in his hands, just to have him touch her. Was this what love did to you?

"Are you listening to me?" he demanded. "You look—weird."

"Thank you. I feel weird." She nodded. "What's this idea?"

"Well, I know you originally wanted to call the place Jessica's Clinic, but after today, after seeing people in this town pull together to stop that fire the accident caused, I started thinking. Maybe they'd chip in and help finish the clinic if they felt they had some stake in it."

"You want me to offer shares?" She frowned at him in confusion. "That would take ages to arrange."

"No, doctor dearest." He brushed her nose with his fingertip. "I want you to sponsor a contest to name the clinic." He moved his fingers to cover her lips and stem her protest. "Just listen. You want the clinic open to honor your sister, right?" He waited for her nod. "But it's getting close to your deadline and opening might not happen. So how does it honor Jessica if the clinic doesn't open?"

She frowned again shifting so his hand fell away from her as she reconsidered.

"People saw you in action today, Doc, and they were impressed. They watched you pitch in unasked. They know you're good at what you do and I think they finally see that you're committed. Sooner or later I'm sure they'll come around, but we need them sooner."

"So?" She still wasn't sure how this could work.

He spread his hands wide and grinned, his whole face alive with excitement. "We make them feel like they have ownership in the clinic by appealing to them to help choose a name. That's inclusion and I think it will turn the tide. You've laid the groundwork, now it's time to see if joining all those committees paid off."

Jaclyn had let go of so many things. She'd had to relinquish the burnt-out building and make do with a smaller one. Brianna wasn't going to be able to join her as soon as she'd hoped because she couldn't sell her home in Chicago. Their friend Shay was supposed to come on board at the clinic in six months but now that arrangement was also in jeopardy. Now she had to relinquish Jessica's name?

"But if it isn't named for Jessica, how will people know about my sister?"

"If they don't know, will that lessen the impact? Will that make Jessica's clinic any less valuable?" Kent leaned forward. "I know it's not the way you planned, Jaclyn. But it might be better. Can you take a chance on that?"

There it was again, the suggestion that she had to

release control. Jaclyn squeezed her eyes closed. She could see her sister's face as if she were here now. She could hear the phrase she'd always repeated—let go and let God.

"Okay." She exhaled and opened her eyes.

"You'll do it?" Kent looked surprised.

Jaclyn nodded. "It's a good idea. How do we do it?"

"I brought some stuff to make signs. I say we hang them all over town." Kent opened the door, drew a big bag inside and began unloading markers and poster boards on her dining table. "We'll tell people to drop off their suggestions at the town hall. I've already talked to the staff there and it's okay with them."

"Pretty sure of yourself, weren't you?" She had to laugh at his confident grin.

"I know how much you want this clinic to happen." His gaze met hers. "I think this will ignite interest more than anything else we can do." He reached out and touched her shoulder then slid his palm up to cup her cheek. "We're not giving up on Jessica's clinic. No way, Doc."

We. She loved the sound of that. Like they were a team.

Overcome with emotion that this wonderful man had done so much for her, she leaned forward and brushed her lips against his cheek. "Thank you, Kent," she whispered, and meant it.

"You're welcome." Kent grinned. "So what are you waiting for? We've got work to do."

She sat down, pulled the cap off a black pen and began to print as the tall, dark and handsome rancher tossed his Stetson on her sofa and sat down beside her to get to work.

* * *

Kent arrived at the clinic at five the next morning with new resolve.

It had come yesterday, after he and his men had extinguished the fire caused by the rollover of a gasoline truck that had caused a three-car pileup. He'd gone to the hospital to have a minor burn treated and instead watched in amazement as Jaclyn dealt with the taxing of the little hospital's resources by assigning volunteers tasks without regard for the town feud. As a result, former enemies had cooperated in a common goal for the community and turned what might have been tragedy into triumph. Her actions had given him the idea for the contest. It had also inspired him to get the clinic finished.

Kent had spent a long time last night wishing he could build on the friendship he'd forged with Jaclyn. It would be so easy to love her.

But that wasn't going to happen.

Kent had failed Lisa—he knew and accepted that, and he was dealing with the guilt. But he could never trust himself to love Jaclyn, couldn't stand to let her down, to disappoint her. And disappointing people was what he did best. His parents, Lisa, even God. Yes, he was trying to change that, trying to be more trusting in God's love for him, but that didn't mean he was willing to risk hurting Jaclyn. So he ignored his feelings for her and got busy on her clinic.

At seven, Zac stopped by with a thermos of coffee and two doughnuts.

"Hey, cowboy, take a break." He looked around. "This place is coming together," he said with approval.

"Thanks, but we've got a long way to go yet." Kent

paused, grateful for the snack since he'd managed only a meager breakfast.

"I can stop by after school and give you a hand," Zac offered. "I'm pretty good with a paintbrush. I could do the trim outside."

"Great! I've been meaning to touch that up. I wish I knew someone who was good with cement. The walkway is in terrible shape and I haven't got time to fiddle with it."

"I'll pray about it. Maybe God will send someone."

"Maybe He will," Kent said, trying to keep the faith.

No sooner had Zac left than someone else pounded on the door.

"Heddy promised us roast beef dinner with apple pie tonight if we helped you out today." Two former town council members stood there smiling. "Put us to work."

Knowing both men were dab handymen, Kent gave them the task of adding trim to the bathroom and examination rooms. He'd barely finished talking when two women arrived and offered to clean. More helpers trickled in throughout the day to repair the waiting-room chairs, to paint a mural, to hang shelves in each of the examining rooms. Each offer allowed Kent to place a tick beside another to-do item—even, finally, the much-needed cement work. God really was giving them a hand and Kent was thrilled.

Zac had just started painting the exterior trim when Joey's parents and three other couples appeared and insisted on tackling the ugly plot behind the building. Kent was dubious about their plans, but when he went to check on them, he found the area transformed into a parking stall for Jaclyn and a tiny walled-off garden bursting with flowers, the perfect place for staff breaks.

"This is lovely," he told them.

"It's the least we can do for Dr. Jaclyn," Joey's mom told him, her face glowing. "Because of her, our son will have an easier life. The specialist says he will walk without the pain after the operation."

So Jaclyn had been right about Joey's chances. Kent cringed as he remembered how he'd questioned her decision.

"If Dr. LaForge hadn't taken our daughter to that healing center in Las Cruces, she would never have entered drug treatment," another woman said. "This is our way of thanking her."

"We need Jaclyn in this town," said the third. "She makes us think about what Hope could be."

A rush of awe filled Kent. Jaclyn had given Hope so much. Now, finally, it was coming back to her. She was going to get the clinic she'd been dreaming of. He could hardly control his excitement. After everyone had left for the day, he did a walk-through and made a new list, much shorter and easier to complete. He'd received enough phone calls offering to help that the following day's tasks should be covered.

Thank You, God.

Part of him wanted to crow with pride at this amazing woman. Jaclyn's presence in Hope made a big difference to the town—and if he was honest, to him. He couldn't escape the truth—Jaclyn had dug herself a place in his heart.

But love? Love was too risky. The thought of failing Jaclyn, of seeing her beautiful face reflect her disappointment in him was untenable. Better not to go there. Better to remain friends…though he yearned to share so much more with her.

"Kent?" Jaclyn stood in the doorway, her confusion evident. "What happened?"

"Hope happened." He watched her smile flicker to life. "People have been stopping by all day to help. Two more days and, with a little push from heaven, the clinic should be ready to open. Early."

Without warning, she threw herself into his arms and hugged him so tightly he could barely breathe.

"Hey, are those tears?" he asked, drawing back to study her face. He wanted to pull her close, kiss her and promise her the world. But Kent contented himself with brushing the moisture off her cheeks. "This isn't the time for tears."

"No. You're right." She eased away and summoned a smile. "Can I see the rest?"

"Sure." He led the way, pointing out the changes.

"This is amazing. I can't thank you enough," she said when they arrived in the small garden.

"Don't thank me. I'm just the guy with the list. The people of Hope did the rest." He grinned, delighted with her happiness.

"Let's celebrate," she said. "I'll buy you dinner."

Watching those incredible eyes of hers sparkle made his heart thud ten times faster. He'd begun to imagine sharing a future with her, and it was dangerous territory. He had to escape before he got in any deeper. "I've got a couple of animals in quarantine. I need to get home."

"Oh. That's too bad." Did the light in her eyes dim just a bit? Good thing he was getting out of here now. Jaclyn LaForge made him want things he couldn't have.

"Hello, you two. I hoped I'd still find you here. This looks lovely." Heddy took her time studying the work that had been done. "Just the place to enjoy the little dinner I brought." She held out a picnic basket.

"Heddy, I can't stay."

She ignored Kent's refusal and set out two plates, cutlery and a bunch of dishes that wafted enticing aromas when she lifted the lids.

"Oh, it smells wonderful." Jaclyn breathed. "Heddy, no matter how many cooking classes I take, I will never be able to make anything like this." She glanced at Kent. "You have to eat. Why not eat here?"

"Listen to the doctor," Heddy ordered.

"Okay, dinner," he agreed, shutting down the warning voice in his head. "Then I have to get home." Kent allowed Heddy to serve him a plate. "It's very kind of you."

"We all want to help," Heddy said. "This is my way. That's the thing, isn't it? Figuring out how you can give. Lots of people in Hope wanted to give to you, Jaclyn. They just didn't know how."

"But—" Jaclyn showed her surprise.

"You joined all those groups, excelled at everything you tried—well, except for the needlepoint." She grinned. "Anyway, you've always pulled more than your share. Nobody believed you needed their help. It wasn't until the announcement about the contest that they started asking questions and learned the clinic might not open. That's when they found they could give to you."

Kent wondered if the blunt words hurt Jaclyn. She prided herself on giving and now Heddy was saying she needed to learn how to take.

"Actually your clinic has been the best thing for this

town. We needed something big to draw us together," Heddy explained. "Now, how about seconds?"

Kent said little as he savored the rest of Heddy's meal and the apple pie she'd brought for dessert. Jaclyn said even less, her eyes filled with wonder as she kept looking at her new clinic.

"I heard about this apple pie from two of my workers today." Kent blinked at the rush of rose that flooded Heddy's round cheeks.

"Oh, those two. They're neighbors on either side. A year after Henry died they both started asking me out. I'm not interested in romance," she sputtered.

"Why not?" Jaclyn touched her hand. "Just because you loved your husband is no reason you can't love again."

"I don't think I could feel what I felt for Henry for another man," Heddy murmured.

"Oh, Heddy, of course you couldn't." Jaclyn leaned forward, her voice quietly comforting. "Henry was special and your bond with him was forged over a long time. But maybe you could find a different kind of love."

"Oh, you'll make me cry now." Heddy patted her shoulder. "Love is strange, isn't it? It's hard to define but you know when you feel it."

"I think love is like elastic. It stretches and grows to allow our hearts to experience many different varieties, if we let it." Jaclyn turned her head and stared straight at Kent.

Discomfited by her penetrating stare, Kent glanced at Heddy and found she was peering at him. He ignored them both and hunkered down, concentrating on his pie.

"Kent, have you shown Jaclyn the glade yet?"

His head jerked up. He couldn't spend the evening with Jaclyn. She was already in his thoughts too much.

"Um, no." He gulped. "I haven't."

"Well, you're always talking about it. Wouldn't this be the perfect evening to show her?" Heddy took their plates. "Get going. Our spring evenings are longer now, but they don't last forever."

"Uh—" He could hardly decline now.

"Kent has some injured animals he has to check." Jaclyn rose and carefully replaced the dishes in the basket. "And I have some medical journals to study."

"You can look at them later," Heddy insisted as she nudged Jaclyn forward. "You deserve some time off, Jaclyn. The clinic will still be here tomorrow. Soon it'll be open and you'll be too busy."

"I'm not sure—" Though Jaclyn protested, Kent saw longing in her brown eyes and in that instant, his resolve evaporated.

"Why not?" he invited quietly. "The glade is really spectacular right now."

She blinked as if she didn't think she'd heard right. "You're sure?"

"I'm positive. Maybe you can bring Arvid back with you. I think his place here is about ready." He smiled at her while his heart thudded in anticipation.

Maybe he was taking a risk by inviting her out. For so long he'd stayed aloof from the possibility of any relationship. He hadn't wanted to be reminded of what he'd lost. But Jaclyn's arrival had shown him how desperately lonely he was—lonely for someone to share things with, lonely for conversation that wasn't just hello and goodbye.

But Kent wanted more than just company with Jaclyn. He wanted to know everything about her, to discover all the little details and file them away in his heart.

"Well, if you're sure I won't be imposing, I'd love to go," she said. "Your glade sounds like the perfect place to restore my sanity."

"Can you be at the ranch in half an hour?" he asked.

"Yes. For once I'm not on call." Jaclyn's gorgeous smile made his heart race.

Kent turned to Heddy and hugged her.

"You're a manipulator, Heddy Grange," he whispered in her ear. "And I shouldn't let you do it. But because you're such a fantastic cook, I'll fall in with your plans. Thank you for everything," he added meaningfully, glancing around. "I know you were behind it."

"No, Kent. Thank you. God has special blessings reserved for those who put themselves out there for others. Hope's going to be fine," she said quietly. "Are you?"

Before he could answer she'd bustled away, toting her empty basket.

"I'd better go. See you in a bit?" he said.

Jaclyn smiled at him and headed out to her car.

Maintaining nothing but friendship between them wasn't going to be easy. Now that he knew he was in love with her, he'd weakened enough to imagine a future that included sharing the ranch, marriage, maybe even a family.

"Don't be ridiculous," he scolded himself. "She's a doctor, a busy doctor. Why would she want to live on a ranch miles outside of town?"

Maybe if he showed her the beauty of the ranch—

"Stop it." Kent recognized his daydreams for what they were—hope. Hope that he could finally be done with the guilt, the shame, the failure, and find peace.

Heddy said God had special blessings reserved for him, but given his record of failure, Kent was pretty sure those blessings weren't going to involve Jaclyn LaForge.

"What if I fail again?" he said as he pulled into his yard. "I'd mess up her future here."

So what do I do, God?

But if God had some wisdom about Kent's future, He wasn't sharing it.

Chapter Twelve

"I can't talk right now, Shay. I'm on my way out to Kent McCloy's ranch for a horse ride." Jaclyn fumbled the phone and so only caught the tail end of her friend's next words.

"...talked to Brianna." Shay sounded hesitant. "Is something going on with you and Kent?"

"Nothing's going on. We're just friends." She found her sweater hanging on a kitchen chair.

"Oh." Shay sounded totally different from the strong, powerful image of her gracing magazine covers around the world. "Brianna said you have feelings for Kent?"

"I do." With a huff of resignation, Jaclyn sat down. "I love him. He makes me feel that I don't have to prove anything, that I'm all right."

"Aren't you all right?" Shay's timid voice strengthened. "Brianna is right, Jaclyn. It's not your job to fix the whole world. I never thought God expected you to make amends for Jessica's death or your parents' marital problems." She paused then asked very quietly, "Do you?"

"No," Jaclyn admitted. "I'm realizing that to honor Jessica, I have to stop trying to live her life. But something happened that has proven to me that I'm on the right track here." She told her friend how she'd given up on getting the clinic finished before her deadline, and about how the town showed up en masse to make opening possible. "It's amazing how much they've done and all because of a little contest."

"So have you chosen a new name?"

"Not yet." Jaclyn eyed the shopping bag full of suggestions that sat by the front door. "I guess I could choose one this evening, with Kent. After all, the contest was his idea."

"When is the grand opening? Will your parents come?" Shay asked.

"No. They feel I made a mistake coming here and that given enough time, I'll change my mind." She squeezed her eyes closed to stop the tears. "I'm worried about divorce, Shay. They haven't said anything but I can tell there's something off."

"Jaclyn, I think fixing their marriage is up to them. You can't do it for them," Shay murmured.

"I know. I'm learning that God has specific things for me to do and that I have to let go of some things if I'm going accomplish His will. I still believe He wants me here in Hope, ministering to children."

"I think the clinic's completion by the townsfolk is proof of that," Shay agreed.

"But I don't know what to do about Kent," she murmured. "I don't want to end up in a relationship like my parents and Kent is so stuck on the past and all the things he did wrong."

"I'm not an authority," Shay said. "But perhaps if

you told him how you feel, he'd realize that there can be a fulfilling future for him."

"Tell him I love him? Oh, I don't know, Shay." Her insides quivered at the thought.

"Isn't it better to see how he feels about it up front? Be honest." Shay paused. "If it was me, I guess I'd tell him, then accept his answer. At least then there won't be any confusion about it."

"I'll think about it." Jaclyn checked her watch. "Much as I love talking to you, I have to go. Call me tomorrow?"

"Okay. And Jaclyn? I hope Kent realizes what you're offering him. You deserve the best." A little catch in her voice stopped Shay.

"So do you, Shay. So do you. Don't forget, when it's finished, the clinic will be waiting for you. I need you here."

Shay hesitated before she finally said, "I'll try to come as soon as I can. I promise. Bye."

Jaclyn hung up, grabbed the bag of contest entries and raced out the door. She made it to the ranch in just over forty-five minutes.

"Sorry," she apologized when she found Kent with the horses, waiting at the corral. "Shay called just as I was leaving."

"Is she coming to join the clinic?" He helped her mount.

"Not right away." A pang of guilt assailed her—all they'd talked about were her problems. "Is this glade of yours far, Kent?"

"Fifteen minutes." He frowned at the bag she'd looped over the saddle horn. "What's in there?"

"The contest entries. I thought maybe we could choose a name tonight."

"Have you read them over yet?" he asked, grinning at her.

"No. I thought we could do that together." She smiled back as she thought about what Shay had suggested. Could she do it? Could she just tell Kent how she felt and leave the rest to God?

They followed a switchback trail halfway up a hill then turned off into a grove of cottonwoods. The bright green of the freshly budded leaves whispered a welcome as they passed under. Jaclyn had to concentrate on negotiating the treacherous stony path and didn't understand why Kent had stopped until she looked up.

"It's an oasis," she gasped. "Kent, it is so beautiful here. I can understand why you want to stay on the ranch. This place is too precious to give up." She dismounted and wandered under a weeping birch tree to the edge of a pretty little brook that bubbled through the glade. She sat on a rock, removed her boots and let her toes dangle in the cool water. "Fantastic."

Jaclyn turned and caught him staring at her. As soon as their eyes met, he looked away. Maybe he did feel something.

"I built a bench," he said when a few moments had passed. She followed his gaze to a crudely made bench—a combination of old logs hammered together into a seat and back. He sat down on it. "I come here a lot. To think."

"It's the perfect place," she agreed, keeping her voice quiet—the clearing seemed to call for reverence. "I suppose we should go over the contest entries before it gets too dark to see." She padded over the lush growth barefoot, carrying her boots. "Would you mind getting the sack from my saddle?"

He'd fastened the horses' reins under a shady cottonwood tree. "All of these?" he asked, as he lifted the sac.

She nodded.

"Wow. I never imagined so many people would enter."

"Me, neither. What it means is that we have a lot to go through." She lifted out a stack of entries. "Why don't we each take half, choose our favorites, switch piles and then compare? I brought a couple of pencils to mark which we like best." She glanced up and found his eyes fixed on her face but she couldn't read them. "Okay?" she asked when he didn't answer.

"Sure." He accepted half and began reading. Jaclyn couldn't help noticing he marked a lot of the sheets.

"We're supposed to be eliminating," she reminded with a grin.

"I know. But some of these are so catchy. Clinic of Cures," he read. "How can you not like that?"

"Trust me, it's not that difficult." She laughed.

They worked together in silence and then traded. Jaclyn waited with impatience for Kent to finish the last half dozen. When he finally raised his head and peered at her through the growing dusk, there was a peculiar light in his eye.

"You have a favorite?" he asked. She nodded. He smiled. "I think I know which one. It's Whispering Hope Clinic, isn't it?"

"Yes." She gathered the rest of the papers and pushed them back into the bag. "We sang that song in youth group, remember? According to the entry, Septimus Winner wrote the lyrics to 'Whispering Hope' in 1868. But those words embody everything I want for Jessica's clinic today." She wondered if Kent was as moved as she. Jaclyn began to sing the words to the song. "'Soft as the voice of an angel, breathing a lesson unheard. Hope with a gentle persuasion, whispers her comforting word.'"

Kent's voice joined her.

"'Wait till the darkness is over, wait till the tempest is done, hope for the sunshine tomorrow, after the shower is gone.'"

She smiled at him as they raised their voices together for the chorus.

"'Whispering hope, oh, how welcome thy voice, making my heart in its sorrow rejoice.'"

The notes died away. Silence filled the lovely glade broken only by the whisper of the cottonwood leaves.

"Whispering Hope Clinic," Jaclyn murmured. "It's the perfect name. Heddy was bang on. She's the winner."

"Yes." Kent smiled, blue eyes aglow. He shook his head. "I don't know what changed, but that woman is not the same one I've been battling with for the past few years."

"People do change, Kent. I've changed." Jaclyn knew it was now or never—this was her chance to tell him what lay in her heart. She was going to do it. "I came to Hope determined to work my way to acceptance. I thought I had to fix things and people. I thought I had to sacrifice myself to deserve life." She held his gaze. "A lot of people, including you, have helped me see how wrong I've been. I look at the clinic and the way the whole town has pitched in and I realize that sometimes people need to give and that the best thing

I can do for them is to accept. Believe me," she said with a grimace, "it's humbling to realize that if I just get out of the way, God is fully able to heal. I've found it hard to learn that I am simply a tool He uses. I'm not the big deal I thought I was."

"I think you're a very big deal, Jaclyn." His solemn face told her he was serious.

"It was you and your questions about me earning my right to live that started me asking questions of myself. Because of you, I'm learning what it means to be a child of God, free of expectations from others and myself."

"That's good."

"Yes, because it opened my eyes to something else." Jaclyn took a deep breath. "I finally accepted that I'm in love with you. I have been for a while."

"Jaclyn, I can't—"

"No," she begged, placing her hand across his lips. "Let me finish. Please?"

He finally nodded.

"I know you've suffered. I know you don't think you deserve love, just as I thought I didn't deserve life unless I could earn it." She moved her hand, her eyes filling with tears as she stared at his beloved face. "That's a lie that we've both believed for too long."

"Is it?" His voice was barely a whisper.

"Yes, it is. You are a wonderful man, Kent. You devoted yourself to your wife, to this ranch, to your father's dream without regard for yourself. You devoted your time to making Hope a better place to live."

"I'm no hero."

"But you are. You're the only hero I've ever known." She swallowed hard. "You're full of love and you share it. Who else would have put up with Heddy for so long? Who else would bother to organize an emergency measures plan and make sure the whole town was included?"

Kent's expression gave nothing away. Jaclyn forced herself to go on.

"Those are just a few things I love about you. Maybe you think you're incapable of love, but I see you giving love every day—in the clinic, as mayor, as a friend. Whenever I think about my future, you're in it, Kent, and no matter how I try to pry out that love for you, it won't go. I love you."

"You can't." His blue eyes blazed.

She had to smile at the vehemence in those words. "But I do."

"Then you'll have to get over it because I can't love you, Jaclyn. I won't." His tanned face hardened so it looked like a mask. "And you know why."

She rose and stood in front of him, mere inches away, determined to force him to explain. "What is it about me you can't love?" *God, please give me courage.*

For a moment his hands rested on her shoulders and she thought he would kiss her. Then he shook his head, backing away when she stepped closer. "I think you're fantastic. If I could be in a relationship with anybody, Jaclyn, it would be you. But I can't."

"Maybe you only think you can't," she answered, her heart sinking like a stone.

"No. I know I can't." He looked over her shoulder, his stare intent, as if he could see the past. "I loved my wife. I loved her more than anything. But I couldn't help her. I couldn't protect her. She died because of me."

"Lisa died because she ran into a fire. You couldn't have known she was going to do it."

"I should have known. I was her husband—that was my job."

"To stop her from doing what she wanted?" Jaclyn shook her head. "Your 'job' was to love her, Kent. And you did. Cherish *those* memories, not the horrible ones you've been dredging up over and over."

She watched a host of emotions flicker across his face. His eyes narrowed and darkened; his jaw tightened.

"Lisa's not the only one I failed," he murmured.

"Kent you have to know your parents never thought you failed them."

"I'm not talking about my parents." Kent held her gaze, his hands clenched at his sides.

Kent stood, grasped the reins of the horses and handed her one set. He waited as she mounted Tangay, handed her the bag of contest entries and then climbed up on his own horse. His face looked like carved stone.

"Lisa was my last mistake, Jaclyn. It doesn't matter how much I might care about you, I will never again put myself in a personal relationship where I can fail someone I care about. I couldn't stand to watch you trying to cope when I let you down."

"But Kent, Lisa was sick."

"And I made it worse. I chose this land over my wife. What kind of a man does that make me?"

She didn't know what to say as she followed him from the sweet peaceful glade back to the ranch. Once there he took Tangay's reins and told her in cold, hard tones that he had to take care of the animals.

Kent's good-night sounded like a death knell. On

the drive home, Jaclyn could only pray that somehow God would heal him. When she got to her place, she phoned Brianna to tell her what had happened.

"What will you do now?" her friend asked.

"Maybe I'll—" She stopped and corrected her train of thought. "That's my old way of thinking, that I could earn his love."

"I think the question is, Jaclyn, is Kent what you want? More importantly, do you think he's what God has planned for your future?" Brianna said.

"Yes, to both. I believe Kent is the man God has chosen for me." The truth of those words sank in.

"So now you proceed to live your best life, walking in faith, being honest with Kent and depending on God's love."

"Exactly." The advice was bang on. "Thanks, Brianna. Sorry I called so late." She hung up with new resolution.

Jaclyn opened her Bible and reread the sections she'd underlined, pressing the promises into her heart and soul. Then she prayed for God to lead her.

"It's not over, Kent McCloy," Jaclyn said fiercely. "Maybe you've given up, but I will not let go of you that easily."

Chapter Thirteen

Through sheer grit and determination Kent finished Whispering Hope Clinic the following day. He attended the grand opening two days later and even managed to give a short speech, but when the event turned into a block party, he left as quickly as he could, pretending he didn't see Jaclyn watching him, and that he hadn't been watching her.

But back at the ranch he found it difficult to concentrate. He did little but sit and daydream as his mind replayed Jaclyn's words of love over and over.

Two days after his rush to get out of Hope, he was back in town, sitting with the old coots on coffee row and hoping to hear something, anything, about Jaclyn. He missed her big smile, her infectious chuckle and the way she always brought him food, as if she thought he was starving.

He missed her voice. He missed talking to her. He missed her.

"What are you doing mooning around here?" Chester Crumb demanded when Kent arrived at his coffee shop, Crumb Cakes, for the third morning in a row.

"Thought you were building some kind of animal refuge or something."

"Who told you that?" But Kent already knew.

"Doc mentioned last night that you had a hankering to do something like that. Keeps awful hours, she does." Without being asked Chester served him a piece of steaming apple pie. "You got that done already?"

"Uh, no. I came to town for supplies," Kent said, knowing he'd now have to go to the building store and get some timber and plywood.

Back at the ranch he changed into his work clothes, faced himself in the mirror and got a grip. First, he needed to focus on clearing up all the things he should have handled long ago. One of those things was the cattle. He picked up his radio and asked his hired hand to come to the house.

"So that's my price for the cattle," he said to a stupefied Gordon. "You more than anyone understand Dad's dream. I hope you're successful."

"All of them?" Gordon frowned at his nod. "You're sure about this?"

"Positive. I failed to make his dream come true but I believe you will." Kent held out his hand to shake on the deal. "Best of luck," he said.

"But what are you going to do with the ranch?" Gordon asked.

"I'm not sure yet."

But he *was* sure. Kent knew exactly what he was going to do. He'd agonized over it too long. It was time to sell. Only before he did, he was going to build some small rescue shelters for the local wildlife department, something better than their current lean-tos. It would keep him from thinking about the future too much. Since he had the material, he set to work immediately.

By the time the supper hour rolled around and Zac stopped by, Kent had made a good start. He invited his friend to stay for a steak dinner.

"Did you say you're selling the ranch?" Zac frowned at the steak Kent had cooked him. "Are you nuts?"

"Maybe I am." Kent appreciated his friend's concern. "But it's time. I listed it today. There are too many memories here. I need to break free," he said.

Zac probably thought he meant Lisa, but in fact, Kent kept seeing Jaclyn—in the kitchen with those ridiculous red towels, chasing after kids at the birthday party, telling him she loved him in the glade. That last one had hounded him through several sleepless nights.

From what he'd heard in town, Jaclyn's clinic was going great. She belonged in Hope. But he didn't. He couldn't avoid her forever and it was getting too painful to see her beautiful face and not pull her into his arms and pretend everything would work out, that he wouldn't mess up again. So he'd move.

"If you're leaving, why bother building stuff?" Zac asked.

"They're a gift," Kent told him. "And I'm building them because they need them. I've talked about it for so long, it's time to put my money where my mouth is."

"What about Jaclyn?" Zac's voice was low and filled with concern.

"I predict a great future for her." Kent had replayed Jaclyn's confession of love over and over in his head, amazed that she'd had the strength to confront him with her feelings and loving her for it. Unfortunately he couldn't do anything about it. That way lay disaster.

"But she's in love with you. Any fool can see that. Didn't she tell you?"

"Yes, she did. It might have been easier if she'd never said those words," Kent told him. "But I'm sure she'll forget them before too long."

"That's not worthy of you or Jaclyn, cowboy. She's not hankering after chocolate. She *loves* you." Zac shoved back his chair and studied him. "What's wrong with you? Where are all those dreams you used to spout?"

"They're gone. I'm finished with dreams. I'm digging into reality now and reality means moving on." Kent pushed away his plate. Not even his favorite food grilled to perfection could ease the ache in his soul. He knew he would never get over Jaclyn LaForge. He rose and carried his plate inside. He had to do something or explode.

"Did you ever get around to reading those Psalms the pastor talked about?" Zac followed him into the house, carting some dishes with him.

"Uh, no, I guess I didn't. I've been meaning to but with the clinic—" He let the excuses trail away knowing his friend saw through them.

"I did. They were quite an eye-opener. Maybe you should read them, too."

Once the meal was cleaned up, Zac excused himself and left, saying that with the end of the school year approaching he was buried with work.

Kent sat in the courtyard listening to the hum of the cicadas.

No matter how I try to pry out that love for you, it won't go. I love you. Jaclyn's words.

No, he was not going to go there again.

Kent took Oreo for a walk, but remembered Jaclyn ruffling the dog's fur. He checked on his chickens and two wolf cubs the wildlife guys had brought him, but that reminded him of the time he and Jaclyn had seen the wolf. He even washed the dishes and dried them on her red towels. Her words would not be silenced.

I love you.

Finally he threw the towel on the counter.

"Please make this go away because I can't do it, God. I will not take the risk of failing her."

Unable to even consider sleeping, Kent returned to the courtyard. Mindful of Zac's words, he took out his Bible and began to read the Psalms from beginning to end. Sometime later the flash of car lights swinging into his yard broke into his meditations. Jaclyn burst out of her car and stomped toward him.

"You're selling the ranch and leaving Hope." It was not a question.

"Yes."

"Because of me. Because I said I love you." She clapped her hands on her hips and dared him to refute it.

"Partly. But mostly because of me." He wanted to hug her, to erase the dark circles under her beautiful eyes. "I need to move on."

"Really. This need hit you all of a sudden, huh?" Her glance was scathing. "Just tell me one thing, Kent. And answer honestly." She waited until he finally nodded. "Do you love me?"

He gulped. She deserved the truth. It would be the last time they'd talk—he'd make sure of that. He'd attend another church until he sold the ranch. He'd already resigned as mayor. He'd get his groceries else-where, anything to keep from hurting her further.

"It's really not that difficult to answer, Kent. Do—you—love—me?" The moon backlit her figure in a hazy glow.

"I'm sorry, Jaclyn, but I can't be what you want me to be." He steadied his voice and continued with reso-lute determination. "I might love you now but—"

"So you do love me." Her face crumpled. "Then why won't you take a chance on us?"

"I can't. I wouldn't be good for you, Jaclyn."

"And the fact that I love you, that doesn't make a difference?"

He shook his head. Pain raced across her face but he couldn't let it sway him. He had to protect her. "I can't be trusted."

Jaclyn stared at him for a long time. Tears dripped down her cheeks and fell onto the white silk shell she wore. Finally she lifted her head and marched over to stand in front of him, eyes blazing.

"You're right, Kent. You can't be trusted. You can't be trusted because you won't be honest, not with me and not with yourself." She dashed away the tears with the back of her hand then reached out and poked him in the chest. "You're running scared. You've hidden out for so long, afraid to really live, afraid to take a chance because something bad might happen. You're willing to sacrifice our happiness because you're an emotional coward who won't take a risk."

She was furiously, blazingly angry. And he loved her.

"Well, guess what? Something bad will happen. Life isn't a sure thing. The Bible says 'Rain falls on the good man and the evil man,'" she quoted. "How dare you tell me or anyone else in Hope to go after our dreams when you refuse to dream at all? Everyone in town looks up to you, but you're an imposter, Kent. You talk big but you're afraid to put your money where your mouth is."

"I guess you're right." He wasn't going to argue. He could take her anger but he would never survive the pain when he failed her.

Jaclyn shook her head at him. "The only sure thing about life is, there is no sure thing. Living is risky, but what's the alternative?"

He had a hunch she had a lot more to say, but she was cut off by her beeper. Then his cell phone rang.

"I have to go," she said when he closed his phone. "I'm needed at the hospital."

"A fire," he told her as fear snaked down his spine and took up residence in his knees. "Some kids playing with matches started a fire in some brush. It's out of control and heading for the hospital. They've activated the emergency response system."

"I told you," she whispered, staring at him. "Bad comes to everyone. No one is exempt. What matters is how you handle it." She leaned forward and touched her lips to his. "Goodbye, Kent. I love you."

It took every ounce of willpower he possessed not to say the same thing to her. But what good would that do? So he climbed in his truck and followed her car down the hill, both of them exceeding the speed limit as, in the distance, the orange-gold haze of flames lit up the desert night sky.

As he drove, Kent prayed that God would keep her safe.

* * *

"They've sent word, Dr. LaForge. We have to evacuate. They can't hold the fire back any longer. We have to move." The nurse stared at her, fear threading through her words.

"Well, we expected that, didn't we?" Jaclyn said calmly. "We always take precautions where our patients are concerned. Do you have the procedure sheet?"

The nurse held it out. Jaclyn took it and began directing the removal of patients from the small hospital. Somewhere out there she knew Kent and his men were making every effort they could to put out the flames before they reached the hospital. All she could do was beg God to protect the man she loved and continue doing her job.

Sometime during the removal of the surgical patients, Heddy arrived.

"I thought you were at central control," Jaclyn said.

"Everything is in order there. They don't need me. Do you?" She looked scared and very pale.

"Indeed I do." Jaclyn paused a moment to hug her. "I need someone capable to keep the children calm while we get them out. Can you do that?"

"If I can't, I'm not much use on this committee, am I?" the older woman sputtered.

"I don't think I've ever told you what a blessing you are to this town, Heddy. Thank you." Jaclyn gave her another hug. "Go with Nurse Becky, will you?"

Heddy hurried away looking less stressed. Jaclyn answered her cell phone.

"Mom, hi. I can't talk now. I'm in the hospital in the middle of an emergency evacuation. A fire is threatening the town."

"What!" Her mother screeched for her husband then asked a flood of questions.

"Mom, I don't have time. Really. I've got to get the kids out of here. I'll call you later. I love you both."

"We love you, too, honey." The phone went silent.

Jaclyn stood where she was, stunned by those words. Her mother loved her. Tears rushed to her eyes and she dashed them away. How long she'd waited to hear those words. Years. Since Jessica's death. She'd tried so hard, done everything she could, but her mother had never actually said those words until today.

"Thank You, Lord," she whispered.

She nodded to the two nurses waiting for instructions. "Okay, let's get the three kids in wheelchairs out first. Sandra, you, Becky and Heddy take them. Once you're safely across, watch for me. I'll walk out the ambulatory ones. Ready?" She smiled at them. "Let's do this."

All they had to do was cross the street to the pool at the community center. The up-to-date fire suppression system there would protect her patients until the fire was out.

"Heddy, you follow Becky. Sandra, you're in the rear. Don't run, but keep moving. Apparently the smoke is fairly heavy outside so I want you both to wear the masks and make sure the kids have them on, too." She followed them to the exit doors and waited until they were ready, then nodded. "Go."

Heddy pushed the wheelchair across the street, battling the wind, the clouds of smoke and the uneven terrain. Every so often she paused to help Becky and Sandra with their chairs. Finally they stood in front of the doors of the complex. They turned to wave. Jaclyn was next. She took a moment to look around outside but although the fire seemed much closer now and she saw firemen racing to and fro, she could not spot Kent.

Please keep him safe.

Heddy's frantic waved signaled Jaclyn to go.

Just as Jaclyn finished explaining what would happen to the two little girls, someone handed her a child to carry. She ordered the other two to hang on to her and they began the crossing. But as she stepped off the sidewalk, a truck bearing a load of oxygen tanks burst onto the street and roared toward them, desperate to escape the licking tongues of flame eating up bushes in the compound where the tanks were kept.

Jaclyn waited for the truck to pass, silently begging the driver to hurry. In the same moment, she heard a snap. The straps holding the load of oxygen canisters broke, releasing everything. One tank flew over her head and hit the curb near a shrub now smoldering from the creeping fire.

"Run!" someone yelled.

Jaclyn ran, dragging the children with her. She was almost across when an explosion shook the ground beneath her feet. Debris flew through the air, smashed into parked cars and covered the ground around her. It was too risky to keep going—she shoved the children down and then covered them with her body.

Something stung as it grazed her hand, but it was the crack against her skull that made Jaclyn woozy. When she reached to touch her aching head, pain flared in a wave so strong she yelped. The world wobbled and stars flew. Beneath her the kids whimpered.

"Lie still, Jaclyn. Lie very still. I'm here. I'll look after you." Kent was there easing the children from under her and handing them to someone nearby. "Hang on, Doc. I'm going to take care of you."

"Kent?" Excruciating pain radiated through her head but she had to speak, she had to tell him.

"Yes?" He leaned near, his face an inch from hers so he could hear her wheezing words.

"I love you."

There was more, so much more she wanted to say but spears of silver light darted through her eyes. The agony enveloped her and everything went black.

Chapter Fourteen

❧

If he lived to be ninety, Kent didn't think he'd ever forget the terror that gripped him when he saw the blood seeping from Jaclyn's head. In a daze he screamed for help. Moments later an ambulance attendant pushed him out of the way and bent over her. After a quick check, he twisted his head to look at Kent.

"Get that fire out," he said, his face grave. "We need that hospital."

Kent took one last look at Jaclyn's pale face, pressed a kiss to her hand then went back to work, pushing himself even harder. More afraid than he'd ever been, he kept a steady stream of prayers for Jaclyn going heavenward as he battled the raging inferno. Nobody had to tell him her injury was serious—he knew it. In the depths of his heart he knew he might never see her again and it was killing him.

Why didn't I tell her I loved her? Why didn't I, for once, take the risk? Because she's right. I am a coward.

All night he fought until finally the fire was extinguished and the hospital was safe. Only then did he give in to his desperation to know Jaclyn's condition.

"How's Jaclyn?" he asked over and over, but no one seemed to know where or how she was. Finally he found Heddy. "Where is she?" he demanded. "Why isn't anyone telling me anything?"

"They air-lifted her to Las Cruces. We just heard that her head injury is very serious." Heddy's somber expression scared him. "One of the EMTs told me the hospital called her parents."

Kent had to see her. He turned to head for his truck, but stumbled from sheer weariness. Someone gripped his arm.

"Come on, Kent. You need to rest," Zac said. "You can pray for Jaclyn at home."

But Kent wasn't going home.

"I have to see her," he said and yanked his arm free. "I need to see Jaclyn."

Heddy exchanged a glance with Zac then nodded.

"I'll drive you." Zac pulled out his keys.

"Wait a minute." Kent shrugged out of his suit, walked over to one of his men and handed it to him. "You're in charge, Pete. I have to leave. Be careful."

"You know it. You tell Jaclyn we're praying for her." The other man slapped his shoulder.

"Kent?" Heddy had never looked more unkempt, but her heart was in her eyes as she said, "I'm praying for you both."

Kent got in Zac's car for the long drive to Las Cruces, wondering what he would say to Jaclyn when he got there. Because the fear he'd carried for so long was now bigger and stronger than ever. He loved her. Kent admitted that. But when had love ever been enough?

"Don't let her die," he begged God. "Please don't let her die."

* * *

When Kent made no headway with the medical staff at the Las Cruces hospital, Zac pushed him aside and told the nurse in charge that Kent was Jaclyn's fiancé. Finally someone agreed Kent could sit with her, but only Kent.

"Don't wait for me," he told Zac but his friend shook his head.

"I'm not going anywhere, cowboy. I'm going to sit here and pray."

"Thanks, pal." Kent followed the nurse down the hall. The surgeon met him.

"She's not fighting," the doctor told him. "Medically we've done all we can. Now it's up to her. If you can think of anything, say anything you think would help, do it. This is the time to pull out all the stops."

Kent watched him go, fear clutching at his throat as he pushed open the door and walked inside.

Jaclyn's room was small with a large window that let in the moonlight. She lay on the bed, pale and lifeless except for the machine that beeped at her side. A rock formed inside him. She gave love so easily. Jaclyn deserved to be loved back. She deserved someone who could appreciate her and return her love. She should be happy.

She still could be.

Kent pushed that thought away. His latest actions proved he couldn't give her what she needed, but he wanted her to be happy.

But when he studied the curve of her cheek, the silvery blond hair framing her face, the rock in his chest grew.

You're willing to sacrifice our happiness because you're an emotional coward who won't take a risk.

He picked up Jaclyn's hand, threading his fingers between hers. The rock grew heavier.

You're always running scared, Kent. You've hidden out for so long, afraid to really live, afraid to find a new dream, afraid to take a chance because something bad might happen.

She was right. He was an emotional coward because he told himself he was trying to protect her when really he was afraid to be vulnerable. He'd always been the strong one, the one his parents and his wife had depended on. But Kent wasn't strong.

And he was sick of pretending he was.

At this moment he was more scared than he'd ever been.

But as he studied her lovely face, he realized that he'd do anything to ensure Jaclyn's happiness, suffer anything to see her smile and laugh again.

He gulped. He'd do anything. Take a chance? But what if—

The Lord is my light and my salvation; Whom shall I fear? The Lord is the defense of my life; Whom shall I dread? The verses of the twenty-seventh Psalm played through his head, pushing light into the crevices and revealing the real cause of his fears.

Me. I'm the reason I'm scared. That's why he'd wasted so many years. That's why he hadn't been able to believe that God understood his situation—because he'd put his faith in himself instead of in God. But God wasn't limited by Kent McCloy's fears. God had a bigger picture. And because God was love, He forgave the past and gave new dreams for the future—a future with Him at the center.

Jaclyn was right. There would be problems in the future, some of them serious if her injury—no. He wouldn't think like that.

Be strong and let your heart take courage. Wait for the Lord.

"Okay, Lord," he prayed out loud. "I'm scared, I've messed up everything. Instead of depending on You to make a difference in Hope, I've been depending on myself to stop bad things from happening. I've been afraid of failing, as I have so often. But that changes right now. I accept Your love for me. I accept Your forgiveness. And most of all, I accept Your will for my life, whatever happens. It's in Your hands. Now, please take my fear and help me move into the future You have waiting for me."

He gazed at the small figure lying motionless under the white sheets.

"It's up to You, God. I'll trust You."

The rush of sweet forgiveness, the warmth of love everlasting filled his heart and chased out the fear that had resided there for so long. He stared into the face of the woman he loved and knew what he had to say. He bent and whispered in Jaclyn's ear.

"I have big dreams, sweetheart. But they can only come true if you're there to help me." Courage grew until the rock inside him crumbled and melted away. "I need you, Jaclyn. I love you. Please, don't give up on me because I'm not giving up on you. I'm here for however long you need me."

Jaclyn had been in a coma for nearly three weeks, and Kent was losing faith. So each day, before Kent drove to the hospital, he rode out to the glade to find a wildflower he could take to her. The glade had always been his special place and it was here he felt closest to God.

Kent spent an hour by the bubbling brook, just talking to his Savior as he sought to renew his waning courage. On the way out of the glade, he cut some daisylike chocolate flowers that were nestled in between some rocks. He dampened his handkerchief and wrapped it around the stems to preserve the delicate blooms for her. Then he rode back home, got in his car and drove to Las Cruces.

When he arrived at the hospital he found the hall outside Jaclyn's room teeming with people.

"What's going on?" he demanded then pushed into her room. Her parents stood by Jaclyn's bedside, hand in hand.

"Hi," he said, confused by their big smiles. They stood in front of the bed blocking his view. "What's up?"

"Me, actually." Jaclyn peeked around her mother.

Kent dropped his bouquet and stared at his beloved doctor.

"She woke up this morning and asked for breakfast," her mother said. "They'll do some tests later, but she seems fine."

"I am fine." Jaclyn stared straight at him. "Just a little confused. Apparently I acquired a fiancé while I've been asleep." Her voice gave nothing away.

Brianna and Shay were also in the room. They grinned at Kent then quickly ushered everyone else out. Now that his prayers had come true, Kent didn't know what to say, where to begin.

"Well? *Are* you my fiancé?" she asked, one haughty eyebrow arched.

"If you want me," he whispered. Kent moved to her bed, touched her cheek then grasped her hands in his. "I love you. I've been an idiot, which you already know, but I love you, Jaclyn."

She didn't smile, she didn't laugh with joy. Instead big tears filled her gorgeous eyes and trickled down her cheeks.

"Don't cry, darling. Please don't cry." He edged onto the bed so he could fold her slight body into his arms. "You don't have to say anything. You don't have to do anything. Just be well. Be happy."

"I am happy." She pushed back to peer into his eyes. "Or I will be if you'll kiss me."

He hesitated. She'd been so ill. She'd been unconscious for days. What if he hurt her? What if—

"You're not scared, are you, Kent?" she asked, her beautiful eyes sparkling.

"Always," he said seriously. "But I'm learning how to give that to God. He's in charge now." He whispered a prayer of thanksgiving then leaned forward and kissed Hope's favorite pediatrician as he'd longed to for weeks, pouring his heart and soul into their embrace.

Jaclyn kept her arms around his neck when he pulled away, her eyes closed.

"What are you doing?" he asked, brushing his fingers over her lovely face.

"I'm going back to sleep so I can savor this dream," she murmured.

"This is no dream." He gave her arm a gentle squeeze. "I need you wide awake, my darling doctor. We have plans to make."

"Plans? What plans?"

"For starters, we're going to get married. In the church in Hope. Since you're in charge of renovations there, you'd better get busy because I'm not waiting long to make you Mrs. McCloy. Or is it Dr. Mrs. Mc-Cloy?"

"You haven't even asked me yet," Jaclyn teased.

A stern-faced nurse entered the room. Kent winked at the love of his life.

"I'm waiting till you get out of here. Then I'll do it properly. But I figured you could start making plans since you're just lazing around here." He kissed her but more medical personnel arrived and the nurse ordered Kent to leave the room.

He sat in the hall for an extended time.

That was okay. He had his own plans to make, his own thanks to give.

Oblivious to the comings and goings in the hall, Kent let the wonder of his answer to prayer, the joy of freedom from his worries and fears and the satisfaction of God's amazing grace flood his soul. The future was his and Jaclyn's, full of promise, waiting for them to discover what God had in store.

Saying thanks hardly seemed enough. But he said it over and over to the One who had given him a new beginning.

A month later, with a clean bill of health, Jaclyn left Hope with no clue about Kent's plans for this impromptu picnic. But she gladly relinquished all control and followed him over the hills on Tangay, every part of her being singing with happiness. Kent loved her. That's all she needed. She was happy to leave the rest in God's hands.

They arrived at the glade just as the sun began slowly sinking behind the hilltops. Glimmers of light illuminated the dusky area thanks to tiny solar lights Kent had planted in strategic places. A quilt lay spread on the ground flanked by candles waiting to be lit. Someone had strewn masses of wildflowers all over the grassy site. In the brook, jars filled with fireflies were tethered to the shore. They twinkled and glowed, chasing away the gloom. The heat of summer gave way to peaceful, tranquil coolness.

Kent helped Jaclyn dismount, not missing the chance to envelop her in his arms and kiss her. Jaclyn reveled in his embrace and kissed him back, wondering if there was any medical evidence to support her suspicion that women in her situation could melt from sheer happiness.

Kent led her to the old bench he'd built and hovered solicitously until she was seated. Her heart boomed in her ears when he knelt in front of her.

"Dr. Jaclyn LaForge, I love you more than anything else in this world. You challenge me and make me a stronger, better person. You give me hope and strength and confidence. Most of all you give me courage to leave the past behind and trust God for the future. You are my future. I want to share each moment with you. Will you marry me?"

She took a moment to savor the beauty of his words. Then she spoke the words she'd held inside for so long.

"I love you, Kent. You're a precious gift from God." She touched his cheek, grazing her fingers across his skin and reveling in the love that welled inside. Her throat clogged for a moment and she fought to gain control. "I can never thank you enough for getting the clinic finished. I thought that was my heart's desire yet you showed me God had more in store for me. So much more. Because of you I learned I was worthy of love, that I didn't have to earn it. Yes, I will marry you, I love you."

"Then this is my pledge to you." He slid a ring onto her finger, a gorgeous sapphire the exact shade of his eyes, flanked by two glittering diamonds. He kissed the ring in place then cupped her face in his hands so he could enjoy the love glowing in her eyes. "I was afraid we'd never have this time, afraid you'd never hear me tell you how much I love you. I've wasted a lot of time being afraid." He smoothed a hand over her gleaming hair, his fingertips trailing down the strands until they rested against the pulse in her neck. "I will never forget how empty my life seemed when I thought you wouldn't be there. Nothing else seemed to matter because you fill my world, Jaclyn. You make me hope and dream. I'm going to trust God and take on whatever challenges He sends. With your help, I'll replace fear with hope."

As she relished the pure bliss of the moment, Jaclyn's thoughts went to her sister. Jessica had brought Jaclyn to Hope, to this man and his precious love.

She savored the feel of Kent's arms around her, his lips on hers. When Kent finally drew back from her, he was as breathless as she.

Jaclyn thought she could sit there forever.

Until her stomach growled.

"Come on, it's time I fed you." Laughing, he took her hand and drew her to the quilt. He'd brought skew-

ers of chicken, golden brown potatoes—the first of the
season—and fresh asparagus. And last but not least,
tiny, succulent wild strawberries he'd picked from his
mother's garden.

"Thank you, darling," Jaclyn said when she was re-
plete with food and love.

He touched his lips to hers then leaned back. "When
can we get married?"

"Heddy is my second in command on the church
restoration and she's insistent that everything will be
done by September. She's chosen the first Saturday of
the month. Is that soon enough?" She couldn't resist
tracing his eyebrows, caressing his cheek, smoothing
her fingers over his smiling mouth.

"Heddy chose our wedding day?" He frowned.

"Well, she insists on being our wedding planner."
Once Kent had stopped laughing, Jaclyn filled him in
on the details Heddy had already arranged. "And by
the way, both Mom and Dad will be walking me down
the aisle. Then they're going on a second honeymoon
cruise. They've certainly mended their relationship."
She studied him, anxious about his lack of response.
"What's wrong?"

"Nothing. I just hope I can get the ranch sold before September."

"Oh." Jaclyn tried to hide her smile. "Well, you
won't."

"Oh." He lifted a quizzical eyebrow. "How do you
know that?"

"Heddy's put the word out that the ranch is officially off the market. According to her you and I need
the ranch to raise our kids properly and Hope needs a
petting zoo and animal sanctuary to bring in tourists."

Jaclyn leaned forward and kissed his nose. "This time, my darling, I heartily agree with Heddy. You cannot sell the ranch. Our future is here." She waved a hand.

"But, sweetheart—"

"No buts. With God, all things are possible. Hey, maybe we could use that on our wedding invitations. What do you think?"

Kent could think of nothing but kissing his beautiful fiancée.

Epilogue

"I've never seen a lovelier September day." Brianna waited until Jaclyn's father had helped Jaclyn out of the car. Then she straightened the bride's veil. "You look stunning. Such a simple dress and yet it's so gorgeous."

"Thank you. Both of you look amazing." Jaclyn was relieved her friends loved the red bridesmaid dresses Heddy had sewn. "It won't be too much for you—going through this with Zac as best man?"

"It would happen sooner or later once I start work in the clinic." She paused. "Zac and I will never get back what we once had. I've accepted that." Brianna's words sounded airy and carefree but a furrow creased her brow.

Never say never, Jaclyn wanted to say. But she didn't. She'd given up trying to control the world. Now she prayed for her friends and left the rest up to God.

"And you, Shay? Are you all right with Nick as Kent's groomsman?"

"Nick and I have been friends forever. I hope we'll have time after the wedding to catch up." The former model smiled her much-photographed grin. "And soon I also hope I'll be moving back to Hope, too."

"Great! Whispering Hope Clinic is ready and waiting for both of you."

"Come along now, dears. It's time this bride saw her groom." Heddy ushered them up the stairs to the church, signaled the organist and handed out the bouquets.

Her heart full, Jaclyn took her parents' arms and followed her dearest friends up the aisle of the old church in Hope to the man who held her heart. The church wasn't finished, not even close. But tons of flowers culled from the gardens of Hope-ites filled the tiny sanctuary to overflowing and hid the imperfections.

The townspeople were all there, squeezed into pews, standing in the balcony. They came because this was *their* doctor and *their* vet and it was up to them to make sure the wedding day went off without a hitch.

Jaclyn's gaze locked on Kent after she'd taken the first step, and stayed there. She saw joy and pride and a host of other emotions rush across his face. But mostly she saw love. When her parents placed her hand in his, she sent a prayer of thanksgiving heavenward.

The ceremony went off without a hitch. Their kiss sealed their promises to each other and then they walked down the aisle of the church, husband and wife. Outside, the people of Hope showered them with a blizzard of rice and good wishes.

Kent escorted Jaclyn into a horse-drawn carriage. A second carriage followed with the attendants. After photographs they returned to the church and the garden reception Heddy had arranged behind the church.

"Are you sure it was a good idea to let her do this?" Kent asked as he helped Jaclyn down.

"I had to, you know that." Jaclyn grimaced. "Being the only doctor in town didn't allow much time for planning a reception. I'm glad we found a locum for the clinic. I refuse to give up my honeymoon."

"You know you would in an instant. And I'd be right by your side." He folded her hand over his arm. "Let's go see what Heddy's created."

What Heddy had created was a flower-filled garden scene with tables scattered across the grass.

"It's beautiful, Heddy." Jaclyn embraced the woman who'd help her find her place in Hope.

"We all worked on it, as a town should. You and Kent have given us our town back. You've helped us heal the rift that threatened to destroy us. Now it's your time for each other." She led them to a table where the attendants already sat. "We love you, Doctors McCloy and LaForge."

As she and Kent enjoyed the reception specially prepared for them, Jaclyn studied the assembly with a full heart.

"What's wrong, darling?" Kent whispered when she borrowed his handkerchief to wipe away a tear.

"I'm just full of blessings," Jaclyn said, snuggling next to him. "You, my parents, my best friends, Hope—my life is full of joy." She paused a moment, studying him. "I'm so glad I came here to start Jessica's clinic. My sister told me to live my life and trust God. She was so smart."

"Yes, she was. Because it all starts with God, doesn't it?" He pressed his lips to hers. "Together we'll pass on Jessica's words and let God use us to reach others. Deal?"

"Deal for a lifetime," she agreed.

Then the minister led all of Hope in a prayer of blessing for the new couple.

* * * * *

PERFECTLY MATCHED

Who then can ever keep Christ's love from us?
When we have trouble or calamity,
when we are hunted down or destroyed, is it
because He doesn't love us anymore? And if we
are hungry, or penniless, or in danger, or
threatened with death, has God deserted us? No.
—*Romans* 8:35

Chapter One

❧

"I hurt, Uncle Nick."

"Aw, I'm sorry, sweetheart." Nick Green tenderly shifted the weight of the little girl clinging to his neck as he stepped into the hospital hallway. "Is that better, honey?"

Maggie sighed and laid her head on his shoulder. "It's okay."

It was so *not* okay that a five-year-old accepted pain as part of her world. A blaze of anger seared his insides, quickly joined by uselessness and frustration. One drunken driver had inflicted so much pain on Nick's family, leaving Maggie bereft of her parents and physically damaged. Not only had she sustained a host of internal injuries, but her legs had also been crushed in the accident. She'd endured many surgeries but she still couldn't walk.

"You did very well with the doctors, darlin'," he encouraged. "Now let's go get some ice cream." He needed it, to wash away the aftertaste of their unappetizing hospital lunch.

"Nick?" A voice with faint vestiges of an English accent made him stop.

"Yeah?" He turned around and blinked at the woman striding down the hall toward him. The hair gave her away—a glorious tumble of copper-colored waves and curls. But if the hair hadn't done it, the famous emerald-green eyes in that heart-shaped face would have. He grinned. "Shay Parker's back in town."

"I always told you I would be back. But what are *you* doing here in Hope?" Shay tapped him playfully against the chest, her smile dazzling him. "You insisted Seattle was your home, yet here you are in New Mexico, and with such a beautiful lady." Shay touched a finger to the end of the little girl's tipped-up nose. "Who is this?"

"This is my niece, Magdalena. We call her Maggie."

"Hello, Maggie. I'm Shay." She held out a slender hand for the child to shake.

"Hi." Maggie kept her hands tucked around Nick's neck. But she did risk a smile before shyly pressing her head into her uncle's shoulder.

"Maggie and I are going for ice cream," Nick explained. "Want to join us?"

He knew she would. For as long as he'd known Shay, she'd never been able to resist ice cream. They'd met when they were twelve, the year she'd moved with her dad from England. When their friend Jessica had died, their shared grief had turned into a close friendship. Taller than most of their classmates, they'd played basketball, picked pecans on her grandfather's farm and gone together to their senior prom. Shay had become an ardent supporter of Nick's football prowess, and she'd actually encouraged his love of inventing and tinkering with machines while most of their peers scoffed.

And yet, as Nick studied her now, he realized he'd never fully appreciated her exquisite beauty. Pretty stupid considering Shay Parker had gone on to become a world-class model.

"I'd love some ice cream, Nick. I can hardly wait to get out of this place." Shay glanced down the hospital hallway and faked a shudder.

"Us either. But why you?" Curious, Nick walked outside beside her.

"I need a break. I've been jumping through hoops to get privileges at this hospital," she joked, touching the unblemished skin at her throat. "They act like physiotherapists are criminals."

"It's probably a security thing. I imagine they're trying to be extra careful given the number of people the new mine is drawing into town." Nick stopped at his truck, which was sheltered under a huge mesquite tree, the only one in the lot that had already bloomed. He'd managed to snag this shady spot by arriving for Maggie's appointment with the traveling neurologist before sunrise. "Want to ride with us?" He glanced around. "I don't see that red dream-mobile you always talked about owning," he teased. "Change your mind about getting a convertible?"

"I think I'm beginning to. My car is in the shop. Again. So, yeah, a ride would be great." Shay paused a moment to study the splashes of green dotting the desert landscape. "Don't you just love the desert in spring?"

"April's nice, yeah." Nick paused a second to look

around then focused on fastening Maggie into her booster seat before he held the front door open for Shay.

"It's wonderful to walk around Hope freely, not like in the big city where you have to be on guard all the time," she murmured, glancing around the parking lot.

Nick frowned. If Shay felt so safe here, why was she looking over her shoulder like that?

But then he remembered. Three years ago he'd been in New York for a meeting with his agent and decided to pay Shay a surprise visit. Confused by her haunted look and nervous manner, Nick had been stunned when she'd confessed that she was being stalked. His temper still blazed at the memory of her trembling tone as she related what she'd gone through. Her stalker had her private number, knew where she lived and had not only snuck onto her set and left gifts for her there, but gloated that he'd even touched her several times without her noticing.

Nick figured Shay's lack of success with the police meant that either they didn't believe her or they'd given up. So, in Nick's mind, it was up to him to help Shay, just as he would have helped one of his sisters. He'd hung around after they'd had lunch, hoping her stalker would call again. Nick figured the guy liked taking chances and probably felt that no one would discover his identity now that the police had given up. No doubt he enjoyed terrifying Shay, making her feel helpless. That infuriated Nick. When the call came, Nick put a lid on his own reactions to the creep's mockery of Shay's vulnerability. Anger still surged at the memory of that snide and gloating voice exulting in the death of Shay's father.

When the guy boasted that Shay now had no one to

protect her, Nick saw red. He'd grabbed her phone and told the slimeball Shay had innumerable friends like him waiting en masse to bring down their wrath on his head if he didn't leave Shay alone. Nick also intimated that the police were ready to haul the guy off to jail. The guy hung up fast. After that, he disappeared and wasn't seen again, according to the bodyguard Nick had hired for Shay.

"Earth calling Nick? Hello?" Shay snapped her fingers in front of his face to draw him out of his introspection. "Where were you?"

"Daydreaming." He tweaked Maggie's nose. He'd ask Shay about her stalker later. "What kind of ice cream are we getting, Maggie-mine?"

"Choc'late, Uncle Nick," she told him without hesitation. She peeked up through her lashes.

"I should know that, shouldn't I, after the number of cones I've bought you." As Nick tugged playfully at a hank of her short, dark hair, he noticed Shay's quick scan of the braces encircling his niece's legs. "Privileges must mean you're starting at Whispering Hope Clinic. When?"

"Yesterday. Jaclyn and Brianna have been nagging me to join them for ages." Shay shrugged her elegant shoulders. "So I have."

Nick knew all about the youthful vow Shay, Jaclyn and Brianna had made to build a clinic for kids after Jaclyn's fifteen-year-old twin sister, Jessica, had died. It was their way of honoring her, making sure no other child went without the medical care Jessica had needed. Doctors had been sadly lacking in Hope when they were kids. But now Whispering Hope Clinic was open and, according to Nick's mom, full of activity with Jaclyn as a pediatrician and Brianna as a child psychologist. Now that Shay had joined the clinic as physiotherapist, Nick figured the place would get even busier.

Though Jaclyn and Brianna were married to Nick's friends, Kent McCloy and Zac Enders, Nick knew Shay wasn't married. He'd heard in Seattle that she'd left modeling but he'd only learned several months earlier, at Brianna and Zac's wedding, that Shay had finished her physiotherapy degree a while ago. He'd had very few moments during that busy weekend to discuss her return to Hope, and Shay had left town the next morning. The following weekend Nick had been injured during a game, and his career as a pro quarterback had ended in the blink of an eye. Then had come Maggie's car accident. Life hadn't settled down since.

Nick wondered what had delayed Shay's homecoming till now.

"I heard about your shoulder injury, Nick." Shay's lustrous green eyes lost their twinkle. "I'm so sorry. I know how much you loved football."

"Thanks." Nick did not want to discuss the demoralizing loss of his career as a pro quarterback.

"How long have you been back in Hope?" she asked.

"About a week. Mom's finding it tough to make all the medical trips to Las Cruces with Maggie, so I came to help." He glanced at his niece, unwilling to discuss the accident that had killed his beloved sister Georgia and her husband. Besides, he'd told Shay the important parts when she'd called with her sympathies. Just hearing her soft, quiet voice that morning had helped him get through what followed.

Nick's throat tightened at the loss he hadn't yet fully

accepted. How could it be part of God's plan for his sister's car to get hit by a semitruck?

"How's your mom?" Shay adjusted Maggie's braced left legs to a slightly different angle, then smiled at the little girl as if they shared a secret.

"She's okay, though her arthritis is really bad. I had hoped she'd stay with me in Seattle, but she couldn't take the cold or the humidity. She always came back here." He paused, glanced at his niece. "Now Maggie's with her. To Mom, Hope is home."

"To me, too," Shay agreed. She grinned as if the little town offered everything she needed. And maybe it did, for Shay. But for Nick, Hope could be only a temporary stop. He had to get back to the city and begin the coaching job that would allow him to provide for his family now that pro ball was out.

"Want to eat outside?" He pulled into a stall in front of the local general store where the owners still piled cones high with real ice cream. "The sun's burnt off this morning's chill by now."

"Maggie and I will find a place in the park while you get our treats." Without waiting for him, Shay slipped from her seat, quickly unfastened the little girl's restraints and lifted her out.

Nick noticed that Maggie didn't make her usual squeal of pain and felt a rush of guilt. He'd been doing it wrong. Disgust washed over him at the thought that he'd even inadvertently hurt his niece.

"I'll have butter pecan," Shay called as she walked away.

"Still supporting the pecan industry, huh?" he teased.

"Have to." Shay's eyes twinkled as she glanced at

him over one shoulder. Gold sparks of mischief lurked in their emerald depths. "I guess you haven't heard. I bought back my grandfather's farm. Support the pecan farmers," she chanted in imitation of a protestor.

Surprise held Nick immobile as Shay chose a grassy spot and set Maggie gently against the smoothed-off trunk of a towering palm tree. A moment later the former model's melodic laughter burst into the sunlit afternoon, her face glowing with happiness and health as she folded her long legs beneath her and settled next to the child.

Nick strode toward the store but jerked to a halt when, for the first time since the accident, he heard Maggie giggle. Choked up by the sound, he hurried inside to buy the ice cream, overwhelmed by the fact that his old friend had made his usually somber niece laugh.

As Nick waited for his order to be filled, he puzzled over Shay's decision to purchase her former home. She was famous—she'd been one of the best-paid models in the world. She'd spent years wearing elegant clothes and expensive makeup—neither of which, in Nick's opinion, she needed to enhance her loveliness. Shay could have bought the nicest house in town. She didn't need to dirty her manicured nails with nuts and soil.

So why buy back the farm?

Nick studied her through the window. The stunning woman now sitting with Maggie seemed worlds apart from the shy, grieving English girl who'd arrived in Hope having just lost her mother. Back then, quiet, reticent Shay had struggled to fit in at school. But Shay had lost that shyness when Jessica, Zac, Kent, Brianna, Jaclyn, Nick and Shay had all become good friends.

Then, in her junior year of high school, Shay's

grandfather died. After that, her dad lost the farm. They'd struggled until, on a dare from Brianna and Jaclyn, Shay had entered a contest at a mall in Las Cruces and won a modeling contract in her senior year. Instead of studying physiotherapy to join the clinic she and her friends were going to build to honor Jessica, Shay had opted to model so she could support her father.

Now Shay Parker was back in Hope. It sounded as if she had her future happily mapped out. Nick wished he felt the same. The assistant coaching job his football team had offered him was not the career he'd planned for himself. Shrugging away his disquiet, he muted his concerns about the future, paid for the cones and carried them outside.

"You're having vanilla?" Shay demanded as he handed over the ice cream. She blinked at his nod. "Forty-one flavors and you chose vanilla? Who are you and what have you done with the adventurous, always unexpected Nick Green? Maggie, are you sure this is your uncle?"

The little girl giggled, and Nick marveled at the sound again.

"Well, I'm shocked. The old Nick would have chosen green bananas with licorice or huckleberry with liver pâté—anything but vanilla," Shay teased.

"You know they don't even make those flavors. Anyway, the old Nick is gone." *And been replaced by whom?* Nick asked himself. Shay had given up her career of her own volition, but Nick felt as if his had been stolen from him.

"I'm sorry—I wasn't thinking. Was the surgery successful?" Shay frowned.

"The doctors said it was a total success. Now it

only hurts when I move," he joked. Shay didn't laugh. "I can't throw a football fifty feet," he admitted. Her eyes darkened with sympathy that Nick didn't want, so he moved the focus back to her. "Why did you buy the farm, Shay?"

"Because it's my home. I know every nook and cranny of that land, and I always liked living there." She smirked. "I like it even more now. The old house was a wreck, so I had it torn down and built a new one. You should visit me. I've got the best view in this county."

"But surely you don't intend to farm? The orchards must be in very bad shape." Nick couldn't fathom what this model-turned-physiotherapist would do with a pecan farm.

"Well, I was told the harvest in December didn't yield much. But I do think the trees will come back eventually. I'll wait and see. For now I have to concentrate on my practice." Her voice softened. "Anyway, it's not the orchard I wanted, Nick, as much as my home. Dad had big plans for the family place. I'd like to fulfill some of them, but that's down the road. For now, I have to live somewhere, so it might as well be on familiar territory."

Nick searched her face. He knew her well enough to know there was something she wasn't saying. Shay avoided his intent look by tossing the scant remains of her cone in a nearby trash can. She offered Maggie a tissue to clean up her hands then asked, "Would you like to try the swing, honey?"

The little girl frowned, her eyes speculative. Finally she nodded, very slowly.

"I'll help you." Shay lifted his niece into her arms

and carried her to the swing. With an ease that surprised Nick, she set Maggie on the seat, told her to hang on then gently pushed until the swing swayed back and forth.

Concern grabbed at Nick as alarm filled Maggie's face.

"Uh, Shay, maybe you shouldn't—"

She pinned him with her world-famous stare. "It's okay, Nick," she assured him, her quiet, firm tone communicating that she had everything under control.

Nick's argument died on his lips. He nodded and she continued pushing Maggie, offering encouragement.

"Can your toes touch the sky, Maggie?" Shay's casual gaze intensified as she assessed the child. "Wow! That's amazing."

Nick sat on the end of a child's slide and observed Shay coax Maggie through a series of moves using little dares that began with "Betcha can't..." Maggie responded every time, engrossed in the tasks as she pushed herself to prove she could do it. After a few minutes Shay slowed the swing, hugged the little girl and said something that widened Maggie's grin. Shay took the swing beside her and together they swayed back and forth, chattering like magpies. Eventually Shay beckoned him over.

"I think Maggie has had enough swinging," she said, tilting her head to indicate Maggie's drooping body.

Nick took his cue, strode forward and bent to lift his niece free. Before he could, Shay reached out and touched his hands, her fingers firm as she rearranged his grip.

"Higher," she murmured in his ear. "Like this. Not under her knees."

So he *had* been hurting Maggie. Inside him, anger exploded at his clumsiness and the seeming hopelessness of her situation. The doctor's words today hadn't been encouraging. Maggie wasn't moving as much as expected. Small wonder. She had missed so many therapy sessions in Las Cruces. It wasn't his mom's fault but—well, at least he was here to help now. If only he could do more.

Using great care, Nick set Maggie in the truck and fastened her seat belt. He waited for Shay to climb inside, but she pushed the door closed.

"I'll walk back. I need the exercise after that gigantic cone." She patted her flat midriff and grinned. "I've gained five pounds since I've been back."

He couldn't see where. Shay looked fantastic in her white fitted pants and navy blue shirt. Her peaches-and-cream skin, flawless except for the trademark spattering of freckles across her elegant nose, glowed radiant in the unrelenting desert sun.

Nick blinked in surprise as a thud of male appreciation hit him. Shay was gorgeous, of course. Always had been. But he wasn't attracted to her—they'd been friends, that's all.

"Uh, we'd better get—"

"Nick, can you come to my place tonight?" Shay asked quietly. "I need to talk to you about Maggie."

Since that was exactly what he wanted to talk to her about, he nodded. "Seven-thirty?"

She agreed. "Good seeing you, Nick." Shay lifted her hand and almost touched his arm before she quickly backed away.

"Good to see you, too, Shay," he said, confused by her abrupt actions, almost as if she were afraid of the contact. "I'll see you later."

As he drove away, he glanced in the rearview mirror. Shay stood where he'd left her, staring after them, copper hair glistening, her lovely face pensive.

"Is Shay your girlfriend, Uncle Nick?"

"Huh? No." Nick laughed. That was absurd, of course. Nick didn't do relationships—well, not with the memory of his father's abandonment melded into his brain. The entire town had gossiped and mourned Cal Green's lack of consideration for his family. When his father had finally walked out for good, Nick had heard enough whispers and pity to last a lifetime. He'd tried once to rebuild his connection with his father and twice to have a romantic relationship and he'd failed badly at all three. Fearing he might take after his father, Nick now avoided those kinds of emotional entanglements.

"Then how come you know her?" Maggie asked.

"Shay's a friend. We grew up together."

"I like her," Maggie said while yawning. She closed her eyes and drifted to sleep as he drove home.

But Nick was wide awake. And foremost on his mind was why Shay hadn't mentioned anything about their encounter in New York. Maybe he'd ask her about that tonight.

He looked again in his mirror and saw her walking across the park, her pace furious.

As if she was running away from something.

Or someone.

Yes, Shay Parker was most definitely not telling him something.

Chapter Two

Shay checked her yard for the third time in less than five minutes, sat down to knit, then rose and peered through the window again, anxious to determine what had caused the crunching sound on the gravel driveway.

Nothing there.

She inhaled and counted to ten while fighting back the burgeoning cloud of alarm now swelling inside her head. This was what no one understood, what she'd only recently learned for herself. Her panic attacks were about losing control. That's what her stalker had left her with—the fear that her world would go careening out of control and that she'd unravel worse than she ever had before.

And there would be nobody there to help her put herself back together again.

Think about Nick, she ordered her jittery brain. Nick was a friend, a very good friend.

Had been a friend, her brain corrected without her permission. Because if he was a friend, why, when Nick's fingers had brushed hers when he'd handed her the cone, had she felt fear? Sure, she'd covered by making a joke about his ice cream choice, but later when she'd almost touched his arm, her pulse had skittered and she'd jerked away because she'd had a flashback.

Her stalker's name was Dom. Or at least, that's what he'd called himself. He'd said he touched her, and she hadn't known.

The memory of someone brushing her shoulder and touching her arm before a shoot still haunted her. Back then Shay hadn't suspected anything untoward, not until she'd received that phone call—*I'm closer than you think. I can touch you whenever I want. In fact, I already have, lots of times.* Almost three years later and she still hadn't rid herself of the panic. That's what had ruined her relationship with Eric. What man wanted to be with someone who froze like a nervous Nellie whenever he embraced her?

Eric had taught Shay that she could never have a normal relationship with a man. The shame, the embarrassment and, most of all, the longing to love haunted her still.

"Shay?"

Shay yelped as she jerked back to awareness. An involuntary rush of fear clutched her throat until she realized Nick stood outside her door.

"Uh, can I come in?" He rattled the handle, studying her with a quizzical look.

"Yes. Of course. Sure. Come on in." She flushed as she unlatched the two locks and pushed open the door. "Sorry. I was woolgathering."

He frowned when she flicked both locks back into place once he was inside.

"You're expecting pecan robbers or something?"

he joked. "Not that you shouldn't take precautions," he added when she frowned at him. His gaze followed her motions as she checked and rechecked the two very solid locks.

"Can't be too careful." Embarrassed that he'd noticed her obsessive security measures, Shay regrouped, led the way into her living room and waved a hand. "Have a seat, Nick. Iced tea or coffee?"

"Whatever you have is fine. Um—" Nick eyed the furniture and remained standing.

Shay suddenly realized all the seats were covered with skeins of wool she'd sorted earlier. "Oh. Sorry."

He remained silent while she scooped her yarn, needles and a pattern book from the biggest, roomiest chair. Then he said, "That looks complicated."

"It's going to be a blanket for Jaclyn's baby. I just hope I can get it finished before she delivers." Shay set the project in a woven basket on the floor next to the chair facing her wall of windows. "There. Now you can sit down."

"Why did you pick something so difficult to make?" he asked.

"If it was easy, it wouldn't be much of a gift," she said with a quick smile. "I want my gift for this baby to be as special as Jaclyn is to me. I'll be right back."

When she returned with a tray that had two drinks and a dish of tortilla chips and salsa, he said, "You weren't kidding about your view, were you? The orchards don't look bad from here."

"I hired someone to prune things a bit." She sat down, aware of his wide-eyed scrutiny of her home.

"Maybe you should hire the same guy to cut all that tall grass in your backyard," Nick suggested. "The rains in January spurred a lot of growth, but now it's so dry that if a wildfire starts, that grass will feed it like gas. Your house could be in jeopardy."

"I'll get it done," she promised, and added "soon" when he kept staring at her.

"Good." Nick's bemused gaze took in the splashes of color on the walls, the floors and the furniture. "This sure isn't what I expected your place would look like."

"What did you expect? Steel and glass and leather? Glitz and glamour?" Shay burst out laughing at his nod. "But, Nick, that's not me."

"Are you kidding?" He scowled. "How is glitz and glamour not you?"

"That's what I did," she said gently. "That's how I made my living." She pointed to the wall opposite them. "That's the real me."

"You made this?" Nick got up to examine an intricately stitched design of a little girl paddling at the seashore. It could have been Shay once, a long time ago. "It's very nice. But—"

"Being a model only looks glamorous, Nick. There's actually a lot of downtime, waiting for the photographer or the makeup person or hairstylist, and more endless hours in airports. Dad encouraged me to do handwork to pass the time. When I finished something, I'd put it away in a box he gave me." She was *not* going to call it a hope chest. "That's it there."

Nick knelt in front of the intricately decorated trunk. "It's lovely."

"I kept putting things in there because I knew one day I'd have my own place, a place I could make into my home." She waved a hand. "Most of what you see here is stuff I've made."

Nick rose, examined cushions, hangings and the little stool she'd re-covered with a tapestry she told him she'd found in Italy.

"Did you make this, too?" he asked, indicating a canvas dotted with handprints that took up the entire wall behind the dining table.

"No. That was a gift from the kids I worked with before I came here." As always, the colorful finger-painted mural made her smile. "I have the other half of it hanging in my office." Shay waited for him to sit down again, sipping her drink as she puzzled over how to broach the subject she'd been musing on since she'd met with Maggie's medical team earlier. "Catch me up on your world, Nick."

"Not much to tell since we talked after Maggie's accident." He returned to his seat and took a drink before he spoke, his voice flat and emotionless. "Tore my shoulder, had surgery, gave up pro ball."

"And now?" she prodded. "I know some athletes go into broadcasting. Is that what you'll do?"

"No. I'm lousy at that. I get too caught up in the game and forget to make the comments they want. The only thing I know is playing football." Nick's face tightened into tense lines. His brown eyes deepened to that dark shade that told her he was brooding over something.

"You know a lot more than football, Nick." Shay could see him mentally reject that but she let it hang, waiting.

"It seems I don't know much that makes me employable. Anyway, I have six months' leave and then I'll go back to the team. They've offered me a job with the coaching staff." Nick sounded—discouraged?

"Six months is lots of time," she told him optimistically. "I'm sure you'll be all healed up by then."

"Oh, I'm healthy now. I asked for the six months so I could help Mom with Maggie, but I have to go back then for sure." His response sounded less than thrilled.

"Well, a job is good. Isn't it?" Shay added when he got lost in his thoughts.

"Yeah, a job is very good. Only I don't like the thought of leaving Mom here, alone, to manage with Maggie," Nick admitted. "It's a lot for her to take on a kid Maggie's age. Mom did so much for us, raising all of us on her own. She deserves to have some time for herself."

"Knowing your mother's great big heart, I seriously doubt she feels that way." Shay sipped her tea and made a mental note to talk to Mrs. Green about her arthritis. But first she had to deal with the past. "I need to say something to you, Nick."

"Go ahead." He leaned back and waited.

"I—uh, never did thank you properly for your help in New York." She swallowed hard and forced herself to continue, feeling nauseous. "What you did for me— well, it was more than I ever expected. I just wanted to make sure you know how much I appreciate it."

"What are friends for, if not to chase away stalkers?" Nick joked. When she didn't smile, his eyes narrowed. "You haven't heard from him, have you?"

"No. Why?" Panic reached out and clamped its hand around her throat, taking away her breath. Her fingers involuntarily pinched the fabric of her capris. "Have you heard something?"

"Me?" Nick shook his head, his face confused as he studied her. "No."

"Oh. Good." She knew she'd just made a fool of herself with her reaction, but she still struggled with a sense of dread. "I—I never heard from him again after you read him the riot act."

"That's great." Nick kept looking at her. "Isn't it?"

Shay offered an unconvincing nod, still unable to shake her memories of those horrible days.

When the police couldn't help, she'd fought to hold her world together on her own. And she'd been losing that war, until Nick arrived. She'd been so relieved to see a friend that day that she'd dumped the whole sorry tale on his broad shoulders. Being the good guy he was, Nick had insisted on knowing the details. Then he'd heard Dom's voice, demeaning, threatening and mocking her.

Shay couldn't believe it when Nick told Dom he'd taped the conversation and threatened police action and reprisals from what Nick claimed were legions of Shay's friends. It worked—she'd never heard from the stalker again—but she'd never been able to shed the panic from those months of persecution. She always felt Dom was out there, lurking, waiting for her weakest moment to appear again.

"Did you ever figure out why this guy focused on you?"

"No. The first couple of times he emailed me through my fan page, he was very nice. He complimented me on my latest cover, said he'd seen me on a talk show, asked if I might throw my support behind a pet hospital, that kind of thing. He was very friendly." Shivers speed-walked up her spine. "But by the time you came to New York, he'd become very aggressive. He told me he'd touched me without my realizing it. I didn't believe him, but then he gave details and I knew he'd been near. Too near."

"Nobody ever remembered seeing him?"

"No, and believe me, I questioned everyone, though I never actually told anyone what was going on. Later I learned some of the other models had faced the same thing, so they would have understood how worried I was, but…" She shrugged. "At the time I was too scared and embarrassed to talk about it."

"Maybe he was someone you worked with." Nick's lips tightened into a grim line.

"I thought of that. But I never had any concrete proof to give police, no personal details. After the fourth or fifth call, I think they stopped believing me. And he knew it."

"Hey, relax now. You're safe here," Nick reminded her.

"Yes." Shay inhaled to regain control. "It's just… I have no idea how he found my number or knew my new address. I changed phones and moved, but that only seemed to aggravate him. Police traced the calls, but they always led to a dead end. Dom was very careful. When he did call—well, you heard him. He'd taunt me with what he'd do when we were alone—" She gulped and forced her breathing to slow. "Sorry. I still struggle a bit with his—you know."

"Abuse." Nick's cold, hard word made her flinch.

"Well, yes." She exhaled. "I tried a hundred different things. I ignored him. I monitored every move I made to see if I could figure out who he was. I became suspicious of everyone. But I was helpless. I had no idea how to—" Shay paused. It sounded weak and pathetic to say escape, as if she'd been a prisoner. Yet that was exactly what she'd felt like.

"Shay, that kind of guy preys on people through fear. But he's gone. You can forget about him now." He studied her.

"I know. I will be fine," Shay said, determined to make it so.

When she thought about how it all began, she felt foolish. Too well she recalled how the innocent-seeming online friendship had changed into something menacing after Dom had found out she'd given the flowers he sent her to someone else. That's when she'd started to feel uncomfortable. But she didn't think of contacting the police until odd messages were left on her voice mail. Crazy, untraceable phone calls showed up on her cell when she went to lunch with her friends or took a break at work. He always seemed to know where she was. But worst of all were his increasingly hateful comments. They seemed to hint that violence could explode if she said or did something to provoke him, and that had scared her into a shivering mass of fear.

Until Nick, her rescuer, arrived.

But even after, even when she'd left New York and modeling, it had taken months of intense therapy to attain an occasional night of uninterrupted sleep, free of his voice, his taunts that he would find her when she least expected it. Those words haunted her, so much so that they'd ruined her relationship with Eric, the man she thought she loved. She could barely breathe when his arms closed around her—all she wanted was to run from him. Finally her memories had pushed Eric away and she'd lost what she wanted most—love.

Still Shay was determined she would vanquish Dom and overcome the terror that he'd planted in her brain.

Please, God?

Nick must have read the tumult of emotions in her eyes. He leaned forward, his dark eyes almost hidden beneath his jutting brow, and spoke slowly but with unshakeable resolve.

"Shay, you cannot spend the rest of your life worrying about whether or not this crazy person will come back."

"I know." She inhaled. "I'm here in Hope to start over. And I'm really trying. It's just—I can't seem to forget the ugly things he said."

"You will."

"Can you imagine if anyone besides you had overheard his words to me?" Her cheeks burned. "I would have felt so ashamed. The things he said—" She couldn't go there. Not with Nick watching her. "I'm ashamed that I couldn't stop him on my own."

"You did the best you could, Shay."

"Did I?" She shook her head. "I wonder about that now."

"Why do you doubt yourself?" Nick demanded.

"It would have been better if I'd told more people about him." Keeping her secret had weighed heavily. Even Eric hadn't known until that last, horrible date, and by then he didn't want any explanations— he wanted a girlfriend who showed her love, not some shrinking violet afraid to let him even kiss her cheek. But tonight, with her friend Nick, it felt good to talk about what she'd kept hidden for so long. "But I was worried that stories would leak out. I had sponsors and a lot of media attention then."

"I remember you came out in support of that kids' charity around that time, too," Nick said. His brown eyes gleamed. "Just getting to share a cup of coffee with you made me feel like I'd won a triathlon."

"Silly." She smiled at him but felt compelled to keep explaining. "My agent was afraid that if I went public, it might have brought more weirdos out of the woodwork."

"Too bad he didn't try to stop the jerk." Nick's grim face expressed his opinion.

"My agent was a she," Shay protested mildly, warmed by his caring. "And she's the one who first insisted I call the police. That didn't help, so I did the only thing I could think to do and pretended everything was all right." She made a face. "But eventually I couldn't pretend well enough. I knew Dad had always wanted me to reach the top but he was gone and I was scared and lonely so I decided it was time to move on, to fulfill my promise to join Jessica's clinic. And now here I am." She was not going to tell Nick about her crippling panic attacks—he didn't need to know everything.

"I'm glad you're here." His brown eyes crinkled at the corners as he smiled.

"Thanks." Her heart gave a bump at his kindness. "Anyway, that brings me to the reason I asked you to come tonight."

"Maggie. Yeah, I wanted to talk to you about her, too. You go first."

"Okay. Well, I met with her doctors this morning. They asked me to start on her therapy immediately." Shay wasn't sure how well Nick understood what Maggie's future would entail so she proceeded cautiously. "Has anyone said anything to you about her progress?"

"The doctor today said Maggie isn't doing as well as he'd hoped, but I don't know exactly what that means."

"Maggie's internal injuries have healed very well, according to the reports," Shay began. "Though her leg muscles were badly damaged when she was crushed inside the car, the surgery appears to have been successful. Yet Maggie hasn't regained her strength." Shay studied his face. "You must have noticed that."

"She can't bear her own weight yet, if that's what you mean."

"She should be able to do that by now, Nick. In fact, Maggie should be walking." Shay reached out and touched his fingers, hoping that would ease what she was about to say. But she had to draw back or risk exposing her anxiety. "The fact that she can't even stand is a bad sign. It means she's losing her mobility much faster than anyone thought."

"My medical knowledge wouldn't fill a teaspoon, Shay. Talk to me plainly and bluntly," he demanded.

"Unless Maggie regains her mobility soon, there's a strong possibility she will never walk normally again." Shay watched horror fill his face.

"But she does exercises," Nick protested.

"Your mom does them with her?" Shay waited for his nod. "All the time?"

Nick's face altered.

"I'm guessing she skips them sometimes because Maggie says they hurt too much." From the look on his face Shay knew she was right. "Your mom probably hasn't felt able to make the long, twice-weekly drives to Las Cruces for therapy either."

"No. But they're just little leg lifts and things. It's no big deal," Nick argued.

"You're an athlete, Nick. You know how quickly the body loses muscle strength if it's not regularly used." Shay tried to make him understand. "You probably still follow a postsurgical therapy program to keep your shoulder from tightening up. Right?"

"Yes." He flexed his arm as if she'd reminded him.

"It's the same for Maggie. In the months she was in traction and healing from her internal injuries, there was little to be done except let her heal. Now she's done that."

"The doctor said that today," he admitted.

"She should be moving by now. Yet on the swing today, you saw that she could barely point her toes. That's not good." Shay wasn't finished, but Nick's sudden shifting in his chair made her wonder if he'd hear all she had to say?

"I don't mean to, but I think I hurt her when I lift her," Nick confessed, his guilt-filled stare lifting to meet her gaze.

Shay nodded. "But that's primarily because she has no strength to lift herself and ease the strain. She's barely using her leg muscles at all from what I saw." This was the hardest part, getting people to see what was only visible to the trained eye. "Maggie's become too comfortable with being carried. She makes no demands of her body. My hunch is that no one's challenged her to do more."

Nick sat still, assimilating her words. Then he looked up.

Sun-streaked wisps of hair had drifted onto his broad forehead, and in that moment he looked very much like the determined teenage boy who'd once proclaimed he would never be anything like the father who had abandoned him.

"I refuse to accept that my sister's child will never walk again if it's even remotely possible that she can," he said, his voice tight with control. "So what do we do?"

"We get Maggie moving, Nick," Shay said with a grin, delighted by his response. "It won't be easy and it won't be fun, but it will work if we don't give up. Are you up for it?"

"Me?" He gaped at her, eyes wide with surprise. "But my mother—"

"Your mother can't do this, Nick. She's too close to Maggie and in too much pain herself. I saw her at the grocery store. Her hands must be killing her."

"Uh—" Nick gulped as Shay held his gaze and laid out the blunt truth.

"If you commit to overseeing Maggie's treatment, this will be totally on you. Are you sure you have what it takes to get it done?"

"Of course I do," he growled, lips drawn tight.

"You won't be Maggie's favorite uncle anymore, Nick. In fact, she might even hate you for putting her through the pain."

Nick's eyes darkened to almost black. "You're saying…?"

"Maybe you should think about finding someone else to do this?" Shay asked, hoping that he wouldn't.

"Like who?" he demanded. "My sisters? Cara's got her hands full with twins. Lara travels constantly for her job. And let's just say Simone has enough trouble that I have no intention of adding to it. There is nobody else, Shay." Nick studied her, old friend to old friend. "To clarify, you're saying that if Maggie follows a regimen you cook up, she will be able to walk?"

"I'm ninety percent sure she could regain all of her mobility."

"Ninety percent?" Nick frowned. "Not completely sure then?"

"No." Shay had to tell him the total truth. "But I am one hundred percent sure that if things continue as they have been, your niece will be confined to a wheelchair in one year. Maybe less."

Nick fell back into his chair as if he'd been slapped. "Are you serious?"

"Very." Shay nodded. The bald truth. He deserved it. So did Maggie. "Left unused, within the year the ligaments will lose their pliability, her leg muscles will degenerate, and then there will no longer be an opportunity for Maggie to regain her mobility."

Nick spent several long moments in silent contemplation. When he finally lifted his head, Shay's heart ached for the sadness clouding his beautiful eyes. He cleared his throat, then spoke, his voice ragged.

"How long will it take?"

"I don't know. Four months, maybe six. Maybe longer." She shrugged. "After I do more tests, I'll have a better idea, but the end result is going to depend on whether or not we can get Maggie motivated."

"I see." He nodded, his head drooped low.

"Think long and hard before you commit to this, Nick," Shay told him. "Maggie needs someone who will be there day after day, holding her accountable. She must have a coach who won't give up, no matter what, and is committed for as long as it takes."

He lifted his head. His eyes, deep-set beneath his broad, tanned forehead, silently begged her to understand his quandary.

"I only have six months here in Hope. Then I start my new job in Seattle. I can't stay longer than that, Shay. I mean, I want to but—" He clamped his lips together.

Shay said nothing, allowing him the space to deal with all he'd just learned.

"I can't just leave Maggie the way she is, knowing she'll never walk again." Nick's tortured tone stabbed her aching heart. "Her mom would hate that. You know how active Georgia was."

Shay did know. Nick's sister Georgia had been her coach when she'd decided to run a marathon in her senior year. No one could have pushed her harder than Georgia.

"But Georgia isn't here anymore, Nick," she said quietly. "You are. You and I."

She hated that she'd added more to his already topsy-turvy world. It had only been a short time ago that Nick had found out his career was over. Then he'd lost his sister and his niece had been orphaned. His whole world was in flux.

"If it's impossible for you, you might be able to hire a personal trainer or someone else to be Maggie's helper," she added, offering him a way out.

"Nobody with those qualifications stays in a little place like Hope," he said, his voice edged with frustration. "So they'd leave and we'd be back in the same situation. Maggie would suffer." He shook his head. "Any other ideas?"

"No. I'm sorry. All I can tell you is that I don't

want to wait on this. I want to get Maggie started on a strengthening routine as soon as possible. Tomorrow would be good." Shay held her breath, waiting for his response.

After a long pause he asked, "What time tomorrow?"

"Eight in the morning. Till noon."

"I see." He rose wearily. "I've got to think about this. About what it will mean," he added. "And I have to discuss it with Mom. She'll make the final decision."

"Of course." Shay stood, too. As she looked up at Nick, she realized that she'd always liked that he stood six feet two inches, just three inches taller than her, tall enough that at the prom she'd been able to lay her head on his shoulder. She wished she could do that now.

"I never finished my college degree, you know. I don't have anything else to fall back on but this job the team offered." Nick's eyes grew muddy with confusion. "Even so, my first priority is always to my family."

"Of course." Anyone who knew Nick knew that about him. "Maybe the team would grant you an extension?"

"They already have—that's why I'm here. But if I'm not back on the appointed day, I have no job." He shook his head. "It probably sounds pretentious, but I have to capitalize on my fame as the winningest quarterback in history while it's still fresh in everyone's mind. I'm only good for endorsements till the next star comes along. If I let this job go—" He left it hanging. After a moment Nick regrouped and straightened his shoulders. "I'll have Maggie at the clinic tomorrow morning at eight. And I'll have a decision for you then, too."

"Great." Shay stood on her porch, watching as Nick

walked slowly to his truck. He opened the door then stopped.

"Shay?"

"Yes?" Her heart ached for the once-fun-loving guy who'd been her white knight. She wanted to tell him it didn't matter, but it did.

"Thank you." His dark eyes met hers. "Telling me all this can't have been easy for you."

"No," she said quietly. "The truth is often very painful. But don't worry, Nick—I make sure my kids get the very best."

"Your kids." A smile drifted across his face then flickered away as he stared directly into her eyes. "And you think I'm 'the best' for Maggie?"

"Yes." She nodded. "I do. You and your mom care about her more than any hired person ever could."

"Yeah, we do. Okay, then. Good night."

"Good night, Nick."

Shay remained standing on her porch until Nick and his truck disappeared from sight. Then she holed up in her study and worked most of the night refining her rehabilitation plan for Maggie. Nick would do it, she was almost positive of that. He was that kind of man. Family mattered to him more than anything else in the world. But what she wasn't so sure of was if he would leave when his six months were up or if he'd continue for as long as Maggie needed him.

A yearning for a family like his—for the knowledge that someone would be there for you, to share the good times and bad—ached inside Shay and would not be soothed no matter how many of her blessings she recounted.

Her parents were gone. Brianna and Jaclyn had their

own lives. Of course Shay was delighted that both of them had found love, but it meant that the tight bond between the three of them had changed. It also meant she was the only one with no one of her own.

Shay had tried so hard to trust Eric when he said he would wait for her to get over her panic attacks. But she'd jerked away one too many times and he had eventually given up on her. He'd left her.

Everyone left.

That's why she had to get these anxiety issues under control.

Because though Shay intended to spend the rest of her life alone, she was not going to spend it mourning the past. She was going to help kids. Especially Maggie.

Nick would help Maggie as much as he could, too, but after six months, she was fairly certain, he would leave Hope and resume his football career. It was up to Shay to get Maggie as mobile as possible before he went. She'd deal with her problems privately, with God's help.

"Thank You for this new home and this new life, Lord," she whispered as the first peach fingers of dawn crept over the jagged tips of the Organ Mountains.

She'd been given so much. Now it was time to give back.

Surely helping Maggie and the rest of Hope's kids would satisfy the longing of her heart.

Chapter Three

Nick sat on his mother's deck with Shay's words running through his mind as warm spring rain pattered down on the awning above him.

Staying in Hope for who knew how long—at least until Maggie was walking—would cost him his future.

Why? he asked God. *You took my career. Okay, so I'll start over. But I only have six months here. Then I have to go.*

It wasn't that Nick didn't love Maggie. He wanted to see Georgia's daughter walk again with every fiber of his being.

But if he took on her therapy and it took longer than six months, what would he do about his future?

Confusion filled him. He'd been so certain the coaching job in Seattle was God's answer to his prayer. Helping his mom with Maggie was supposed to give him time to prepare for the only job he felt qualified for.

But if I'm not supposed to do that job, what am *I supposed to do, God?*

When no miraculous way out presented itself, Nick considered his options.

He could take Maggie with him, back to Seattle.

He discarded that immediately. Even if he did hire someone to work with Maggie, his mom wouldn't want to move back there. And Nick was pretty sure his mom would never allow her grandchild to live so far away from her.

Maybe he could hire someone in town, as Shay had suggested.

Nick scratched that idea, too. He'd already phoned around. Hope didn't have someone of the caliber he needed for Maggie. And if he hired a certified trainer to come to Hope, he'd be too far away to keep an eye on things. Plus, if he spent his savings on Maggie, what would he do if his mom or sisters needed money? His savings would be gone and his dad sure couldn't be counted on to help.

Defeat swamped Nick as he finally accepted that he had no choice. He would stay in Hope for however long it took to help Maggie. He'd stay and play the heavy and push her even when she cried for mercy.

He dreaded that most of all.

Nick had been through therapy. He remembered too well the days it took every effort just to show up. But he'd done it because, in the back of his mind, he'd hoped he could get back in the game, get his life back. Maggie wouldn't have that drive. She was just a little kid. The intense therapy Shay was talking about would hurt her. But if, as Shay said, the only alternative was a wheelchair, he could not—would not—back down. She had to do it.

"What are you doing out here, son?" His mother handed him a steaming mug.

Nick took it and smiled. Peppermint tea, her panacea for all of life's ills.

"You do know it's past two-thirty?"

"I know. Just thinking." He couldn't tell her what was on his heart. His mother would feel responsible. If she guessed his fears, she might insist on moving back to Seattle for his sake, and he knew how little she wanted to leave her friends, her home and the desert dryness that eased her arthritic pain. "Shay's plan— it's going to be hard on Maggie, Mom. Really hard."

"I know. I should have pushed the child to do more, but—"

"No." He wouldn't let her feel guilty. "What you did was good. But now it's going to get intense. Shay says Maggie has to get walking, and soon."

"I've been praying about that." His mother sat down next to him on the built-in bench that ran the length of the deck, a small part of the extensive renovations he'd had done on her house after he'd signed his first big contract. "I know God has a plan in all this, but I just can't see it," she said, sniffling.

"Me neither," Nick muttered, trying to suppress his frustration. As his mother's tears spilled down her cheeks, he lifted his arm and hugged her against his shoulder. "Don't cry, Mom. We have to be strong now. For Maggie."

"You've always been a pillar of strength to me, son. I thank God for you every day." Before Nick could say anything further, she'd launched into a prayer that included him, Maggie, Shay and half the town of Hope.

That was Mom, always talking to God about every detail in her world.

Nick only half listened. Lately his communication with heaven seemed distinctly one-sided. Probably had something to do with what he felt was the unfairness of his world. First his career, then his sister. Now it seemed God wanted his job, too.

When his mom finished praying, she lifted her head to smile at him.

"I'm going to bed. You should go, too. You'll need your rest to help Maggie." She rose, held out a hand.

"Don't worry about me. I'm fine." Nick took her hand, gently squeezed the gnarled fingers and brushed a kiss against her silvery head. "I'll be up shortly, Mom. You go ahead."

"Don't fret, Nick. God will handle everything. After all, He sent us Shay. Aren't you glad she's back?"

"Yeah." And he was, Nick realized. He didn't know anyone else he'd rather work with on Maggie's care.

"You two always made such a great pair. You always seem so perfectly matched, as if you can read each other's minds." She smiled. "You were always inseparable."

"Maybe when we were kids." But Nick heard a note in her voice that made him study her face. "There's nothing between Shay and I now, Mom. We're just friends."

"But good friends, right? And who knows when that could change."

Oh, yeah, she was implying something more than friendship all right.

"It's not going to change, Mom. It can't. Shay knows that in six months I'm leaving town. And she's staying here, at the clinic. But in the meantime we're both going to do the best we can for Mags."

"I know you will," his mom said soberly. "You'll be perfect together."

"I don't know about that." He grimaced. "We'll probably argue. As Shay reminded me, therapy isn't fun. I don't mind for myself, but I wish I could make things easier for Maggie."

"You and Shay will find a way to help her," his mother assured him. "Put you two together and the world of possibilities is huge. I just need to have faith that God is going to use both of you to do wonderful things for my granddaughter." She kissed him on his forehead the same way she did with Maggie, took his empty mug and walked inside.

Nick waited until the light in her room blinked out, doubting she'd heard his warning that nothing more than friendship was going to happen between him and Shay. Knowing there was no way he could sleep with everything whirling around in his head, Nick walked over to the old shed he'd taken refuge in when he was eleven, the day his dad had left them. It wasn't much back then, but it was where he'd first begun tinkering with his mom's vacuum and later found out he had a knack for adapting machines. The old shed had been revamped and modified as his inventing took over. When he'd had his mom's house renovated, Nick had more electrical outlets added and installed more tools and a better workbench to the shed.

Christmas, holidays, celebrations—he came out here every time he came home, relishing the fact that no matter how long he was away or how far removed Hope seemed from the rest of his world, the peaceful ambience in the shed never changed. Coming in here gave him the same satisfaction it had as a kid—here, he could let his imagination take flight. He flicked on the light and studied the assortment of his inventions that he'd unearthed the past few days.

His mom had said God sent them Shay. He had to agree. The fact that Shay was going to help Maggie walk again filled him with a feeling he couldn't quite describe. It was deep gratitude, of course, but it was also something else, something that made him a little uneasy. All he knew was that he had to bring his A game to this whole process—he didn't want to let anybody down. Least of all Shay.

Nick reached down and picked up a gizmo he'd invented years ago. It gave him an idea. If he could come up with something fun, something that kept his niece's attention off her pain and encouraged her to take another step, that would push her to work harder and help both Shay and him be more effective. And it would also help him keep his mind off whatever it was he was feeling about Shay Parker.

"Uncle Nick? Where are you, Uncle Nick?"

Nick jerked awake, suddenly aware that the desert sun shone through the small shed windows with a strength that said he was very late.

"Uncle Nick!"

"I'm coming." Nick shut off the lights and laid a tarp over his work. Fiddling with it felt good but it was probably a waste of time because, despite the hours he'd spent scouring the internet for information on Maggie's injury, he still wasn't sure of exactly what he was trying to accomplish. He turned his back on the mess he'd created and walked into the yard.

"Hey, pumpkin."

"Did you go to bed last night?" Maggie's brown eyes stretched wide.

"Nope. Working." He let one of her ringlets twine itself around his finger.

"Can I see?" Maggie asked eagerly. She was sitting on the porch swing he'd had installed last Mother's Day. From the corner of his eye, Nick saw Maggie move. With the tiniest movement of her body Maggie had managed to put the swing into motion. It was the first time he'd seen her extend such an effort. Excitement filled him, but he kept his cool.

"Uncle Nick, did you get something working?" Maggie pressed.

"Not yet. It won't do what I want."

"It will. You can build anything. Remember that robot you made at Christmas? I love your inventions." Maggie's smile had a child's blithe confidence of a world where good always triumphed. If she could see the good in things, Nick felt challenged to rid himself of his feelings of defeat.

"Grandma says you're taking me to see Shay today."

"What do you think of that?" he asked, watching her face.

Maggie shrugged. "Is she a doctor like Aunty Jaclyn?"

"No. She works at the same clinic, but Shay's a physiotherapist. She helps people use their muscles," Nick explained.

"Grandma says she's going to help me walk again." Maggie's voice trembled slightly.

"Would you like that?" He held his breath waiting for her response.

"Yes!" Her eyes glittered with excitement. "Staying with Grandma is nice, but I want to go to school like other kids do."

"It's going to take a lot of hard work, Mags, and it might hurt," he warned.

"It hurts now," Maggie said, fear in her eyes.

"Once your muscles get used to working, I don't think it will hurt so much anymore. We can ask Shay about that. Okay?" Nick waited for her nod, satisfied that at least she was willing to try, even if she didn't yet know what was to come. "Well, I'd better shower and get changed. Are you okay here for now?"

Maggie nodded. Then, with the slightest stretch she again touched her toe against the floor and pushed. A hiss of pain escaped her lips, but as the swing moved she grinned. "I prayed and asked God to help me to walk again."

"Good for you." Nick stemmed the urge to tell her not to try too hard. Because according to Shay, that was exactly what Maggie would have to do in the coming months.

She seemed up for it. But was he?

You have to be. This is no different from when Dad walked out and left Mom with five kids to feed.

As the eldest, Nick had taken very seriously the responsibility of making sure his family was okay. Just as he had back then, he would now put aside his own plans for the good of the family.

He'd ignored his counselor's advice to get his engineering degree because football was in his heart and a career with the pigskin was the quickest way to give his family all the things his father hadn't. And he'd never regretted that choice. But now that playing football was over, Nick felt he'd lost the one thing that had provided him with a sense of security and made him feel competent in his caregiver role. He needed the coaching job so he'd be able to confront his father in his mind and say, "See, even though I'm out of the game, I'm still not like you. I'm not walking away from my family."

Like his father cared. He'd written them all out of his life.

"I need that job, God," Nick whispered, self-conscious about his prayer. "But I want Maggie walking more. Can You make both of them happen?"

As prayers went, it wasn't stellar. And Nick didn't hear a heavenly response inside or outside his head. He'd have to check in with God again later. Right now it was time to take Maggie to Shay's office for her first therapy session.

"Maggie, do you want to walk again?"

Shay crouched in front of the little girl, blocking her view of Nick watching from the sidelines.

"Yes."

"Do you want it enough to keep trying when Uncle Nick asks you to, even though it hurts?" She saw fear creep into Maggie's big round eyes and laid a reassuring hand on the child's thin arm.

"I—I think so," came the whispered response.

Shay lifted one eyebrow.

"I want to walk." Maggie's chin jutted out. "I am going to walk."

"Atta girl." Shay hugged her, loving the spirit she saw in the child's brown eyes. "Now that we've

stretched, let's see how your legs feel about walking."
She ignored Nick's gasp and eased Maggie into a standing position. She carefully guided one foot forward,
ensuring Maggie had a hold of the rails on each side
of her.

"Ow!" Maggie cried out.

Shay sensed more than saw Nick jerk upright.

"I know it hurts, honey. Your legs are mad. You
haven't used them for a long time and they've gotten
lazy. They like having Uncle Nick and Grandma carry
you around." Shay kept working as she spoke. "You
lazy legs! You've been on a long holiday, but your vacation is over now. It's time for you to get to work."

A couple of minutes were all Maggie could bear
upright, but that was okay. They'd taken the first step,
literally. Shay helped her lie down on a floor mat then
massaged her muscles until they were relaxed.

"See over there, Maggie?" She pointed to the corner of the room. "There's a video camera there. It took
pictures of you when you walked today. Each time you
come here we're going to take more pictures. Then, in
a little while, you'll be able to see how the exercises
are helping. Are you ready to do more now?"

Maggie frowned. "I guess so."

"Good." Shay motioned Nick over so he could watch
and repeat each stretching move she made. When Maggie winced and attempted to pull away, Shay reassured
her, keeping her distracted with a silly game for each
exercise. When Nick didn't use enough force, Shay
laid her hands on top of his and guided his movements.
The contact gave her a nervous quiver in the pit of her
stomach. She wished his touch didn't make her want
to jerk away from him.

When would she be able to move on from those memories?

"Good job," Shay praised after an hour had passed. She grinned at Nick. "And you, too."

"Are we finished now?" Maggie's red face shone with perspiration. "'Cause I'm tired."

"It is time for a break. You worked very hard, honey. I'm so proud of you." Shay hugged the little girl.

"Uncle Nick worked hard, too," Maggie said. "Aren't you going to hug him?"

"I think Uncle Nick's too big for hugs," Shay said, nonplussed by the child's comment.

"Nobody's ever too big for a hug. That's what Grandma says." Maggie waited.

Uncomfortable, already way too aware of Nick, Shay had little choice but to place her arms around his waist and hug him. She pulled away quickly as panic knotted her insides.

"Shortest hug in history," Nick complained. His teasing grin made her blush.

Shay swallowed hard and admitted the hard truth to herself. It wasn't just panic that had her pulling away from Nick so quickly. It was something else, something that made her wonder what it would be like to really hug him, not as the friend she remembered from high school, but as the devastatingly handsome man he'd become, a man who made her wish he'd hug her back.

That made her really nervous.

"Now, Maggie," Shay said, hurrying to get her focus back on task. "I want you to rest—I'll give you a juice box and a book. Then, after you have rested, there are a few other things we need to go through."

"I can't really read yet," Maggie mumbled, her cheeks reddening.

"Oh, you'll be able to read this." Shay handed her a book specially designed for preschool kids. Soon the room was filled with the recorded sounds of barnyard animals telling a story. "We'll be back in a minute. You stay there, okay, honey?"

Maggie nodded absently, already enthralled by the story. Shay motioned to Nick to follow her outside. She led the way to her office, made them each a cup of coffee and then sat down.

"So that's the first part. What do you think?" Shay deliberately chose the chair behind her desk instead of sitting next to him, where she usually sat with most caregivers. But then again, most caregivers didn't have the strange effect on her that Nick Green seemed to be having today. Just thinking about that hug made her take a minute to control her rapid breathing. "Okay?" she asked.

"I think I can manage. As long as I don't hurt her."

"She'll tell you if you do. Go slowly. Warm up thoroughly at first with the stretches." She leaned forward, intent on making him understand. "Don't skip anything, Nick. Each move is designed to prepare for the one that follows." She checked the closed-circuit monitor on her desk to ensure Maggie was still resting and reading. "She's a great little girl. I think she'll do well."

"As long as I don't mess up," Nick muttered as he stared at his hands. His troubled gaze met hers. "She's so—delicate."

A rush of heat warmed Shay's heart. Nick was always concerned about his precious family. One glance at her appointment book told her she shouldn't make the offer she was about to make, but Nick had been there for her when she'd needed him most. She had to help him now.

"I could come to your mom's place tomorrow morning to watch you go through your paces the first time. If you'd like," she offered.

"Would you?" Relief flooded his handsome face. "I'd really appreciate it. That way Mom could watch, too, just in case I have to be away or something."

Shay's heart sank at the words, but she struggled to sound detached.

"Nick, I told you last night. This can't be hit or miss. Maggie needs the same routine every day. Besides, I doubt your mom could manage all the manipulations Maggie needs. You have to do it, no matter how unpleasant."

"You're making it sound like I'm trying to get out of helping Maggie." His face tightened with irritation.

"Are you?" she asked, keeping her voice even.

Anger lit a fire in his dark eyes. "I'm here, okay, Shay? I will be here for however long it takes. In the event something comes up, we'll work it out together. Okay?" When she nodded he put his cup down and rose to his full height. "Let's get on with it," he said in a flat voice.

Nick walked out of the room. Knowing he was frustrated with her, Shay kept her distance until they reached her treatment room.

"I'm sorry if I irritated you, Nick. But Maggie has to be my first concern. You understand that, don't you?"

"Yes." He sighed. "Forget it, okay?"

"Okay," she agreed. She laid her hand on the doorknob then froze when his covered hers a millisecond later. In a flash, panic swamped her and she flinched away from his touch.

"Shay?" When she didn't answer, Nick tipped her chin up so she had to look at him. She tried not to flinch again. "What's wrong?"

Stupid. Stupid. Stupid. She tried to avert her eyes but couldn't. "N-nothing. I'm fine."

"That's not true." His brows drew together as their gazes locked. "You're shaking," he said in surprise.

"I'm fine, Nick."

"Sure you are. That's why you're acting like I'm going to hurt you." His eyes blazed. She could almost hear his perfect, even teeth grit together. "I am not your stalker, Shay."

"I know that." She tried to move away to gather her composure, but he blocked her path.

Nick's face softened. "He sure did a number on you. Did you ever get some help?"

"I'm fine." Shay laid her hand on the knob again, eager to get his attention off her.

"You're not fine." Nick reached out as if to touch her cheek, saw the way she recoiled from him and let his hand fall to his side. "Obviously," he murmured.

"I will be."

"Oh, Shay. You can't make yourself be fine any more than Maggie can." He lowered his voice. "Promise me you'll talk to Brianna."

"The thing is, I have to handle this myself, Nick, in my own way. And I will." Embarrassed, she dragged open the door and pasted on her brightest smile. "Okay, Maggie. How was the book? Are you ready for some more work?"

Behind her Nick said nothing. But throughout the

entire session she could feel his intense scrutiny. Shay knew she had to get a better grip on her reactions or risk Nick seeing just how out of control her panic attacks had become.

Coming home, back to Hope, was Shay's fresh start. She would not allow the past to tarnish her life here. A nice guy like Nick—her friend—didn't deserve the way she shrunk away from him.

Tonight she'd study her self-help book some more, see if she could discover a new technique to suppress her fear. She'd pray longer, harder. Somehow she would figure out a way to be whole again, to heal that scar her stalker had left her with.

She knew there was nothing to fear in Hope. Nothing at all.

So why was she still terrified?

Chapter Four

❧

"A little more pressure right here, Nick. More. Good."

Two mornings later Nick steeled himself against Maggie's whimper of pain while Shay's hands guided his. She'd had to cancel yesterday but had shown up bright and smiling right after breakfast this morning. As she bent to smile encouragement at him, her shimmering hair brushed his cheek. He caught his breath at the soft floral fragrance and immediately recalled that day in New York when he'd helped her untangle her hair from her sunglasses. Despite everything that had happened, Shay Parker was still the most beautiful woman he knew. His heart-thudding reaction to her was perfectly normal. Any red-blooded male would respond to Shay's smile.

They'd been at it for an hour and Nick was more tired than he'd ever been, including after his first championship game. Would he ever get used to the feeling that he was torturing Maggie?

"Sweetie, that was fantastic." Shay apparently had no issues with hugging his niece, though she still edged away from Nick whenever he got too close. He despised her stalker for that legacy.

"Grandma and I prayed God would help me." Maggie swiped at a tear that lingered on her cheek. "It didn't hurt *too* much."

"I promise it will hurt less each time and pretty soon it won't hurt at all. Okay?" Shay squeezed Maggie's shoulder. "Just don't give up."

"I won't." The child thrust out her chin. "I want to walk by my own self."

Nick heaved a sigh of relief. Maybe he hadn't done so badly today.

"When can I ride Uncle Nick's roly-poly?"

"His what?" Shay looked from Maggie to him, then back to Maggie, one perfect eyebrow arched. "What's a roly-poly?"

"It's an invention Uncle Nick made. And it's way cool." Maggie's eyes danced as she struggled to sit up. "It's kind of like—it makes noises and—you tell her, Uncle Nick."

"It's just a gizmo I've been fooling around with. Roly-poly is Maggie's name for it." Once he'd figured out exactly which muscles Shay was targeting, Nick had spent most of yesterday tweaking his prototype.

He was *not* ready for anyone to see it, but he should have expected Maggie to tell Shay about it. She was enthralled with the bells, whistles and whirly gigs he'd attached so that every movement made a noise.

"Can I see it?" Shay must have remembered his reluctance in high school to show off his devices before he'd completed them because she paused a moment, then softly added, "Please?"

He guessed she wanted to see if what he was making would cause Maggie problems.

"Sure." Nick rose from the floor, helped Maggie into her chair and pushed it up to the table, where his mother waited with a drawing tablet and art pencils. "I'll be back in a few minutes, Mom."

"No rush," she said with a smile. She was always smiling, in spite of the pain he knew plagued her joints. Nick remembered asking her once why she was always so happy. "Because God loves me," she'd told him. He'd never quite grasped the comfort she found in that, though he'd often wished he could. Once, in high school, after he'd told Shay he struggled to feel God's love ever since his dad had dumped them, Shay had admitted she felt the same way after her mom died. He wondered if she still felt like that.

"You've been working in the shed again," Shay exclaimed as she followed him outside. "Remember the time you were trying to figure out a sequence for the Fourth of July fireworks? You almost blew off the roof." She laughed, her eyes crinkling at the corners.

"Go ahead, make fun of me," he growled and blocked the door. As he looked down at her, he realized he wasn't that much taller than Shay, but somehow she always brought out a protective urge in him. Maybe it was the innocence in her wide-open gaze or the way she always looked directly at him, as if she expected nothing but the truth from him. His heart seemed to skip a beat at the thought, and he cleared his throat. "Maybe I shouldn't let you see what I've been working on."

"I'm just teasing." Her smile softened. "I also remember how you constructed that ladder thing that let

Mrs. Smith get what she needed from her attic without endangering herself. And the way you rigged that gizmo in Mr. Murphy's garage so he could raise and lower shelves. And—"

"Okay. Enough ego boosting," he said in his drollest tone.

"Your inventions have made a difference to quite a few people in Hope, Nick."

"For that you are permitted to enter, kind madam." He bowed and waved a hand as if granting passage into a secret cave. Well, it *was* his man cave.

Shay walked inside and stopped, her head swiveling to take in the assortment of projects on his workbench. "It's not exactly the same as it used to be."

"I should hope not. I'm older and smarter now." He grinned when she rolled her eyes. He directed her to his left. "This is what Maggie was talking about," he said, pointing to the roly-poly.

Shay bent to study his work. "Interesting. What is it, exactly?"

"I researched Maggie's injury. Then, after watching you work with her, I put this together. It's like a walker. Sort of." Unnerved by Shay's silence, Nick lifted it and set it in front of her. "When you push it, it makes noise. I figured it might keep her from getting bored with the exercises."

"Clever guy," Shay murmured. She pushed the handle and grinned at the noise that followed.

"Once she's mastered this, it won't take much to change it up a bit," Nick explained. "Maybe I'll make it more like a bicycle that she has to pedal. That would build strength in her legs, wouldn't it?"

"Yes, it would." Shay asked him to demonstrate so

she could watch which muscles he used—Nick began to sweat bullets wondering if he'd made a huge mistake. Then Shay tried it herself. "It's amazing," she said. "Ingenious, actually. Obviously Maggie can hardly wait to try it, and those things that whirl and click and beep will be an excellent incentive for her to push harder to make them go faster, louder, whatever."

"I hope so." He adjusted one of the handlebars trying to hide his delight that Shay thought his work was amazing. "It needs a few modifications but it'll soon be finished. When do you think she could start using it?"

"Whenever she wants to give it a shot." Shay straightened. "But only where it's flat and smooth. And only if you're right beside her. She will tire quickly at first and may overbalance. Don't let her overdo."

"I could add something like training wheels," he mused. "That would provide stability."

"Good idea." She moved to study another machine he was deconstructing. "What's this?"

"It was going to be an adaptation to the pedal system on Mom's old bike, to make riding easier. She promised Maggie they'd take a bike ride when she's able," Nick explained. "But I can't get it to work right so I've gone back to the drawing board. These are just a bunch of spare parts at the moment."

"Actually—" Shay frowned, her gaze far away on something Nick couldn't see.

"What's wrong?" he asked, steeling himself for her criticism.

"Nothing. It's just that I was thinking—" She touched one wheel thoughtfully then looked straight at him. "Can I play inventor for a minute?"

"Be my guest." Nick stepped back, disconcerted by

the way she studied him. Once he'd been able to read her thoughts so easily, but he couldn't tell what she was thinking, only that it made his stomach do a little flip and he had no idea why that was.

Shay grasped two hard, round balls from a nearby basket filled with sports paraphernalia from his youth. "Could you attach these to the wheels?"

"I suppose." Nick frowned, considering how he could do it. He turned to glance at Shay. That speculative look of hers was leading up to something. "Why?"

"Because then this machine would be exactly what your mom needs to work her hands and arms. It's a strange thing, but in the world of arthritis, moving, even though it hurts, means gaining mobility." Shay demonstrated what she wanted and waited while he attached the balls. "Yes. That's better." She tried it out. "Can you make it a little harder to move?"

Nick caught the flowery scent of Shay's perfume as he bent to adjust the tension. Had she always smelled like the desert in bloom? "How's that?" he said, standing back, trying to regain his focus.

"It's perfect."

"We make a good team." He grinned at her.

"I didn't do anything, but you sure have a knack for inventing." Her gaze moved back to the machine he'd created for Maggie. "I wish I had something like this for another client. A boy, Ted Swan. I don't suppose..." Her head tilted to one side as she favored him with an odd look.

"No, I can't," he said when he realized she wanted him to build something else. "I don't know anything about therapy. This is just a toy."

"It's a very useful toy," she said. "You can help people with your toys."

"My field is football, Shay. That's what I intend to stick with." He felt oddly unsettled by the calculating look she gave him. She liked the machine he'd made, but if he tried to create something for this client of hers and failed, he'd look like a fool to her. He couldn't figure out why it suddenly mattered so much that Shay didn't see him as a failure; he only knew it did. "If this thing helps Maggie, great. But that's as far as I'll go."

"Okay." Her voice was quiet but her eyes brimmed with sadness. "Can you carry this inside so your mom can try it now, while I'm here?"

Nick lifted the machine they'd collaborated on. Shay led the way back to the house, her long legs easily eating up the distance from the shed. He followed more slowly, wondering about the other client she'd mentioned. It had to be a kid because that was primarily whom she worked with. He found it endearing that Shay managed to think about someone else while helping Maggie and his mom. She had always gone the extra mile for something she believed in.

But then Shay and Brianna and Jaclyn had always rushed to fill a need where they saw it, often before others even realized it was there. Zac and Kent were the same. They all pitched in whenever and however they were needed in the small community. Nick was starting to realize how much he'd missed the sense of togetherness and common purpose that Hope offered.

And how much he liked being a part of it. Maybe he'd think about something for this boy, but not till he'd finished Maggie's machine.

Inside the house, Nick stood back as Shay gently

led his mother through a regimen that had her panting with effort, much to Maggie's delight.

"Hey, Grandma, we can do our exercises together," the little girl said with a grin.

"Speaking of that, we'd better get cracking with the rest of Maggie's therapy, Nick." Shay smiled at him. "I have another client to see this morning."

The rest of the time passed quickly. Shay's quiet encouragement never faltered though Maggie burst into tears at several points and Nick grew so tense he kept making mistakes.

"Don't get frustrated, Maggie. You either, Nick. You can't think of this as something you'll do and be done with. You have to practice it every day. Maggie, every morning, before you get up, I want you to do ten of those little leg lifts when you're lying in bed. Your legs will soon get used to working," Shay assured her. "But only if you keep making them do it."

"Like 'sparagus," Maggie puffed as she worked to flex her knee. "Right, Uncle Nick?"

"Right." He chuckled at her distasteful expression.

"Huh?" Shay glanced at him, her eyes questioning.

"Well," Maggie said with a deep concentration. "Grandma says 'sparagus is good for you," Maggie explained to Shay. "Uncle Nick and I don't like it, but she said if we eat a bit every time, then we'll get to like it."

"Grandma is very smart about a whole lot of things," Nick agreed as he shared a smile with his mom. "Though maybe not 'sparagus," he whispered in Shay's ear. She turned to smile at him, a wistful look on her face. He wondered at that look, but it quickly disappeared.

Ten minutes later Shay headed out the door.

"You're doing fine," she said. "Call me if there's a problem. Otherwise I'll see you in the office next week, Maggie." With a flutter of her fingers Shay was gone, her small red convertible vanishing in a cloud of dust.

"It's like a light goes out when Shay leaves," his mother mused as she lifted her hands off the machine he'd created. "It's no wonder she was a success at modeling. How could the camera bear to look away from such inner beauty?"

His mother had always loved Shay. In high school she'd never made any bones about the fact that she liked seeing the two of them together. But Nick knew she'd always hoped something else would develop. He wasn't exactly sure how he was supposed to tell her not to hope for more than friendship. Because he couldn't offer Shay more.

A moment later she and Maggie began preparing lunch. Nick wandered out to his workshop, his thoughts on that wistful look on Shay's face when he'd teased about the asparagus. What was that about? She had looked—what? Envious?

Come on, Nick. Shay Parker, envious of you? Get real. You've got nothing she'd want.

Nick's cell phone broke into his train of thought.

"What are you doing tonight?" His friend Kent McCloy was a very busy local vet and prone to short, clipped phone calls.

"I'm guessing I'll be doing something with you," Nick shot back. "Wanna tell me what?"

"Jaclyn and Brianna have planned a housewarming for Shay. It's tonight," Kent said, sounding harried. "According to them, you, Zac and I are in charge of the food. So what are you bringing?"

Strange noises erupted in the background.

"What are you doing?" Nick asked.

"I'm waiting for a colt to make his first appearance in this world, so I can't stand here talking to you for long. Are you in, Einstein?" Kent used the old moniker he'd tagged Nick with years ago after he'd debuted his first invention.

"I'm in, Cowboy," Nick shot back, using Kent's old tag. "What do you want me to bring?"

"Some of those chocolate cookies your mom used to make the team back in high school wouldn't be hard to take," Kent said. There was a disturbance in the background. "Gotta go, Einstein. Seven at Shay's. We're going to surprise her. Bye."

A housewarming—which meant he needed to buy Shay a gift. Nick almost groaned aloud. The thought of shopping in town where everyone stopped to say hello and ask his plans now that he was out of pro ball made his stomach tighten. But he'd weather their questions today because he wanted to give Shay something special.

As he walked to the house, Nick flashed back to the night he'd visited her and the fear that had filled her eyes before she'd realized it was him at the door. Shay said she had moved back to the farm because she was trying to recreate her dad's dream, but given the way she drew back whenever he got too near, Nick now realized that dream was costing her. She'd been terrified that night, before she'd realized he was her caller.

Maybe a surprise party for Shay wasn't the best idea.

Nick dialed Kent to alert him, but his friend's phone went to voice mail. He tried Zac before recalling Zac was out of town for an all-day conference. Nick would have to think of something else.

At the sound of a neighbor's dog barking, Nick had an idea. A dog—he'd give Shay a watchdog. Nick was pretty certain her stalker didn't know where Hope was, and he was even more certain that if the man was going to make another move against Shay, he would have done it before now. But maybe having a dog would make Shay feel more secure. At least she'd have something to befriend and love with that soft heart of hers.

"Do you know if Sam Levine still has those German shepherd pups? I thought I might get one for Shay." He told his mom the plan, delighted when she offered to bake cookies and his favorite chocolate cake for the housewarming.

"I'm sure Sam has one or two left. A dog is a great idea. I believe Shay's a little nervous about being alone on the farm, though she would never admit it," his mother said, urging him to eat the bowl of soup she'd set out for lunch. "She nearly jumped a mile when I stopped out there one evening."

"When were you out there?" he asked, surprised that his mom had been to the farm.

"It was before you came home. She said there were pecans left unpicked in the orchard." His mom avoided his stare.

"Mom, I can afford to buy all the pecans you need. You don't have to go pick them." It infuriated Nick that she still acted as if she was as poor as they'd been before his success. "I'll increase the grocery budget if you need it."

"You've already spent a small fortune on us and this house." She shot him a severe look. "And I don't need more grocery money. I just wanted an excuse to talk to Shay. She misses her dad. I don't think she's had anybody to confide in for a long time. I believe she's lonely."

"I doubt that," he said in a dry tone. "Shay attracts friends like moths to a flame."

"Because she's so kind and generous." His mother paused. "You know, it sounded to me like Shay bought the place hoping she'd live there with her own family someday."

A shot of envy speared Nick in the gut.

"She's seeing someone special?" he asked, irritated that Shay hadn't told him.

"Actually, I heard she broke up with someone before she came back to Hope. But she'll probably settle down soon. Shay's always been a family girl."

Somehow Nick couldn't quite wrap his mind around Shay, the world-class supermodel, being content to settle on the farm forever. That had always been her father's dream. Hadn't she been affected at all by her big city lifestyle and fancy surroundings? As he drove over to Levine's, Nick chuckled at his mom's comment. It seemed highly unlikely to him that Shay would find a suitable husband in Hope.

Or was that wishful thinking?

Nick frowned at the errant thought. Now, what made him think a thing like that? Shay was his friend. He wanted her to be happy and to have everything she wanted. He wanted her to find the man of her dreams.

Didn't he?

Shay drove slowly toward the house, puzzling over the flicker of light she thought she'd seen inside. She was imagining it, of course. There was no light. Just as there had been no one outside last night when she'd sat peering through the window at 3:00 a.m.

"You're getting weird," she murmured to herself as she turned the wheel toward the garage. "Get a grip on yourself." She breathed in and out twice, just to calm her nerves and pulled inside.

Her whole body stiffened as her headlights picked out someone standing inside the garage, on the step that led into her home. But she couldn't see who it was. Shay cringed against the seat, drawing as far back as she could. The person came down the stairs toward her but she still couldn't see their face. The light was so dim—why hadn't she put a bigger bulb in the garage? A hand reached in to touch her on the shoulder. When he moved toward her side of the car, she opened her mouth to scream but her throat sealed, stifling the sound.

Lessons from a self-defense class replayed in her head. *Fight!*

Shay pushed the car door open to pin the intruder against the wall. A moment later Nick's head appeared in her side window. "Relax. It's me." Nick pushed the door closed so he could free himself. "Shay? Sorry if I startled you."

"Of all the—what are you doing here?" Anger spilled from her like water from a burst dam. "How dare you sneak into my garage and scare the living daylights out of me—"

"Shh," he hissed. "They're inside. They'll hear you if you don't calm down."

They? Fear clung to her, but at least she wasn't alone. Shay slowly eased out of the car, overly conscious of his hand on her elbow.

"Who is inside?" she whispered.

"Everybody. Practically the whole town."

Shay frowned at him. Maybe Nick was losing it, too. She backed away, letting his hand slide off her arm, leaving the sensation of warmth where chills had been. He leaned down to rub his injured knee. "What are you doing in my garage, Nick?"

"I'm here for the housewarming, the *surprise* house-warming," he enunciated in a hushed voice. "Only I thought you might not like the surprise part so I figured I'd give you advance warning." He shot her a wounded look as he straightened his leg. "I didn't realize I'd get attacked by your car door."

"Ever hear of a phone?" Shay winced at the caustic tone in her voice. That's what fear did to you.

"I left about twenty messages. You never called me back." Nick's brown eyes flickered with frustration in the dim light of the overhead bulb.

"I shut my phone off," she remembered and blushed. "I was with a client and it kept ringing and then I forgot— I'm sorry." A housewarming? That would be Jaclyn and Brianna's idea. Warmth filled her, easing the panic that had banded her throat. She glanced down at her wrin-kled work clothes and groaned. "Oh, boy. I am so not ready to party."

"They're just friends. And you look great, Shay. You always do." Nick gave her a cheering grin. "My house-warming gift to you is here." He motioned to a box on the floor in which a dark brown puppy lay curled up, fast asleep. "I wanted to give him to you before you get swamped by everyone."

"Oh, Nick." Tears welled at his thoughtfulness and the abashed way he looked at her, as if he was embar-

rassed by his thoughtfulness. She wanted to hug him
but couldn't make herself do it. Instead she watched
as he lifted the small body and cradled it in his strong
arms. She reached out to touch the wiggling pup with
a fingertip. "How did you know I wanted a dog?" The
puppy lifted his head, licked her finger twice with his
tiny pink tongue and then chewed on her a little bit.
"Thank you so much, Nick. He's darling."

"He's not darling," Nick snorted in disgust. "He's a
purebred German shepherd. He has dignity and pride
and distinction!"

Nick had never been more wrong. The puppy was
darling. And so was he, his big strong hands delicately
caressing the tiny vulnerable ball of fur so she could
check him over.

"He's so sweet." Shay laughed, pressing a kiss
against a small paw. She wanted to kiss Nick, too, for
his thoughtfulness. But when she looked up at him
there was something in his eyes that unnerved her. It
wasn't fear. It was—something she'd never seen before. Something she'd have to think about later, alone.
"Thank you again, Nick."

"You're welcome. We'll have to put off further intro-
ductions until after the party though." He put the pup
back in the box and laid Maggie's pink doll quilt over
him to keep him warm. "That was all I could find," he
muttered when their gazes met.

"Very pretty." She grinned at his aggrieved groan.

"You'd better go inside or they'll wonder what's taking you so long. I'm going to stay out here with him
for a bit before I 'arrive.' I don't want anyone to know
I spoiled the surprise."

"Okay." She smiled, grateful for his thoughtfulness. "It was nice of you to do this, Nick."

"Yeah, 'cause I'm such a nice guy," he mumbled, his handsome face flushed. "Go. And act surprised," Nick ordered as he backed into the shadows.

"I won't have to act," Shay whispered. She glanced at the puppy once more then unlocked her door, switched on the lights and blinked as a bunch of voices yelled, "Surprise!"

"What took you so long to come in?" Brianna demanded, grabbing her hand and leading her forward.

"I—uh, couldn't find my keys." Shay blinked at the host of people filling her home. "What's going on?"

"We're giving you a housewarming," Jaclyn said, grinning. "For once we pulled off a surprise without you guessing."

"Did you ever. Well, welcome to my home, everyone. Please be comfortable." Nick wasn't kidding—half the town *was* scattered throughout her home. She owed him big-time. If he hadn't warned her she'd have made a fool of herself in front of all of them.

Instead she'd made a fool of herself only in front of him.

She'd make it up to him later. For now she'd pretend everything was fine.

"I hope you all brought something to eat with you," she said as cheerfully as she could. "Because the fridge is empty and I'm starved."

Everyone laughed. As Shay turned, she saw Nick come in from the garage. He stood at the back of the room, his brown eyes steady as they met hers. At the thought of the way he'd taken her arm in the garage, she felt her face flush and she had to turn away.

Shay started chatting with the well-wishers who swarmed her. But she couldn't help recalling the moment when Nick's hand had rested on her arm, and she realized that the sensation had pushed away the terror that threatened to swamp her. She'd felt safe, for the first time in a long time.

And cherished.

Precious. Cared for.

Shay glanced at Nick again across the crowded room. To hide out in the garage like that just so he could take care of her...

Oh, Nick. Why can't you stay in Hope forever?

Chapter Five

"Ted says he's gonna walk by himself before I do," Maggie confided from her perch on a nearby chair the following Friday. "But I don't think he will."

"Who is Ted and what makes you think he won't?" Nick asked, glancing up from his second prototype of Maggie's roly-poly. She called it Tiger. She'd used the first one only a few times before it had broken. He'd fixed it, of course, but figured she needed a stronger machine.

"Ted's my friend," Maggie explained. "He was riding his bike and a car hit him. Shay's helping him, too."

Maggie's presence did nothing to help Nick's concentration. But he had to watch her for an hour after lunch so his mom could take a nap she desperately needed. Nick checked his watch. Ten minutes left until that hour was up.

It wasn't that he didn't enjoy spending time with Maggie. But the sooner he had this machine done, the sooner Maggie could regain her mobility, ensuring he'd make it back to Seattle in time to start his job.

"So why do you think he won't walk before you?" he asked. "Isn't this Ted kid willing to work hard?"

"He works as hard as me," Maggie assured him, her dark head bobbing. "More hard, even."

"So?" He paused and turned to look at her. "Why won't he walk before you?"

"'Cause he doesn't have a roly-poly. They're really poor 'cause his dad is sick and he can't work. Don't you think that's sad, Uncle Nick?"

"It's very sad," he agreed, checking that she hadn't yet finished sorting the box of screws he'd unearthed.

"My Sunday school teacher said we should help anyone who needs help," Maggie told him. "I wish I could help Ted."

"Yeah, me, too," Nick muttered absently. If he could make the rotating arm a fraction more pliable...

"But you *can* help Ted, Uncle Nick," Maggie crowed excitedly. "Shay and I talked about it and we know you can do it."

"You weren't supposed to tell him that yet, Maggie," Shay said from the doorway, laughter enhancing the lilt in her voice as she shook her head at the little girl. "Remember?"

"Oh. Yeah. I forgot." Maggie's face fell. "Sorry, Shay."

"Sweetie, it's okay."

Nick raised one eyebrow and scowled at her.

"Don't give me the evil eye, Einstein," she teased, her eyes sparkling. "Maggie and I were simply chatting about how Ted can't do all the exercises he should. We got talking about how the roly-poly could help him and, well, we thought how wonderful it would be if you built one for him."

"Uh-huh." Nick watched the two females share a look and sighed. "And I suppose the two of you think I should do this in my 'free' time?" he said in his drollest tone. "Which would be when, exactly?"

"I could do my exercises myself," Maggie offered. "I'm getting lots better at them."

"You are getting better, sweetie." Shay brushed back the brown strands from Maggie's face. "In fact, you're getting to be an expert. But for now you still need help."

"Let's leave sorting those screws for now, okay?" Nick said. He lifted Maggie off the stool. "What are you doing here at this time of day, Shay? I thought you'd have appointments."

"Cancellation," she said, following him as he brought Maggie out into the sunshine. She reached up to brush her fingertips against a lemon that hung from the bottom branches of a tree he'd given to his mom in ninth grade, the year he'd spent his summer vacation working in a nursery. "I thought this would be finished bearing by now."

"It always bears late, remember? You want some lemonade?" It wasn't a question Nick needed to ask. Shay's green eyes brimmed with longing. She loved lemon anything, but she couldn't resist lemonade made from fresh lemons. "It'll cost you," he said as he set Maggie on the side of her sandbox.

"Everything costs, Nick." A haunted look flashed in Shay's eyes as she studied him. The intensity of those words and the wariness of her gaze sucker punched him. It hurt his heart to think that this was how Shay now viewed the world.

"I could use your help designing Ted's roly-poly," he said. "Unless his issues are identical to Maggie's."

"You'll do it? You'll make him a roly-poly?" A smile started at the corners of Shay's eyes and spread across her face. She stepped forward as if to hug him and then wrapped her arms around her middle instead. "Do you mean it, Nick?"

"You and Mags make it kind of hard to say no," he said, struggling not to grin at her obvious delight. Nick started plucking lemons and handing them to her.

"Don't worry. I won't be calling on your services right away because I'm at the thinking stage. I have to let the design roll around in my brain a little longer before I can begin."

"I know Ted and his family will appreciate it. So do I. And I'll be happy to help however I can. Thank you." Standing there in the sun, her arms loaded with lemons, her pink-tipped toenails peeking out from her white sandals, Shay glowed with happiness.

Something in Nick's gut gave such a wrench that he nearly jumped. *What is going on here?* He fought to get his reactions under control.

"Maggie-mine, I'm going to make some lemonade for us. Will you keep Shay company out here?" He waited for the little girl's nod then took the lemons from Shay, trying not to notice how quickly she edged away from him when her arms were empty.

Funny how much that bugged him.

It didn't take long to squeeze the fruit, add sugar, water, fresh mint and ice cubes, and carry it all out-side, along with slices of the cake he'd brought home from her party.

"Oh, good! I was wishing I'd sampled this cake at my place," Shay said, sliding into a place at the picnic table, across from where he'd set Maggie. "But there was just too much food."

"You should have kept it," he said.

"If you'd left that cake at my place I'd have eaten it." She sipped her lemonade, closed her eyes and savored.

He loved watching her enjoy the cool tart drink, knowing that he'd made it for her.

"You're eating it now," Nick teased when she took a bite of her cake.

She stopped, blinked at him, her eyes wide. "Oh. Yeah." She set down her fork. The longing in her eyes made him chuckle.

"Eat the cake, Shay. You can run your six miles later."

"I'll have to. That puppy you gave me demands a lot of exercise. I named him Hugs, by the way."

"You named that masculine dog Hugs?" Nick grimaced. "Why?"

"Because he's always up for one." She munched away happily, sharing a smile with Maggie, her emerald eyes shining as she told tales of Nick's housewarming gift. "He's such a sweetie. Thank you again for giving him to me. I love him."

"I'm glad. I was told he could be trained for different things, if you want." Somehow Nick couldn't add "as a watchdog."

"I'll train him when he's older. For now I'll just love him and ignore the way he chews on my Manolo Blahnik shoes." She drained her glass then dabbed at the frothy mustache it left on her upper lip. "Your lemonade is superb, Nick. The cake was, too. Tell your mom I said thanks."

"I will." He watched her rise. "Going already?"

"I need to get back to work." She tilted her head to one side. "When would you like me to come help you in your shed later?"

"I'd be happy to have your company anytime, but actually I've had an idea about enhancements to revise the old roly-poly. I think it could be ready to try out tomorrow." He tousled the little girl's hair. "Maggie broke the original one," he teased, "but pretty soon she'll have her Tiger-version. Maybe even tonight." He winked at Maggie. "If she doesn't mind, maybe we could give the old one to Ted."

"I knew you'd help Ted, Uncle Nick." Maggie flung her arms around his neck and hugged him.

"I knew you would, too," Shay said softly.

"You did?" Nick frowned. "How?"

"Because that's the kind of guy you are. That's why your family loves you."

Nick met her gaze, and the look on her face made him want to take her in his arms. Instead, he turned his attention to Maggie.

Shay checked her watch.

"I have to go. If you bring the old roly-poly on Monday morning, we could let Ted try it. Then you could fine-tune it for his needs." She checked her watch. "I have to go. Thanks a lot, Nick."

"My pleasure."

She stopped to unlatch the fence gate just as something behind the house made a noise. Shay tensed and glanced around hurriedly, then straightened and forced a squeaky laugh. "That startled me," she said.

"Probably just mourning doves." But Nick could

tell his reassurance didn't ease her anxiety. She slowly loosed her fingers, passed through the gate before she got in her car. She had to crank the ignition a couple of times to start it. Nick wasn't sure if that was Shay's fault or the car's.

"Don't you think Shay's the most nicest person in the world?" Maggie said.

"You can say 'nicest,'" Nick told her. "But I don't think 'most nicest' is grammatically correct, Maggie-mine."

"It is for Shay," the little girl declared. "She helps everybody. When I get big, I want to be just like her."

"You already are like her. You're a sweetie." Nick left her to finish her drink as he carried the dishes inside, musing on Maggie's words.

Shay *was* always trying to help people. But based on her reaction to that noise, maybe it was time for somebody to help her. Would she let him? Would he know how?

He heard Maggie talking to someone, and saw her speaking into the telephone he'd left lying on the picnic table as he headed back outside. "Who's that, sweetie?"

"Emma White's mom. Emma has casts on. Could you fix her bed so she can get in and out?" Maggie held out the phone.

Nick had to keep from rolling his eyes. With his mom, Shay and Maggie offering his services to the citizens of Hope, he wouldn't have to worry about having time on his hands. He would miss all the small-town interactions. He spared a thought to wonder who'd fix beds and other assorted issues when he returned to Seattle. *I can't worry about that*, he thought. He tousled Maggie's hair and took the phone.

* * *

Shay used the ride back to the clinic to recover her sense of equanimity, embarrassed that squabbling birds had unnerved her so badly, and that Nick had witnessed it. She had to figure out a way to get over this.

Utter frustration burned deep inside. No matter how much she steeled herself and tried not to react, she could find no way to control her panic attacks. But she could not go on living like this. Even more humiliating than freezing at the slightest noise, however, was seeing Nick's eyes brimming with sympathy. *Nick's gorgeous eyes*, she thought, before she could stop herself.

As she headed into the clinic, she realized she'd been having a number of thoughts like that about Nick lately. What exactly did *that* mean?

Just as she reached her office, Shay ran into Jaclyn. Weariness marred her friend's pretty face.

"You need to go home and rest," Shay chided.

"And you need to tell me what you were just thinking about. Whatever it was, it must have been good."

Shay blushed, and the obstetrician sank into a chair as Shay dragged forward an empty plastic box so her friend could put her feet up.

"Don't put me off, Doc." Shay frowned. "I don't need a medical degree to see you're exhausted."

"I am," Jaclyn agreed. "That's why Kent's picking me up in a few minutes. I'd planned to cook us dinner, but I think I'll ask my husband to take me out instead." She patted her baby bump. "This little one tires me out."

"You should take the advice you're always handing out to your patients and remember that having a baby is hard work," Shay scolded. Her grin faded when a rattling sound came from the front of the clinic. She checked her watch. "Aren't all the staff gone?" Dread oozed up from the pit of her stomach.

"I thought so. I'll go check it out," Jaclyn offered after a glance at Shay's white-knuckled grasp of the desk.

"No, you won't. Stay put." Shay rose, summoning her courage as she did. She walked into the hallway. "Anyone there?" she called. There was a bump, then a crash like the splintering of glass.

A band of terror tightened around Shay's throat. "We do not keep any drugs here, if that's what you're after," she said, her voice barely more than a whisper for the fear choking her words.

Who could be there? And why didn't they answer?
Oh, God, please help.

"Shay? What's wrong?" Jaclyn called. "Do you need help?"

The sound of Jaclyn getting to her feet penetrated Shay's fear. No way could she allow Jaclyn or her baby to be hurt. Shay licked her dry lips and forced out the words.

"Stay there! I'll handle this."

Her whirling stomach mocked her words. How could she handle anything when her knocking knees held her captive? The only weapon at hand was a huge medical tome sitting on a file cabinet in the hall. Shay grabbed it, swallowed hard and inched forward.

Maybe their intruder had left at the sound of their voices.

No. There was a distinct padding noise in the waiting room. Someone was still there.

With growing trepidation, Shay stepped into the front of the clinic with her book upheld. She stopped short at the sight before her. A laugh burst from her—shaky, nervous, but at least it was a laugh. She set the book down and held out her arms.

"Hello, kitty. How did you get in here?"

"I'm coming out there, Shay." Jaclyn's worried voice carried down the hall.

"Don't bother. I've caught our intruder." She cuddled the big tabby in her arms, where he seemed perfectly content to rest as she walked back to her office. "Meet our cat burglar. He broke a vase."

"Where did he come from?" Jaclyn took the cat, petting his fur.

"No clue. He must have snuck in somehow. What will we do with him?"

"I'll take him home till we find his owner," Jaclyn said. "Goodness knows we have enough space at the animal sanctuary. I hope we haven't put you out too much, Mr. Cat," she murmured dryly, smiling when he made a circle in her lap before nestling down for a rest. Jaclyn returned her scrutiny to Shay, who was making a cup of coffee. "Your hand is shaking. Are you all right?"

"It was just a bit nerve-racking. I started imagining…well, imagining a burglar in Hope is a bit silly, isn't it? I think the last time that happened here, we were in fourth grade." She turned her back, added some creamer to her coffee and took a sip, hoping it would calm her.

"You're still bothered by thoughts of your stalker, aren't you?" Jaclyn asked. "Did you talk to Brianna?"

"I did. A lot." With a sigh over the fact that she wasn't going to be able to avoid this discussion, Shay returned to her chair behind her desk. "It doesn't seem to make a difference. Something happens and boom! I freeze up."

"You didn't freeze up just now," Jaclyn said. "Did you?"

"For a minute or two." Shay realized that her stomach still hadn't settled. "I don't know why I get so freaked. I'm going along, doing fine, and then it hits me. Suddenly all I can think about is that he's returned and it will start all over again. There's not a thing I can do about it."

"You know that's not true, don't you?" Brianna said from the doorway. "Sorry—I slipped in the back door to put some stuff in my office. I didn't mean to eavesdrop."

"You know all my secrets anyway." Shay shrugged. "We're just laughing at my latest panic attack."

"No one's laughing, Shay," said Jaclyn.

"What sparked it this time?" Brianna asked.

As they related the cat story, Brianna smiled, but her eyes grew serious. "I'm worried about you, Shay. From what you've told me, it's this fear that ruined your relationship with Eric. Now it's affecting you here in Hope. Why?" She bent, kicked off her high heels and massaged her toes. "New shoes are the worst." Her focus returned to Shay. "Have you heard from the stalker guy? Is that why you're so on edge?"

"No. Nothing like that." Shay felt like a fool once again. "It's just—I know he'll be back."

"Honey, you don't *know* that. You said he hasn't bothered you since Nick threatened him," Jaclyn reasoned. "It's your fear talking."

"She's right," Brianna agreed. "You can't let this fear overwhelm you, Shay."

"I'm trying not to," she said helplessly. "But I can't seem to control it."

"That's key. Control. I've been thinking and praying about this a lot." Brianna's gaze encompassed both of them. "It seems to me, given what happened with Eric, that you've never resolved your trust issues. And you must, because this is a fight for control of your mind, Shay."

"I agree. And I think we need to pray about it." They bowed their heads, and Shay listened to each of her friends ask God to grant Shay the strength and wisdom to combat her fear.

"I appreciate your prayers," she said when they'd finished. "But why don't I feel any stronger?"

"It won't happen overnight. You must actively fight every negative thought," Brianna insisted. "Only then will you be able to finally let go. Just don't expect it to be easy. These thoughts have taken root in your mind like weeds. But you can do it."

"I hope so."

"No, Shay." Brianna shook her head. "There's no 'hope' about it. You put your trust in God. Keep your mind fixed on Him and when it strays to fear, recite Scripture to combat it."

"Which Scripture?" Shay read the Bible every day,

but she'd never given a thought to reciting it like a shield.

"Last night I was thinking about you and I wrote down a few passages that have helped me in the past. Maybe they'll help you, too."

"I'm sure they will." Shay folded the paper. "You guys are the greatest. Thank you." She hugged them both, chuckling when Brianna's phone chirped a text message in a ring she recognized. "Didn't you just see Zac a few minutes ago at the school office?"

"Yes." Brianna blushed. "What can I say? We spent ten years apart. Now that we're finally married, we're making up for lost time." She winked. "We've got dinner plans tonight."

"Well, get going then," Shay urged, smiling as Brianna scrambled for her shoes, slid them on and eagerly hurried away.

"I've got to go, too," Jaclyn said. "Kent's probably waiting outside." She inclined her head. "I was looking for you after lunch, by the way. RaeAnn said you'd had a cancellation and went out?"

"Our office nurse is all-seeing, isn't she? And you're nosy," Shay teased. Jaclyn merely lifted one inquiring eyebrow. "I went to Nick's, to ask him to build one of his machines for that client you referred to me. Ted Swan."

"And did Nick agree?" Jaclyn's implacable stare was hard to ignore.

"Yes." Shay frowned. "Well, sort of."

"Sort of?"

"Well." Shay felt her cheeks warm at Jaclyn's scrutiny. "He said he'd do it if I promised to help him with it."

"Help him how?" Jaclyn eased the cat off her lap and rose.

"However I could. But before I left he said he'd had an idea to revamp the first machine he made for Maggie, which she calls a roly-poly, into something for Ted. Maggie broke that one. But I think Nick was thinking ahead and figured she'd get bored with it because he's already started something new. Maggie calls this one Tiger. You know Nick," she said. "He can't help inventing."

"I do know." Jaclyn shared a smile with her.

"Anyway, he's agreed to give the roly-poly to Ted so it seems that everything is fine." Shay grabbed her purse and followed Jaclyn, who carried the cat to the front door. "I'd be very willing to help Nick if he needs it, though."

Jaclyn looked straight at Shay, her gaze swirled with questions. Shay knew exactly what she was going to ask.

"Honey, are you feeling something for Nick?"

"Yes," Shay confessed. "Friendship, of course. Thankfulness that we've begun a kind of a renewal of the bond we shared in high school."

Jaclyn frowned. "Do you trust him?"

"Why wouldn't I trust Nick?" Shay asked.

"It's none of my business and as you mentioned, I am too nosy for my own good." Jaclyn touched her arm. "But I know you've always wanted to be married, to raise a family. And I know your panic attacks have made you wary of relationships. I just want to be sure—"

"Jaclyn, stop." Shay shook her head. "Nick's a friend. That's all. There can't be more. I freeze up if he even touches my arm. Believe me, I, better than anyone, know I'm not a candidate for another relationship. I doubt I ever will be. I've accepted that I'll stay single, and that's okay."

"I'm not sure it is okay," Jaclyn murmured, her lovely face brimming with doubt. "Just because Eric wasn't the one doesn't mean—"

"Yes, it does." Shay forced herself to sound upbeat. "Anyway, I think God meant for me to learn to stand on my own two feet. You know how hard that's always been for me, especially since Dad died. The panic attacks must be a test or something."

"I don't believe God sends fear," Jaclyn said.

"I love you for fussing, pal, but I'm going to be fine. You worry about yourself and that baby." Shay hugged her, petted the cat and pulled open the front door. "Now go have dinner with your husband and relax. That's an order, Doc."

"Yes, ma'am." Jaclyn brushed her cheek with her lips. "I love you, Shay."

"Back atcha. Now git." She stood watching as Jaclyn strode eagerly toward her husband. Kent kissed his wife, took the cat from her and stowed it in a kennel box he always carried in the back of the truck. Then he helped Jaclyn inside, waved at Shay, and the two drove off.

A rush of envy suffused Shay. Both Brianna and Jaclyn were blissfully happy in their marriages. Shay craved the love and security they enjoyed with men who treasured them and showed it. That love was something she'd seen between her parents, and it was what her father had showered on her every day of her life. She yearned for it now. But ever since Eric had told her that when she cringed from his touch it made him feel like an attacker, Shay had begun to question whether an intimate relationship was for her. She told herself that was okay, she'd settle for feeling safe.

Nick made her feel safe. But Shay was beginning to realize that he'd be leaving soon. The only one she could depend on was herself. Jaclyn and Brianna were right. She had to deal with this apprehension that dogged her. To let it continue was to remain a prisoner.

The only question was—how would she do it?

Shay locked the office door then climbed into her car after an automatic check of the backseat. The motor didn't catch till the third try, but once it did and she was moving, she put the top down. She loved the breeze in her hair as she drove home.

The sun was beginning its colorful descent below the jagged rims of the western mountains as Shay drove into her yard. She paused outside the garage, caught up in the glory of vibrant reds, peaches and oranges that painted the horizon. Only when the scrabbling noise of an animal startled her did she realize how quickly darkness had fallen. She pulled into her garage and closed the door.

As Shay stepped out of her car, the slip of paper Jaclyn had given her with a list of verses tumbled from her pocket onto the floor. She picked it up, determined to get a handle on this fear thing starting tonight. She entered the house, then let Hugs out to run while she made dinner. Afterward, with the dishes done and Hugs curled up at her feet, she started to study the list.

God has not given us the spirit of fear; but of power, and of love, and of a sound mind.

2 Timothy 1:7.

Power, love and a sound mind—those were God's gifts to her.

It was up to her to use them.

Her thoughts strayed to Nick. He was a gift, too. A wonderful, sweet, helpful friend. But that's all he could ever be because deep down inside her secret heart, suspicion still lurked and Shay couldn't lay it to rest—not even for a wonderful man like Nick.

Nick drove the back route to Shay's, surveying every vehicle he passed, noting the driver, or, if he didn't recognize them, the kind of vehicle. It was probably obsessive and unnecessary, but Shay's face today—the panic that had filled her gorgeous emerald eyes when she'd looked at him—wouldn't leave him.

Shay wasn't a wimp or a weakling. She was a strong woman. Fresh out of high school, she'd built a career that supported her dad and herself, and then she'd found a second career when the first was no longer viable for her. She'd never been prone to flights of fancy.

But since she'd returned to Hope, he'd seen her suddenly drawing back several times. He'd heard her quick gasp when he'd touched her that day outside her office, and since then he'd taken note every time she drew away from him. He knew she was still fearful.

Though she pretended otherwise, Shay had never fully recovered from that stalking. That made Nick angry. Angry enough to ensure there was no foundation for her fears.

Nick parked his vehicle at the edge of Shay's land and walked over the perimeter, even though it was 11:00 p.m. He stood behind the leafy foliage of a paloverde tree to study her house. He had to guarantee—if only to himself—that no one was there playing tricks on her, taunting her, cashing in on her unsteady nerves.

By midnight Nick had seen nothing. But he would be back tomorrow night. Shay was a friend, and friends took care of friends.

That funny little burst of affection he'd felt for her this afternoon bubbled up again, unsettling him. He shoved it away and drove home. But back in his workshop, Nick couldn't focus on the adaptations needed on Maggie's Tiger machine. Instead, memories of Shay cropped up, and all the things she had done for him when they were teenagers.

It was Shay who had pushed him to see himself as more than his father's son when he'd hidden his shame in this very shed after overhearing local gossip and rumors about his father. *Cal Green—you remember Cal, the no-account who'd abandoned his wife and kids for other folks to tend? That poor family, left all alone.*

Nick's fists clenched as memories of gossip and innuendo cascaded through his brain. Shay had thought his house was fun, his sisters were great, his mom the salt of the earth. In those days, whenever she'd come to his home, it was as if she suddenly came alive. The quiet introvert allowed herself to relax among his family.

That's what he wanted for Shay now—to let go of the fear that shadowed those gorgeous eyes and let joy fill her completely. He wanted to see her free and fully participating in life. That's why he'd keep making these trips at night, to make sure his friend was all right.

But friendship was Nick's only motive. It had to be, because he was Cal Green's son. Nick figured the two relationships he'd botched proved he'd inherited his dad's legacy of failure when it came to personal relations. No matter what he might or might not be feeling for Shay these days, he wouldn't risk repeating that lesson with her. Better to concentrate on loving his family to the best of his ability, and being Shay's best friend.

That would have to be enough.

Chapter Six

"That's fantastic, Ted." Shay beamed as the little boy showed off his newly learned skills, thanks to Nick's roly-poly. "My goodness, it seems like you've been working with that thing for a lot more than just a week."

"That's 'cause Uncle Nick's been helping him," Maggie chirped from the sidelines of the therapy room. "I helped, too, by cheering for him."

"Good for you, Maggie." Shay studied Nick with a smile. Despite his family obligations, and his initial refusal to take on the work, Nick still couldn't bypass an opportunity to help others when needed. She wasn't surprised. He'd always been that way.

Courtesy of a little bird named Maggie, Shay now knew that Nick had volunteered to help restore the seniors' center. He also chauffeured his mom on errands, took care of Maggie's therapy and clearly spent hours thinking of ways to help speed his niece's recovery. Yet he'd still made it a point to refine the roly-poly and help a little boy learn how to use it.

Shay's brain hummed with possibilities as she watched Nick and Ted interact. Maybe, if she went

about it the right way, she could show Nick the impor-
tance of his contribution. There were so many other
kids who needed someone like him to help them.

"Ta-da!" Ted completed his last feat, spread his arms
wide and bowed.

"Amazing job, buddy." She wrapped Ted in a fierce
hug, knowing how hard he'd struggled. "You keep
working like that and soon you won't need the roly-
poly."

"You mean you think he's going to walk before me?"
demanded Maggie.

If Nick meant that strangled cough as cover for his
laughter, it didn't work. Shay shot him a silencing look
before she turned to comfort Maggie.

"It's not a contest, sweetheart," she said gently. "The
goal is for both of you to walk."

"But it's my roly-poly! I don't want him to beat me!"
Maggie glared at Ted as if he'd done something wrong.

Shay glanced at Nick, and she knew that making
Maggie understand was up to her. So she tried reason.
She tried calming words. She tried everything, but to
no avail. Maggie's sour look telegraphed her irritation.
Exasperated, Shay turned her glare on an amused Nick
and refused to be charmed by his smile. Which, some
part of her brain acknowledged, was devastating.

Funny she'd never noticed that before. Even funnier
that she was noticing now, when she should be concentrating on her clients and not her client's hunky uncle.

"Do something," she growled sotto voce.

"You know, Shay, it's refreshing to know that you
don't excel at absolutely everything." With a grin that
took the sting out of his words, Nick knelt in front of
his niece. "Listen, Mags," he began. "You offered the

roly-poly to Ted. You can't take it back. That would
be mean."

"But—"

"Hear me out. The important thing is that both you
and Ted walk again." He pushed the brown bangs off
her forehead. "*When* you walk doesn't matter. It's like
Shay said—all any of us care about is that you *do* walk
again, on your own, both of you."

"But Uncle Nick," Maggie sputtered, her indignation
obvious. "I started before Ted so I should walk first!"

"Sorry. That isn't how it works, kiddo." He shrugged
at her mutinous look. "Be as mad as you want. All I
can say is if it matters so much, then it's up to you to
do something about it."

"How?" Maggie perked up, suddenly all ears.

When Nick winked at Shay she had to suppress her
smile, remembering when Nick used a million coer-
cion tactics to get his younger sisters to do something
they didn't want to.

"Let's see." He pretended to think about it. "I know.
Maybe you'd walk first if you worked at your exercises
harder. Harder than you did this morning," he hinted,
though he kept his expression neutral.

Shay watched Maggie's face color and realized that
the stiffness she noticed in Maggie this past week was
because Maggie had apparently sloughed off on her
workouts. Shay had mistakenly attributed the slow-
ing progress to Nick, assuming he'd become tired of
pushing his niece. She'd misjudged him.

Maggie's bottom lip thrust out under her uncle's
steady regard. She huffed her indignation before she
turned to join Ted on a pile of exercise mats at the far
corner of the room. Shay took advantage of the privacy.

"I owe you an apology," she admitted.

"Me?" Nick blinked his surprise, his bittersweet-chocolate eyes widening. "Why?"

"I assumed Maggie's lack of progress today meant you'd been slacking off. Now I realize it's Maggie who isn't putting in the effort." Shay stared straight at him. "I apologize, Nick."

For a moment his lips pinched tightly together and his brows lowered, shielding his gaze from her. Then his frustration released in one irritated sigh.

"I am not my father," he said, enunciating in a clear, harsh tone.

Stunned by the bitterness underlying each word, Shay blustered, "I never said—"

"When I say I'll do something, I do it. You should know that about me by now, Shay."

"I do know that," she assured him, rushing to make amends. "I've always known that about you. It's not that I doubted your commitment. Not exactly." She motioned for him to sit on the nearby chair. "I guess I jumped to conclusions."

"Why? What have I done that would make you think I'd stop before Maggie has recovered her mobility?" Nick folded his long body into the chair.

"Actually, nothing," she admitted. "You've done better than I ever hoped for."

"Then why assume I'd slack off now?" The rigidity did not leave his face.

"It's not just you. Trusting isn't my strong point," she admitted. "But the way you responded when I first laid everything out, you sounded as if you could hardly wait to get away from Hope. Well, you *did*," she said more forcefully when he raised one imperious eyebrow.

"Okay, maybe," Nick conceded. "But now your doubts about me are settled, right? You know I'm here for the duration, so you can relax."

"I do?"

"You have to know I'm not going anywhere for the next couple of weeks, for sure."

"How would I know that?" She waited for an explanation, but all she got was a cute smile that bloomed across his sun-tanned face. She ignored the giddyup of her pulse. "Tell me what's going on, Nick," she demanded.

"You know, you haven't changed all that much since we were in high school. You still can't stand it if there's something happening that you don't know about." Laughter burst from him in a great roar of amusement when she made a face.

"So what is 'happening,' as you so succinctly put it?" She wished she didn't sound so eager.

"I'm surprised somebody in town hasn't already told you, even though it's supposed to be a secret."

"I've been a little busy with work." She inclined her head. "So?"

"So I'm planning a surprise sixtieth birthday party for Mom two weeks from Saturday. The girls and their families are coming Friday evening. Saturday we'll all have breakfast together, and then in the afternoon I intend to invite the town to come help us celebrate. I'm not sure about the evening yet. Maybe we'll have a family dinner."

"It sounds fun." It had been a very long time since Shay had been part of a family event, and she felt just the tiniest bit envious. "Can I help?"

Nick slowly nodded. "Actually, you can."

"Great. How?"

"I don't know if I should ask this or not." Nick's smooth forehead pleated in a frown.

"You can always ask. If I don't want to do it, I'll say no," Shay promised. "But remember, I was a kid when we moved here, and your mother became like my own. I love that woman dearly. There's not much I wouldn't do for her."

"Good to know." His eyes narrowed. "Because there's a glitch in my plans and I need some advice. I'm afraid Mom will feel like she has to be the hostess if I ask people to come to the house. I want her to be the guest of honor, to enjoy her day, not spend it waiting on other people."

Nick gazed at her intensely, and Shay started to feel strange, as if he was somehow intruding into her personal space. "Of course you do," she said, breaking eye contact with him. "Knowing your mom, you are right to be worried. She'd be rushing around, seeing to her guests, trying to make everyone comfortable."

An idea flashed in Shay's brain but she was still feeling flustered by the way Nick had been looking at her, and she couldn't seem to get her thoughts together.

"I thought maybe a reception in one of the halls in town would work, but they're already booked." Nick shook his head in frustration, but his eyes held hers, narrowed even, holding hers so that she couldn't look away. "I should have started planning earlier."

"Uh-huh." Shay found it hard to breathe under that intensity, let alone say anything halfway intelligent.

The slap of a workout mat hitting the floor startled them both. Shay and Nick blinked at each other then hurried to ensure both Maggie and Ted were all right.

The kids rolled on the floor, howling with laughter, best friends once more.

Once again Nick's eyes met hers. Thankfully he spoke first, giving Shay a moment to regroup.

"Maybe I can hire some of the high school girls to act as servers or something," Nick said as he lifted Maggie. "Don't worry about it, Shay. You've got enough to do."

"Oh, I *am* going to help." Shay eased Ted onto the parallel bars. "But right now I've got to finish Ted's therapy. Can you come over to my place tonight?"

"Yeah. Sure. Okay." Nick smiled at her, which made her stomach do a funny little backflip. "I'll be there after dinner. Mom's serving asparagus, so I might even be early."

She laughed at the face he and Maggie made before they turned to leave.

Shay put Ted through his paces. He pushed himself so hard she had to remind him that he couldn't do everything at once, even with the roly-poly.

"The secret is to work hard, but not too hard," she said as his mother rushed in looking harried.

"I'm so sorry I'm late. I agreed to decorate a cake for a friend and I had to pick up some supplies. There was a long line at the grocery store."

"No problem." After updating Susan Swan on her son's progress, Shay ruffled Ted's hair.

"No overdoing it now, Ted," she warned.

"But I want to beat Maggie." His big eyes blinked at her from his too-thin face.

"This isn't a race. Be patient. Do everything I showed you, slowly, carefully. Okay?"

His face demonstrating his frustration, Ted finally nodded. Then he and his mother left.

Since Ted was Shay's last appointment of the day, she hurried to reorganize her workout room before returning to her office. Once seated behind her desk, she let her imagination run free as she sketched out rough ideas for Nick's mom's party. By the time she leaned back in her chair to ease the crook in her neck, she was certain her plan would work. And it would be a huge surprise to the woman who always labored so hard giving to others, the woman who'd become like a mother to her.

Suddenly the ticking clock seemed overly loud in the office. Shay's nerves stretched taut as she realized she was alone. She checked her watch—almost six-thirty. Everyone had left. The eerie silence sent fear skating over her shaky nerves. Uneasiness mushroomed into anxiety.

"Don't be ridiculous," she said out loud. "There's no one here."

Though psychologically Shay knew the only danger was in her head, the rattle of a window pane against the desert wind tightened an invisible band around her dry throat and made her so skittish that all she could think was, *Get out of here!*

She grabbed her keys and her bag and hurried to the front door, only then realizing how dim the office was. One meager nightlight glowed in a losing battle to fight back the shadows of the room. She flicked on a desk lamp and immediately felt better as illumination chased away the worst of the darkness.

"Bogeymen? You're being silly," she told herself. "Go home."

Shay stepped outside and locked the door. Then she racewalked to her car. She flicked her key fob, scanned the backseat, got inside and snapped the door locks.

"Stupid habit, Shay," she mocked as she did up her seat belt. "If the guy's going to come after you again, he's certainly not going to sit in your backseat and wait for you."

She drew deep, calming breaths when the car wouldn't start. Stupid thing—she'd taken it to the garage twice this week and no one could find what was wrong yet the car still didn't start properly.

She decided to try once more before calling a tow truck. The engine finally caught. Heaving a sigh of relief, she negotiated her way through town. After a few minutes she put the top down, remembering the verses Jaclyn had given her.

God has not given us a spirit of fear.

Meaning, God wanted her to get on with her life. He certainly didn't want her skulking around, afraid of her own shadow. Afraid to be alone in the office. Afraid to trust…Nick.

Shay shoved a praise CD into the player and, once she was out of town, sang along loudly as she drove toward home. But no matter how hard she sang, she couldn't dislodge the questions that lay at the back of her mind.

A spirit of fear—about Nick? Why would she fear him? Because she'd begun to feel something for him? Because she was afraid of those feelings? Because when he came over to her house tonight he might figure out that he was becoming more than a friend to her?

Shay had found no answer to those and other questions by the time she pulled into the garage. She only knew that the fear was there. Like a cactus thorn, it had dug in deep. It would take a lot of verses to excise.

"Please help me learn to trust again," she whispered before she climbed out of the car.

Nick drove to Shay's to discuss his mom's birthday a little faster than usual, eager to talk to her. But he did savor the scenic evening drive while he wondered what brilliant idea Shay had come up with. He loved his family but was more comfortable doing the mundane stuff that needed doing. Shay was the party girl. She'd know the best way to make his mom's day special. He'd do anything to make his mom happy. No way did he want her remembering that his deadbeat dad had chosen to walk out on them on her special day. Why hadn't God given him any ideas for his mom's party?

Or any solid assurance that the job in Seattle was where he ought to be. Though it was supposed to be a sealed deal, his concern about being so far from Hope and his family gnawed at him more with every day that passed. Especially now that he realized how much his mom had come to depend on him.

That wasn't the only issue though. Nick had also begun to appreciate his time in Hope. Helping the seniors renovate the building where they'd built lifelong relationships made him covet the same sense of connection with his surroundings. And Maggie and Ted's bragging about the machines he'd made for them had brought calls from several parents who wanted him to build stuff to help their kids. Though Nick grumbled about more work, he'd appreciated Shay's efforts to scrounge old rehabilitation equipment for him to use. The satisfaction of watching each child experiment with his unique invention surprised Nick. He loved being involved and had agreed, despite his misgivings, to let a couple of the kids' fathers help him work on the machines.

But the best part of working on those machines was the time he spent with Shay.

She made everything fun. Because of her Nick had a new appreciation for his hometown and all it offered. He hadn't really been surprised by Shay's remark that she'd love to raise her own family here. She was so caring and generous—she'd make a great mom.

And working with Shay and her kids had shown Nick fathers who gladly got involved in their kids' lives, men totally unlike his dad. These guys were wholly vested in seeing their kids thrive and offered to help on their weekends off or until late at night if Nick needed them. When it came to their kids, these dads were totally unselfish.

Was that what had sparked his own desire to know what being a father would be like? Would he be a better dad than his own had been to him? Could he love and guide his own son or daughter better than his father had?

Yet each time Nick dared dream that, the vision was snuffed out by bitter memories of his last meeting with his father. He'd thought a reunion might work but his father's rejection of him, his sisters and his mom showed Nick how silly it was to imagine he, the son of a man so uncaring, would be any different. Hadn't he already messed up twice? What had changed?

Nothing. Nick wouldn't risk another relationship. He certainly wouldn't involve a child in his failures. That's why his own dreams had to be suppressed to allow him to fulfill his primary duty—to care for his family.

As if to emphasize that, his cell phone rang. It was his sister Cara.

"I'm so sorry the twins aren't feeling well, sis," Nick said after she'd revealed her doubts about making the drive for the party. "But they'll be over this bug soon, won't they? You guys can't miss out on Mom's special day."

"I don't want to miss it, Nick, but driving four hundred miles with the twins is going to tax all of us." He heard the hesitation before she said, "Besides, I'm not so sure bringing my kids would be good for Mom. She'll already be ramped up. The twins don't sleep through the night yet and the noise they make will prevent Mom from getting the rest she needs. Maybe we should come later, when the fuss has died down."

"No way, Cara. You can't miss this party. And Mom will be hurt if you and the munchkins aren't there." He thought for a moment. "Why don't all of you fly into Las Cruces? I'll pick you up. The tickets will be my treat," he insisted, knowing Cara and her husband couldn't afford the expense. "We'll get you a hotel room if need be. We'll figure it out."

"Nick, that's too much—"

He cut off her interruption. "Just come and enjoy yourself. I've got it all taken care of."

As Nick said goodbye and pulled into Shay's driveway, he hoped Shay would help make his words come true. A minute ago he'd been regretting that he had to leave Hope, but here was another reason for showing up for that assistant coaching job—his family needed him. Without a steady job he'd run out of funds to pay for things like spur-of-the-moment plane tickets. Then he'd be as useless to his family as his father. Leaving Hope for that job was the right choice and he needed to stop doubting his decision.

Nick climbed out of his truck and blinked in surprise. Shay had all the outside lights on—every single one of them. Something must be wrong.

He strode to the front door and rapped once, hard, before he called out, "Shay? It's me."

She opened the door a few seconds later, struggling to hold back the madly wriggling puppy. Her laughter bubbled out to greet him, eliminating his worry. Despite her efforts, Hugs burst free of her grip and in one giant leap had his front paws on Nick.

"Hey, guy. What's got you so excited?" Nick squatted to pet the animal. When the dog had calmed, he rose and shook his head. "Giving you this fellow may have been a mistake," he muttered, swiping his thoroughly licked face with a tissue.

Shay brushed off her jeans. "He gets a little— exuberant. That's all."

"Exuberant? That's one word for it." He was about to pull the outside door closed when Shay stopped him by laying her hand on his, for one tiny second. Then she pulled it away. "What?"

"Don't close the door. We're going out again. I need to show you something."

She didn't sound scared, he noted with relief. She sounded sort of—keyed up.

"Is anything wrong?" He searched her face for the fear he often saw buried in those beautiful eyes.

"Just—come with me. Wait. I need my shoes." She thrust her pink-tipped toes into the rattiest pair of sneakers he'd ever seen. The shoes did go with her worn, almost threadbare jeans and the chunky, red-checked flannel shirt with holes in the elbows. Swaying pigtails made the picture complete. Nick smirked. Supermodel indeed.

And yet, even in work clothes, there was something exquisitely elegant about Shay, something that made him want to protect her.

"Okay, let's go." The dog bounded out in front of them. Nick went next, waiting while Shay locked the door behind her.

"Is that really necessary?" he asked as she pocketed the key.

"Let's say, I'm not sure that it's not. Come on." She avoided his stare by leading the way to the harvest shed. Once there, she unlocked the big double doors and threw them wide. "Well, what do you think?" Shay was so keyed up her copper curls almost vibrated with anticipation. She danced from one foot to the other, eyes wide and expectant. When he didn't immediately answer, she looked at him as if he'd become particularly slow-witted. "For the party, of course."

Nick took in the room, touched that Shay had wanted to offer her home for his mother's celebration. For a moment, he couldn't speak.

"Think of the advantages," she continued. "There's plenty of room to park in the yard, space for people to spread out, shelter if the sun gets too strong, and best of all, it's easy to decorate."

Nick studied the big shed, his nose twitching at the aroma of past pecan harvests. It was clean, rustic and, best of all, not too fussy—his mother would definitely approve.

"There's a company in Las Cruces that rents those big white tents. We could get one for that side." She glanced at him, waiting for his nod before she continued. "A band could set up over there. There are a couple of local bands that play country music—your mom loves country music," she reminded. "There'd be lots of room over here if folks wanted to dance."

Nick hadn't seen Shay so vivacious in years. Her skin bloomed a rosy peach. Her green eyes, lit by the gigantic yard light, radiated pleasure and eager anticipation. She was the most beautiful woman he'd ever seen.

Ever.

"You don't like it." In a flash, her delight snuffed out. "I'm sorry. I thought—"

"It's perfect," Nick said. And it was. His mom was going to love it.

"You don't have to say that. It was just an idea." She turned away.

"I'm not just saying it." He stopped her with a hand on her arm. Though she drew away from his touch, Nick wouldn't let her escape so easily. He grasped her fingers in his and hung on until she faced him. "I think it's absolutely brilliant, Shay. But it's a lot of work. Are you sure you want to take this on?"

Shay looked down at their entwined hands, and for a moment Nick thought he saw her smile at the sight. And then she slowly pulled her hand from his.

"Are you kidding? I'd love a chance to make the old place come alive with a party. Dad always said we had the best land for partying."

Nick almost laughed as that glimmer of pure joy flared to life in her eyes again.

"The stove is old, but it still works. So does the fridge. We've got enough power out here to make coffee, string fairy lights and whatever else we dream up." She continued, listing one asset after another until she ran out of breath.

"You've done some serious thinking about this." Her generosity amazed him, but then, that was Shay. "There's only one thing." Nick had to say it before she went any further. "What about Maggie? Will she be able to handle it out here?"

Shay looked at him. He could tell she was now considering all the aspects of the day from his niece's viewpoint. She was silent so long it made him nervous.

"Well?" he demanded when he couldn't wait any longer.

"I don't know." Shay's mouth stretched in a smile. "But we can find out."

"How?"

"Tomorrow you bring Maggie out here for her session and we'll see how she adapts." She chuckled when he blinked in surprise.

"Seriously? You want to do this?" He wasn't sure about it—it seemed a lot to ask. But nothing else he'd come up with came even close to Shay's plan.

"Absolutely serious." She grinned at him as if he'd given her the biggest gift anyone could. "Let's go back to the house. There are a lot of things to discuss." She tugged him along beside her as she talked. "For one thing we'll need tables and chairs…"

As Shay talked, Nick wondered if she realized she was touching him. Apparently she hadn't because halfway to the house, she yanked her hand from his arm as if she'd been scalded.

"Sorry," she mumbled. "I didn't mean to drag you."

"Hey, what are friends for?" He changed the subject before she could get more flustered. "Do you think we could wrangle a campfire? Your dad used to have an old tractor wheel we used when we held our youth group out here. Is it still around?"

"Yes! I saw it in those bushes where the barn used to sit." Shay skipped up the stairs with the dog nipping at her heels. She motioned Nick to follow her inside. "I've got iced tea. I think it's probably too sweet but—"

"The sweeter the better," Nick told her, thinking that Shay looked very sweet as she bustled around to offer him some cinnamon buns she'd made to go with the tea.

"They're your mom's recipe," she said.

"When do you find time to make cinnamon buns?" he asked.

"I couldn't sleep last night so I baked." Before he could ask her why, she handed him a filled tray. "Come on."

Though he wanted to say more, Nick followed her to the table in front of the wall of windows. She took his tray and set it on the table, beckoned him to a chair then folded herself onto the floor in what he'd once heard termed the Lotus position.

As Nick munched his cinnamon bun and sipped his tea, he couldn't help but think how he felt completely comfortable in Shay's home, sharing her baking and talking about his mom's party and what would happen next week, next month. Gradually his worries about the party seeped away. Shay's place was far homier than his condo and Nick had a hunch the exterior would soon boast that same relaxed, beckoning feel she'd created inside.

Too bad he wouldn't get to see what she did with the place.

He'd be in Seattle.

Alone.

Chapter Seven

"I can't do it, Shay. I can't!"

Maggie's mournful wail pierced Shay's heart. Everything for Mrs. Green's birthday was coming together so perfectly. But if Maggie couldn't manage the rough terrain around Shay's pecan shed with her braces and her Tiger machine, they couldn't have a party for her grandmother here.

Shay glanced at Nick and saw her worries reflected in his eyes. If Maggie couldn't handle the ground, their party plans had just flown out the window.

Nick sighed and nodded. "Okay then."

"But I'll practice lots, really I will," Maggie promised Nick as tears streamed down her cheeks. "I don't want to miss the party, Uncle Nick."

"Whatever happens, you are *not* staying home from your Grandma's party, Maggie-mine." Nick hunkered down until he was at her eye level. "No way."

"Do you promise?" she asked with a sniff.

"Cross my heart." He brushed away her tears with the tenderest of touches then gently set her on a nearby stump. "Here's the deal. You keep working your hardest. Don't say a word to Grandma about her party. I'll think about this some more. So will Shay. Okay, darlin'?"

"Okay." Maggie huffed a huge sigh of relief, which turned into a giggle when Hugs jumped into her lap. She obviously trusted her uncle to sort everything out. But from the way Nick looked at Shay, she knew he was as stumped as she was.

"Maybe we should go with the wheelchair," she suggested, hating the very idea of it.

"After all the work she's put in to get herself walking?" He shook his head, his gaze on something distant as he turned over the problem in his mind. "No way. A wheelchair would be no better in this gravelly sand anyway."

"Well, we have to come up with something." Frustration at the seeming hopelessness of the situation gnawed at her. "Maybe a new machine?"

"I haven't got time to design and build another machine before Mom's party!" he exclaimed, eyes widening. "Even if I had a clue what to build, which I don't."

"Then we're back at square one." Shay bit her bottom lip as she checked her watch. "I have to get back to the office."

"You go ahead." Nick sighed as he raked a hand through his already mussed hair. "Maggie and I have to pick up Mom at the hairdresser's. Thanks anyway."

"I'm not giving up yet, Nick, and don't you either." For a second, Shay felt tempted to reach out and reassure Nick with a touch. Startled by her impulse, she offered him a smile instead. "Your mother deserves the best party we can put together for her. With Maggie present."

"Hey, Uncle Nick and Shay," Maggie called. When they walked to her side, she tilted her chin and stared at them.

"What's the matter, honey?" Shay touched her cheek. "Do you hurt?"

"No. But do you remember last Sunday when Pastor Marty said God wants us to talk to Him about the hard stuff *and* the easy stuff? This is really hard. I'm gonna pray for God to help me walk for Grandma's birthday."

"That's the spirit, Mags." Nick hugged her and pressed a kiss against the top of her head. He scooped Hugs from her and handed the wriggling bundle to Shay then swung Maggie into his arms. "Now, come on. You and I need to let Shay get back to work."

"Okay. Bye, Shay." Maggie wagged her fingers at Shay then blew a kiss.

"Bye, sweetie." Shay caught the kiss in her outstretched palm and blew one back. She laughed when Nick reached in front of Maggie and caught it. After pretending to swoon, he tucked his clenched hand to his heart mimicking his performance of Romeo in their high school play. "That kiss was for Maggie," she chided, laughing again when he pretended to pout. Nick was just so much fun. What would she do when he left?

Shay walked over and brushed her lips against Maggie's forehead. "Don't give up."

"I won't." Maggie's brown eyes shone. "I'll pray about it when she's not listening."

Shay watched them drive away, waving until she couldn't see them anymore, then returned to the house just as the phone rang.

"Hello?"

No one answered.

Immediately, memories of the innumerable calls she'd answered with the same result swamped her.

Is it him? Is he back?

Fear crept up her backbone as she laid the phone down.

God has not given us a spirit of fear.

Shay repeated the words, but before peace could fill her soul, the phone rang again. She wiped her damp palms against her thighs, and then picked up the receiver a second time.

"H-hello?"

Nothing. No dial tone. No voice. Just an empty yawning silence.

"Who is this?" she whispered.

Click.

God, help. The fingers of fear clamped hard around her throat. *Not a spirit of fear,* her brain chanted. But it seemed her heart didn't get the message because when the phone's shrill peal broke the silence for the third time, it took every ounce of courage Shay had to answer it.

"Shay? Shay, are you there? Oh, this stupid cell phone. Three times I've dialed this number and I still can't hear if anyone is answering. I should have let Nick get me a new one and tossed this dumb thing in the garbage. Doris, do you know how I tell if this thing is working?"

Nick's mother. It was Nick's mother calling.

Shay's throat suddenly opened.

"Mrs. Green, this is Shay. Can I help you with something?"

"Oh, good. You're there." She let out a huff of irritation. "Nick said he was driving out to talk to you while I was getting my hair cut. I wanted to tell him to pick me up at the grocery store, but I can't reach his cell phone."

"He's already left, Mrs. Green. I'm sorry." Shay smiled at the hiss of irritation. "But I'm sure if you leave a message with Doris, she'll pass it on to Nick." The town's hairdresser had an uncanny knack for being able to relate most messages before the telephone did.

"Oh, yes, I know that, dear. It's just that I was hoping to get him to look at Faye Campbell's granddaughter's old tricycle on the way. Faye's throwing it out. I thought he might be able to adapt it somehow for Maggie. Faye says it has special tires that work in any conditions. With all the gravel in my yard, I thought…"

The rest of Mrs. Green's sentence disappeared into oblivion as Shay registered what she'd said. Special tires—

"Shay? Are you there? Oh, this stupid phone." The line went dead.

Shay hung up and tried call return but Mrs. Green's number was busy. Faye Campbell. She'd said Faye Campbell had this tricycle.

Shay patted Hugs, grabbed her car keys and left, glad that for once the car started without a problem. Maybe she could catch Nick on the road to town. When she reached town without seeing his truck, she dialed the office and asked RaeAnn for directions to Mrs. Campbell's.

"Your next client is here," RaeAnn warned.

"I'll be a bit late, but I'll be there," Shay promised.

When Shay pulled up in front of Faye Campbell's big Victorian home, she saw a pile of discarded things, obviously waiting for trash pickup. But it was the big tricycle that snagged Shay's attention. The wheels were not like the usual bicycle tires. They were the old-fashioned very wide kind—Was this the answer she'd been praying for? She hopped out of her car and rang the doorbell.

It took a bit of convincing but Shay finally persuaded the older woman to allow her to store the tricycle in the side yard until Nick could pick it up. She'd no sooner disentangled it from the other items when a truck pulled up and two men began loading the junk into the back.

"Want us to take that, too?" one of them asked.

"No, thanks. I've got an idea for this," Shay told them.

"A project, huh?" The burly driver surveyed the rusted fenders, torn leather seat and bent handlebars. "Good luck. You'll need it."

"Thanks." Shay pushed her treasure to the area under a big cottonwood tree where Mrs. Campbell had directed. "Thank you very much," Shay told her. "I'll have it out of here by tonight."

"As long as it's gone when I get back, I'll be happy," Mrs. Campbell said.

Shay said goodbye and got back in her car, her heart light. That was a heavenly answer, wasn't it? Surely a clever guy like Nick could figure out how to make those big tires work. He had to. Nick was pouring his heart and soul into this party so his mom would have a wonderful day. Shay was going to do everything she could to make sure the day was absolutely perfect.

For Mrs. Green, of course.

But also for Nick. Her very dear friend Nick.

Because she wanted to see Nick happy.

What could be wrong with that?

* * *

Saturday, the morning of his mom's birthday, Nick stood outside the doors of Whispering Hope Clinic, anxiously shifting from one foot to the other. Getting the wheels on Maggie's Tiger was supposed to be the hard part. He'd managed that without any problem. But this—this had him panicked.

On the phone Shay had promised she'd meet him here in five minutes. So where was she?

"Nick? What's so urgent?" came her voice from behind him, gilded with laughter. "And what's that on your pants?"

He twisted to get a better look at his backside and groaned. "It figures."

"It looks like—icing?" Shay frowned. Then her eyes widened. "Your mom's birthday cake…?"

"…is now mush," he finished, trying not to grit his teeth.

"Because?" She waited for his explanation, but her gaze slid back to the icing.

"Because some kid went racing through a stop sign. I hit the brakes to avoid him and the cake—well, it flew all over the place." Nick grimaced. "Trust me when I tell you there is no way to salvage any of it for this afternoon."

"I see." She arched one eyebrow, but he caught the flicker of a smile at the corner of her mouth.

"This is not funny," he barked.

"Yes, it is. Kind of." She giggled as she reached up and touched the top of his head, then showed him the pink icing on her finger. "You're wearing a lot of this cake."

"What am I supposed to do, Shay?" He realized his

entire right sleeve was also plastered with mashed cake and icing. "I checked with the bakery. They don't have another cake that big, or anything close to it. I also checked the grocery store. No big cakes. Just a ton of little round ones. Buddy Simms is pretty mad. Their delivery got doubled or something."

"Cupcakes?" Shay asked, her green gaze narrowing.

"I guess that's what you call them." He waited impatiently. Shay had come up with the answers to so many other issues—was it expecting too much to think she could solve this, too? He watched as she pondered the dilemma while he found himself pondering just how beautiful she was. He caught himself—now was not the time.

"Go and buy them," she said.

"Buy the cupcakes?" He frowned. "How many?"

"We guessed there'd be over a hundred people to come for your mom's party, but yesterday Heddy Grange said there will probably be more like two hundred."

Heddy Grange knew everything about everyone in Hope. If she said they'd have a full house—well, he wasn't going to argue.

"How many does the store have?" Shay asked.

"I think he said—maybe around six hundred?" Nick frowned. "I can't remember. Apparently they always order a bunch for some school event, but the company shipped way too many. Buddy told me he was going to freeze the overage until the truck comes back next week."

"Maybe he won't have to." Shay tilted her head to one side, her copper hair shining in the sun. "Maybe he'll give you a deal, just to be rid of them."

"But they don't have any icing or decorations," Nick sputtered. "Why do we want a bunch of plain little cakes?" This was not the solution he'd hoped for.

"Never mind that. Just go over there and buy them. Tell him I'll pick them up in twenty minutes. After that," she said, pushing his shoulder, "go join your family for breakfast at the restaurant. I've got an idea."

"You always seem to have an idea." He had to smile. "Bike wheels, birthday parties, cake messes. The mind boggles."

"Don't worry, Nick. It will be fine." She was scanning numbers on her phone. "If there are leftovers, you can take them to coffee time at church tomorrow morning."

Somehow, Nick knew Shay would handle it. Again he was struck by how much he was willing to put his trust in her when he wouldn't have afforded anyone else the same, especially if it involved his family.

"Sure you don't want help?" he asked. "I feel like I'm dumping this in your lap and running."

"You are dumping it in my lap," she teased. "But at least there's no icing on me. Yet." She laughed when he groaned. "Anyway, I'll have help—Brianna and Jaclyn are at my place now with Zac and Kent. I came to pick up the coffee I bought yesterday and left in my office. Everything's under control. You go enjoy your sisters and their families."

"Okay."

"You might want to wash some of that icing off first, though. Your mom might guess about the cake."

"I owe you, Shay," Nick told her sincerely. "Big-time."

"And I intend to collect soon. But that day is not

today." She waved at him. He started to walk away but then she called him back.

"Yes?"

"Maggie?" she asked, her beautiful face telegraphing her anxiety.

"Will be moving around like a hummingbird searching for flowers," he told her. Nick cupped her cheek in his palm, loving her for her concern about his niece. How could one woman have such a generous heart? How lucky was he to have her in his life? "For now, and that is thanks to you and that tricycle. But Mags wants to surprise you, so I can say no more."

Shay's eyes sparkled. "That little girl has got the faith of a giant. And the heart of a champion. Just like her uncle."

"Then we're in good company," he said, brushing the end of Shay's nose with a fingertip of icing. His heart felt huge in his chest. Shay Parker thought he had heart. What a compliment. He hoped she'd never think less of him.

When she didn't immediately back away from his touch, Nick's heart rate accelerated until he could barely breathe. Could that be because she wasn't afraid of him anymore? He checked her eyes and found no fear lurking there. That made him want to hold her close and reassure her that he'd always be there for her.

Only—he wouldn't be.

So all he said was, "Later."

Nick headed to his car, fully aware that he would never be able to get enough of the icing and cake off his clothes for his family not to suspect something was amiss. Well, let them suspect. He wasn't going to explain. This was his mom's day, and nothing was going to ruin it.

Thank heaven for Shay. As Nick drove away, he saw her talking on her phone a mile a minute wildly gesticulating. Before he turned the corner, he watched her hesitantly peek into the rear of her car before climbing in.

So Shay wasn't afraid of him, but she was still afraid of something. Nick made a decision. He was going to help her let go of the past and move into the future. No way could he let that beautiful woman who held such a special place in his heart suffer any longer. It was time for Shay to embrace life, and he was going to help her do it.

He owed her at least that much.

Shay watched as Nick led his mother to the table where the cupcakes were assembled into a beautifully decorated birthday display.

"I can't thank you enough, Susan," she murmured to Ted's mom. "You've made them look so beautiful—far better than the ordinary cake we had planned. A lot of people are going to ask who made that masterpiece."

"I'd be happy to get another job," Susan said. "I used to work in a bakery. It's something I really enjoy."

"You're certainly good at it," Shay said.

Nick's stunned surprise on seeing the cupcake cake was gratification enough. The "thank you" he now mouthed at Shay was, well, icing on the cake. A quiver that started in her stomach moved up to hug her heart. Did he know she'd do almost anything for him?

"I'd better get home. Ted's with his dad. They probably both need rescuing." Susan's eyes widened when she saw the check Shay handed her.

"This party wouldn't have been the same without a cake. Thank you." Shay smiled as the grateful woman left, thinking she'd be sure to mention Susan's name this afternoon. Maybe she could help Ted's mom get more work. The woman was talented, and it had to be tough for her to manage on part-time cleaning wages and her husband's disability check.

When Nick led everyone in a slightly off-key rendition of "Happy Birthday," Shay joined in, clapping with everyone else as Mrs. Green made a vigorous effort to blow out the relighting candles Nick had chosen. Then Shay motioned to the girls from the cheerleading squad, who'd agreed to act as servers, to begin handing guests a beverage.

A sweet sense of satisfaction blossomed deep inside Shay as she noted how easily people mingled through the yard, enjoying the food and the company. A local group—old friends of Nick's sister Cara—played music that soon drew a few dancers. The babble of conversation and Mrs. Green's glowing face proclaimed this party a total success.

Kids squealed and giggled nearby as they jumped and bounced inside the blow-up castle Nick had rented. But it was Maggie who caught Shay's eye.

Shay knew Nick had attached the wheels from Mrs. Campbell's tricycle to Maggie's Tiger machine, but how he'd done it so successfully was a mystery. Maggie moved freely over the gravelly ground, captivating everyone with her bubbling laughter.

"The party's a success, isn't it?" Nick murmured in her ear a few minutes later.

"It certainly is," she agreed. There was that quiver again and the rush of warmth to her heart that Nick always brought.

"It's because of you, Shay." Nick's dark gaze held hers. "None of this could have happened without you. I don't know how to thank you."

"Are you kidding?" She shook her head. "You were the driving force. Anyway, look at your mom's face. That's all the thanks I need."

"Me, too."

They stood together, watching Mrs. Green hand out cupcakes to her friends. The fatigue of the previous day had vanished, leaving a carefree woman who interacted with each grandchild who rushed up for a hug before disappearing back inside the jumping castle.

"Excuse me, Shay," Brianna said. "Hey, Nick. Great party."

"That's Shay's doing," he answered, smiling at Brianna. Brianna turned to look at Shay and gave her a wink that made Shay blush a little.

"I just wanted to let you know, Shay. We're running a bit low on coffee and I can't find any more grounds," Brianna said. "So I'm going to take a run into town."

"I'll do it. I'm the one who miscalculated." Nick dug his keys out of his pocket. "I guess I'm not very good at planning for parties."

"Everyone here thinks you're great at it. Including me." Shay grinned at him. "And you didn't miscalculate. There's lots of coffee. I just forgot to take it out of my car after we finished unloading those cupcakes. I'll go get it."

"I'll join you in a sec," Brianna said. "First I want

to ask Zac to put together those treat bags Jaclyn and I plan to give the kids later."

"Great idea." Shay touched Nick's arm to gain his attention. She waited for the usual sense of panic and realized with surprise that it wasn't as strong as usual. "Maybe you and your sisters could take over passing out the cupcakes and give your mom a rest. She's scrunching up her hand as if it's sore."

"Really?" Nick took a quick look at his mom then faced Shay again. "Don't miss a thing, do you?" For a moment, Nick stood there, looking down at her as if there were something else he wanted to say, but after a moment he seemed to change his mind. "Thanks. Again," was all he said.

"You're welcome." As she walked back toward the house, Shay felt a surge of satisfaction. The party was everything she'd wanted for Mrs. Green. Maggie was as mobile as possible. The day was sunny and warm without being stifling. And Nick—Nick was happier than she'd seen him in a long, long time.

"Thank You for answering Maggie's prayers," she whispered. "And mine."

It felt odd to walk inside her house without unlocking the door, but there was no way to keep the house locked up when so many people needed access. She walked through the kitchen, trying to ignore the chaos. The place would need a good cleaning when the party was over, but a little mess was well worth the amount of joy the party had brought. She opened the garage door to get the coffee out of her trunk and flicked the light switch. With a flash the bulb burnt out.

"Great timing," she grumbled. Shay grabbed for the flashlight she kept hanging by the door for just such emergencies. Then she remembered leaving it in the pecan shed last night. "Oh, for goodness' sake," she muttered in exasperation as she hesitated. "Just get the coffee out of the car, Shay."

Her voice sounded shaky in her own ears. Suppressing her disquiet over the darkness, she felt her way along the car's fender until she found the door. She opened it and reached inside, flicking the trunk switch. At least the interior car light provided a little illumination.

The quiet snick of the trunk lock releasing did not drown out the rustle of something behind the car.

Shay froze.

"Is someone there?" she asked, peering into the shadows.

Nothing. And then it came again, a sound that was like shuffling footsteps.

"Who's there?"

No answer.

The ominous dread of knowing someone lurked in the shadows made Shay's knees knock. As she cowered in the semidarkness, she tried to remember the verses she'd read.

But all she could think of was, *Please, God, send Nick.*

Chapter Eight

"Have you seen Shay?" Nick asked Brianna.

"No, and we're getting really low on coffee." Brianna frowned. "I'll go check on her."

"I'll go. You finish the kids' bags," he told her with a wink. "Your work is much prettier than what my feeble attempts would produce."

Waylaid by several people on his way to Shay's house, Nick took longer than he intended to get there. His concerns ballooned when he didn't find her in the kitchen.

"Shay?" Her name had barely left his lips when he noticed the door to the garage standing ajar. He reached for the doorknob then paused when he heard a soft whimper. "Are you in here, Shay?" No answer. Then he saw her.

The dim glow of the car's interior lights made Shay a ghostly figure as she huddled on the hood of her car, hugging herself. Nick spotted a switch on the far side of the wall. He negotiated his way over, flicked it upward and then pushed the door opener. As the garage door slid up and daylight flooded the space, he hurried back to her.

"Shay, what's the matter?" he asked. He had to repeat himself twice, until finally she lifted her head.

"Someone's there," she croaked in a hoarse voice. "Behind the car." Her emerald eyes stretched wide with terror.

Nick glanced over one shoulder. "I don't see anyone."

"They were there," she insisted. A shudder made her body tremble. "I heard someone."

"Okay, I'll check." Nick walked around the car to see a plastic bag caught in the door hinge rustling as the wind toyed with it. He grabbed it and returned to stand beside her. "It was just a bag. It must have caught in the door from all that wind last evening. You're safe, Shay."

Her glazed green pupils gradually narrowed into focus. "A b-bag? That's it?"

"That's it. There's nothing else there, Shay. I promise. Come on." Nick held out a helping hand as she slid off the hood of her car. Her fingers clung to his. Nick had no intention of letting go. For the first time since New York Shay needed him and it felt good to be able to be there for her when she'd done so much to help him.

Maybe it felt too good?

It was great she'd begun to trust him. But who would be there to help after he'd gone back to Seattle? The realization that he might not be there when Shay needed him most made Nick clasp her hand that much tighter.

"I feel so s-stupid," she stuttered, avoiding his gaze.

"You aren't stupid." She was shaking. Nick wrapped

his arms around her and held her. "You got spooked. It can happen to anyone."

"Sure it can." She inhaled then pulled away from him. "Does it happen to you?" she demanded, her green eyes furious. She strode up the stairs into her house. "What an idiot I am."

"You're not." He followed her then suddenly stopped. "Shay?"

"Yes?" She turned.

Her beautiful face was so pale. Nick's breathing hitched at the pain he saw. He wanted to hold her until the fear dissipated. He wanted to comfort her. But he knew she'd pull away. All he could do right now was give her some space and be there if she needed him.

"Didn't you come out here for the coffee?" he asked.

"Oh. Yes, I did. It's in the trunk." She scurried inside.

Her distress gutted him. To see her so shaken—well, Nick was grateful for this small reprieve to regain his equanimity. He retrieved the cans of coffee then followed her into the kitchen. When she saw him, she reached for the doorknob. Her hand was trembling, and she knew he'd seen it. But she pretended all was normal.

"I hope no one's gone thirsty." The tremble in her self-conscious laugh gave her away.

"I doubt it. We've only been away a few minutes." Nick frowned.

"Oh." She inhaled deeply. "Good."

"Listen, Shay, you should get the light switch moved over beside the house door. It's not a good thing to go out there in the dark," he said quietly. "A rattler could have gotten in, and they don't like being disturbed."

"It's the one mistake the contractor made that I haven't rectified," she agreed. "I had the hall light on when I went out. It didn't seem that dark then." She visibly struggled to keep her tone even. "Besides, I always close the garage door as soon as I drive in. A snake couldn't get in that fast."

"You were never afraid of rattlers anyway." Nick suddenly recalled a high school biology presentation she'd made about handling dangerous snakes. It had included a hands-on demonstration. "Snakes don't bother you, but people do," he said half-jokingly.

"Totally irrational, isn't it?" Chin thrust forward, she headed out the door and walked toward the party.

"Nobody ever said fear was rational."

Shay didn't answer. Nick touched her arm, and she jerked away.

"Talk to me, Shay," he begged. "You thought your stalker was back, didn't you?"

"It's—Nick, I'm fine. I just let my panic get out of control."

Or you lost control. But Nick didn't say that as Shay turned away.

As he walked beside her back to the birthday party, which was still going full swing, his gut roiled at his powerlessness to help her. Beautiful Shay Parker had gone above and beyond for him, for his mom, for Maggie and for the community of Hope. But inside she suffered terribly. She'd tried to hide her fear from him but he'd seen it in those beautiful eyes, and it stabbed him with a fierce anger every single time.

Why? he demanded of God. *Why does Shay have to go through this?*

Nick hated the image of Shay cowering on her car,

hunched over, afraid. He wanted to set her free, to see the old Shay return, laughing, copper curls tossed back, wide open to everything life sent her way.

Can't You help me, God? She's such a special woman, a very special friend.

Like an echo, a question came into his mind.

Friend? Is friendship all you want from Shay?

"I don't know how to thank you, dear." Mrs. Green enfolded Shay in a tight hug. "Today was simply fantastic."

"I'm glad." Shay basked in the love she felt emanating from Nick's mother. Mrs. Green always made her feel as if she was a favored daughter. "I was thrilled Nick allowed me to help out with your party."

She helped the weary woman ease into a lawn chair then sank into the one beside her. Brianna and Jaclyn had banished Shay from the kitchen for cleanup while their husbands disassembled the tables.

The Green girls chattered together as they picked up the refuse left from Chinese buffet Shay had provided for the family dinner. Maggie and the other kids were grouped around Nick. In the glow of the campfire, each child's eyes expanded as they leaned forward to hear every sensational detail of the story he was telling them.

The perfect ending to a perfect day, Shay mused. The growing dusk seemed to invite introspection.

"Which part of today did you enjoy the most?" she asked.

"I appreciated every moment, dear. But do you know why this particular birthday you helped me celebrate is such a blessing?"

"No." Shay frowned. Nick hadn't said a word.

Mrs. Green smiled. "Years ago my husband left us on my birthday," she murmured. "I was devastated."

"Of course you were." Shay clasped her gnarled hand, smoothing the knotted knuckles with her fingers. Mrs. Green hadn't given a sign that she had bad memories or was less than blissfully happy today. "I can't imagine how upsetting it must be to face that every year on your special day. All this time—how did you manage?"

"I didn't at first." Nick's mom chuckled. "I was bitter toward my husband, angry at God and so afraid."

"Afraid?" Shay blinked in surprise.

"Terrified, actually." The small woman peered into the dusk. "I felt so alone and felt I had no control over anything. I prayed as hard as I have ever prayed."

"Did that help?" Shay backtracked. "I'm sorry. That's too personal a question. I guess I identify with you—I've prayed often for help, but sometimes it seems like God isn't listening."

"He is, my dear." Mrs. Green's fingers tightened around hers. Perfect assurance filled her voice. "He hears every word you say. And yes, it did help me."

At that moment, Shay lifted her head and found Nick's gaze on her. He lifted one brow as if to ask if everything was okay. Shay nodded. He studied her for several moments before he went back to his storytelling.

"So, if God hears me, why doesn't He answer?" Shay asked the older woman.

"My dear girl, what makes you think He hasn't?"

Confused, Shay frowned.

"We must have a firm grip of knowledge about the love of God to fight our fears."

"I don't understand," Shay admitted, unsure where this was going.

"After I stopped ranting at God for allowing my husband to abandon me and our family, after I got past telling Him how He should fix my world, after my heart was completely empty and I couldn't fight any-more," Mrs. Green said as her eyes, so like her son's, met Shay's. "After I got past all of that, a wonderful thing happened. I began to listen."

Listen to what? Shay waited, needing to understand how this brave woman had conquered her fear and her anger.

"Perhaps I should say I began to hear." Mrs. Green smiled. "I remember the moment so clearly. I read a verse in Romans that said because of our faith Jesus brought us into this place of highest privilege where we now stand." Her laughter bubbled up into a chuckle. "You may believe me, my dear Shay, when I tell you I didn't think I was in any place of privilege, trying to feed and clothe five hungry kids on my own."

Shay smiled at her self-mocking tone, but she couldn't wait for the older woman to continue. Maybe here, at last, she'd find the solution to her panic.

"The next part of that verse says, 'We confidently and joyfully look forward to becoming all that God has in mind for us to be.' I was curious about that," Mrs. Green continued. "What could God have in mind for me, a single mom who didn't know where her next dollar was coming from? Was I going to be rescued, like Cinderella?"

Shay chuckled.

"I know." Mrs. Green shook her silvery head. "Me as Cinderella? Hardly. The next part says, 'We can rejoice when we run into problems and trials, for we know that they are good for us—they help us learn to be patient.'"

Shay nodded, familiar with the verse.

"I really, really *did not* want to learn patience just then, but what choice did I have? I repeated those words to myself day after day until I had them memorized."

Was there a way that Shay could put them into practice for herself? What would her life be like without the fear?

"'And patience...helps us trust God more each time we use it until finally our hope and faith are strong and steady.'" Mrs. Green beamed, her brown eyes shining with a joy that flowed from deep inside. "Isn't that wonderful? God so loves us that He teaches us to trust Him."

"But—" Shay started to argue.

"I realized that God always gave us enough. My children ate, they slept safely in their own home, they finished school." She touched Shay's shoulder, her fingers gentle. "I learned the truth of that passage. 'We are able to hold our heads high no matter what happens, and we know that all is well, for we know how dearly God loves us.'"

But God's love hadn't ended her panic attacks. Frustration nipped at Shay.

"You see, Shay, our part is to trust in Him and move on in our faith." Mrs. Green touched her cheek with a swollen knuckle. "The Bible promises, 'His peace will guard your hearts and minds as you live in Christ Jesus.'"

Silence stretched between them. Shay replayed the words mentally. *His peace will guard your heart and mind.* Peace from her fears sounded so wonderful.

"Jaclyn gave me a verse about God not giving us fear but power. I've been reciting it over and over—"

"Honey, it's not the repeating so much as it is letting His words sink into your heart so that you believe them." The older woman searched her gaze. "Nick told me about the stalker, Shay. I hope you don't mind?"

"I don't mind. The thing is," Shay murmured, "I'm not sure if God abandoned me or if I've abandoned Him since then. I've tried to make it better, only it seems like God is doing nothing to help me. I feel like I don't matter to Him."

"You *do* matter, Shay. You are His beloved child and He cares for you." Mrs. Green leaned toward her and pinned her with that intense gaze. "I know you were terrorized. That opened the door to fear. I know exactly how it creeps up. I've felt its tentacles sink into me."

"So what do I do?"

"You have to listen to another voice." Mrs. Green leaned closer, her face somber. "Listen to the whisper that says, 'I am God. I am here and I am in control. I know the things I have planned for you, to prosper you and not to harm you.' That voice is stronger than anything you'll ever face. It can help you overcome your fear, if you'll only listen to it."

"Story time is over." Nick stood before them.

Shay hadn't even noticed him leave the fire. She looked around. Their marshmallows roasted, weary, drooping children looked ready to climb into their beds without complaint.

"I'm coming, son." Mrs. Green rose then bent to

cup Shay's cheek in her palm. "Any time you want to talk, let me know."

She held out her arms and Shay went into them. She could at last see a flicker of light at the end of the tunnel. She wasn't sure how it all worked. Not yet. But she knew she wanted the peace Mrs. Green had. She wanted to overcome defeat, to refuse to let the fear control her world any longer.

"Thank you," she whispered in the woman's ear. "Thank you so much."

"Grandma, what are you and Shay whispering about?" Maggie moved her Tiger machine with the big bicycle wheels alongside her grandmother, yawning mightily as she did.

"I was just telling Shay about God and how much He loves us," her grandmother explained.

"But Shay's big," Maggie said with a frown. "Doesn't she already know that? I'm five and I know God loves me."

"How do you know, Maggie?" Shay asked.

Maggie leaned her head to one side to think about it. "Like how I asked Him to please help me come to Grandma's party." She shrugged. "I'm here, so that's how I know God loves me."

"Thank you for explaining that to me." Shay smiled at Nick over Maggie's head as she hugged the sweet child.

"Time to get you home, darling." Her grandmother shared a look with Maggie. Their faces glowed with the knowledge that they were loved.

That, Shay realized, was what she longed for most of all. To be loved.

The Green family took their leave, each one hugging Shay and thanking her, until only Nick remained. He walked with her to the house and switched off the lights they'd strung.

"Are you sure there's nothing more that needs doing?" he asked.

"No. It's all finished. Everything is back to normal," Shay said with a smile.

"Everything?" He tilted his head to one side, brushing a strand of hair from her eyes.

She bit her lip and forced herself not to ease away from Nick. "I know I lost it there in the garage. Thank you for coming to my rescue. Again."

"Listen. I've been thinking." He shuffled his feet in the gravel then lifted his head, his dark eyes hidden in the shadows. "This fear—it's tearing you apart. I thought maybe I could help. There's supposed to be a meteor shower in a couple of weeks—in the desert," he emphasized.

Dread of being alone in the desert's vast expanse surged. Shay opened her mouth to say no. Then she remembered Mrs. Green's words.

Face it. Trust God. Overcome.

"I promise you'll be safe, Shay. I'll—"

She reached up and with the briefest touch, laid a fingertip against his lips to stem his words. "I want to go," she said quietly.

Nick looked stunned by her acceptance. Or maybe it was that she'd touched him. When he finally snapped back to awareness, his dark eyes grew intense, his face earnest.

"Then we'll go. Together. I'll be right there, Shay."

"Thank you." Doubts about her decision swarmed. *What if, what if, what if...*

"I guess I'd better get going."

"Okay." She pressed her hands behind her, wishing he didn't have to leave, wishing he could stay and talk, help her chase away the panic that always came at night.

Wishing she could just be with him.

"Thank you for giving my mother this wonderful day, Shay." His gaze held hers. "We couldn't have done it without you."

"That's what friends are for." The way Nick stared at her made Shay's knees liquefy. Did he want to stay as much as she wanted him to?

"You went a long way past friendship today. So thank you."

Then Nick Green leaned forward and pressed a kiss against her cheek.

A moment later he was gone and Shay was left standing in her yard, staring after him. She lifted one hand and touched the spot of tingling skin where his lips had landed for one brief second.

Now why had he gone and done that? she wondered as her heart skipped a few beats before it began to soar.

And if he was going to kiss me, why did it have to be on the cheek?

Shocked by the yearning that surged through her to be held in Nick's strong arms, Shay rushed into the house.

How come the prospect of such a thing filled her with joy and not fear?

Chapter Nine

"So Nick kissed you?" Brianna put her elbows on her desk and tucked her chin into her cupped palms. The gleam of interest in her eyes couldn't be disguised by the scholarly glasses she always wore for their sessions.

"Yes, he kissed me. On the cheek." Shay closed her eyes, still able to feel his lips. In fact, little else had been on her mind ever since it happened. Her brain kept replaying the scene over and over and her skin still tingled at the memory. That's why she'd made an appointment to talk to Brianna. Because she was so confused.

"And? What happened when Nick kissed you?"

"Nothing." Shay blinked at the realization.

"You didn't panic? You didn't freeze?" Brianna smiled at her surprise. "You trusted Nick enough to let him get that close."

"Or I was too stunned to react," Shay mumbled. Nothing seemed straightforward since Nick's kiss.

"You've never been that stunned before." Brianna smiled as she tented her fingers. "You've always managed to react before anyone else could get too close, including Eric."

"Nick surprised me, that's all. Don't you think?" Shay frowned.

"Is that what you want to believe?" Brianna asked.

"I don't know. Everything seems so mixed up." Shay rubbed her shoulder. "I can't make sense of myself."

"Because things are changing," Brianna suggested.

"Changing?" Shay couldn't make sense of what her friend meant. Or maybe she didn't want to? "You know, maybe this fear thing—maybe it's a personal flaw, something that can't be fixed."

"Why would you think that?"

"Because I look around and everyone else is happy. So I start to think, 'I can be happy, too. Today I'm not going to be afraid.'" Shay sighed as she slouched in her chair. "And then some stupid little thing happens and all I can think is—Dom's back."

"I wonder if that *is* what you think." Brianna fixed Shay with a serious stare.

"Huh?"

"Hear me out. I wonder if somewhere deep inside, when you're uncomfortable, your mind protests with fear because your subconscious is trying to protect you, to prevent a repeat of the out-of-control situation with the stalker."

"You think?" Shay rubbed her arms, desperate to get rid of the chills she was feeling.

"Tell me when you're most comfortable, Shay."

"When I'm at home, working on a project."

"Really? You're not getting up every five seconds to see if someone's out there?" She nodded at the look of surprise on Shay's face. "I thought so. Try again. When are you the *most* comfortable?" she prodded.

A second passed before Shay found the answer.

"Working with the kids."

"You're not afraid then?" her friend asked.

"Of course not." Shay blinked. "Why would I be? They're smaller than me—usually."

"I doubt that's the only reason." Brianna raised an eyebrow. "Can I tell you why I think you're totally comfortable with yourself when you're with the kids?"

"You're the shrink." Shay wondered if she was going to like hearing this.

"Technically, I'm a psychologist, but moving on." Brianna leaned forward. "You're completely relaxed when you're with kids because your focus is off you. You're thinking about how you can help them."

"Okay. So?" Shay didn't get it.

"Your panic stems from when you start thinking about what might happen. You're letting 'might' dictate how you live your life, Shay."

"I'm not that bad." Shay bristled at the intimation. "I have a...normal life."

"Really?" A tiny smile played at the corner of Brianna's lips. "You're a young, beautiful woman. You broke up with Eric, what, eight, ten months ago? Have you had a date since then?"

"No, but Eric was a doctor. He understood my situation."

"And yet, he broke up with you." Brianna's implacable expression told Shay she had to face facts.

"Right. But—" Shay bit her lip. "It doesn't matter anyway because I don't think God wants me to be in a romantic relationship."

"God doesn't? Or you don't, because you don't want to get hurt again?" Brianna stood, moved around her desk and sank down next to Shay. "Tell me—what would happiness look like to you?"

"Living on my farm with a family," Shay replied with a promptness that surprised her. "Helping kids during the day, sharing life with someone."

"A family." Brianna paused to let that sink in. "In that world you're safe because you've got everything under control. Only you don't, do you? Because life isn't like that. It's messy and things happen when you least expect them. Like Nick kissing you." She smiled. "You can't preprogram your life because you're afraid, darlin'. And you have to stop expecting you can revert back to the woman you were before the stalker."

"Then what do I do?" Shay demanded, frustrated.

"Stop trying to keep yourself safe." Brianna shook her head when Shay tried to interrupt. "Face your fears, sweetie. It's time."

"You're saying I should go with Nick and watch the meteor shower?" Heat scorched her cheeks at the thought of it. "What if he…kisses me again?"

"Would that be so terrible?" Brianna asked.

"What if he kisses me and I end up in the middle of the desert, cowering under a cactus? What then?"

"Who better than your responsible best friend, Nick Green, to make sure you get home safely?" Brianna asked. "*Let go*, Shay. Trust Nick. He might surprise you. You might surprise yourself." She wrapped an arm around her shoulder. "Just remember, you're not alone. And you're certainly not helpless."

"What do you mean?"

"You have God on your side." Brianna grinned. "If God be for us…" she said, reciting the mantra she, Jaclyn and Shay had often used back in high school.

"...who can be against us?" Shay finished.

Who indeed?

Nick sat in Shay's yard, reliving the memory of the kiss he'd planted on her after his mom's party. Two weeks later and the joy he'd felt that night wasn't any easier to suppress. But it seemed as if he was alone in that reaction because when Shay started showing up several evenings a week for Bible study with his mom, she pretended nothing had changed between them.

Maybe for her, nothing *had* changed.

But for Nick, things were definitely different. First of all, he couldn't stop wondering what might have happened if Shay had turned her head and let him kiss her lips. He was pretty sure there would have been fireworks.

What was new was that Nick had finally accepted that he wanted more than that little peck on the cheek from Shay—and knew he couldn't have it. God's plans included him leaving Hope, so despite his over-the-top reaction, there was no way he and Shay could be anything more than friends.

And he wanted to be her friend. But he also wanted more...

Nick forced himself off that subject to think about whether he'd included everything they'd need for this evening in the desert, and then spent a few minutes praying for guidance. He was no longer certain this trip was the right thing for Shay. After all, what did he really know about anxiety attacks? How could he possibly understand what she was going through?

And yet, in a way, he did know. Nick got that same throat-clenching worry every time he thought about that job in Seattle. What if his family needed him and he wasn't there for them? His stomach dipped when he imagined Maggie and his mom on their own, maybe needing his help but too proud or too embarrassed to let him know.

Every day Nick watched the two of them and knew the situation couldn't last forever. Though she loved her granddaughter dearly, his mom was overtaxing herself. Maggie was a little kid. She wanted to run and jump and yell, as all kids did. Even with him here to help, his mom tired easily. She needed time for herself. When Maggie went to school, that would help. But...

The what-ifs tortured him.

And what about Shay? Who would be here to help her? Who else knew exactly how deeply the stalker had affected her life?

Nick had no answers to any of those questions.

"Hi." Shay's quiet voice jerked Nick out of his introspection.

"Hi, yourself."

"Any particular reason you've been sitting out here for the past ten minutes?" She waited, her head tipped to one side in a quizzical look.

"Not really." He climbed out of the truck. "Shay, I'm not sure about this—"

"I am, Nick." She lifted her shoulders and looked him straight in the eye. "Your mom told me how her faith changed after your dad left. As we've studied together, she's shown me how childish I've been about my panic. Even Maggie's faith is bigger than mine." Her wide, generous mouth tipped down at the corners as if she was fighting back tears. A moment later Shay was back in control. "But that is going to change. Starting tonight."

"Oh?" Nick couldn't imagine what his mother had said to ignite the light of battle in Shay, but he was glad to see it. The very thought of brave, strong Shay huddled up on her car hood pierced an arrow right through his heart every time.

"I've been letting my fear cast out God's love. No more. I'm trusting God now."

"Good." He smiled at the flash of fire in those emerald eyes.

She threw her jacket over one shoulder and arched an eyebrow at him. "You have my permission to remind me of those words. Now, are you ready to go?"

"Sure." Nick grabbed his knapsack from the truck and slipped the straps over his shoulders. "Let's go see what movie God's playing on the big screen tonight." He slung two folding chairs over his shoulder then held out his hand.

Shay hesitated just long enough that he started to drop his hand. Then she stretched out her arm and threaded her fingers into his. Her laugh had a wobble in it, but her grin was all Shay-of-the-old-days.

"I'm thinking it's going to be a double feature," she joked.

"I even brought popcorn." His pulse skipped at the touch of her soft skin against his palm.

She's a friend. That's all. Remember?

They weren't far into their walk when Shay withdrew her hand, ostensibly to brush a strand of hair from her face. Nick was pretty sure she'd done it to put distance between them. But that was okay—she'd managed to keep hold of his hand for a few minutes. It was a start.

Part of him mourned that he wouldn't be around to see her triumph, but he was going to make every moment he did have with her count.

"Nick?" Shay touched his arm to stop him.

"Yeah?" He glanced around, searching for something that might have startled her. He saw nothing.

Shay said in a perfectly normal tone of voice, "I've been trying to figure out how you made those bicycle wheels on Maggie's Tiger work."

"Top secret," he said, crossing his fingers and placing them against his heart as if he'd made some kind of promise.

"You know I hate secrets. Tell me." Shay gave him a fake glare.

"Uh-uh." The urge to tease grew. "If I told you, I'd have to—"

Kiss you? Stunned by how much he wanted to, Nick gulped and struggled to regroup.

"You'd have to what, Nick?" she prodded, waiting for him to finish.

Now was so not the time. But later he was going to have a strict talk with himself about a certain lady named Shay. Nick grabbed her hand and tugged.

"We have to talk as we walk or we'll miss the show."

She drew her hand out of his after only a few steps and rapped his shoulder in reproof.

"Seriously, how'd you figure it out?" she demanded as she returned her fingers to the cradle of his.

Nick looked at her and his stomach knot tightened. That had been happening a lot lately—like whenever he was around Shay. When Shay was near, Nick saw pure possibilities. Which was stupid, because there was no future possibility for them, he reminded himself.

"I stopped by the seniors' hall to pick up something for Mom," he explained. "They were working on an old Model T, so I pitched in." He drew her near as they sidestepped some low-hanging mesquite trees. "While we were working, one of the guys mentioned he was struggling to adapt his current project. I fiddled with it and figured it out, and it gave me the idea for Maggie's wheels."

"Well, that was good." Shay inhaled deeply.

Nick noticed her eyes dart from side to side for a moment. He kept talking, hoping to distract her.

"Maybe not. I got talked into meeting with them after their coffee hour on Saturday mornings." Nick rolled his eyes. "They think I'm some kind of super-repairman. They're going to bring stuff from home so I can show them how to fix it."

"How can that be bad?" Shay's forehead creased in a frown.

"Shay, I tear stuff apart. I don't put it back together."

"So now you will." She laughed at the face he made.

"Unlikely. But they won't take no for an answer, so I'll do my best to help."

"Like you helped Mrs. Campbell get her thirty-year-old dishwasher working?" she asked, her lips curling in a coy smile.

"Exactly. Look how that turned out. I nearly flooded her house in the process." He stepped around a teddy bear cactus. "I was trying to do her a favor, to thank her for giving us that old bicycle."

"A favor, huh?" Shay nodded, her face solemn. "The same kind of favor you did Susan Swan and her sink?

And of course, you couldn't walk away without fixing some kind of weight machine so Susan's husband could exercise his arm, could you?" she said, tongue in cheek.

"Don't make me out to be some kind of hero, Shay. I just like to tinker." Nick grabbed her arm when she misstepped on a rocky area. "Careful. Stick close."

"As close as a tick." Her fingers tightened around his. He couldn't deny how he loved the feel of her hand in his. It was almost more than he could stand. "I could continue to list things you've done around town to help people, Nick," she went on. "Seems like everyone has a story about you." She chewed on her bottom lip for a moment before she blurted out, "I think you should advertise. You could start up a business."

"A business?" Nick frowned at her.

"Don't look at me like that. It's a good idea."

"Doing what? I don't have any training or certification. Who would pay me to tinker with their stuff?" He appreciated the thought, but it had taken him four hours to figure out he needed a two-dollar seal to get that wreck of a dishwasher working. No one would pay him by the hour to learn on the job, and Nick needed the assurance of a steady income.

They walked a little farther in silence, each lost in their thoughts. Then Shay's small hand started to squeeze his.

"How much farther?" she whispered. He knew she was fighting back her panic at the blackness surrounding them.

"Just up that rise." Nick pointed and heard her breath catch as she recognized where they were. She inhaled in short gasps as they climbed the steep hill.

"This is where Dad taught me about astronomy."

Her voice wasn't exactly calm—more like determined. But it wasn't full of panic, and that made Nick happier than he could have imagined. "I used to love coming up here."

"I remember. Look."

Ahead of them stars twinkled and glittered like diamonds tossed onto black velvet. Nick kept his grip on Shay's hand, just to make sure that she was okay, that she knew he was there if she needed him.

At least, that's what he told himself.

In truth, standing here with her, sharing this moment, made his own breathing uneven. Beautiful Shay, so near he wanted to draw her into the protection of his arms and kiss her. But that would betray her trust.

Nothing more than friendship, he reminded himself.

Beside him, Shay gasped. "Our heavenly star show is starting. See that?" She pointed upward, tracking a meteor as it flew across the sky. "And that?"

"I see it." Nick fell silent, awestruck by the glorious shower of lights.

"It's like God is lighting them especially for us." Shay's eyes blazed with excitement. "Look how they sparkle and blaze and then fizzle away, their tails glowing. Beautiful."

Shay's words chided him, reminding him that his faith wasn't as strong as it should be. It wasn't only Shay who needed to stop trying to be in control.

Her breath tickled his neck when she turned her head. "Fearfully and wonderfully made," she whispered.

Yes, she was. But he had a hunch Shay wasn't talking about herself. "I've heard that before somewhere," Nick said.

"It's a verse your mom quoted." Shay turned her head to smile at him. "The Bible says we are fearfully and wonderfully made by God. Everything in the universe has a purpose, a reason, a private beauty."

Moonbeams cast Shay's hair in a golden sheen. Nick's gaze tangled with hers, and for a moment neither of them said anything. Just as Nick was wondering how to fight off the urge to kiss her again, a noise startled Shay. Her green eyes widened as she asked in a shaky tone, "What was that?"

"I've got you, Shay." Nick slid an arm around her waist and hugged her against his side. "Nothing bad is going to happen. And God's on duty, too. Relax and enjoy His show."

It took a few moments before she relaxed enough to lean against him. When she turned her head to study him, a tiny smile pulled up the corners of her lush lips.

"You're my very best friend, Nick." She tilted her head to rest it on his shoulder for a brief moment before she stepped away and hugged her waist. "Thank you."

"For what?" he asked. He had a hunch Shay was about to say something important, something she didn't tell just anyone.

"For being you. For not caring that I'm scared all the time. A coward." She didn't look at him as she continued speaking, her voice dropping to a near-whisper. "I think it's only here, tonight, with you, that I realize how great a gift you are. Eric claimed to love me, but he was never as patient with my fears as you have been."

"Eric?" Nick went cold inside at that name. His stomach tightened and his heart skipped a beat. It took a moment to define what he was feeling. Jealous—he was jealous of Shay's former boyfriend.

"We were a couple." Her husky laugh made a mockery of mirth. She seemed oblivious to the burst of emotions exploding inside him. "He said he loved me. I thought I loved him, too. But whenever he touched me, I'd freeze up."

"He didn't force—" Nick couldn't say it.

"Oh, no. Eric was kindness itself. He tried hard to understand what I was going through. For months he tried. But he wanted a wife. He needed someone who could respond to his love."

The shame in those words lit an angry fire inside Nick. "You couldn't have been that bad."

"I was." In the flare of a meteor, her green eyes looked wounded by the admission. "We would be having fun and then he'd put his arm around my shoulder or hug me and it was like being choked. I couldn't breathe. But I couldn't tell him what was wrong, either."

Nick didn't give a fig about Eric but he hated that Shay looked so decimated, that she felt she was to blame for the breakdown of the relationship.

"I'm sorry," he murmured, feeling utterly helpless.

"Your mom says I didn't trust Eric." She stopped abruptly and tilted her head to one side. "She's right. I find it hard to trust anyone after…"

"The stalker." Everything always came back to that. "But why? That guy was never someone you trusted. Was he?"

"I didn't even know him!" Shay turned and stared at him. "Why did you ask that?"

"I guess because you blame your lack of trust on the stalker."

"And?" Those world-famous lips pressed into a straight line.

Nick had never been good with words or emotions. But he was going to say this because he'd thought about Shay's problems a lot and he figured maybe he was on to something. "Everything started after your dad died, right?"

Shay nodded but said nothing. As she listened, her focus returned to the dance of meteors above them.

"Well." Nick watched the flash and dazzle of the light show as he spoke from his heart. "I wonder if you felt abandoned by his loss and that made you more... susceptible."

"You're saying it's all a trick I'm deliberately playing on myself?" Anger threaded through Shay's voice and she turned on him. "You think I get myself up in the middle of the night to check outside because I'm nuts?"

"That isn't what I'm saying." Nick unfolded one of the chairs and held it for her. "Sit down and let's talk about this. We're alone here. You can say whatever you want. Nothing you tell me will shock me."

She thought about it for a while.

"You said you were going to face your fear," he reminded.

"I did, didn't I?" Shay flopped into the chair, slouched and thrust her long legs out in front of her. "But if I'm crazy, so are you."

"I'm willing to explore the possibility," he said as he unfolded his own chair and sat down beside her. "Exactly why am I crazy?"

"Because your family—the most precious thing in the world—is right here in Hope, and you're bound and determined to leave them and go off someplace where you won't be able to see them." She crossed her arms as if daring him to deny it, her gaze on the sky. "That's about the craziest thing ever."

"I have to work," Nick told her flatly.

"Why can't you work here?" She turned her head, her hair swishing around her face. "There are lots of things you could do, lots of people you could help in Hope."

"I have to earn a living, Shay." Nick ignored her irritated glance. "I can't do that in Hope."

She'd turned the tables, focusing the conversation on him. But before he could explain again why he needed to go back to Seattle, Shay's eyes filled with unshed tears.

"Lately it seems everyone's telling me I have trust issues. You just did, too," she reminded, her voice tight. "But everyone has them."

"Of course they do. Trust is one of the hardest things to give."

"That's why you're determined to leave here," she said so quietly he almost didn't hear. "You don't trust God."

Nick was stunned by her comment. Suddenly one meteor blazed brighter than all the rest and set off the desert in stark relief before it winked out, plunging them into darkness again.

"All that caring you have inside you will fizzle out, just like the meteorites, because you don't trust God or me or your mom," Shay continued. "You don't even trust Maggie."

Nick opened his mouth to reply, but he couldn't tell her that for years he'd trusted God to bring his dad back, or about how he'd been bitterly disappointed. He couldn't tell her why it was so hard to keep trusting.

"I think you're the most admirable man I've ever known, next to my dad. You care for everyone. You've done your best to do that from the day your dad left." Shay's green eyes met his. "But Nick, you can't make up for what your dad did."

"Yes, Shay, I can. And I am."

But Shay shook her head. "You can't because it isn't your mistake to make up for." She touched his arm, her sweet face intent. "Your mother loves you, Nick, and she loves everything you do for her and the rest of the family. But you can't erase the hurt your father caused her. You shouldn't even try."

"I have to," he said, his jaw clenched. "She's a wonderful person. It's not fair that she should—"

"When did we get a promise of fairness in this life?" Shay's smile eased the sting of her words. "I know I have problems, Nick. But don't spend all your time trying to help me. Help yourself, too."

"I don't know what you mean." He couldn't look at her.

"I mean that you don't have to prove that you're not your dad. I doubt there's a single soul in town who thinks you'd abandon those who count on you." Shay cupped his cheek in her palm. "The only one who doesn't seem to believe in you is you."

She was right, and he knew it.

"The job in Seattle—you don't really want to take it, do you, Nick?" The intensity of Shay's gaze and the wistfulness of her words prevented him from lying.

"No." A wave of relief washed over him as he finally admitted the truth. "It's not the work," he assured her as another blaze exploded above them. "I could enjoy helping the guys reach their potential. It's just that with Georgia gone—" Why did it still hurt so much?

"You're worried about your mom and Maggie," she finished, her fingers squeezing his.

"My mother puts up a good front, but being responsible for Maggie is wearing her out."

"So stay here in Hope."

"Shay, we've been through this." Frustrated, Nick raked his hand through his hair. "How can I stay in Hope and still support my family?"

"I don't know, Nick. I don't have all the answers. But I know who does. Why don't you try asking Him what His will for you is?"

A wry smile lifted his lips. How could he tell her he didn't have enough faith to do that? How could he admit that he'd been so deeply disappointed by the loss of his career, so shattered by Georgia's death, so angry God hadn't answered his prayer about his father that he now was afraid of God, afraid He'd dole out another sucker punch and that it would completely destroy the threadbare remnants of faith Nick now clung to? Nick was so scared of what God would do that he was afraid to even consider that the growing feelings he had for Shay could ever be realized.

"You're just like me, Nick." Shay's whisper was all the more emphatic in the silence of the evening. "Neither of us trusts God enough. And we must. It's time you and I began trusting God with our futures."

As they sat silently together in the darkness of the desert, watching heaven unfold its mysteries, lost in their own thoughts, Nick glanced at Shay. Her attention was riveted on the flashing spectacle above. Her lips moved in what he thought was a prayer.

Nick claimed he was a Christian. He professed to believe in God's love. Maybe Shay was right. Maybe it was time to prove it.

Moments, maybe hours later—he wasn't sure how much time had passed—the last flash blinked into nothingness and the world finally returned to normal. Shay rose. Her face glowed with radiance only a transformational inner experience could have given.

She said nothing as they walked back to her house, and Nick was content with that. But he was surprised when she wrapped her fingers around his as he walked her to her front porch.

"Would you like to come inside?" she murmured.

That surprised him even more. Shay looked and sounded different. Not exactly serene, but not filled with the panic he'd glimpsed earlier. Clearly the meteor shower and their talk had affected her. He wanted desperately to go inside, to talk some more, to be near her.

To stay.

But what he wanted wasn't possible.

"It's late. I'd better get home."

"Okay." Her lovely smile flashed white in the gloom as she stared at him. "I want to thank you for such a wonderful evening, Nick. Now, whenever I go into the desert, I'm going to think of this meteor shower and remember that God's love is like a cloak of meteors showering down all around me, protecting me."

He debated about the best way to say what was on his mind but in the end decided it would be wrong to keep this from her any longer. Besides, something about the change in her tonight made him believe that she could deal with what he had to say, and he so wanted her to be able to get rid of the past.

"Shay?"

"Yes?" Her innocent green eyes held his.

"I've been in contact with the New York Police Department."

"Wha—why?" she stammered. He could almost feel her anxiety building like static in the air around them.

"I wanted to know if they'd ever caught your stalker." He waited but she said nothing. "They haven't." Her reaction, the way she seemed to freeze up, told him he should have waited. But he couldn't stop now. Nick struggled to find the best way to say it, but there was no way to put a good spin on this. "For over a year they've been chasing a guy who's stalking other women."

"I'm sorry." Her face froze into an ivory mask.

"The thing is, Shay, he has almost the same M.O. as your stalker. If it is the same guy, he's become much more adept at hiding his identity. His victims are terrified."

Her posture grew increasingly rigid until finally she burst out, "What do you want from me, Nick?"

"I was hoping you'd agree to talk to the police, review your experience to see if there are any clues that could stop this creep and save other women the harm you've suffered." His heart ached for the rush of emotions that cracked her mask of calm.

Shay seemed frozen to the spot. Though not a muscle moved, he knew her panic battled for control. Then she lifted her head and looked straight at him. Her lips lifted in a mirthless smile.

"So it's time to put my money where my mouth is," she said. "Time to prove that I will trust God."

"Shay, I didn't mean—" One look from those green eyes silenced him.

Her shoulders went back, her spine straightened and her chin thrust out.

"Okay," she said. "I'll talk to the police in the morning." She seemed somehow frailer, somehow diminished, but her tone was resolute. "I will not be a coward anymore."

"You could never be a coward."

Nick couldn't help himself—he drew her into his arms, pressed her head to his shoulder and breathed in the soft lemon scent of her hair. "You're the strongest, most amazing, most caring and most compassionate woman I know." He cupped her face in his palms and drew back to look into her eyes. "I'll be with you, Shay. I'll be right by your side. We'll do it together."

"Together." A spark of gold flared in her green eyes. "Can you arrange a conference call for eight a.m. tomorrow?"

He nodded.

"Okay then." She exhaled then eased away. "You really know how to show a girl a good time, Nick."

The right words wouldn't come to him, the words he needed to tell her how much he admired her, how she was the most special woman he'd ever met. So Nick did the only thing he could think of. He drew her close and kissed her on the lips, pouring the kaleidoscope of his feelings into that embrace.

When he released her, Shay's glazed look made him want to do it again. But he couldn't.

Nick said good-night and strode to his truck.

Shay said his mom had taught her about trusting God. Maybe it was time he sought some parental advice for himself. Nick knew nothing would change between him and Shay—no matter how much he wanted things to be different, he was still responsible for his family.

But maybe he could do something about the gulf between him and God.

Chapter Ten

"So you've got *another* machine? How many is that now?"

"I don't know." Maggie frowned as she pushed her foot against Shay's hand. "There's my roly-poly, my Tiger and the giggle machine."

"The giggle machine? What is that?" Shay glanced at Nick standing nearby in the physical therapy room and blushed, remembering his kiss after the meteor show. It had been two weeks and she still couldn't stop thinking about that kiss, or the way he'd held her hand through every conference call they'd had with the NYPD.

"Uncle Nick calls it a giggle machine because it makes me laugh when I use it." Maggie puffed with exertion.

"Think of a weird version of a treadmill," Nick said to Shay. His brown eyes twinkled when she lifted one eyebrow. "Really weird."

"It is weird," Maggie agreed, brown eyes widening. "Because sometimes when I walk on it, nothing happens. And then all of a sudden, something does. Once a balloon blew up right in front of me!"

Shay smiled as she urged Maggie to push a little harder.

"If you came to Grandma's, I could show you," Maggie hinted.

Shay had deliberately stayed away from the Green home because of Nick. Or, more accurately, because of his kiss. It set odd feelings alight inside her, and that made her nervous. She was coming to rely on him too much. So she'd buried herself in helping Jaclyn with restorations on their old church. And slowly, solace began to replace fear as Scripture seeped into her heart.

The hours of discussion with the police tested Shay's baby steps of faith, leaving her feeling wobbly, her fragile sense of security shaken. Reliving the terror of those days when she'd been so vulnerable to her stalker had challenged her determination to trust God. Some days it felt as if she was hanging on by a mere thread, but Shay *did* hang on, refusing to give in to the fear.

Nick, with his unswerving comfort and support, had now become such an integral part of her world that Shay wasn't sure how she would fare when he left. But she was only too aware that her time with him was running out. And then she'd be alone.

Again.

But that's the way it had to be because she couldn't love or be loved…until she'd defeated the panic for good.

I can do all things through Christ who strengthens me. I can do all things through Christ who strengthens me…

"Shay?" Maggie touched her arm. "When will you come to see my giggle machine?"

"I'll stop by as soon as I can," Shay promised before leading Maggie through the rest of her exercises. "You're doing much better," she said, surprised by the child's progress in the past week. "Uncle Nick's machines are really helping you, huh?"

"Or maybe it's her excellent therapist," Nick chimed in from the end of the bars.

"Well, naturally that's a given," she joked. "But if you polled the folks in Hope, I'm guessing Nick Green would be the one they'd nominate as most valuable citizen." She tossed him a grin. "There doesn't seem to be anyone who doesn't think you deserve the town's top award, maybe even a crown."

"It's a distinct possibility Heddy Grange might crown me with something, but I doubt it would be gold or jewels," Nick said in a droll tone. "I didn't exactly fix that fountain of hers. In fact, she said I broke it."

Shay looked at Maggie. They tried to keep straight faces but a second later they burst into laughter.

"When she plugged it in," Maggie spluttered, "the water came out of the swan's mouth and hit Uncle Nick in the face!"

"Go ahead and laugh," Nick said, his pique evident in the spots of bright red dotting his cheekbones. "I told you, Shay, I am not a handyman. But I could easily come up with a list of things I'd like to do with that swan." His gorgeous eyes glinted. "And most of them involve a hammer."

His malevolent glare only made Shay laugh harder. She caught Maggie's eye and winked.

"At least your debacle didn't make it into the paper,"

she said. "Heddy loves to get her name on the front page, you know."

The words had no sooner left her lips than an idea dawned. "Maggie, what would you think about showing off what you and the others have achieved these past months? You can invite your grandma and anyone else you'd like. Uncle Nick can come, too."

"Like a demonstration?" Maggie breathed with shining eyes. "Ted, too?"

"Yep, for all of my kids. Saturday afternoon. I want you to bring your giggle machine and your Tiger machine, Maggie. Nick, you bring that new gizmo you've been working on for the seniors' fitness class you started."

Shay thought if she could show Nick the difference he and his machines had made in people's lives, if he realized that he was needed here—maybe then he'd reconsider staying. Shay wanted Nick to be happy. Wouldn't he be happier in Hope, with his mother and Maggie, than in Seattle?

Of course she wanted Nick to stay for her, too. Shay wanted him to stay because she was sure he was as affected by that kiss as she was, because she wanted to spend more time with him, because...

Wait! This is about Nick's happiness. Not my...feelings.

Shay made a mental note to phone the newspaper to suggest a human-interest story. The whole town was talking about Nick—surely it wouldn't be hard to steer a reporter toward a profile of Nick's work. And once her buddy recognized the difference he made here in Hope, he'd change his mind about leaving.

"So, uh, anything else?" Nick asked.

"Oh, sorry." She helped Maggie put her braces back on. "Pretty soon you won't need these," she whispered in the child's ear.

"Really?" The brown eyes expanded. "When can I walk all by myself?"

"If you keep working hard, pretty soon." Shay's heart warmed at Maggie's whoop of joy.

"I am going to beat Ted," she said, a fierce determination filling her face.

"Don't think about that," Nick said, scooping her into his arms. His gaze rested on Shay, as if he were trying to transmit a secret message. "Forget everyone and everything. Keep your eye on the goal."

That was good advice—for Maggie and for her.

Because at this moment, the goal was to get Nick to see that he was needed here. Shay couldn't imagine life in Hope without Nick.

Actually, she couldn't imagine *life* without Nick. Period.

"So what's your role in this?" Ben Marks demanded as he snapped several shots of Shay's kids.

"Me? I'm just the fix-it guy. And a cheerleader." Nick deliberately downplayed his contribution to the local reporter because he wanted all the focus to be on Shay and the wonderful things she'd done for these children. Fierce pride filled him as he watched her instill confidence in each of her clients. "She's a miracle worker, that's for sure."

The reporter moved in for another shot and Nick headed for his seat. Maggie was onstage next and he didn't want to miss a second. As he sat down beside his mom, he heard her gasp and glanced up. What he saw made his own heart skip a beat.

Maggie stepped free of her braces and walked three steps in a halting, jerky gait.

But she *walked*.

A lump the size of Gibraltar lodged in Nick's throat. He couldn't say anything. He could only stare as his niece, triumphant, stood grinning as Shay put her braces back on.

When her last clients finished their display, Shay introduced each one again, beaming with joy and satisfaction. The kids took a final bow then hurried over to their loved ones, eager to crow about their achievements. Maggie was no different and moved quickly toward them with her Tiger machine.

"I beat Ted!" she blurted, her joy boundless.

"So that's what you and Shay have been doing the past few days." Nick hugged her tightly, thanking God for the gift of healing He'd given this precious child. "That's quite a secret you've been keeping, Maggie-mine. I'm surprised you didn't burst with it."

His mother, tears flowing down her cheeks, couldn't say anything. All she could do was wrap her granddaughter in a hug until finally Maggie squealed.

"Too tight, Grandma," Maggie protested and eased herself free. "Shay's got doughnuts and cookies with pictures on them and fruit punch!" She waved at Ted and rushed toward him.

"I give thanks every day for that woman," his mother murmured as she dabbed at her eyes. "Shay Parker is a walking, talking blessing."

Yes, she is. Nick stood in the background, as proud as any parent, watching as Shay spoke with the families of her clients. How Nick wished he could stay in Hope and watch her break free of the fear that had kept her imprisoned for so long.

How he wished he could help her finish that part of her journey.

Shay posed for pictures with her kids. When Ben would have moved on, she asked him to take some with Nick and his inventions.

"He's a big part of the reason these kids have made such astounding progress," she bragged.

"This is your moment, Shay," Nick protested to no avail.

"It's a moment that wouldn't have happened at all without you, Nick. His work is amazing," she said to the photographer. "He has a gift for seeing what the kids need and creating exactly what will help them achieve their goals."

Nick's cell phone buzzed to let him know he had a text. He took out his phone as Shay and the photographer began setting up the shot. NYPD was trying to reach Shay, who had apparently turned off her phone. So they'd called him.

Why today? Nick could hardly bear the thought of extinguishing her joy, but it probably had to do with the stalker, and if it did he would be there for Shay.

He couldn't do anything about his burgeoning feelings for her. But he *could* stick by her side and be a true friend, regardless of the fact that his heart wanted more.

Nick got through the photos and waited until the last person had left to tell her. As he worked beside Shay to restore the room to its rightful appearance, he said, "Shay?"

"Yes?" She led him out of the room then locked the door. When he didn't immediately speak, she frowned. A guarded look filled her eyes—he hated being the cause of it. "What's wrong?"

"New York texted me," he told her quietly. "Our guy has been active again. They'd like to review what you told them and see if they can find something new."

She didn't protest, didn't argue that she'd told them all she knew. Shay Parker wasn't that kind of woman. Instead she inhaled, pushed back her shoulders and nodded. But the clouds in her eyes told him she was battling hard to retain her calm. "I'll go call them now." She turned.

"Shay?" Nick waited for her to look at him. "I'll stay. If you want me to."

"Yes," she said very quietly. "I do want you—to be there."

He caught the slight hesitation, but there was no time to think about that. He followed her into her office and while she dialed, he pushed a chair next to hers. When the questions began, he grasped her hand in his and held on all through the heart-wrenching process of re-living the worst days of her life—again.

And that's when Nick realized that leaving Hope and this amazing woman was going to be the hardest thing he ever did.

But he couldn't ignore the only opportunity God had given him to care for his family.

Could he?

Three hours later, all joy in her afternoon's achievement had drained away, leaving Shay tired and defeated. Nick hated that.

"I doubt they'll catch him," she said as she hung up the phone. "I couldn't give them enough. I don't *know* enough." She ran a hand through her copper curls, rubbing her scalp to ease her tension. "Or if I do, I can't remember."

"You did the best you could."

"It wasn't enough. They know it and so do I. I should have tried harder to figure it out back when I was going through it. I shouldn't have been so afraid."

"Anyone would have been afraid, Shay. Anyone would struggle as you have if they'd gone through what you did. Don't beat yourself up with what-ifs."

"I'll try not to." She summoned a tired smile. "Thank you for staying with me. I appreciate it."

"That's what friends are for." Which was true, except that Nick felt guilty for saying it because he knew he wanted to be a whole lot more than just Shay's friend. He returned his chair to its rightful place facing her desk then followed her to the front office. He paused by the door. "What now?"

"I'm going home to take a nice long bubble bath. Maybe that will ease this crick in my neck." As Shay locked the door she exhaled a puff of air that rustled the damp strands of hair on her forehead. "It's so hot today. I'm glad I left Hugs inside with the air on."

She would go home defeated and probably spend the night dreaming about the creep and the terror he was causing someone else. Nick couldn't allow that.

"I can trump the bubble bath," he said as he waited for her to unlock the car.

"Right this minute a bubble bath sounds like heaven to me," she said. "What have you got in mind?"

"A swim. At the lake."

"The lake, huh?" Her green eyes flickered with interest.

"Think about it." Nick figured he'd have to sell this if he wanted to spend more time with Shay this evening—which obviously, against his better judgment, he did. "Cool, refreshing water lapping over you. A soft breeze floating through the pines. You can swim, relax and work out the kinks. Hugs could run around—" Nick blinked. The wimpy name had slipped out without him even thinking about it. Because that was Shay's name for her dog. Because she'd chosen it with love.

Man, he cared a lot for this woman.

"Mmm. Perfect." Shay closed her eyes and stretched. "You're right, the lake will be far better than a bubble bath. When would we go?"

"I'll pick you up in half an hour." He hesitated, wishing he could spend the evening alone with her but knowing that his mom desperately needed some free time. "Do you mind if I bring Mags? Mom could probably use the break."

"Of course I don't mind. Swimming will be good for Maggie." She nodded. "I'll put a picnic together. We could roast some hot dogs if you build a fire."

"Now you're getting the picture." Nick paused, unsure of the words that would tell her how deeply affected he was by what she'd done today. "I can't thank you enough, Shay. Seeing Maggie walk those few steps this afternoon—it was incredible."

"No thanks needed. It's my job." She grinned, her green eyes sparkling. "I love that kid. And her faith is incredible. Georgia would be so proud of her."

"Yeah." He swallowed hard.

"Yeah." Shay touched his arm then got into her car.

She cranked it a couple of times before the engine caught.

"You should get that checked," he told her.

"I've had it in the shop several times but they never find the problem. I guess I'll have to take it in again." She revved the motor. "See you in half an hour," she called before driving away.

"Yes, you will," he promised. As he drove home, Nick caught himself whistling the melody to a hymn and realized belatedly that it was "Only Believe," a song he hadn't heard since he was a kid. "All things are possible," the lyrics claimed. "Only believe."

All things?

Nick wasn't sure he understood that. This morning he'd received an email from his football squad wanting to know if he could start work a month early. The bonus the organization was offering was substantial enough to make him seriously consider it, despite his overwhelming reluctance to leave Hope and his family—and Shay.

Maggie was doing so much better now. Daily she grew more independent. As for his mom, well, Nick had talked to Heddy Grange about finding people to help with Maggie after he'd gone. That eased Nick's mind. His team's offering of a bonus would solve another worry; that cash would make a nice dent in the purchase price of a new minivan for his mom so she could retire her problem-plagued vehicle.

But no matter how he spun the benefits of that offer, Nick couldn't find a positive in leaving Shay. Talking to her, sharing their problems, finding ways to surmount them—that part of his life had become more important to him than he'd ever imagined it would.

Because Shay Parker was more than his friend.

Nick sat in his mother's yard and let the knowledge seep into his soul. He admired Shay's giving heart and the way she refused to back down. He treasured the way her enthusiastic laugh bubbled up from deep inside and spilled onto everyone around her. He adored the way she included all people and didn't care about opinions. How could he feel anything but the deepest respect and affection for a woman so generous she had to help every child she encountered?

But even if Nick did believe he could have a relationship with Shay, he wouldn't dream of asking her to leave her new life and the joy she'd found in Hope. And he couldn't stay here without a job.

For a moment he let himself dream of Shay with him in Seattle, riding up the Space Needle for dinner, cheering for his team, walking through the fine spring rain.

All things are possible? Not this time.

"This is one of those memory-making nights," Shay murmured, staring into the dying embers of the campfire. "In fifty years, I'll lie in my bed and still remember how bright the stars shone, how sweetly the birds sang, how fresh the air felt on my skin. Mostly I'll remember how alive I feel." She turned her head toward Nick. "Thank you for suggesting this."

"I'm enjoying it, too," he said. *Enjoy* seemed such a tame word. He'd never laughed as hard as he had watching Shay and Maggie revel in the buoyancy of the water as they turned somersaults. When he couldn't match their feat, his two ladies had splashed him mercilessly.

And Nick loved every moment.

"This is a God time," Maggie said, scooping another charred marshmallow into her mouth.

"A 'God' time? What do you mean, Mags?" A flush of amazement filled Nick at his niece's certainty of God's leading in her life. She sounded exactly as Shay had years ago in high school, when her faith was so strong his felt puny beside it. Lately Shay had begun to sound confident in her faith again, which made Nick very happy.

Maggie pointed up at the full moon. "That's what tonight feels like to me. Like God is here."

Shay brushed the damp curls off Maggie's forehead and hugged her. "How did you get so smart about God, Maggie?"

"My mom." Maggie peered into the night sky, her voice very soft. "She told me lots of things about how God loves us so much."

"Your mom was a smart lady, honey." Nick swallowed hard, thrilled that Georgia's very strong faith still lived on in her child's heart.

"Grandma teaches me, too. She knows lots of stuff about God, too."

"Like what?" Nick prodded.

"Grandma said that if I had questions, I should ask God about them. So I do."

Such easy faith. A flush of shame suffused Nick that he'd ever doubted God.

"I was worried when Pastor Marty talked about God's plans for us."

"Worried?" Nick frowned. He didn't want his niece worrying about anything. "Why were you worried, Mags?" Nick asked, anxious to hear what she'd say. Shay seemed captivated, too, for she leaned forward, arms clasped around her knees and waited as Maggie assembled her thoughts, her face scrunched up with the effort.

"I couldn't figure out why He made it so I couldn't walk." Maggie's forehead furrowed. "Sometimes it's hard to understand what God's doing." She peered at Shay, her eyes earnest.

"Yes, sometimes it is very hard," Shay agreed, her face solemn.

"Grandma told me, 'You don't have to understand. You just have to work hard and trust God to do the rest.'" A huge yawn interrupted her words.

Shay snuggled Maggie against her side. "That's right, Maggie. Are you warm enough?"

"Toasty." Maggie rested her sleepy head against Shay's shoulder.

Do your part. Trust God to do the rest.

Nick suddenly felt himself getting angry. *Trust God to do the rest.* Wasn't that what he was doing? He believed that job had come from God. So why didn't he feel at peace?

He faced the same quandary with Shay. He cared so deeply for her, but the thought of promising her anything and then failing her—something inside him twisted into a knot.

He just couldn't, wouldn't do that.

"I think Maggie's asleep," Shay murmured. When he didn't answer, she looked at him. "Why are you so quiet, Nick? Are you okay?"

"I'm thinking about what Maggie said."

"In regard to your dad?" Shay asked. "You told me once that you wanted to reconcile with him, that you hoped you would someday be able to rebuild a bond with him."

"I'm not hoping for that anymore, Shay," Nick told her grimly.

"Why not?" Her wide emerald eyes brimmed with innocence.

"Because my father doesn't want anything to do with any of us." The words spilled out of him with an acrid bitterness Nick hadn't realized he still clung to.

"You don't know that," Shay protested.

"Actually, I do know that." Nick didn't want to risk Maggie hearing this so he lifted her from Shay's arms and carried her to the truck, where he settled her on the backseat. After ensuring he had a clear line of vision to the truck, he returned to Shay. He stabbed at the fire viciously as he sat down, struggling to tamp down his anger.

"Nick—" Shay touched his arm for a moment, her eyes brimming with empathy.

"You can't tell Mom any of this." He locked her gaze with his. "Not one word."

"Okay." She looked mystified by his harsh tone.

"After Georgia's death, I hired the same private investigator that tailed you in New York to find my father."

Shay's eyes widened but Nick kept going. Better to get it all out in the open.

"I thought that surely, after all these years, he'd be over whatever he'd been going through, that he'd finally want to know us, his family." He snorted his derision. "Turns out I couldn't have been more wrong."

"Oh, Nick." Shay scooted closer so she could slide her hand into his. "I'm sorry."

"Yeah." He exhaled. "He said he had his own life now." He threaded his fingers through hers. "My father," he said, enunciating the words, "didn't want the responsibility of a family and never had, even though he had five kids. It didn't matter that we're all grown now, that we didn't want anything except to know our father. He said he'd made a clean break when he walked away years ago and he had no regrets."

Shay said nothing, simply held his hand. But Nick could feel her comfort as a tangible thing. Perhaps that was why he had to say it all, to release the pain in one torrent of bitterness. Maybe then he could heal. Maybe.

"I tried to show him pictures of his grandchildren," Nick muttered. "But he pushed them away. Can you imagine not wanting to know Maggie?"

"No, I can't imagine that," Shay whispered. "It's his loss, but we should feel sorry for him."

"Sorry?" Rage burned in Nick's heart. "Why?"

"Because your father hasn't the slightest clue as to what he threw away." Shay leaned in so her face was inches from his. "He has no idea that he has a wonderful son, a son who gives deeply of himself to others. A son the whole town is proud to call their own."

"Thanks," Nick said, looking away from her as if he didn't believe what she was saying.

"Don't thank me. It's true, Nick." Shay grasped his chin and turned his face toward hers. "The fact that your father doesn't get it, even after all these years, is sad. But it's no reflection on you. Let it go."

"I don't know if I can," he admitted.

"You have to. Hate is corrosive. It will ruin your life." Her fingers brushed his chin.

"But he—"

"God has blessed you with a wonderful family, with a community where you are appreciated." Her voice softened. "Think about that, and leave your father to God."

As Nick stared into Shay's eyes, the longing to kiss her grew until it was an ache that had to be satisfied. He leaned forward and covered her lips with his, seeking the comfort she offered, but asking for more than that. Asking for a response that would show she felt the same rush of joy that he did whenever they were together.

He felt her still then felt the slight tremble ripple through her. He shifted to move away, but then she was kissing him back, her hand curling around his neck, moving into the kiss, gently, without fear. She tasted of toasted marshmallow. Her skin felt soft as silk against his five o'clock shadow.

When Nick finally pulled back, Shay wore a bemused look.

"You're the best friend I ever had, Shay."

"Me, too," Shay said in a slightly choked tone.

Friend. But he ached to be so much more than that.

When Shay shivered, Nick wrapped an arm around her and drew her against his side. They sat there silent.

"The team wants me to start work a month early."

"Oh?" Shay's body tensed.

"They've offered a really good bonus if I show up a month early."

"In two weeks," she whispered. "After the Fourth of July."

"Yes."

She tipped her head to study him. "Will you go?"

"I don't have a choice." She didn't argue but still Nick felt he had to defend his decision. "Mom needs a new car. The old one's ready for the scrap heap, but her pension check won't stretch enough for a new one. I can't leave her with an unreliable vehicle."

"No." Shay said nothing else. But she didn't move away either. Was it because she was comfortable with him? Because she knew she could trust him?

But *should* she trust him if he was just going to leave?

"What else?" she whispered.

"Cara needs to get out of that apartment and into a house where the twins can thrive, but her husband just got laid off."

"Oh," Shay murmured.

Nick could feel her withdrawing.

"It's not that I want to leave Hope," he tried to explain. "But I can't take the risk of trying to start a new business or waiting for a job to find me. I'm the one my family depends on."

"Your mom depends on God," Shay reminded in a soft but firm tone.

"Yes, and God uses me to help her. These past months—you've become a lot more than just a friend, Shay. You've helped my mom and my niece. And me," he added with a smile. "I really wish I could stick around." *Maybe if I stayed long enough I could figure out how to have a relationship with you.* "I'd like that more than anything."

"You're a lot more than a friend to me, too, Nick." She bit her lip, lifted her head and stared into his eyes. "I care about you more than I have ever cared for anyone but Dad." She touched his cheek.

This woman had his heart. He couldn't bear to think about leaving her.

"Lots of people have long-distance relationships." Her whisper warmed his heart—how he wanted more with this special woman.

"I don't think I'm one of those people, Shay," he said, wishing it wasn't true with every fiber of his being.

"Why?" Her fingers curled into his as she met his gaze head-on, her green eyes swirling with questions.

"I'm terrible at relationships." He shook his head when she smiled. "I'm serious, Shay. You and I—we've always been friends." He gulped. "But there's a lot you don't know about me."

"I doubt that. You're the most trustworthy person I know." She leaned her head on his shoulder.

Nick's heart almost burst at the vulnerability he saw on Shay's face. Vulnerable, yet she trusted him enough to bare her heart to him. He had to be honest with her. She deserved nothing less that the complete truth.

"Tell me," she invited.

So Nick did. He told her about his last two relationships and how he'd failed to be who the person he'd loved said she needed.

"I'm just like my father," he said, his teeth grinding as he got the words out. "I don't want to be, but when push comes to shove, I get cold feet, just like he did, and rather than risk making a mess down the road, I walk out before I hurt someone."

Shay was silent for such a long time, he finally turned his head to look at her. She was grinning.

"This isn't funny," he said.

"Yes, it is, Nick. It's very funny that you of all people— Mr. Responsible—would think that you failed someone. It would never happen," she said. "Not if the moon turned purple. Not if we had a month of Sundays. Not even if someone mistreated you. It just isn't in you to dump your responsibilities."

Nick stared at her. He opened his mouth to argue but Shay shook her head.

"Impossible," she said. "I know you."

"You don't understand. You haven't even heard the details yet."

"Details don't matter. I know who you are inside." She shifted so she was facing him, her eyes flashing.

Nick thought he could lose himself in those eyes.

"I know you, Nick Green. I know how seriously you take your obligations. If your relationships ended then it was because there was something wrong with the relationships themselves, not with you. You don't walk out, Nick. Not on anybody. Not ever." She smiled again, and he felt warm all over. "You have an abundance of integrity. I'd trust you with my life."

"Did I hear you right?" Nick blinked. "You *trust* me?"

"Yep. Weird, isn't it?" Shay grinned a wicked smile then threw her arms around his neck and kissed him with a carefree abandon he'd wished for only in his dreams—until now.

Nick kissed her right back. If Shay Parker wanted to kiss him, he wasn't about to turn her down.

But, Good Lord, what happens next?

Chapter Eleven

"Happy Fourth of July!"

Shay stood on Main Street watching the parade, waving her little flag in one hand while the other was firmly tucked into Nick's. She couldn't remember when she'd been happier.

She'd made him dinner several nights in a row. He'd treated her to pizza and Mexican food. They'd shared campfires and walks and another evening at the lake, just the two of them. And they'd talked. My, how they'd talked—about everything—except the future.

Shay had skirted around the subject, longing for Nick to tell her he couldn't leave her, but purposely not asking about his decision. Staying in Hope had to be Nick's decision and though she desperately wanted him to say he was staying, she would just have to wait for his decision and keep praying about it.

She'd put her trust in God to find a way for Nick to stay.

The bubble of Shay's perfect world burst when the sound of gunshot cracked through the laughter surrounding her. For an instant, fear perched on her shoulder and told her to be afraid. But Shay was no longer a novice.

She squeezed her eyes closed and repeated a newly memorized verse.

For I hold you by your right hand, I the Lord your God. And I say to you, "Don't be afraid. I am here to help you."

Shay repeated it twice then opened her eyes just as an old Model T huffed and puffed past them and continued down the parade route.

"I think that thing backfires once every parade. Are you okay?" Nick leaned past Maggie to ask, obviously sensing something amiss.

"Everything's perfect," she said and smiled. It was true. Everything *was* perfect.

The day was gorgeous, one of those not-too-hot summer days that had a soft breeze to fan you. This year the parade was on time, marching bands and cheerleaders filling the air with excitement. Maggie's joy in each entry reminded Shay of the many times she'd come here with her father and she took a moment to savor the memory.

But it was the seniors' float that made Maggie dance and point, her anticipation visible.

"Grandma, Grandma!" she called, waving her little flag and jumping up and down. "Throw me a candy. Please, Grandma."

Shay chuckled when the entire float of seniors aimed their goodies in Maggie's direction, forcing the little girl to use the hem of her blouse like an apron to collect her treats.

Just behind the seniors, someone began to sing

"America The Beautiful." When it was finished Nick touched her shoulder.

"Is perfect too strong a word to describe today?" he murmured into her ear, his hand resting against her waist.

"I think it's a perfect word for a perfect day," she told him, loving the gentle yet strong support he provided.

Then her cell phone rang. She glanced at the number and swallowed. *Don't be afraid.*

"Anything urgent?" Nick asked.

"I didn't expect the New York detectives to call me again. I'll just be a minute." She stepped away to find some quiet.

But it was a very long minute, and when it was over, Shay wished she had left her phone at home.

"You missed most of the parade, but at least you won't miss lunch." Nick grinned when she returned. He helped Maggie stand then frowned at Shay's non-response. "Shay? What's wrong?"

"I, um, I can't go for lunch right now. The detectives in New York are faxing something they want me to look at."

"Not a problem. We'll swing by the police station on our way to Mom's. Okay?" He waited for her nod while Maggie got settled into her crutches. Then they walked to his truck. After only a few steps, Maggie gladly relinquished her bag that brimmed with goodies thrown to her from the floats in the parade.

"Didn't Grandma look nice on that float?" she said.

"Very nice," Nick agreed.

"I like the dress Shay helped her find. And I'm glad you helped them get their float working, Uncle Nick.

Grandma said they wouldn't have been in the parade this year without you."

Shay grinned at him. "Always on hand to help out, aren't you?"

"It was just a motor thing. No big deal." He avoided her knowing look.

"It is a big deal for the seniors," she said. She was about to reiterate that a lot of people in Hope needed Nick when Buddy from the grocery store called out to her.

"Nice article, Shay. Looks like Whispering Hope Clinic is a real success!" he said.

"What article?" Nick asked.

"Remember Ben Marks and all the photos he took that day at the clinic? The paper must have run the story today." And maybe, Shay mused, it would be enough to persuade Nick he was needed here. That's what she'd been praying for. "Can we stop at the store and pick up a copy? Your mom did say she needed some whipped cream for her strawberry pie," she reminded.

"Right." Nick lifted Maggie into her seat then paused. "What about the police station?"

"Oh, right." This was a holiday—Shay didn't want to be the damper. "Why don't you and Maggie go to the store and I'll meet you at your mom's place as soon as I'm finished?"

"You don't want me there?" Nick frowned. "It's not a problem."

"Nothing is ever a problem for you, is it?" Shay squeezed his hand. "But you know what? I think I'm ready to face this on my own. I feel like I have to."

"You don't have to. Just give me a few minutes to get Maggie—"

"Nick." Shay smiled and shook her head. "I need to do this. I need to stand on my own two feet. It's time." *Actually, it's past time*, she thought.

He studied her for a long moment but finally nodded.

"Okay. I'll be praying," he promised.

"Thank you. That I will gladly accept." She waved at Maggie then set off at a crisp walk across the town square toward the police services building, needing the exercise to help work off the nervous energy that filled her.

Perfect love casts out all fear.

With her shoulders back and her courage high, Shay walked into the station. Moments later Chief Dan Burger ushered her into his office.

"I've been briefed by the New York police, Miss Parker. What they'd like you to do is look at this picture and see if you recognize this person." He handed her a sheet of paper as he sat and motioned for her to do the same.

Shay looked down and inhaled sharply. He was facing the camera, smiling as if he had not a care in the world. He looked like an ordinary man.

"Miss Parker?"

"I know him," she said.

"So who is he?" The chief leaned forward, pen in hand, poised to take down her information.

"That's the thing," she whispered as a cold, clammy sweat began to form under her bangs. "I know him— that is, I'm familiar with this face. He was on the set of a number of shoots I did. But I have no idea who he is.

I don't believe I ever knew his name or what, exactly, he did. I just—know him." She bit her lip. "I wish I could tell you more."

"Don't worry about it." The relaxed tone of the chief's voice calmed Shay. "Can I ask you something? I'm just curious. What was this guy doing on the set? Can you recall?"

Shay began to shake her head but Dan leaned forward.

"Close your eyes for a moment and see yourself there. What are you doing?"

"I'm in the makeup chair," she said.

"Someone's doing your hair?"

"Yes. It's a shoot of evening gowns. Very formal. I have to wear an up-do and it's not quite right. I had some sparkly clips—they're missing." She gasped, opened her eyes. "He must have been somebody's assistant because Mario, my hair guy, yelled at him to find those clips."

"I see." Dan tented his fingers. "Did this guy work with Mario?"

"No. Mario worked alone. He always made me look beautiful. So did Cerise, my makeup artist." Shay got lost in her thoughts of those hectic, frantic hours when nothing mattered more than giving the client the very best picture she could. She didn't want to model anymore, but she didn't resent it because it paid for her education and everything she had. Modeling had allowed her to come home to Hope.

"Could the guy have worked for her, this Cerise?"

"I don't know. Maybe. She always had someone cleaning her kits, her brushes. But I don't remember *him* doing it." She stared at the picture, chilled. "Is he the stalker?"

"For now, he's just a person of interest."

"I see." She had a hunch the chief wasn't going to tell her any more. "Well, I'm sorry I couldn't help more."

"You've done fine. I'll relay what you've told me to New York and they'll take it from here." He shook her hand. "But if you remember anything else, you let me know."

"Of course," she promised.

"And Ms. Parker? I can't tell you how much that clinic you work in means to this town. I know how hard it is to keep folks in a place where medical services aren't up to par. Whispering Hope has become a tremendous asset. It's even drawing people to get help for their children."

"That's what we hoped for." A rush of satisfaction surged inside and almost dislodged the unsettled feeling that photo had left her with. Almost.

"Listen, tell Nick I said thanks, will you? My mother's been nagging me to get her golf cart fixed for ages. He did it in about ten minutes at the seniors' hall when they had their fix-it time last Saturday morning. Saved me another bungled attempt with the thing." He scratched his chin. "There are plenty of regular folks who'd pay him good money if he could get some of their broken-down stuff going."

"Really?" That caught Shay's attention.

"Sure. I was talking to some of the guys on council. They wish he'd open a shop. He'd never have a spare minute."

"I will tell him what you said," Shay promised. "I've

been trying to talk him into staying. After all, his mom and his niece are here. But Nick thinks that the work he does in town wouldn't support a business. He feels he has to go back to Seattle to earn a living."

"Well." The chief rubbed his head. "I don't suppose he'd earn a pro-ball salary in Hope, but then it doesn't cost as much to live here either." His eyes narrowed and he seemed to get lost in thought.

"I'd better get going. Nick's mom is planning a big July Fourth barbecue and I don't want to be late." She pushed the photo toward him, less than eager to look at that face again, and stood up. "I hope they catch the right guy."

"Yeah. Creeps like that think they can get away with their nasty tricks, but sooner or later they get found out. God has a way of evening things up. Maybe not on our timetable, but always on His."

"Thanks, Chief." Shay left, lost in thought as she walked back through the town square, got in her car and drove to the Green home.

She couldn't help brooding over the picture she'd seen. The familiarity of that face struck her, but she couldn't recall exactly why. Despite the many Scriptures she recited as she drove, an aura of disquiet rattled her nerves. She was glad when she arrived at Nick's and hurried to the backyard, where laughter spilled over the fence.

Shay stood still, soaking in the happy atmosphere. Friends and neighbors filled the yard, laughing while kids played games. Maggie, moving as best she could now that she was using canes, was the life of the party.

Shay's observant eye noted that the little girl was almost lifting the canes up so she could go faster, prov-

ing that the strength in her legs was almost normal. In a
very short time, Maggie would be walking without aid.

"You're back." Nick wound an arm around her waist.
"Everything okay with the police?"

"I'll tell you later," she said sotto voce. "I don't want
to spoil the afternoon."

"You couldn't." He grinned as his mother, conned
by the kids, took a turn—and failed—at flying a kite.
"I don't think anything could put a damper on this day.
It's time to celebrate, Shay. Want a frank?"

"And some lemonade. You do have lemonade?" she
asked, one eyebrow arched.

"Is the sun shining?" He drew her forward into the
circle of people he'd been talking with.

Shay accepted compliments about the paper's feature on the clinic. When she saw Nick busy manning
the grill, she found a quiet corner inside and sat down
to read the newspaper article for herself.

"It's good, isn't it? Bob covers how the clinic idea
started with Jessica's illness, and how it's grown and
is now impacting people from here and far away." Jaclyn sat down across from her. "It's also very good pub-
licity for you and the results you've achieved for your
clients."

"I guess." Shay closed the newspaper with a sigh.
"I was hoping for more."

"More?" Jaclyn looked surprised. "More of what?"

"I was hoping he would write about Nick and the
roly-poly, the Tiger, the giggle machine…" She met
Jaclyn's inquiring look. "I've been trying to persuade
Nick that Hope needs him more than Seattle does."

"Because?"

"Because I want him to stay. Because I'm in love

with him, Jaclyn." Saying the words solidified something inside, made her feelings more real.

"In love—wow." Jaclyn grinned. "You told me, several times I might add, that it was only friendship between you. I didn't expect love to develop this soon."

"Neither did I." She sighed. "And I can't see how it is going to work out."

"Because he doesn't care about you?" Jaclyn asked, her voice soft.

"I think he does care about me."

"So what's the problem?" Her friend frowned. "Oh. You're still feeling skittish?"

"No." Shay blinked in surprise. "I'm not like that around Nick. I was at first, but now—I guess I'm learning to trust him."

"Oh, that's wonderful! I'm so glad, honey." Jaclyn hugged her then returned to her seat.

"It is an amazing feeling. The only thing is, I don't know what can come of it." Shay told her about Nick's determination to leave and about her visits with the police. "Even if he stayed, I'm not much of a bargain. Seems like I still have to fight back the fear every step of the way."

"At least you are fighting. That's a huge step." Jaclyn frowned when she didn't reply. "Something else is troubling you?"

"I've been studying with Nick's mom. She's shown me that I have to learn to trust God. And I'm trying. I really am. But—"

"But you feel that maybe He has abandoned you? Or forgotten you?" Jaclyn asked.

"It sounds juvenile, I know. But after all the verses I've learned, all the praying and Bible studying I've done, I thought I'd feel empowered or not so alone or—something. But I don't." Shay stared at her hands. "I keep praying, I keep reading the verses, but it's beginning to seem like I'm only going through the motions. Like today, looking at that picture, even though I was inside the police station—the fear still rises up."

Jaclyn remained silent, listening as Shay released her pent-up feelings.

"Look around at all the love in this home. You and Kent are making your family together. Brianna and Zac are doing the same. I know beyond a shadow of a doubt that what you all have is exactly what I want." Tears welled but she dashed them away. "But I'm beginning to doubt I'll ever get it. Especially if Nick leaves."

"You've always talked about having a family. You said you trusted Nick. Now you have to trust God, too, because He knows what your heart desires." Jaclyn shook her blond head. "Nothing works without trusting God, Shay. Do that, then go for it. Go for the heart. Nothing else is good enough for you. Just remember, Nick will never be able to guarantee you safety. Nobody can."

"I know. That's why I have to get this fear thing sorted out, so that I'll be whole and able to love in return. Only—" She bit her lip, unwilling to voice her thoughts.

"Only it would be easier if Nick actually said he loves you and he's staying in Hope?" Jaclyn finished.

"Yes."

"I wish I could tell you there's some kind of easy way to guarantee he will, but the truth is, there isn't." Jaclyn shrugged. "It all comes back to faith. I think the way to put your faith into action, in this case, is to cherish whatever moments you have with Nick, put yourself on the line and tell him how you feel."

"Live with no regrets," Shay mused. "That's what my dad used to say. 'Live your best life right now.'"

"I think there's a lot of wisdom in that." Jaclyn rose. "And remember that just because you don't 'feel' different doesn't mean things aren't changing inside you. How often did our youth leaders remind us that the Christian life is founded on faith, not on feelings?"

"They taught us a lot, didn't they? And we probably didn't appreciate them enough back then." Shay rose, too, and hugged her best friend. "That's why this place is so important to me. I have a history here. I belong."

"Then live like that. Don't wait for things to change," Jaclyn advised as they strolled back outside. "Be honest with him, do what you can and trust God to handle what you can't. Now, where is that husband of mine? This music is too good to ignore."

"Blame it on Maggie. She found some of my old cassettes and insists on playing them," Nick said, walking toward them. "I wondered where you'd disappeared to. Want to dance?" he asked Shay.

Shay waved as Jaclyn headed toward Kent. While they'd been talking, the sun had set and candlelit paper lanterns now created a soft, intimate glimmering in the backyard. A pretty ballad about love floated through the evening air. Shay turned toward Nick with a smile. "Your music? But this isn't that awful hard rock you used to love."

"It wasn't that I loved that music as much as I fancied myself a guitarist back then." Nick held out a hand and led Shay to a back corner of the yard covered with beautifully fragrant tea roses. No one else was there.

"I don't think we've danced together since prom night. I'll try not to step on your toes." His arm closed around her waist and his hand enveloped hers.

"I don't mind," she said.

I don't mind? What an understatement.

In Nick's arms, swaying to the music, with laughter and love of his family and friends surrounding them, it felt intimately right to be sharing this moment. Jaclyn was right, Shay mused. The Bible said God had a plan for her life. She had to trust in that and enjoy the special moments He sent her way.

"You're awfully quiet. Tired?" he asked, his breath brushing her cheek, only inches from his mouth.

"I feel wonderful," Shay told him.

"Good." He grinned. "Because if I remember right, the next song is a bit more energetic."

Shay laughed with abandonment as he swung her wide and then pulled her back to him. Though she'd forgotten some of the old moves, Nick remembered all their favorite steps. Soon they had drawn a crowd of onlookers who clapped them on to an exuberant finish.

Flushed and slightly embarrassed, Shay tucked her arm in Nick's and bowed at their applause but shook her head when he inclined his to ask if she wanted to continue.

"Too thirsty," she told him.

"And you haven't sampled any of my fantastic burgers," he said. "Actually, I didn't either. I was too busy cooking. I'm starving. Let's go see what Mom's got left."

The buffet table was, in usual Green style, loaded. They helped themselves. Nick snagged two Adirondack chairs that had wide enough arms to hold their heaping plates and the tinkling glasses of lemonade he brought.

"You're not supposed to eat the watermelon first," he said, eyebrows lowered in a fake scowl when she took a bite from the triangle of red fruit.

"Who says?" Shay munched happily on her watermelon.

"I do." He reached out with his napkin and dabbed at a trickle of juice dribbling down her chin. "It messes up such a pretty face."

"Pffffft to pretty faces," she told him and blew a raspberry to emphasize her words. "Life is about so much more than a pretty face."

"You seem different tonight." Nick set aside his plate and studied her. "Something happen that you want to tell me about?"

Shay took a few moments to tell Nick about what had happened at the police station and about her conversation with Jaclyn. "I guess I've decided I'm going to get out of the control seat and leave things up to God." She laughed when Nick blew his own raspberry. "Go ahead, laugh. But I have decided. Being here tonight, seeing the love your mom shows everyone has been a real eye-opener to me. She went through such tough times when your dad left. Her arthritis is getting worse, yet she faces each day with abundant joy and love. She's on top of her circumstances because she trusts God, always. That's where I want to be."

"I thought the newspaper article showed you were already there." Nick sipped his lemonade thoughtfully.

"The newspaper article showed what my clients have achieved," she corrected. "What needs to happen inside me isn't for the newspaper."

"Uncle Nick?" Maggie stood in front of them, holding her canes. "Are you sure we can't have the fireworks?"

"We talked about it, Mags. You know the fire chief said we're too close to other houses. I'm sorry." Nick ruffled the little girl's hair.

"But my place isn't too close to other houses." Shay winked at Maggie before she turned to Nick. "Do you think we could set off the fireworks at my place? Do you even know how to set off fireworks anymore?"

"Please." He shot her an offended look that said she should know better than to ask. "We'd need to hook up a hose, in case any grass caught. That rain last week helped, but the monsoon season hasn't really soaked anything enough to be fully safe yet."

"I have hoses. And lots of water," Shay told him. "But I don't want to drag anyone away from your mom's party. Look at her. She's having a ball."

Mrs. Green tipped back her head and laughed at something Ned Barns said. She was flushed, her smile beaming.

"We'll wait until everyone leaves," Nick said. "Then, when everything's cleaned up, we'll go."

"But I'll get too tired and fall asleep. Then I'll miss everything," Maggie wailed.

"If you go to your room and rest now, I promise I'll wake you up when it's time to go to Shay's." Nick squatted in front of her. "But no fuss and no telling Grandma. She's enjoying herself, and that's what we want. Right?"

"Right." Maggie high-fived him then grinned at Shay.

Two hours later the three of them stood in the desert,

waiting for the time-delay mechanism to click and ignite the first in the series of fireworks Nick had set up.
Finally it did. Noise burst across the desert and flares of
color lit the night sky as rocket after rocket exploded.

"It's not a meteor shower," Nick murmured in Shay's
ear. "But Maggie seems to be enjoying it."

"So am I." Shay was very conscious—too conscious—
of his arm draped around her shoulders. She couldn't help
wondering if he'd kiss her tonight. Memories of their evening at the pond and a rush of feelings bubbling inside
made her catch her breath.

She knew now that she loved Nick, loved him with
everything she possessed. She wanted to spend her
days by his side, to push into the future with him, to
share Maggie and his mom and all the happy moments
family could bring. He was still her very best friend,
but now he'd become much more than that.

If only she could know if he felt the same. Did he
love her?

"Here it comes, the grand finale," Nick said. "Make
sure you don't fall asleep, Maggie-mine."

"I won't." Maggie sat on the lawn chair Shay had
provided, her eyes huge as she watched the display.

"Happy Fourth of July," Nick murmured in her ear.

"Happy—" Shay never got to finish her sentence
because Nick's lips touched hers. Her heart exploded
as his lips moved over hers and he pulled her into his
embrace. She let herself melt into him as she kissed
him back, pouring her feelings into that kiss, pleading
silently with him to say the words that she desperately
wanted to hear. That he wasn't going to Seattle next
week. That he wasn't going away at all. Ever.

This, she prayed when Nick finally ended the kiss

by turning her to stand in front of him and looping his
arms around her waist, *is what I want, Lord. Please let
him love me. Please let him decide to stay.*

Nick, however, said nothing.

Chapter Twelve

"Is that what you wanted?" Nick stood back and watched Shay's newest client turn the handles of Nick's giggle machine with bandaged hands.

"Perfect." Shay assessed the movement, her emerald eyes shimmering. "Try again, Robbie, honey," she encouraged in a very soft tone.

The child complied, chuckling with delight when his actions made a clown pop up. He kept going, working a little harder after a balloon inflated. Under Shay's direction Nick tweaked the machine until it was a perfect fit for the little boy who'd been burned in a cooking fire. When Nick's phone kept interrupting, he finally switched it off.

"You're certainly getting popular," Shay said, waving goodbye as Robbie left with his mom and the precious machine. "Everybody wants Nick."

"Everybody wants Nick to fix their broken stuff," he corrected, pretending annoyance. "The Girl Scouts are coming to the seniors' hall on Saturday morning, and on Monday the Rotary Club wants help with one of their service projects. I suggested they get the seniors group to pitch in. There is a lot of knowledge there that could be tapped."

"Your mother said you're also booked for Tuesday nights." Shay readied the room for Maggie's session, which would start once her checkup with Jaclyn was finished.

"Yeah. About that." Nick wasn't sure how this would go over. Not that Shay would ever balk at helping anyone, but she was already so busy.

"Uh-oh. That doesn't sound good." She glanced over one shoulder at him.

For the hundredth time Nick admired how stunningly beautiful Shay was. Though her work clothes—baggy cotton tops and pants that let her move easily—were hardly haute couture, Shay always looked stunning. Today she'd bundled her gorgeous hair onto the top of her head and secured it with a big comb that was the exact color of her eyes. A few wispy tendrils of richly glowing copper escaped to caress her cheeks and her long, slim neck. He got that warm feeling remembering just how perfectly his lips felt on hers.

"Nick?"

"Yeah?" He gulped and refocused.

"Are you sick?" Shay studied him with concern.

"Maybe." He stepped nearer, holding her gaze, wondering if she'd back away if he tried to kiss her. This *was* her workplace, after all, and even though no one else was here—

"Nick? Hello?" She snapped her fingers under his nose. "You *are* ill."

"No. But sometimes when I'm near you I get this weird feeling in my chest." Apparently that hadn't come out exactly the way he'd intended, because now it looked as if Shay thought he needed a defibrillator. "Uh, never mind."

"You were saying about the seniors?" Shay glanced at her watch. "You need me to step in and take over some of your classes when you leave town?"

"Not exactly."

So she was okay with him leaving? Nick ignored that for the moment as he swallowed the golf ball in his throat. "You know how old people get."

"How they *get?*" Shay's arched eyebrows rose. Her lips twitched. "Old, do you mean?"

"No. We all get old." Now she was laughing at him. *Get a grip, Green.* "I mean stiff. Achy. Hurting. Hard to move. Joint issues. Like Mom. You know?"

"Oh." She nodded. "Yes, I do. And it's not just old people who suffer with those issues, for your information."

"Right." He was putting this so badly. "Well, I figured that maybe, if you could fit it in, because I know how busy you are now that you're working with Jaclyn on those church renovations—"

"Just say what you want, Nick."

"I want you to teach a yoga class to the seniors," he blurted. "If you know yoga, I mean. If not, maybe you could teach them some stretching exercises, stuff that will help them limber up a bit. Sort of like you did for Mom."

She stared at him for a long time, obviously suspicious about his request. He couldn't blame her. Shay knew he didn't have much time left here.

"Is that what you really want?"

"What do you mean?" Nick shifted, unable to break the hold of her gaze as it locked with his.

"I'm wondering why you're asking me."

"Uh, because you know yoga. I think."

"You just can't help it, can you? You have to help everybody. And now you're trying to draw me into it." She leaned against the parallel bars, a tiny smile tipping up her kissable lips.

"Well." No point in trying to deny it—those big eyes of hers saw everything. "Yes."

"Okay." Her smiled faded. "I guess I could teach a few yoga moves on Tuesday night, but only if you attend."

"Can do." He shifted uncomfortably. "Uh—"

Shay's eyes narrowed. After a moment she sighed. "What else?"

"I was speaking to Heddy Grange today. Her granddaughter and some other girls want to learn to play soccer. Lots of people have volunteered but no one wants to coach. So since you were captain of the soccer team in high school, I was wondering—"

"When?"

"Thursday nights?" Nick held his breath. He'd promised Heddy he'd find someone to coach. If Shay wouldn't help—

"You do realize what you're doing, don't you?" She looked up at him through her thick lashes. "You're making yourself an indispensable part of Hope. You belong here, Nick."

He hated it but he had to say it.

"I have to leave next week."

Shay stared at him.

"That's why I'm trying to get all these things settled. I want to ensure I've kept all my promises. I want to make sure everything's up and running so nobody is put out when I'm gone."

She stood there, staring at her toes for several long moments.

"I see," she whispered.

Two words and yet they so perfectly expressed her obvious disappointment in him. How he wished it could be different but he just couldn't shirk his duties to his family.

Nick wanted to wrap his arms around her and promise her he'd be back. He wanted to hold her once more, pour heart and soul into a kiss, but that wouldn't make leaving any easier.

"I have to go, Shay."

"Do you? So it was all just talk about trusting God." With a hiss of frustration, she clapped her hands on her narrow hips and glared at him. "Who do you think is going to see the needs in Hope and fill them when you leave?"

"Somebody will. I was just the—facilitator. A temporary one."

Her eyes darkened. She tried to turn away but he stopped her with a hand on her arm. "I have to leave, Shay. I need this job. Please understand."

For a moment she avoided looking at him. But when she finally did, her green eyes were glossy—with tears? For him?

"You haven't even looked for a job here," she said, her voice wobbling.

"I've spent the past six months looking for a way to remain in Hope. I've prayed about it endlessly." He put his hands on her shoulders, forcing her to look at him. "You and I both know there's no getting around this."

"Everyone's always telling *me* to have faith," she said, her green eyes turning glacial. "*You* have to have faith that God has an answer to this. We need you here, Nick."

We need you.

Shay needed him. And Nick needed her. Boy, how he needed her. He needed her in his life to give the days meaning, to share the highs and lows.

He'd tried to have faith, to believe something would come up at the last minute. But nothing had. And his mom's car was sputtering worse than ever. He needed that bonus.

"You'll all manage very well on your own." She stepped back and he let his hands drop. "I wish I could stay here, Shay. I truly do."

"Nick—" She stood staring at him, her brows drawn together in a troubled frown. Her hand reached out to touch his cheek, stayed a second longer, then fell to her side.

His gut clenched with wanting, but he fought back.

"You're getting your fear under control, Shay. Whispering Hope Clinic is on the rise, just as Jessica would have wanted." Nick lowered his voice, trying to make her see the truth without revealing how hard this was for him. "Your kids will heal and walk and run because this is where you belong, here, helping them."

"I love you, Nick."

Her words shocked him into silence.

"I have for a while. If I've fought my fear, it's because of you, because you stood with me through the worst of it, because you showed me I am not alone." She stood straight and tall. She'd never looked more beautiful to him. "It's you, Nick, with your nightly visits to my place to make sure I'm safe, who has made me feel I was secure and that I could trust again."

He hadn't realized she'd known about that.

"You make me laugh, Nick, and you help me when I cry. You cheer me on when I want to give up. You hold me up when I stumble," she whispered. "You helped me face the worst issue in my past, and you're here now, helping me again. I love you for all of that."

"Shay, don't." He couldn't bear to hear her say those words.

"Why? I'm only telling the truth. Hope and I have both changed because of you. You make us see what we could be." She folded her arms across herself as if to shield her body. "You, Hope, me—we're perfectly matched. God has a place for you here. If only you could see that, you'd understand that you can't leave. You can't give up on us."

"If God has a way for me to be here, I'm totally open to it." A twinge of bitterness prickled inside. "But so far I'm not seeing it."

"Because you want God to show you before you'll trust Him." Shay's smile held sympathy, understanding, sadness. "You know the most important thing I've learned since I've started facing my fears? Faith is just that—faith. Faith is when you don't see a way and you don't see how you can get through. You don't even see a sign that what you hope for is possible. But you believe anyway. You trust God to work it out."

Maggie opened the door and walked in, thumping her canes on the floor.

Nick did a double take. Maggie wasn't really using those canes—she was walking totally on her own strength. Shay smiled at his surprise.

"Hey, Maggie." She took the canes and set them aside. "Today our whole time is going to be spent without these because you don't need them anymore, sweetie."

Maggie whooped with joy. Nick stood on the sidelines watching while they worked, his heart in his throat as his niece completed every exercise without any help or support. At first her steps seemed hesitant, but as she adjusted her balance and gained confidence she moved more easily. By the end of the session, she was triumphant and flushed with success.

"Now, wasn't that worth all the hard work?" Shay asked with a grin.

"Yes! Thank you, Shay." Maggie wrapped her arms around Shay's legs.

"Don't thank me. You're the one who believed in yourself and hung on to that belief even when it hurt and you didn't feel like doing it anymore." She drew the little girl away so she could hunker down to her level. "I'm very proud of you, Maggie."

"I'm proud of me, too."

Shay laughed and hugged Maggie. As Nick watched the two embrace, he felt left out. This was what he'd miss when he left, this intimacy, this closeness, this sharing.

This love.

Shay's love.

He didn't want to go. He couldn't stay.

"We can't forget to thank Uncle Nick either," Shay reminded. "All those amazing machines he made for you really helped your recovery."

"Thank you, Uncle Nick." Maggie walked slowly toward him, standing straight and tall, brown eyes shining with joy. She held up her arms as she had so often in the past months.

Nick swung her into his arms and hugged her close to his heart, his throat choked with thanksgiving and joy and love.

"You're so welcome, Maggie-mine."

Over Maggie's head he caught Shay watching them. Her gaze locked with his, and after a long moment she nodded as if to say, *This is the kind of faith I'm talking about.*

He wanted to believe. He wanted to have that kind of faith.

But—

He couldn't do it. He couldn't give up his only means of security for a faint hope that somehow, someway, sometime, something would come along that he could depend on. He needed more than hope.

Maggie wiggled and he set her down. "I love you, Mags. You know that."

"I know, Uncle Nick. I love you, too." She leaned in and kissed his cheek. "I couldn't have walked without you."

"You would have," he told her, tweaking her nose. "You would have found a way."

"But I didn't have to, 'cause God sent you."

God sent him? Nick couldn't wrap his mind around that.

"I want you to sit down, Maggie, because I have a few things I need to say to you." Shay pulled forward a child-size chair and waited until Maggie was seated. Then she folded herself on the floor in the Lotus position. "You have done amazingly well. But I want you to remember that your body gets tired. When it does, you use this." She held out one of the small canes.

"But—" Maggie's face pinched tight "—I'm better."

"You are. But your body is still healing. Some days it will be tired. That's when you use the canes."

"I won't get tired." Maggie's stubborn tone made Shay shake her head.

"I know what I'm talking about, sweetheart. I helped you get this far, didn't I?"

"Yes."

"Then listen to me now and trust me," she said with a sideways look at Nick. "You walk as much as you want, but take a rest when you get tired, just like you did with the exercises."

"I won't get tired." She thrust out her determined chin. "I'm strong."

"Maggie." Shay took her hands and held them, her voice compelling. "God made your body and He did an excellent job. But He made it to work and to rest, to play *and* to sleep."

From Nick's viewpoint, Maggie remained unconvinced.

"You said God healed you," Shay said.

"He did." Maggie had no doubt.

"So are you going to undo all His work, ruin His gift, by trying to get your own way?" Shay leaned forward. "I'm not trying to punish you, Maggie. I'm trying to tell you what to expect and how to be prepared for it. You know I'm your friend."

"Okay." Maggie heaved a heavy sigh. "I'll do what you say. I promise."

"Good. And if you are still feeling strong and

haven't overdone it, I'll have a surprise for you on Saturday afternoon."

"Really?"

Shay grinned as Maggie plied her with a thousand questions, but she offered no further clues. "Saturday afternoon," was all she would say.

As Nick watched Maggie leave the workout room, he couldn't find the words with which to thank Shay. Anything he thought of seemed too small, too simple to express his gratitude. But he said it anyway.

"Thank you."

"You're the one who inspired her to keep going." Shay walked to the door with him, both of them watching Maggie navigating the hall.

Near the far end the little girl paused. Several moments passed before she transferred her cane to her other hand and leaned on it. Then she glanced back over one shoulder.

"Good girl," Shay murmured.

"Will she need to come back?" he asked.

"I'd like to see her twice more this week, just to make sure everything is fine." Shay held his gaze. "Then once a week for a month after that, barring anything unforeseen. I'll call your mother with the appointment times."

Because he wouldn't be here. Anger made him say, "It's not as if I'm choosing to go, Shay."

"Aren't you?" She touched his arm so he would look at her. "I love you, Nick," she said in a very soft but clear voice. "I think you have feelings for me, too. You couldn't kiss me the way you have unless you did." She touched his cheek with her fingertips. "I believe that together, with God's help, we could do something wonderful here in Hope. But you're afraid to take a chance on me and on God's ability to provide for you."

"I'm not afraid," he denied.

Shay let her hand drop to her side. "What do you call it?"

"Duty to my family. Obligation. Sense."

"All excuses," she said. "Faith doesn't have excuses. It simply says 'I believe.'"

"And we're back to where we started, Shay—where this conversation always starts. How will I provide for my family if I don't have work?" he demanded, irritated that she wouldn't see this from his perspective, as if he wanted to leave.

"The same way you've always provided for them." Her voice dropped to a whisper when Maggie looked back at them. "You'll ask God to help them and you, and then you'll get on with doing what you can with whatever God gives you."

"It's not that simple, Shay."

"But you see," she said with a smile, "it is. You either trust, or you don't. That's what your mother taught me. It all starts with a choice." She lifted her hand and waved as Ted passed Maggie at the end of the hall. "Hi, Ted. Come on in. I've been waiting for you."

"It's all very clear for you, isn't it, Shay?"

"I'm a work in progress," Shay replied, angling her head toward Maggie, who waited at the end of the hall. "Like her. Like all of us. But I will get there. God will get me there if I continue to put my faith in Him. He has plans for me."

Shay ushered Ted into her workroom and gently closed the door, leaving Nick standing there. Feeling bereft and more alone than he had ever been, Nick walked toward Maggie as he struggled to assimilate Shay's words with what he knew in his heart.

He had to leave, to take that job, to build security for his family.

But oh, how he longed to stay and accomplish all the things Shay spoke of.

She loved him. How could that be? The wonder of it simply didn't compute.

Did he dare imagine that God had used Maggie's horrible accident to draw the two of them together because He meant for them to share a future? Maybe even a family?

Finally he dared imagine it. A family with Shay, sharing each day, each trial, each joy. Impromptu picnics with Maggie, face-to-face chats with his mom and Shay, by his side. Always.

Are all things really possible, God?

Chapter Thirteen

❧

"What's the surprise, Shay?" Maggie's eyes sparkled with excitement as she almost danced across her grandmother's front porch late Saturday morning.

Overly conscious of Nick sprawled on a chaise longue behind her and swamped by a rush of love that threatened to swamp her, Shay hid her emotions by hugging his mother. It hurt so much to be so near him and not go to him, not wrap her arms around him and tell him that she loved him. But nothing had changed. She whispered a prayer for help.

"How are you, Mrs. Green?" she asked.

"Never better, my dear. I don't know how to thank you for your hard work with Maggie." She dabbed at the tear forming in the corner of her eye. "To see her walking again is a total answer to prayer."

"Yes, it is. A special answer to a little girl's faith." Shay squeezed her hand then turned toward Maggie. "Sneakers, jeans, jacket—check?"

"Check. And cane." Maggie held it up. A burst of barking from Shay's car made her eyes widen. "Are we taking Hugs?"

"Your uncle said he'd look after him while we're gone." Shay's face burned. She explained that Hugs had escaped his pen and found his way into her closet, where he'd chosen an expensive pair of silver Versace shoes—her favorite—to chew on. For peace of mind and the safety of her wardrobe, she'd asked Nick to watch him while she was away with Maggie today.

Nick made several jokes at her expense and then suggested she'd have to figure out another solution for the dog while she was at work, but she sensed he was keeping things light as a way of withdrawing from her, because he didn't like what she'd said the other day.

Shay couldn't help that. All she could do was pray he'd see the truth and put his trust and faith in God to supply his needs.

"Major and I have several events planned for today," Nick said.

"Major?" Shay lifted one eyebrow. "Who or what is Major?"

"That's my name for your distinguished animal."

"Uh-huh." She watched him balance his coffee cup on his flat midriff and asked, "Events such as—?"

"A nap is first on the list."

"Good luck with that." She returned to the car, put her dog on a leash and led him to the house. "Under any circumstance, do not let this animal into your house," she said to Mrs. Green as she handed the lead to Nick. "He is death to expensive clothing."

"Well, I don't have any, so we should get along fine. Bye, Maggie. Be good." She wrapped her granddaughter in a hug.

"I will, Grandma. Bye, Uncle Nick." She hugged him, too, then presented herself to Shay. "I'm ready."

"Call me when you need me, Shay. And you will need me—argh!" Nick's parting shot was cut off as Hugs knocked over his coffee cup and stained his shirt.

"You'll probably be the one to call me," Shay shot back and laughed at his grumbled comment. "We'll be back before dark," she told Mrs. Green. She allowed herself one last glance at Nick before making sure Maggie was belted in. Her car started on the first turn and she drove away without looking back.

"Where are we going?" Maggie asked.

"I thought we'd head to the lake for a swim and a picnic at a special place I used to go years ago with my dad." Shay felt an inward tickle of delight. Maggie couldn't possibly know that Shay had chosen this isolated location as a test to herself, to prove she hadn't just spouted words to Nick but had truly found the trust in God she'd touted. "I love swimming."

"So do I." Maggie grinned. "And diving."

"We'll do both, I promise." She pressed the button so the roof would retract. The feel of the warm breeze against her skin made everything better. "You'll be so tired when we get home that you'll sleep for a week."

The sparkle in Maggie's eyes told Shay she intended to make those words come true.

The previous evening Shay had scouted out the road to the place her dad had called Mooney's in memory of an old silver prospector. Confident in her route, she drove to the site of their picnic, a small tree-enclosed glade that required a short hike from where they parked. Once Maggie was out of the car, Shay handed her the cane.

"Take this just in case," she said. "You can use it like a walking stick up the hill." She spared a thought to wonder if she should have chosen such a remote spot, but Maggie loved to fish and the best spot was at this secluded part of the lake. Maggie would love it when she saw the rod Shay had tucked into her rucksack.

Breathless from lugging the picnic basket uphill, Shay felt her efforts were well worth it when they arrived at the small lake. Once immersed in the water they'd have a fantastic view for miles in any direction of the desert floor below them. When the sun grew too warm, they'd have plenty of shade under the cottonwoods that clung to the hilltop.

"I have to sit down." Maggie puffed out the words, her voice trembling.

"Okay. Sit here and rest a moment." Shay worried she'd tired the child too much. She knew better than anyone that Maggie's mobility wasn't yet back to normal. But once she'd tucked their picnic in a nearby shady spot, Maggie had found new energy. She peeled off her clothes to reveal her pretty red swimsuit beneath.

"Let's swim," she said with a giggle.

"Go slowly," Shay directed. "It's slippery in spots." Glowing with perspiration, she dragged off her own jeans and T-shirt, glad she'd put on her suit in the cool of her house. She helped Maggie over the stones and into the water. "Oh, this feels good," she breathed as she glided into the water.

Time stood still as they paddled lazily for a while. The screech of a hawk disturbed Shay's calm once and she glanced around nervously, wondering if she should have asked Nick to come. Immediately, the bubble of anxiety began building.

God has not given us a spirit of fear.

Shay let the words swell and fill her mind as she reminded herself who was in charge. The fear ebbed. She whispered a prayer of thanksgiving just before Maggie swamped her with a cannonball splash. The little girl's squeals and giggles drove away whatever fragments remained as they played in their paradise.

When they climbed out of the water and dried off, Maggie sat on her towel while Shay laid out the feast she'd prepared. Shay was delighted as the little girl devoured her favorite foods.

"This is so fun." Maggie leaned against a tree trunk and drank her lemonade.

Shay leaned over and hugged the child who'd grown into her heart. "You're a very special girl, Maggie." She swallowed past the lump in her throat, refusing to dwell on the thought that she might never have a daughter like Maggie, someone to hold and hold on to. Someone to love.

There were those doubts again. As if God didn't know her heart's desire.

Trust, she reminded herself.

For God has said, "I will never, never fail you nor forsake you."

"I have a surprise." Shay reached back to grab her pack and swung it in front of Maggie. "Dig in here and see if you find something."

"A surprise?" Maggie hunched over the bag. She gave a squeal as she pulled out the rod and reel. "I love fishing!" she said as she popped open the small tackle box and took out a hook.

"I think I've heard you say that once or twice." Shay grinned at the studiously bent head. A movie played in her head of fifteen years ago when Nick had insisted she learn how to fish. He'd been as intent as Maggie on setting the hook just right.

Dear Nick. Her heart pinched with longing.

Trust.

They spent the next hour fishing. Shay had been half hoping that nothing would bite because she hated taking fish off the line, but Maggie caught four. As deftly as any expert, she slid the squirming creatures off the hook and set them back into the water to live another day.

When it was time to pack up and go, Maggie said, "We should come again and bring Uncle Nick. He likes doing things with you."

Shay's breath hitched. If only—

"I wish he didn't have to go away next week," Maggie said with a mournful face.

"Well, maybe he'll come back for a visit soon," was the only thing Shay could think of to say. She wanted Nick here, too, but maybe that was just her own selfish desire. Maybe God's plan for him did lie in Seattle.

Maybe she was supposed to live alone.

"Ready to go back?" Shay asked.

"Yes." Maggie glanced around one last time. "Thank you, Shay."

"You're welcome, darling."

Shay went ahead of Maggie so she could help when needed. And help was needed because a very hard wind starting whipping across the desert floor, raising sand as it moved in gusts and whorls. The grit bit into their skin with a ferocity that surprised Shay until she saw a voluminous yellow cloud forming in the distance.

"A sandstorm is coming," she told Maggie as panic wrapped its tentacles around her heart. She threw her gear in the back of the car. "You get inside while I put the top up."

But the top wouldn't move because Shay's engine wouldn't start.

We're stuck out here, alone, and no one knows where we are.

For a moment panic rendered Shay immobile, until the slash of sand in her face jerked her back to awareness.

Shelter. They needed shelter.

She struggled to manually lift the top into place but the wind was fierce and almost ripped it out of her hand. In the midst of struggling with it, she caught sight of Maggie's face and knew she had to get the scared little girl to safety. But first she would call Nick for help. He would find them—Shay knew that as certainly as she knew her own name.

Only her cell phone had no reception.

As another blast of grit pelted her bare arms and face, Shay knew she could not delay. They had to move.

"Come on, sweetie. We'll hide in one of these caves until this passes. I'll help you." She half boosted Maggie up the first step of the incline they'd just descended. It was too rocky to carry her and risk a fall that would undo all Maggie's hard work to walk again. "There's a place here where I used to stay when Dad and I played hide-and-seek. We'll wait in there. We're going to be fine, Maggie. Don't worry."

"I'm not worried. I'm praying." Maggie's lips moved as they struggled upward.

"You stay, honey. I'm going back for some stuff," Shay said when they were finally inside. She saw Maggie's face tighten and hugged her. "Don't worry. I just want to get the rest of the food and a blanket, in case we have to camp here for a bit. You keep praying."

"I'll ask God to send Uncle Nick," Maggie said.

"Good idea." Shay paused in the opening of the cave. But how would Nick know where to find them?

The wind tore at her as she scrambled down the rocks to her car. It didn't seem to be dissipating. Moving as quickly as possible, she bundled as much as she could carry into her rucksack, including the leftover lemonade. Then she scrambled back up to the cave.

"I'm back," she called to Maggie, raising her voice to be heard over the wind. "I'm just going to step outside and try my phone again to see if I can let your grandmother know that we'll be late." She was grateful when Maggie didn't argue. If only her own faith was that strong.

Shay's heart sank when she saw there was only one bar of reception.

"Please let this work," she whispered as she dialed.

The fourth time she edged a little closer to the precipice and extended her arm. To her amazement the call went through and was immediately picked up by Nick.

"Shay, there's a bad storm…" he said, his voice fading.

"Nick!" She stretched her arm an inch farther and yelled, hoping the wind wouldn't obliterate her voice. "My car's dead. We're at Mooney's. Please help."

The phone blinked out; the battery was dead. All she could do was pray he'd heard her. She walked back into the cave slowly as she tried to come up with a way to tell Maggie she wasn't sure when help was coming. What were they going to do? If she could carry Maggie out, they might get caught in a rainstorm and that meant getting wet and risking hypothermia when the desert cooled off as it always did at night. They wouldn't have enough clothes to keep warm even if they snuggled together inside the cave. Rattlers came out at night. Javelina pigs and mountain lions stalked and fed at night.

They were in trouble.

"I'm c-cold, Shay." Maggie sat huddled inside, lips chattering.

"This should warm you up." Shay wrapped the child in the blanket then, after checking to be sure there were no animals inside the cave, sank down beside her and drew her close. "Better?"

"Yes." Maggie was silent for a few moments then she asked, "How long do we have to stay here?"

"I'm not sure." Shay had to be honest. "It's a big storm, honey. Listen." As if to emphasize her words, the wind chose that moment to send a shower of sand into the mouth of the cave. "But we're safe here." Shay didn't *feel* safe, but she would not let Maggie see her fear. "I brought the rest of the picnic for when you get hungry."

"Okay." Maggie peered through the gloom for several moments. When she finally spoke, her question surprised Shay. "Uncle Nick said your dad died. Did you have a good daddy?"

"I did, darling." Shay snuggled the girl close against her and bent her head to rest her cheek against Maggie's still-damp hair. "I had the best father a girl could want."

"So did I," whispered Maggie. She sniffled.

"I know." Though she tried to ignore the hiss of wind into the cave, worrisome what-ifs plagued Shay.

"We were lucky to have had such good fathers," she said, struggling to blot out her unease.

Maggie frowned. "When I was in the hospital, a lady told me I was an orphan. I asked Grandma what that meant."

"What did Grandma say?"

"She said I wasn't an orphan because God's my daddy and Jesus is my brother." Maggie lifted her head. "And you know what else Grandma said?"

"Why don't you tell me, sweetheart?"

Shay's admiration for Mrs. Green's ability to teach her faith to her granddaughter was shattered by a strange noise. She leaned forward a little, concentrating on where the sound came from. Was it just the hiss of sand in the air as it hit the stones outside? Or an echo that kept rebounding inside?

Or was it something more sinister? They were near the front, but perhaps something had taken refuge in the back where she hadn't seen it. She shuddered at the thought.

Shay couldn't quiet her rising panic when a shadow on the cave wall moved. Her breath jammed in her chest. Every brain cell told her to grab Maggie and run.

God? The one-word prayer whispered straight from her heart to heaven.

Suddenly there was a lull in the wind. The whole world seemed to hush. Maggie's pure, confident tones rang out.

"Grandma said God isn't like other daddies. He knows how to take care of His kids." With that, Maggie closed her eyes and fell asleep.

I will never, never fail you nor forsake you.

This morning's verse bloomed crystal clear in

Shay's head. The promise was hers. Maggie had accepted it. Now Shay could choose to believe it or she could fret and make herself sick with worry.

Either way, sooner or later, Nick would show up.

Because that's who he was.

Shay made her choice.

"I will trust You," she whispered. "We are safe in Your hands."

The wind raged again. The sand pelted the cave opening, and the sky was just as dark. But inside Shay's head, a reassuring presence blossomed, pushing out panic and fear.

Even if she never had her own family, she was part of God's family and He would never let her down.

Shay closed her eyes and worshipped. And in that moment she remembered a detail so startling, she knew it had to be from God.

"Shay? Shay!" Nick glared at the offending phone but no one answered. He dialed Shay's number but it went immediately to voice mail.

"What's wrong?" His mother hovered at his elbow.

"I'm not sure but I think they're in trouble, Mom." Nick met her gaze.

"Then you'll find them." Her confidence in him was reassuring.

"There was a lot of static. Nothing Shay said came through clearly. It sounded like she said they were at the moon." He shook his head, his hands fisted at his sides. "I'm pretty sure she also said her car was dead."

"The moon?" His mom frowned. "Is that some kind of amusement park?"

"Not that I know of." Why hadn't he gone along

with them, or at least asked her to tell him where they were going? He glanced down at Hugs. The dog lay flopped on the floor at his feet, his big eyes fixed on Nick as if he knew something was wrong.

"If we don't know where to look, how can we find them?" Worry lines appeared at the corners of his mom's eyes.

"We'll get help." He dialed Kent. "Hey. Are you and Jaclyn okay?" He listened for a moment then explained the situation and what he thought he'd heard Shay say. "The thing is, I can't figure out what 'the moon' means."

"I haven't got a clue either. Hang on a sec." Kent talked to Jaclyn then returned. "Jaclyn says the Weather Channel is claiming this storm will let up in about an hour. I'll call Zac and Brianna. We'll head over to your place as soon as we can and go from there."

But go where?

"They're coming as soon as they can," Nick told his mother.

"But it will be dark soon, Nicky." The old nickname that his mother used only at the most stressful times told him how worried she was. "I'll pray."

"I hope that's enough to help Shay," he muttered.

"Prayer is always enough." His mom frowned. "If you say you trust God, you have to trust Him with everything, son. He has plans for Shay and Maggie. He isn't going to let harm come to them."

Worry chewed at Nick. This was exactly why he'd been so hesitant about that job in Seattle. What if this had happened when he was away? Who would be there for the ones he loved?

Loved?

Maggie, yes...but Shay, too?

The knowledge blindsided him, but he knew it was true. He did love Shay, and somewhere deep inside he'd known it for a while. So why hadn't he told her that when she said she loved him? Because he was afraid?

But fear was exactly why he wanted so desperately to see her healed, to see her happy, to look after her.

Because he was in love with her.

"Nick?"

"Yeah?" Half-dazed by this new understanding, he glanced at his mother.

"Why is it so hard for you to trust God? He's your Father."

"Sorry, but that analogy doesn't exactly inspire me, Mom." He let out a harsh laugh.

"God is nothing like your earthly father," she said. "But you're not just talking about God's trustworthiness, are you? You're also worried about your own."

"I am my father's son," Nick said bitterly. "I am just as bad at relationships as the old man was. I even walked out on a woman I said I loved," he admitted. "Twice. I can't be trusted with love."

"That's why this decision to take the job in Seattle is tearing you apart," she said. "You want to be here with Shay, but you won't take the risk."

"I love her." It felt good to finally say that aloud. "I want her to be happy. I want to *make* her happy. But I can't stay."

"Because?" his mother prodded.

"Because I don't think I will make her happy. Besides, the family needs me and I can't fail them. I can't fail you, or my sisters, or Maggie."

"Nick, you won't fail us no matter where you work.

You've been there every time your sisters and I needed you." She touched his cheek. "Sometimes I think you've been there too much for us."

Nick gaped at her, stunned by her words, words that turned his entire perception of himself upside down.

"Your sisters and I all find it too easy to turn to you at the first hint of trouble, and like the dependable man you are, you rush in to rescue us." His mother smiled. "You always have, because you think no one else will. But that's a lie, Nick. God uses you when you let Him, yes. But God doesn't expect you to give up your life for us. If you're not available, He'll find some other way to see His will done."

Nick couldn't assimilate her words. For so long he'd been the go-to guy in his family. To just back off and let them deal with whatever—well, that just wasn't his way.

"You can't always be there for us, even though you want to be." She wrapped her arms around his waist and laid her head on his shoulder. "I am so immensely proud of you, Nick. You are everything a son should be and more. But you can't run yourself ragged trying to be all the things your father wasn't. You deserve to find happiness with Shay."

"But what if I fail Shay, like Dad failed you?" That memory of his father turning his back on his family still burned. "What if I mess up and hurt her?"

"Then you apologize and ask for forgiveness." She sighed. "Humans fail, dear. All of us. I failed your father, too." She smiled at his look of disbelief. "It's true."

"But Mom, if I stay in Hope, if I don't take that job—" Nick gulped. "What will I do?"

"I don't know, sweetheart. Take the time to woo the

woman you love? Start thinking about what you want your own future to look like? Keep blessing people with your inventions?"

"You make it sound so simple."

"It is simple, Nicky." She leaned back. "Now, are you ready to pray with me?"

Nick thought of Shay and Maggie out there somewhere, alone and probably frightened. And then he thought of God wrapping His arms around Nick's loved ones, protecting them and keeping them safe, just as he wanted to.

Nick reached out and took his mother's hand as she led a prayer asking for the Father's guidance. Then Nick prayed his own prayer.

"God, You know how much I love Shay. But I can't keep her safe all the time. I trust You to bring Shay and Maggie home safely. I trust You to direct my future. Put me where You want me." He inhaled. "You know what the future holds, and You know how much I want a future with Shay. I leave it in Your hands, Father. Help us find Shay and Maggie. Please."

Nick lifted his head, met his mother's tearing eyes and smiled.

Now all they could do was wait for God to show them the next step.

Chapter Fourteen

Shay sat motionless with Maggie sleeping in her arms as the storm raged, waned and finally died away. The sky cleared, the wind calmed and the world around them returned to normal. She had just begun to nod off when she heard the pad of footsteps outside the cave.

Outlined by the moon, the shadow of an animal filled the cave opening. She couldn't tell exactly what it was. Only that it stood there, poised, waiting.

In that instant fear rose up like a tsunami and prepared to engulf Shay. Every muscle tensed. She wanted to scream but couldn't.

"The Lord is my shepherd, I shall not want." Maggie's soft but unfaltering voice surprised her, cutting through the cloud of fear.

As Maggie continued, the animal twisted its neck to watch them. Its eyes seemed to glow through the shadows, joining the host of stars behind it that glimmered and shone. On seeing those stars, Shay's fears melted away. God had created the stars and the animal and Maggie and her. Like a shepherd He led them all on the best path. Nothing happened that He wasn't in control of.

She joined Maggie, her voice growing more confident with every word.

"Even though I walk through the valley of the shadow of death, I fear no evil for thou art with me." Loudly, their voices raised in triumph, Shay and Maggie finished the verse. When Shay looked again, the animal was gone. All she could see now were stars. Laid out across the desert sky, they shone. Some were brighter, some were dimmer, but all of them shone, proclaiming the power and glory of God. Then, suddenly, a star burst out from the others and shot across the sky, scattering particles of light in a path behind it.

"Did you see that, Shay?"

"Yes, darling, I saw it," she said, remembering the night when she and Nick had watched the meteor shower. A powerful certainty filled her.

God had led her back to Hope, to Whispering Hope Clinic, and to Nick. He'd given the love she felt filling her heart. God would finish what He started.

"I can do that," she whispered.

"What?" Maggie asked.

"It's getting light. We should get our stuff together and be ready to leave. Your uncle will be here soon."

"Really?" Maggie's big brown eyes studied her.

"I'm positive." She grinned at the little girl. "Want to take a dip in the lake before he gets here?"

Maggie laughed and Shay laughed right along with her. God was in charge. He would take care of them. Always.

And that wasn't the only thing she held in her heart.

She could hardly wait to tell Nick what she'd remembered. It could change everything—for both of them.

When Nick saw the red convertible, his heart jumped with relief. She was here.

He saw a picnic basket sitting on a ledge above him. As he scrambled up toward it, he saw a cave behind it. He climbed quickly, using his hands to propel him faster.

"Shay? Maggie?" They weren't inside.

Nick moved back outside and dug out his cell phone to let everyone know he'd found the car. But he couldn't find cell service so he climbed a bit higher. And that's when he heard the singing.

His heart jumped for joy. Maggie's childish soprano accompanied by Shay's strong voice filled the hills and the valleys, echoing back to penetrate even the tiniest crevices.

"Our God is an awesome God," they sang.

"Yes, He is," Nick agreed, his heart skipping in time to the tune. "Thank You, God." He moved higher up the hill, anxious to hold his loved ones in his arms. He ducked through an overgrowth, and when he stepped free he saw Shay and Maggie seated at the edge of a small lake, legs dipping in and out of the water as they swayed together, arms around each other's waists. As far as Nick could tell, Shay looked perfectly calm, with no sign of panic marring her lovely face.

Thank You, Lord.

"Do you think that was loud enough for Uncle Nick to hear?" Maggie asked.

He stood silent, curious to hear Shay's response.

"Whether he heard it or not, Nick will find us. He won't let us down."

Such faith in him. For a moment the old worries besieged him, but he shoved them back and stepped forward. "You sure have a lot of faith in me," he said, his eyes meeting and holding Shay's.

"Yes." Shay gave him the most heart-stopping smile he had ever seen in his entire life.

"Oh, Uncle Nick, we had the awesome-est picnic." With Shay's helping hand, Maggie rose and walked over to encircle his legs with her arms.

"I don't think awesome-est is a word," he said with a chuckle, swinging her into his arms.

"It is when you're talking about Shay's picnics. We missed you." She hugged his neck then leaned back to look into his face. "You should come next time, Uncle Nick."

"I intend to, Maggie-mine. I intend to be at every one of Shay's picnics in the future." He set his niece down and locked his gaze on Shay. "If she'll let me."

"Every time you're home, you mean?" Shay swung her feet out of the water and rose. She tilted her head to one side, watching as he smiled.

"I am home." Nick waited for her to get closer, and when she did he reached out and pulled her into his arms, burying his face in her hair. "This is my home, Shay. With you." He leaned back just a little, so he could see her face. "I love you. I want a future with you."

"But—" She stopped, though her arms were already winding around his neck. "What about your job?"

"They'll have to find someone else. My life is here in Hope." It felt so good to say that. "I love you, Shay.

Will you marry me and share whatever future God gives us together?"

"Say yes, Shay," Maggie chanted, her dark eyes shining.

"Yes," Shay repeated. "I love you, Nick."

Nick didn't need anything else. He pulled the gorgeous Shay Parker as close as he could and kissed her. He poured everything into that kiss—his worry about her and Maggie, his relief that God had answered his prayers in a way he'd never expected, and his dream of a future with the most beautiful woman he'd ever known. He would have kept on kissing her but a small hand tugged so hard on his pant leg, it broke his concentration.

"Excuse me a minute—don't go anywhere," he said to Shay. He peered down at his grinning niece. "What?"

"Are you and Shay going to get married?" Maggie asked.

Nick looked at Shay. She smiled at him. "Yes," they said together.

"Can I be in it? I'd practice ever so hard to carry the rings or whatever you want. I promise I wouldn't mess up or…"

Shay eased out of Nick's arms and hunched down to lay a finger over Maggie's lips to stop her words. Then she drew the girl close.

"Maggie, my darling Maggie," Shay said. "Do you think Nick and I would even think about getting married without you?"

"I don't know," came Maggie's muffled response.

Shay turned to smile at him, and Nick's knees turned to mush. Lord, he loved this woman. He squatted down beside them and folded them both into his embrace.

"You're the one who brought Shay and me together in the first place. You're the one who taught us to trust God. We watched your faith and we learned how to trust Him." He smiled at her. "You have to be in our wedding, Maggie-mine."

Maggie beamed. "Good. Can I wear a pink dress? I love pink."

"You can wear whatever you want, sweetheart," his wife-to-be said. "Maybe Uncle Nick will wear a matching pink tie."

"Pink? Shay, come on." He straightened, ready to plead his case.

"And we could get a big pink ribbon for Hugs," Maggie agreed. "He has to be part of the wedding, too."

"No. Absolutely not. That dog is a—" Nick stopped short. His two ladies were looking at him as if he'd doused them with water from the lake. His heart melted. "So, is this what it's going to be like?" he asked meekly.

Shay grinned. "Want to back out?"

"Not on your life." He held out a hand, pulled her upright and pressed another kiss on her mouth. "We are getting married, pink ties and dogs and bows notwithstanding. You hear me?"

"I hear you, Nick. I can hardly wait." Shay wrapped her arms around him and kissed him back with a fervor that drew no complaints from Nick.

He checked his heart and felt only anticipation about their future and what God would show them.

"Not that kissing again," Maggie grumbled. "I want some breakfast."

Nick burst out laughing. "Okay, Mags, we'll go get breakfast." He took her hand and helped her down the path, glancing at Shay, delighted to see the same joy reflected on her face that warmed his insides. "But if you're going to be in our wedding, I've got a condition."

"What condition?" Maggie planted her hands on her hips.

"I get to kiss Shay whenever I want and you don't get to complain about it." He set her inside his truck and fastened her seat belt. Then he held out his hand. "Deal?"

With a heavy sigh, Maggie shook his hand. "Deal," she agreed.

"Good. Now sit tight for a minute, will you?" He closed the truck door then turned to face his best friend. "I don't know how this will turn out," he said. "I have a verbal contract with the team. I might have to go back and work a couple of months until they find someone else."

"God will work something out," she said, her lovely face glowing. "However He does it, we'll keep trusting Him to lead us."

"Sounds good to me." Conscious of Maggie's peering eyes, Nick contented himself with one last quick kiss.

"Nick, I remembered something important last night." She took a deep breath. "I know who the stalker is. I remembered him talking to the maintenance man one time, and the man called him 'son.'" She smiled at his quick intake of breath. "It should be enough for the police to catch him, shouldn't it?"

"It should be more than enough, sweet Shay." Nick hugged her. "Are you okay?"

"Yes, thank God. I am very okay." She hugged him hard. "Let's get on with the rest of our lives."

"Deal." He helped Shay into his truck and drove to his mother's house, where Maggie, after wiggling out of her grandmother's arms, broke the news about their upcoming wedding.

"I'm so delighted." His mom hugged him then embraced Shay. "You've always been a daughter of my heart. This will make it reality." She stopped. "How was it up there? I remember you told me you had a fear of the desert at night."

"I gave all my fears to God," Shay explained. "I don't know what He has planned for my future, but with Him by my side, and Nick," she added, grasping his hand, "I know I can do anything He sets before me."

"That's quite a lesson."

Shay gave Mrs. Green a smile. "I learned it from someone very special, and very wise."

A few minutes later Jaclyn, Kent, Brianna and Zac arrived while Shay was on the phone with the NYPD. Once her friends had heard the story of the cave ordeal and her returned memory, Shay told them she and Nick were getting married. After a lot of hugging and congratulations, the ladies tipped their heads together and began wedding planning. Nick led the men out to the deck, where they sat drinking his mom's lemonade.

"So what will you do in Hope?" Zac finally asked the question Nick figured was on everyone's mind.

"I have no idea. Odd jobs, maybe." Nick shrugged, pretending it didn't matter. "I'll do something. The important thing is that I stay here."

The other two men were silent for several moments. Finally Kent spoke, scuffing his toe against the deck as he said the words slowly. "I think the Lord's got more in store for you than odd jobs. I think He brought you back here for a reason." He slapped Nick on the back. "Just hang in there. He'll show you His plan soon enough."

Nick opened his mouth to respond but a squeal from inside had the three men jumping out of their seats.

Brianna stuck her head out the screen door.

"Kent, you need to get your wife to the hospital. Apparently she's been having contractions for a while but didn't want to interrupt the search. Well?" she demanded, hands on her hips. "Why are the three of you staring at me like that? A baby's coming."

"Baby. Right. Hospital." Kent jumped up and stalked toward the truck—without his wife.

Nick started laughing. "You hold him there," he told Zac. "I'll go help Jaclyn. We'd better follow them in. I have a hunch he's going to need us before this day is over."

"What are friends for?" Zac high-fived him. "Congratulations, by the way. You and Shay are perfect for each other."

"Perfectly matched," Jaclyn agreed as she stepped onto the deck. Then she groaned and grabbed her friends' hands. "Oh, boy." She puffed through the contraction with Brianna's coaching, then muttered, "I need to leave. Now."

"You think?" Nick said as Kent roared up, lifted his wife into the truck and roared away.

"Keep praying, Mom," Nick whispered in her ear as he hugged her. "This is turning out to be a day when we need a lot of God's help."

"All we have to do is ask." She nudged him. "Now,

take Shay to the hospital. Maggie and I will work on the wedding. We know exactly what we want, don't we, honey?"

"Pink," Maggie said with a nod. "Lots and lots of pink. It's Shay's favorite color."

"I see." His stomach clenched at the thought of what the two of them would create, but he tamped down his misgivings, helped Shay into his truck and followed the others.

"Is your favorite color really pink?"

"No." She laughed. "But it really doesn't matter, does it? I just want to marry you."

He picked up her hand and kissed her palm.

"Now, that's what I call having your priorities sorted," Nick told her. "Because I want to marry you, too. And soon. As soon as possible." He turned to look into her beautiful face. "What do you know about women having babies?"

"Not a thing, but I guess we'll trust God to teach us something new."

For the first time in a long time, trusting God sounded absolutely perfect to Nick.

Epilogue

"I can't believe a world-class designer just gave you this wedding dress. It's spectacular." Jaclyn sat on the living-room sofa holding her sleeping daughter, Lily Grace. Liam Kent lay nearby, wide awake but quiet in the blanket Shay had made.

"Evan is a dear friend and an amazing designer. I love his work. His dresses have always made me feel as if I'm a princess. This one certainly does." Shay smoothed a hand over the feather-light silk creation, a one-of-a-kind design made especially for her, more beautiful than anything she'd ever worn.

"I can't believe you look more lovely today than you ever did on any magazine cover," Brianna said as she watched Shay bend to press a tender kiss on each baby's cheek.

"Well, thank you, Jaclyn. But what *I* can't believe is how a doctor can be pregnant with twins and not know it! You always were an overachiever, Jaclyn."

Jaclyn grinned as Shay and Brianna admired the babies.

"Those things are all true, of course. And wonderful besides. You girls are right to notice them. But what I can't believe is that the New York police finally caught Shay's stalker." Mrs. Green shook her head. "That memory she had in the cave with Maggie was certainly God timing, wasn't it?" She asked Shay to give them more details.

"Dom was the son of the building maintenance guy. He was supposed to be helping his dad but he'd often disappear for hours at a time. His father thought he was playing video games or something since it had been happening for years." It didn't bother Shay at all to talk about it. "Maybe that was true when he was younger, but when the modeling agency bought the building as a shoot site because of its roof terrace, Dom apparently became mesmerized by the models. Of course he had access to everything and he'd keep the pink telephone message cards we threw away. He started spying on us and got fixated on me."

"Who wouldn't?" Jaclyn asked with a proud smile.

"Nick said he started by stealing some of the jewelry you were modeling," Mrs. Green said.

"Yes, but his dad found out and put it back. He never knew Dom was following me or threatening me. And that only started because Dom saw me give away some flowers he'd sent. Though I didn't realize that."

"I'm just glad they got him. That Dom would have gone on deceiving women and terrorizing them if you hadn't remembered who he was and given the police enough information that they set a trap that he couldn't get out of. Now, thank God, he won't hurt anyone again." Mrs. Green reached out to brush Shay's cheek with her hand, a fond smile lighting her face. "God answers. He always answers."

"Yes, He does," Brianna agreed. She checked her watch. "Hey, we've got to get this woman to the church on time. Let's move it. Where's her veil?"

"Where are the flowers?" Jaclyn asked.

"Where's my phone?" Shay said as the familiar peal sounded. She found it and saw Nick's number. "I have to take this," she said. "It's my groom." Her heart swelled with joy as she said his name. "Nick?"

"Hey, gorgeous. Why aren't you at the church? I'm waiting."

"I'm on my way. Be patient," she said. "After today we'll have forever."

"Yes, we will. Listen, God really came through for us, sweetheart." Nick sounded ecstatic.

"What's going on?" Surely nothing would go wrong now—no. *Trust God*, Shay ordered herself. He didn't bring you this far to leave you. "You sound excited, Nick."

"I am. We just received the most perfect wedding gift."

"You opened it without me?" Shay asked.

"I was told to. It was a letter. You won't believe this, Shay. Thanks to a little push from Chief Burger, the town of Hope just offered me the job of activities director," he told her, his voice jubilant.

Shay closed her eyes, her heart exploding with praise. "Go on."

"They said that while I was in Seattle working out my notice to the team, they realized there were so many groups that had worked with me that they needed someone on staff to keep them running. I am employed full-time starting the first of next month."

"Praise God," she whispered, trying not to cry and ruin her makeup.

"You'd better double that praise, sweetheart." His excitement transmitted clearly over the phone. "Because they've also initiated a fund to create that wellness center you and I proposed. They believe it will benefit the whole town and are anxious to get together with us as soon as we return from our honeymoon to hammer out details!"

"Fantastic!" Shay couldn't help but whisper a prayer of thanks.

"I love you, Shay Parker."

"That's soon-to-be Mrs. Green, to you, buddy. And I love you, too, Nick." The enormity of the love that filled her heart and soul swamped Shay.

"Uh-oh. Maggie just texted me." Nick chuckled. "She wants me to get my boutonniere. Now."

"You'd better obey our 'wedding planner.' I'll follow shortly," Shay promised.

"And then we'll begin our future," he murmured. "I can hardly wait."

"Me, either." Shay saw her friends gesturing at the clock. "I love you. Bye."

"The flowers are at the church," Mrs. Green said, emerging from the bedroom. "Someone put them in the fridge in the basement. That's why we couldn't find them. We're good to—oh, Shay. You look so very happy."

"Because I am." She explained about Nick's new job. "Thank you all," she said, studying each dear face. "You've made this the most wonderful day of my life."

"Well, us and Nick," Brianna teased.

"Yes, especially Nick," she agreed.

Jaclyn looked at her watch. "We're behind sched-ule. Is Kent here?"

"Outside with the limo," Mrs. Green confirmed. "Give me one of those babies to carry, Jaclyn. Brianna, you help Shay. We don't want the bride to be late for her own wedding."

They arrived at the church and were escorted into the bride's dressing room by a very excited Maggie, who looked sweet in a pink sundress that Shay had picked out for her. She held Shay's bouquet and a small rectangular box.

"This is for you, Shay," she said holding out the sil-ver box. "With lots of love from Uncle Nick."

"Oh." Shay lifted the lid and found a silver filigree necklace with a tiny heart nestled inside. In the center of the heart sparkled an emerald.

"It's lovely," Mrs. Green said. "Shall I put it on for you?"

"Yes, please." Shay leaned over while the necklace was fastened. Then she drew out a tiny card that said, *You have my heart, Shay. Always. Love, Nick.* "It's the perfect wedding gift," she whispered, eager to tell him thanks in a more personal way.

"Here, Shay!" Maggie said, holding out a sheaf of dark pink sweetheart roses. "These are from Uncle Nick, too. He chose them from Grandma's garden."

"They're lovely." Shay sniffed. She glanced around, overcome by the generosity of everyone who'd helped make her wedding happen in such a short time.

"I just wish we could have finished renovations on the church before your wedding," Jaclyn said, tracing a finger across the worn paneling on the wall.

"I don't think we'll ever be done with that," Brianna

said. "We'll probably still be working on it when all of our kids graduate from college and come back to Hope to be married. That's how it should be, isn't it? The church growing and changing as our lives do?"

"I like the sound of that," Shay murmured as she set her veil in place.

"Brianna and I wanted to give you a special gift, because you're our best friend and because we're glad you joined us in the clinic, and because we're so happy you and Nick are getting married." Jaclyn grinned.

"Yes." Brianna smiled at Jaclyn. "We wanted something really special and something lasting. So we're going to make a special donation to the wellness center you and Nick put forward. It will be funding earmarked for a children's section so that no child who uses it will ever pay a fee."

"I can't imagine a better gift," Shay said, embracing the pair. Of course she was crying. Of course it took a few moments to repair the damage. But her joy was so great that nothing could dim it.

"Shay, Uncle Nick is waiting at the front," Maggie said after she'd peeked out the door. "The church is full and everyone's ready." She clutched the door. "Can we start now?"

"Yes. We can start now." Shay nodded. Maggie opened the door wide. They all walked to the back of the church. "Thank you for making our day so special," Shay whispered to Maggie. The little girl started down the aisle first, walking proudly with no limp. Shay's heart gave a bump of pride. God had certainly brought her to this place—Maggie was confirmation of that. Brianna followed in a lighter pink press, then Jaclyn in the palest pink of all. Both of them stood next to their husbands, Nick's best men. The organ sounded and the congregation rose. Shay fixed her eyes on Nick.

Shay spared a thought for her father. He'd have been so proud to walk her down the aisle. She missed him desperately, but she knew he was watching.

She focused on Nick until she was finally by his side. His gaze held hers as Brianna and Jaclyn, Kent and Zac linked their hands together. Cherished and protected in his grip, Shay listened as he recited the age-old words that would bind them as husband and wife before God for the rest of their lives. Nick said his vows slowly, his eyes locked with hers, his voice quiet, the promise meant for her ears alone. He didn't stumble over the words as he'd teased he would. And when he slid the ring on her finger, it was as if her heart locked with his.

Then it was her turn. Nothing had ever felt more right than this moment.

"I, Shay, take you, Nick to be my lawfully wedded husband. For better, for worse, for richer, for poorer, in sickness and in health. As long as we both shall live."

After a short homily on what marriage meant, Pastor Marty told Nick he could kiss his bride. As his lips covered hers, Shay knew she was finally at home.

It was when they moved to sign the register that Shay saw it—a spray of the tiniest pure white roses in a silver vase on the table. While Nick was signing she leaned forward and peeked at the card tucked in with a pink ribbon.

To Shay, with love, Jessica.

"What's wrong?" Nick whispered as Shay gasped.

"Everything is right. An old friend of ours sent her

blessing." She showed him the roses. "Everything's perfect."

When the ceremony was over, the pastor announced, "Ladies and gentlemen, may I present Mr. and Mrs. Nick Green."

The congregation clapped as they walked together down the aisle. Outside the church, they formed a receiving line with bubbles filling the air around them, sparkling iridescence in the summer sunshine.

The reception was held under a huge white tent as the sun dipped behind the mountains. Tiny paper lanterns strung all over the ceiling were switched on as everyone found their place. Anyone who wanted to come had been invited to celebrate and that's exactly what they did, toasting the beautiful bride and her handsome groom. There was much tinkling of glasses to encourage the couple's kisses. Then Shay threw her bouquet which Mrs. Green caught. Finally Shay and Nick cut the wedding cake Susan Swan had made and passed it out to their guests.

It was while her friends were helping her change out of her wedding dress that Shay's friend Jaclyn asked, "Any idea where Nick's taking you for your honeymoon?"

"New York." Shay smiled at her two friends' dismayed looks.

"Why?" Brianna asked.

"It's time for us to make new memories in that city. It's only the beginning of what God has in store for us." Shay hugged them both then walked out the door and tucked her arm into Nick's, delighted to know that God had given her such a wonderful gift of love out of such a terrible time.

When everyone had wished them well and they were on their way out of town in her convertible, Shay took a moment to look at the man by her side—her husband.

"Do we have time for a side trip before we catch the plane?" she asked. Nick frowned but nodded. "We need to stop by my place."

"We've got a pretty tight schedule," he said, but he drove there quickly, casting her questioning looks but remaining silent until they arrived. Then his eyes widened. When he looked at her, he seemed stunned.

"You gave me the most lovely wedding gift," she said, fingering the chain at her neck. "This is mine to you. With all my love."

Nick caught her close and kissed her. Shay laughed at his quick glance over her shoulder.

"Go and check it out quickly," she said. "Then we have to go."

"Yes, ma'am." Nick vaulted over the side of her car and raced toward the building she'd had moved onto the property last night. He dragged open the door and peered inside. A moment later his woohoo echoed across the desert.

Shay sat content, unable to suppress her smile as she waited. After a few minutes Nick came racing out of the building, yanked open her door and caught her in his arms, swinging her around and around.

"I take it you like it," she said with a laugh, twining her arms around his neck. "I hope you enjoy your new shop, my darling husband. I know you'll use it to help those who need you. Those God sends your way."

"I love you, wife," he whispered. "And not because you gave me the most wonderful inventing shop in the world. You are the most beautiful woman I've ever known and your beauty starts in your heart. I love you." He kissed her, pouring his heart and all of his feelings into that kiss.

And Shay kissed him back until Nick finally drew away, set her in the car and took his place behind the wheel. But before he drove away he cupped her chin in his palms.

"From here on it's you and me and God. I love you, Shay."

"I love you, too, Nick." She leaned her head against his shoulder as they drove into the sunset.

Sometimes the unscripted moments when you let go of the controls and just trusted were the best of your life.

* * * * *

SPECIAL EXCERPT FROM

*When Amos Burkholder steps in to help the
Miller family, he soon discovers that middle daughter
Deborah disappears for hours at a time.
Where does she go?*

Read on for a sneak preview of
Courting Her Secret Heart *by Mary Davis,
available September 2018 from Love Inspired!*

Amos Burkholder looked out over the Millers' fields to be plowed
in the spring. He couldn't help but think of them as partly his. Of
course, they weren't his fields, and he might not even be here to do
the plowing and the planting. But if he was, he would take pride in
that work.

Bartholomew Miller appreciated everything he did around the
farm, so Amos worked harder than he ever had at home.

Bartholomew had never had a son to help him with all the work
around the farm. How had he run this place without sons?

But on the flip side, Amos's *mutter* had been alone doing the house
chores, cooking, cleaning and laundry for six men. How did she do it
without help?

On the far side of one of the fields, a woman emerged from a bare
stand of sycamore trees nestled next to a pond. She walked across the
field.

The woman came closer and closer.

Deborah.

Where did she go all the time? She had disappeared every day this
week and would be gone for hours. He was about to find out.

With her head down, she didn't see him approaching. He stepped
directly into her path a few yards in front of her. When it looked as
though she might literally run into him, he cleared his throat.

She halted a foot away. She was so startled to see him there, she
appeared to lose her balance. Her arms swung out to keep herself
upright.

LIEXP0818

He reached out and took hold of her upper arms to stop her from tumbling to the ground. "Whoa there."

She gasped. "I'm sorry. I didn't see you."

"Where have you been all day?"

"What? Nowhere." She tried to pull free of his grip, but he held fast.

He shook his head. "You've been somewhere. You've left every day this week and been gone for most of the day."

"I—I went for a walk."

"Where? Ohio?"

"We have a pond just over there. I like to sit and watch the ducks. It's a nice place to think and be alone. You should go sometime."

"I did. Today. You weren't there."

Her self-satisfied expression fell. "I was for a while, then I walked farther."

He sensed there was more to her absence than a walk. "Where?"

"Why do you care?"

"With your *vater* laid up, I'm responsible for everyone on this farm."

"I'm fine. I can take care of myself. May I go now?"

He didn't want to let her go but did. "I don't want you to leave the farm without telling me where you're going."

"Are you serious?"

He gave her his serious look.

She huffed and strode away.

Where did she go every day? He had wanted to follow her, but he realized it was none of his business. But curiosity pushed hard on him. He still might follow her if she didn't obey. Just to see. Just to watch her from a distance. Just to know her secret.

Something inside him feared for her. Feared she would walk out across this field and never return. Feared her secret would consume them both. She was a mystery.

A mystery he was drawn to solve.

Don't miss
Courting Her Secret Heart *by Mary Davis,*
available September 2018 wherever
Love Inspired® *books and ebooks are sold.*

www.LoveInspired.com

Love Inspired®

Save $1.00

on the purchase of **ANY**
Love Inspired® book.

Available wherever books are sold,
including most bookstores, supermarkets,
drugstores and discount stores.

✂- -

Save $1.00

on the purchase of ANY Love Inspired® book.

Coupon valid until October 31, 2018.
Redeemable at participating retail outlets in the U.S. and Canada only.
Limit one coupon per customer.

52615896

Canadian Retailers: Harlequin Enterprises Limited will pay the face value of
this coupon plus 10.25¢ if submitted by customer for this product only. Any
other use constitutes fraud. Coupon is nonassignable. Void if taxed, prohibited
or restricted by law. Consumer must pay any government taxes. Void if copied.
Inmar Promotional Services ("IPS") customers submit coupons and proof of sales
to Harlequin Enterprises Limited, P.O. Box 31000, Scarborough, ON M1R 0E7,
Canada. Non-IPS retailer—for reimbursement submit coupons and proof of
sales directly to Harlequin Enterprises Limited, Retail Marketing Department,
Bay Adelaide Centre, East Tower, 22 Adelaide Street West, 40th Floor, Toronto,
Ontario M5H 4E3, Canada.

5 65373 00076 2 (8100)0 12379

U.S. Retailers: Harlequin Enterprises
Limited will pay the face value of
this coupon plus 8¢ if submitted by
customer for this product only. Any
other use constitutes fraud. Coupon is
nonassignable. Void if taxed, prohibited
or restricted by law. Consumer must pay
any government taxes. Void if copied.
For reimbursement submit coupons
and proof of sales directly to Harlequin
Enterprises, Ltd 482, NCH Marketing
Services, P.O. Box 880001, El Paso,
TX 88588-0001, U.S.A. Cash value
1/100 cents.

® and ™ are trademarks owned and used by the trademark owner and/or its licensee.

© 2018 Harlequin Enterprises Limited

LICOUP89584

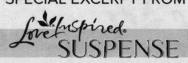
First Lieutenant Heidi Jenks, news reporter for CAF News,
blew a lock of hair out of her eyes and did her best to keep
from muttering under her breath about the boring stories
she was being assigned lately.

Heidi shut the door to the church where her interviewee
had insisted on meeting and walked down the steps. She
shivered and glanced over her shoulder. For some reason
she expected to see Boyd Sullivan, as if the fact that she
was alone in the dark would automatically mean the serial
killer was behind her.

After being chased by law enforcement last week, he'd
fallen from a bluff and was thought to be dead. But when
his body was never found, that assumption changed. He
was alive. Somewhere.

Heidi's steps took her past the base hospital. She was
getting ready to turn onto the street that would take her

home when a flash of movement from the K-9 training center caught her eye. Her steps slowed, and she heard a door slam.

A figure wearing a dark hoodie bolted down the steps and shot off toward the woods behind the center. He reached up, shoved the hoodie away and yanked something—a ski mask?—off his head then pulled the hoodie back up. He stuffed the ski mask into his jacket pocket.

Very weird actions that set Heidi's internal alarm bells screaming. She decided it was prudent to get out of sight.

Just as she moved to do so, the man spun.

And came to an abrupt halt as his eyes locked on hers.

Ice invaded her veins. He took a step toward her then shot a look back at the training center. With one last threatening glare, he whirled and raced toward the woods once again.

Like he wanted to put as much distance between him and the building as possible.

Don't miss
Explosive Force *by Lynette Eason,*
available September 2018 wherever
Love Inspired® Suspense *books and ebooks are sold.*

www.LoveInspired.com

Looking for inspiration in tales
of hope, faith and heartfelt romance?

Check out **Love Inspired**® and
Love Inspired® **Suspense** books!

New books available every month!

CONNECT WITH US AT:

Facebook.com/groups/HarlequinConnection

Facebook.com/HarlequinBooks

Twitter.com/HarlequinBooks

Instagram.com/HarlequinBooks

Pinterest.com/HarlequinBooks

ReaderService.com

Inspirational Romance to Warm Your Heart and Soul

Join our social communities to connect with other readers who share your love!

Sign up for the Love Inspired newsletter at **www.LoveInspired.com** to be the first to find out about upcoming titles, special promotions and exclusive content.

CONNECT WITH US AT:

Harlequin.com/Community

 Facebook.com/LoveInspiredBooks

 Twitter.com/LoveInspiredBks

LISOCIAL2017